THE FIRST VICTIM

RIDLEY PEARSON

THE FIRST VICTIM

HYPERION
New York

The stories and characters in this novel are the product of the author's imagination and are not based on real or actual events, nor on real or actual characters. Although the author strived through research to make the factual basis of the writing as accurate as possible, liberties are always taken in fiction, and the author apologizes up front for any mistruths or location inaccuracies required by the story, and, as always, begs the forgiveness of the reader and the people of Seattle and King County, Washington, for any such errors, intentional or otherwise.

Library of Congress Cataloging-in-Publication Data

Pearson, Ridley.
    The first victim / by Ridley Pearson.—1st ed.
      p. cm.
    I. Title.
    ISBN 0-7868-6440-0
  PS3566.E234F57   1999
  813'.54—dc21   98-49992
                              CIP

Designed by KimShala Wilson

FIRST EDITION
10 9 8 7 6 5 4 3 2 1

ACKNOWLEDGMENTS

This novel was edited by Leigh Haber at Hyperion Books who deserves none of the criticism, if any, for its successes or failures, but all of the credit for both holding me to the page and expanding my horizons. Thanks, Leigh.

Also a note of thanks to Al Zuckerman for editorial consultation and literary representation.

The author wishes to express his gratitude to the variety of professionals who helped with *The First Victim:* law enforcement, Sergeant Donald Cameron; medical examiner, Dr. Donald Reay; oceanographer, Dr. Alyn Duxbury; friends at the FBI and at Washington D.C.'s Metropolitan Police Force and Capitol Police Force.

THE FIRST VICTIM

CHAPTER 1

PUGET SOUND, WASHINGTON

It came off the northern Pacific as if driven by a witch's broom: the remnants of typhoon Mary, which had killed 117 in Japan, left 6,000 homeless in Siberia and flooded the western Aleutians for the first time in sixty-two years. In the ocean's open waters it drove seas to thirty feet with its eighty-five-mile-per-hour winds, dumping three inches of rain an hour and barreling toward Victoria Island, the San Juan Islands, and the largest estuary in North America, known on charts as Puget Sound. It headed for the city of Seattle as if it had picked its course off a map, and it caused the biggest rush on plywood and chipboard that King County had ever seen.

In the partially protected waters west of Elliott Bay, one nautical mile beyond the established shipping lanes that feed Seattle's East Waterway docklands, the pitch-black night was punctured by the harsh illumination of shipboard spotlights that in clear weather might have reached a half mile or more but failed to stretch even a hundred yards in the dismal deluge that had once been Mary. The freighter, *Visage*, a container ship, rose and sank in fifteen-foot swells, rain drumming decks stacked forty feet high with freight cars. The Asian crew followed the orders of the boatswain who commanded a battery-operated megaphone from an upper deck, instructing them to make ready.

The huge ship pitched and yawed and rolled port to starboard, threatening to dump its top-heavy cargo. The crew had been captured inside Mary's wrath for the last three hundred nautical miles—three impossibly long days and nights—rarely able to sleep, some unable to eat, at work all hours attempting to keep the hundreds of containers on deck secure. Early on in the blow a container had broken loose,

1

sliding across the steel deck like a seven-ton brick and crushing the leg of an unsuspecting crewman to where the ship's medic could find no bones to set, only soft flesh where the shin and knee had once been. Three of the crew had tied themselves to the port rail where they vomited green bile with each and every rise and fall. Only four crewmen were available for the transfer that was to come.

The neighboring tug and barge, seventy feet and closing off *Visage*'s starboard bow, were marked by dim red and green running lights, a single white spot off the tug's bow, and a pair of bright halogens off the tower of the telescoping yellow crane chained down to the center of the barge. The tug and barge disappeared into a trough, rising and reappearing a moment later, only to sink once again into the foam, the crane as ominous and unnatural as an oil platform. The storm prevented any hope of docking the barge to the freighter, but both captains had enough motivation in their wallets to attempt the transfer nonetheless. Like two ends of a seesaw, the vessels rose and fell alternately, the crane's tower pointing like a broken finger into the tar black clouds. Radio communication was forbidden. Signal lights flashed, the only contact between the two captains.

Finally, in a dangerous and daring dance, the two vessels drew close enough for the crane's slip harness to be snagged by the freighter's crew on an upward pendulum swing. Briefly, the barge and container ship were connected by this dangling steel cable, but it broke loose of their hold, the barge lost to another swell. It was twenty minutes before the crane's steel cable was finally captured for a second time.

The vessels bobbed alongside one another, the slack in the crane's cable going dangerously tight with each alternating swell. The exhausted deckhands of the *Visage* worked furiously to be rid of this container, to a member wondering if it was worth the bonus pay they had been promised.

When the moment of exchange arrived, the crane made tight the cable and the deckhands cut loose the container's binding chains while lines secured to winches on both vessels attempted to steady the dangling container, for if it swung too violently it was likely to capsize the barge. As the first of these four lines snapped, the container, dangling precipitously over the void of open foam between barge and ship, shifted awkwardly, suddenly at a treacherous angle. Above the deafening whistle of wind and the lion's roar of the sea came the muted but unmistakable cry of human voices from within this container.

A crewman crossed himself and looked toward heaven.

A second line snapped. A third.

The container swung and slipped out of the harness, splashing into the water. It submerged and then bobbed back up like a whale surfacing.

The captain of the *Visage* barked his orders. The mighty twin screws spun to life, the gigantic ship lumbering to port and away from the barge and crane in an effort to keep the container from being crushed between the vessels.

The spotlights on the freighter were ordered extinguished as the ship was consumed by the storm, lumbering back toward the shipping lane where it belonged.

Behind it, in its wake, the abandoned container, singing of human screams and cries of terror, rode the mounting swells into darkness, lost to the wash of the waves and the whim of the wind.

CHAPTER 2

On the evening of Monday, August 10, when the coattails of typhoon Mary had receded into little more than a torrential downpour, a rust orange container appeared bobbing in the churning green waters and whitecaps of Puget Sound. Spotted by a copilot of a test flight returning to Boeing Field, it was immediately reported to the Coast Guard. Loose containers were not an uncommon occurrence in the Sound. The urgency behind the Coast Guard's efforts to recover the orphaned container began as a result of the threat to navigation, especially with night closing in. "Metal icebergs," they were called. This urgency was heightened, however, as the Coast Guard's patrol boat came alongside the partially sunken container and human cries were heard from within. At that point, the call went out to the Seattle Police Department.

The piano sounded better than ever. For an old beat-up baby grand in a smoke-filled comedy bar where no one paid the instrument any attention except for the homicide cop who presently occupied its bench, his large hands and stubby fingers evoking a somber rendition of "Blue Monk," its tone was earthy and mellow, just the way jazz and blues were supposed to sound. The notes flowed out of Lou Boldt without conscious thought or preparation, sounding of the torments born of forty-odd years of life and a job involving all too much death.

Boldt aimed his interpretation toward the table where his wife and friends sat. If his five-year-old son and three-year-old daughter had been there he would have had everything and everyone that mattered to him in this one room: Elizabeth, his sweetheart, wife and partner;

Doc Dixon, the county medical examiner who'd been his friend for most of Boldt's twenty-plus years with Seattle Police; John LaMoia, who had taken Boldt's place as a Crimes Against Persons' squad sergeant; Bobbie Gaynes, the first woman cop to join that squad; Daphne Matthews, forensic psychologist and confidante; and the lab's Bernie Lofgrin, with his Coke-bottle glasses and leaking-balloon laugh.

He didn't need to invent an emotion behind his playing. Liz's lymphoma had been in remission for one full year, and Boldt's happy hour performance that night at Bear Berenson's club The Joke's on You had developed into an impromptu celebration of her progress, a celebration that only a cop's wife could tolerate, but one that Liz would actually appreciate. Morbid humor was a way of life with this group, and while Liz didn't totally fit in with the others, they were family to her, just as they were to her husband.

While few at the table were above teasing Liz about how she'd looked when her hair had fallen out during treatment, or about smoking pot to bring on a taste for food, no one was really talking about anything, either. No one discussed that his new desk job was a problem for Boldt, that he ached for the opportunity to slap on a pair of latex gloves and get back out into the field. Similarly no one talked about the fact that for Liz's doctors her long remission was both unexpected and still unexplained. They wouldn't recommend breaking out the champagne for another three to five years. But Liz herself was sanguine: She credited God with her healing; and Boldt kept his mouth shut on that one. He felt that he and Liz had yet to recapture their comfort zone, but he wasn't about to talk about that, either. So that night no one discussed much of anything. They joked. They drank. They drank some more.

When the pagers started sounding, it seemed like something orchestrated for a comedy sketch, except that everyone knew immediately that it must be serious, since one call simultaneously summoned the lab, the medical examiner and the Homicide squad.

LaMoia flipped his cellphone closed and said, "It's a shipping container. Sinking out in the sound. People screaming inside. Still alive. Coast Guard's towing it ashore."

"Still alive," Liz echoed, watching as all but Daphne Matthews headed for the exit. Those words meant more to her than anyone at the table.

Liz offered a look of surprise that Daphne stayed behind.

Daphne explained, "They don't need me."

"Well I do," Liz replied, though retreating into silence, both confusing Daphne and making her curious.

When club owner Bear Berenson got the jukebox going a few minutes later, the rock music clashed with the earlier mood set by Boldt's piano.

"He doesn't understand it," Liz told Daphne. She meant Boldt. "The prayer. He can't accept that I was healed by something outside of that hospital."

"His background," Daphne said, uncomfortably attempting to explain the woman's husband to her. "If he wasn't a detective, he'd be a lab guy. You know?"

"Yeah, I know," Liz agreed. "But it's more that that. He won't give it a chance. It drives him crazy."

"He's glad you're well, however you got there."

"He doesn't trust it. Has he talked to you about it?"

"No," Daphne lied. She and Boldt had once been more than friends, just briefly. She knew well enough to protect the deeper friendship they had now.

"He doesn't say anything," Liz continued, "not directly, but I know he's waiting for the other shoe to drop. Not that he *wants* it—I'm not saying that! Of course not! It's just that he doesn't *believe* in it. It's inconceivable to him that prayer, that God, can have that kind of power, that kind of consequence." She organized the dirty glasses on the table for the waitress.

"He doesn't believe it," she repeated. Liz looked toward the door as if he were still there.

"What if I talked to him about it?" Daphne offered.

"It's not something that can be sold."

"He needs to hear that from all sides," Daphne suggested.

"He needs to hear this from within, Daphne. That's the only way it's going to make sense, to have any resonance. Especially to him."

Liz reached for Daphne's hand and gave it a squeeze.

Daphne felt this woman's cold fingers held in her own warm palm, and thought how quickly things change. There had been a time when she would have cheered for Liz to leave her husband. Now she was cheering for Liz's survival. "You're an amazing woman," she said, as a chill whispered through her.

Boldt marveled at the emptiness of the docklands at night, the wide streets and warehouses deserted. Huge shipping cranes towered along the shoreline, silhouetted against dull gray clouds that reflected back the glow of city light, reminding Boldt of his son's Construction Site Legos kit that currently occupied the far corner of the living room.

The August air blew both warm and heavy, laden with salt spray, forcing all who awaited the raising of the container to squint and turn a shoulder toward shore. Boldt wore his hair trimmed short, which didn't quite fit with his otherwise professorial look—the wrinkled khakis and favorite tweed jacket worn threadbare at the elbows and sleeves. His tight jaw and erect posture belonged to a man who meant business. Few people interrupted him when he was locked in thought, eyes distant and yet strangely focused. He deservedly owned the respect of all who worked with him, due to his attention to detail and dedication to procedure that many in law enforcement preached, but few practiced. He occasionally spoke at law enforcement seminars and conferences and at graduate criminology courses on the role of homicide victims as witnesses. "The Victim Speaks," his talk on the subject, had been transcribed and posted on the Internet.

Boldt grumbled to LaMoia about how long it was taking the Coast Guard to recover the container. The cries and screams continued. Patience was running thin.

LaMoia had stood at Boldt's side for the last seven years, working in his shadow, studying his every movement, then rising in rank to take not only the man's stripes but even his desk and office cubicle.

LaMoia wore his jeans pressed, his shirts crisp, his hair perfect and his cowboy boots gleaming. He was focused less on Boldt and more on his boots—brand new boots that had cost him a month's salary. This salt spray was beginning to really piss him off. He kept rising on tiptoe to pull his boots out of the puddled water.

"Piano sounded great tonight," LaMoia said.

"Are you kissing my butt?" Boldt asked. "What are you after, John?"

"I want to keep these new boots dry," LaMoia confessed.

"So get out of here. I'll cover." As a lieutenant, Boldt was expected to have no active field responsibilities. Technically, the case was LaMoia's, he was lead detective, though under Boldt's direct supervision. Both men understood this. Boldt resented it. Despite his two decades of experience he was expected in the conference room, not the street. Under a different captain, he might have been given more latitude, but Sheila Hill paid attention to rank and procedure. A ladder-climber and well connected in the department, Hill was not someone to cross. "Make it quick," Boldt said. "They're going to get this thing up and open any minute now." LaMoia was famous within the department for his casual attitude and his willingness to stop and chat with any and every woman he encountered.

"Okay, Sarge." LaMoia still referred to Boldt by his former rank. He jogged back toward his fire-engine red 1968 Camaro and the police line established to hold back the press from where television news crews were already shooting.

The detective left. Briefly the field belonged to Boldt.

"Polly's broken down in traffic. She's not going to make it. We need you."

"Slow down, Jimmy," Stevie McNeal said into the phone.

Jimmy Corwin was among the station's best producers, but he worked in a constant state of high anxiety. Stevie found his energy infectious, even over the phone. He was proposing she take a live segment for Polly. As an anchorwoman, Stevie picked her reporting work carefully.

"What are we looking at?" she asked.

"We've got a shipping container found by the Coast Guard. Human cries coming from inside. Channel Seven is already on-air. We need you on-camera in the next ten minutes."

"You'll post it up on the feed."

"Sure we will."

"I need a promise on that, Jimmy." The national feed could bring offers from the larger market.

"When we see the piece, we'll determine—"

"Now! You commit now or I—"

"Okay. Agreed."

"And it's my follow-up, my story," Stevie negotiated.

"It's going to mean original segments for us, not just the five o'clock leftovers."

The phone crackled and the window flashed blue with the light of an approaching thunder cell. She said, "Tell the crew I'm on my way."

The Coast Guard crew had attached inflatables to stabilize the container while it was being towed to shore. Those same inflatables currently kept the steel box afloat.

As the cries from inside continued, swimmers climbed up and connected the cables to all four corners. A supervisor signaled the all clear and the crane's mighty diesel growled loudly. The cable lurched and snugged tight as the slack was removed, and a pillar of slate gray exhaust rose from the crane's rusted stack. The container's sunken end lifted from the black water that spilled from every crack, and the cries grew sharper, splitting the air and running chills down Boldt's spine. A cheer rang out from the workmen as the container cleared the water altogether, suspended and dangling as the crane moved it to dry land. Boldt was not among those cheering, his nose working overtime. He pulled out his notebook and marked the time. *Dead body*, he wrote alongside the numbers.

A man stepped through the police line, the officers clearing the way as he displayed his ID. Broad-shouldered, he exuded a confidence that advertised the sports he'd played in college, while the inexpensive suit clearly said "federal agent." Brian Coughlie introduced himself as the INS investigator in charge. Shaking his hand was like taking hold of a stick.

Boldt didn't know many agents from the Immigration and Naturalization Service and said so. He added, "Glad to have your help on this one."

"What you're going to find in there, once they get the doors open, is anywhere from fifteen to seventy illegals. More than likely, all of the adults are Asian women in their teens and twenties: better for the sweatshops and whorehouses, which is where they all would have ended up. These container shipments have been a thorn in our side for over a year now. Glad to finally have one with something inside."

"Part of that something is dead," said Boldt, who was a little put off by Coughlie's arrogance. Boldt touched his own nose, answering Coughlie's quizzical expression.

"You think?" Coughlie asked. "These things arrive pretty damn ripe, I'll tell you what."

"Dead," Boldt ventured. "And that makes the others in there witnesses."

"You already jockeying for position, Lieutenant?" Coughlie asked calmly. "A reminder, lest you forget: These are illegal immigrants, so my boss is calling this ours. I pick 'em up and I deliver them to federal detention. You want to visit our house and have a chat with them, we got no problem with that. But your boss will have to clear it with my boss. Okay? Meantime, these visitors—the live ones, anyway—take a trip on federal tires, not the local variety."

"And the dead ones?"

"Yours to keep," Coughlie said. "That okay with you?"

"So long as you keep them apart from your general population. I don't want them hearing stories, getting coached."

"We'll clean 'em up, shave 'em, and give 'em their own custom chain-link cage," Coughlie agreed. "No problemo. Barracks K. Our detention facility is part of what used to be Fort Nolan. You know Fo-No?"

"I know of it."

"You golf?"

"No," Boldt answered.

"Too bad. They've got a great eighteen out there. Maintained courtesy of the taxpayer. You and me—we'd a been smarter to be military. Can't beat that retirement package."

LaMoia approached at a run. Boldt made the introductions. LaMoia shook hands with Coughlie but on his face was the expression of someone who'd picked up a sticky bottle of honey by mistake.

"We've got the turf problems all worked out," Boldt said, easing LaMoia's concerns.

"Somebody's dead," LaMoia remarked.

"Ahead of you on that," Boldt said.

LaMoia reached into his coat pocket and brought out a pair of plastic gloves and a tube of Vicks VaporRub.

Boldt accepted the tube after LaMoia had smeared a line under his nose. He passed it to Coughlie, who did the same. Some things a person couldn't live without.

When the container was finally opened with a bolt cutter, a hush overcame the crowd as one by one, nine Chinese women—partially naked, bone thin and weak—were helped into waiting ambulances. Some on their feet, some on stretchers.

Three women came out in body bags.

Coughlie suggested Boldt give it a few days before attempting interviews. "I seen worse, Lieutenant. But I've also seen better, too."

"Thing about our squad," LaMoia informed Coughlie, "the victims don't typically get up and walk away."

"Three of them didn't," Boldt reminded somberly.

"Whereas in mine," Coughlie explained, "we're not in the habit of sending them home in a pine box."

Stevie McNeal arrived by Yellow Cab and was met by two of the remote crew, one who handed her an umbrella and a wireless microphone, another who explained camera position. Stevie headed straight
for the yellow police tape that she was prohibited to cross, and crossed
it anyway.

"Hey!" a black uniformed officer with a young, boyish face
shouted from beneath his police cap, "You can't—"

Stevie stopped and faced the man, allowing him a moment to recognize her.

"Oh," he said.

She looked him in the eye, putting just enough juice behind her
determined expression and said, "Who's in charge?"

"LaMoia's lead," he answered obediently. "But the lieutenant's
here too." He pointed out a group of silhouettes.

She stood facing LaMoia, Boldt and Coughlie. There weren't
enough ambulances on hand. A few of the illegals, wrapped in EMT
blankets, were being offered water to drink. Between the Coast Guard
and the police, there were uniformed officers everywhere.

LaMoia said, "This is a restricted area. Press has to stay on the
other side of the tape."

"The rumors are wild back there, Sergeant. Some say serial killer,
some say illegals."

"Illegals," Coughlie answered. Stevie locked eyes with him. He
wore an INS identification.

"We'll have a statement shortly," Boldt interjected.

Stevie tried to determine who to play to. She asked the INS guy,
"Is this yours or SPD's?"

Coughlie answered, "Believe it or not, we're working in concert
on this."

"So who's in charge of this love-in?"

One of the body bags was carried past them by a team working for
the King County Medical Examiner.

"Not ready for prime time," LaMoia quipped.

"We'll have a statement shortly," Boldt repeated.

Stevie nodded, suddenly unable to speak.

CHAPTER 3

They met in the International District on a clear and sunny Tuesday afternoon, the intense sunlight capturing all the surroundings in a golden luminescence. Stevie McNeal arrived early, unusual, if not unheard of for her, charged with excitement.

She dressed down for the meeting in blue jeans, a black cotton T-shirt and a new khaki safari overshirt she'd recently bought. Despite her American heritage, she still spoke with a faintly British accent, courtesy of her father's overseas service.

House of Hong, a dim sum restaurant alongside an elevated stretch of I-5 south, occupied a plain cement block of a structure with a large red plastic sign on the roof for all to see. Its modest parking lot, the asphalt cracked and heaved, was surrounded by a wilted chain-link fence draped like bunting from rusting bent stanchions. The clatter inside was Mandarin, which was the language Stevie used to greet the maitre d', who was clearly surprised by her perfect inflection. He led her toward a table where a Chinese woman sat with her back to the door.

Melissa was Chinese, twenty-six years old, with a simple, confined beauty, more radiance than pure looks. She wore a white man-tailored button-down shirt and blue jeans, her only jewelry a rubber watch that had extra buttons for lap times. She swam two miles every day at the YWCA, and she kept her hair unusually short so that it fit easily under her cap.

Stevie said, "You look good, Little Sister."

"And you."

"Thank you for coming on such short notice."

"I love seeing you. You know that," Melissa said. "A chance at a job as well? What could be better?"

"I just don't trust men arranging secret meetings, even ones offering to sell important information."

"If I'd been through what you've been through . . ." Melissa said.

A year earlier, Stevie had been stalked for over three months. When the private security firm the station hired finally caught the man, he turned out to have an arrest record for sexual assault, rape and kidnapping, though no convictions.

A waitress interrupted, offering fresh dim sum from a steaming bamboo container. Melissa politely declined. She removed a stenographer's pad from her purse and placed it on the white linen tablecloth. Everything in its place: that was Melissa. "So?" she said.

Stevie explained, "He claims to have information tied to that container that came ashore. You like the stories with teeth. It's not a documentary, but—"

"No, listen, I appreciate it. Freelancing, you take what you can get."

"Not that I haven't offered to get you a job with the station."

"Not that you haven't offered," Melissa echoed. "When I *earn* a job at a station, then that's different." They'd been over this a dozen times. "We grew up in the same house. We spend our weekends together, our holidays."

"Our vacations," Stevie interrupted.

"But if you used your celebrity to get me a job . . ."

"I understand perfectly well."

"Even this," Melissa said, indicating the restaurant, "makes me uncomfortable."

"You're perfect for this. You're Chinese and you're a freelancer. If this bozo has anything worthwhile, who better to pursue the story?" Stevie added, "Besides, what a great excuse to charge a lunch off to the station!"

Melissa grinned and nodded. She sobered and said, "All that you've done for me. And don't deny it! If I could repay one-tenth of these favors—"

"What good is anything if you don't use it? These are my fifteen minutes of fame. When yours come—and they *will* come—I'm counting on you to let some of it rub off on me."

"Not likely."

"Don't say that. Your production work is the best around. You'll see. A story like this . . . if it proves to be good information . . . This could break you out, change everything."

"I'm not holding my breath."

As the only Caucasian male in the restaurant, the man they were expecting stood out upon his arrival. Balding, overweight, with a drinker's nose and cheeks and an apparent taste for ill-fitting discount sports jackets, he arrived carrying beads of perspiration beneath his unfashionably long sideburns and down his equally florid neck. He searched the restaurant, looking a little distraught until recognizing Stevie. She signaled him and he sat down, eyeing Melissa guardedly. He said to Stevie, "You look different than on TV."

"Your phone call," Stevie said. He was not a man with whom she wanted to lunch. She ordered an iced tea, wanting this meeting over as quickly as possible.

"Your eyes? Your hair? I don't know." He mopped his face with the restaurant's napkin and glanced around for a waiter. He ordered a Cape Cod, a vodka and cranberry, and also waved off the offer of food.

Melissa used her Chinese to request they be left alone, stopping the onslaught of dim sum.

"I watch you every night. The news." He lowered his voice conspiratorially. "I thought you were the one to make the offer to, you know?" Again, he glanced at Melissa.

"She works with me," Stevie clarified. "Let's talk about this offer," she said.

"I'm a state auditor."

"I thought it was King County," she corrected.

"State. I oversee inventories of a half dozen state agencies, everything from road cones to, I don't know, fax machines."

"How fascinating," she said.

"We're with you," Melissa said, salvaging Stevie's breach.

"This is a big story," he said.

"Then perhaps we should hear it," Melissa encouraged.

He touched Stevie's hand and she instinctively jerked hers away. "Maybe I called the wrong person," he said.

"Maybe you did," Stevie agreed. "You touch me again and you're having pepper spray for lunch."

He apologized. "I've never done anything like this: whistle-blowing to the press. It's not something I'm comfortable with."

"You count police cones," Stevie said, recovering slightly from her malaise. "Are you comfortable with that?"

"What else do you count, Mr. . . ." Melissa asked, attempting to drag his name out of him.

He mopped his face again. His teeth were stained from smoking. "Do you know how movie houses keep track of the popcorn they sell?"

"Popcorn?" Stevie blurted out. "You're passing me a hot tip about movie-house popcorn?"

"It's not by how much they pop, because it only takes a few kernels to make a cup of popped popcorn, and it's too random to estimate how many kernels go into each cup . . . and also because they end up throwing out the stuff they haven't sold at the end of the night, or between shows."

"Listen . . . Really . . ."

"They count the bags, the cups," Melissa said.

"Exactly! The owner, the manager, tracks the number of bags used. They inventory the bags—small, medium, large—and that's how much cash the employees behind the counters are responsible for putting in the till. It's that simple. Not enough cash, the employees make up the difference, so the employees watch those bags closely. Same with soda cups. Exact same method. The number of cups used in an evening determines cash flow."

"Bags and cups," Stevie repeated, somewhat curiously.

"At the LSOs—the Licensing Service Offices—it's the laminates. The number of plastic laminates that go through each department.

These days the laminates have some printing embedded in the plastic to help cops sniff out counterfeits: Washington State Department of Transportation, it reads. That laminate validates the driver's license. It's very important to—"

"Counterfeiters," she supplied.

He glanced between the two women.

"We're listening," Melissa said, beginning to jot down notes. She flashed a look to Stevie. Melissa's eyes were hot black pinpricks of excitement. Stevie felt a rush of heat pulse through her.

He said, "One of my responsibilities is to inventory the LSO laminates. Discards are tracked as well, so the numbers have to work out."

"Counterfeit driver's licenses?" Stevie said. "These connect to the container how?"

"Ask yourself why the state would have me counting laminates. Why bother? They cost the state two-point-six cents per laminate. Even at a few hundred, we're talking three or four dollars' worth."

"Three or four hundred," Melissa repeated, writing it down.

"You lost me," Stevie said. "The state's waste of your manpower?" she asked, a little more interested. "Is that the story you're pitching?"

"It's the IDs," Melissa said.

"What's the street value of a fake ID?" Stevie asked.

"Now you're catching on!" the man said. "What value would *you* put on a counterfeit driver's license, Miss McNeal?"

"It's Ms.," she corrected. "I don't know . . . Depends if it's kids trying to buy cigarettes or illegals trying to buy their freedom."

"It certainly does," the man agreed.

She reconsidered. "Two hundred?"

"Five hundred?" Melissa asked, when the sweating man only returned a grin to Stevie.

"How about thirty-five hundred *per* license."

Stevie spit some ice back into her tea. "What?"

"Legal residence is the first step toward a work permit. A work permit is the first step toward a green card. The green card leads to—"

"Citizenship."

He grinned. "It's a big story. See?" He said, "I have a name."

"How much?" Stevie asked.

"Five thousand," he replied without hesitation.

Stevie coughed out a laugh. "This isn't *Nightbeat*. We're not *Hard Copy*." She returned, "Five hundred."

"Maybe I should call *Nightbeat*."

"It's a long distance call," Stevie said.

She won a laugh from him. "It's the hair, isn't it? You wear it different on the show."

"It's not a show," Stevie replied. She felt cold all of a sudden. She didn't like the business of fans. "It's a broadcast. It's news."

The man took a moment to consider the offer. "A thousand," he countered.

"Five hundred up front. Five hundred more if the piece runs."

"You think I'm giving you my name? Some way to find me?"

Melissa said, "You've told us you are a state auditor. You think we can't find you?"

"The condition of my cooperation is that you leave that alone . . . leave me alone. Leave me out of it." He added, "I happen to like my job."

Stevie repeated, "Five hundred if our producer goes along with it. Melissa here will bring you the money. You'll provide her the name of the LSO employee with the bad laminate count. If we run the piece, you get a second five hundred. You want to call us and set up the meetings, that's fine. Give me two hours to run it by my producer."

"I'd rather deal with you," he objected. "No offense," he said to Melissa.

"It's Melissa's story, not mine. I'm an anchorwoman, not a reporter. You let us do our jobs. You do yours."

"You were the reporter did that container," he reminded.

Melissa said, "We like our jobs, too. Let us do them."

He left the restaurant a few minutes later, trailing some bad cologne.

They ordered food once he was gone.

Melissa said, "You're asking for five two-minute segments: a review of the container tragedy; this LSO exposé if it proves out; and a piece on the detention center and what awaits illegals who've been detained."

"Correct."

"I have no problem with any of that, but if it leads to a bigger story—if I can connect these counterfeit driver's licenses to legal illegals, if I can deliver the people behind it, I need to know you'll stay with me, that no one's going to push me out and steal it from me."

"It won't be me," Stevie said. "That's about all I can promise. As long as I'm a part of it, no one takes this from us."

"Fair enough. And if it gets political?"

"I'll run with this wherever it leads, wherever you take it, Little Sister. In the meantime, I keep the dialogue alive—the story alive—by interviewing anyone and everyone who's a part of this: the INS, the cops, the detainees, whatever it takes."

"And if Corwin doesn't want it going that way?" Melissa asked.

"What did we do when Su-Su didn't want us doing something?" Stevie asked.

"Appealed to your father," Melissa answered.

"If Corwin puts up road blocks, I'll take it over his head to New York. I have plenty of contacts left."

"You'd do that?"

"I'm agreeing to do that. For this story, yes."

"This story, or for me?" Melissa asked.

"The story."

"Because I—"

"I know your principles," Stevie reminded, interrupting. "This isn't a handout. Honestly. If it proves to have legs, and you want to pursue it, I'll stick by you. You want to go undercover, I'm with you—but only if it's exposure, not entrapment. That's all I'm saying."

"Then we've got a deal," Melissa suggested, having never discussed her pay. "You get the story. I get creative autonomy."

"Yes," Stevie agreed, "we have a deal."

CHAPTER 4

LaMoia delivered the medical examiner's preliminary report on the three Chinese illegals who had died in the container. The report, though scientifically stated, remained indecisive, an enigmatic confusion that did little to support the investigation's pursuit of homicide charges for the three deaths. The illegals had succumbed to malnutrition and dehydration, "aggravated by symptoms consistent with those caused by a virulent strain of influenza, *as yet unidentified*." Doc Dixon's emphasis expressed his unwillingness to draw firm conclusions—at least at the stage of the preliminary report. The prelim went on to say that the corpses had sustained postmortem contusions, likely the result of being tossed around at sea. Tissue samples were being forwarded to the Centers for Disease Control (CDC), Atlanta, in an effort to identify the particular strain of flu. The extent of malnutrition and dehydration suggested to Boldt the possibility of filing charges of "depraved indifference to human life" against the captain and crew that had transported the container. This, in turn, might lead to plea bargaining and names of those responsible for the trafficking in human lives. A strategy began to reveal itself, not much different than a drug raid or organized crime sting. But more than anything, he also recognized Doc Dixon's underlying interest and curiosity in the unidentified flu strain, and the memo's carefully worded, intentionally vague language. Dixie was holding his cards close to his vest, buying himself time for that CDC report.

For Boldt, the fastest way to the name of that ship, to the captain and crew, was the illegals themselves—the passengers—the nine women who had survived the passage and were currently being detained by the INS.

Fort Nolan was no longer an army base. Only its golf course had survived the budget cutting of base closures in the late 1980s. Congress could evidently see its way clear to losing a few hundred civilian jobs and a thousand infantry, but an eighteen-hole course was not to be sacrificed under any conditions. The result was that retired and active officers alike regularly shanked, hooked, pitched and putted only a hundred yards from former barracks that currently housed indigent Asians and Mexicans unlucky enough to have been caught and detained by the INS. The more fortunate among them found themselves in service as ground maintenance crew or caddies, enjoying a limited freedom, spending their days outside the razor wire and receiving the occasional gratuity.

The base's hasty remodel by the INS had come as a boon to the chain-link contractors in King County. Boldt pulled his department-issue Chevy Cavalier to a stop at the guard gate. He and Daphne Matthews displayed their badges and stated their business. In the far distance a man wearing khakis and a lime green crew shirt made a nice chip shot onto the green. Attorneys and government employees came and went with regularity at Fort Nolan, but a pair of Seattle cops was clearly something new, for the guard studied their identification badges carefully and, asking Boldt to pull over inside the gate, made a phone call. They were provided an over photocopied map of the facility upon which the guard hastily drew directional arrows. Daphne navigated.

"Shouldn't John be with us?" Daphne asked. "In fact, shouldn't you be at the office and John be here?"

"He's lead. He gets the joy of the paperwork," Boldt replied.

"Are we in denial of our rank, Lieutenant?"

"Hill and I disagree as to the job description," Boldt said. "Let's just leave it at that."

"Will she leave it at that? Would you have tolerated Phil Shoswitz in the field?"

"It's different."

"Why? Because it's you, not Shoswitz?"

"Exactly."

"Have you heard the term *bullheaded*?"

"Are you familiar with the word *experience*?" he fired back at her.

"I certainly am. And my experience," she said, intentionally cutting him, "is that both you and Hill are bullheaded. Something's got to give there—and she's got rank on you, Lieutenant."

Boldt pursed his lips and pulled up to the curb. She shot a look at him that could have caught a bush on fire.

The interview room, plain and bare, contained two long metal tables with Formica tops surrounded by metal chairs with worn plastic cushions. On the wall hung framed portraits of the president and the regional INS director, Adam Talmadge. The interpreter was a Japanese-American woman in her forties who stood five feet tall in shoes with heels and dressed with a simple elegance.

The detainee was young and silently defiant. Her head and eyebrows were shaved, lending her an otherworldly look. She wore overwashed denim pants and a thin denim shirt with no bra. Her blue rubber sandals slapped the gray cement floor in a steady, insistent rhythm. An aide delivered four cups of tea.

Boldt cupped his hand and whispered to Matthews, "Do you recognize her?"

"No," Daphne answered. "But I only saw photos."

"Yeah? Well I was there, and she . . . I don't know." Boldt went through the formalities of introductions. Through the interpreter he attempted to explain that the police had no interest in pressing charges against this woman or any of her companions. Then, pen ready, he said to the interpreter, "Please tell her we need the name of the ship that transported the container."

The interpreter told him, "You'll never get that out of her. To give you that would put not only her at risk, but her relatives here and at home. Perhaps agent Coughlie should brief you before—"

"Translate the question, please," Boldt said, interrupting.

"Wait!" Daphne interjected, catching the interpreter's warning eye. She whispered into Boldt's ear.

He shrugged and deferred to her saying, "Go ahead."

Daphne addressed the detainee, "You paid a great deal of money to be brought to this country. What if we could get that money back for you, erase that debt?"

Boldt wrote on his pad where Daphne could read it: *smart*.

The Chinese woman replied through the interpreter, "Yes. We pay money to be brought America. We in America. Yes?"

"She's an illegals poster child," Boldt mumbled.

Daphne tried another tactic. "What if we arranged for you to remain in the United States legally? Would you help us then?"

The interpreter interjected, "I will not be party to this kind of sham."

"What sham?" Daphne argued.

"The Service will never agree to such a deal. Have you spoken to Agent Coughlie? Of course you haven't! Brian Coughlie *never* makes such deals."

Boldt inquired, "Then how do they obtain information from these people?"

"Listen, I'm only the translator, but I'm telling you: I've never offered a deal to any female detainee. It just isn't done. The operating premise is that the women don't know anything. They are rarely, if ever, even interviewed. The male detainees, the various gang members occasionally rounded up—the coyotes—they're a different story. But in terms of the women, Fort Nolan is nothing but a big bus terminal, with all the buses headed home."

"All the more reason she should cooperate with us," Boldt reminded. "We're giving her a chance to be heard."

"But you don't control their destiny, the INS does. Agent Coughlie does."

The subject's eyes ticked back and forth between her interpreter and Boldt, who was beginning to dislike Coughlie already.

Daphne said politely, "Please translate the lieutenant's offer. If we cut her a deal that included a legitimate green card and her money returned, could she supply us with the name of the ship and any details of crossing?"

The translator spoke quickly behind poorly contained anger. The detainee listened carefully, looked surprised and then studied both Boldt and Daphne carefully. After a long hesitation, she shook her head no.

"Why," Daphne pleaded. "Why volunteer for deportation?"

The interpreter answered, "Because—"

Boldt chided, "Not you. Her!"

The Chinese woman shook her head a second time upon hearing the translated question.

The interpreter tried again with Daphne. "They are warned before they leave the mainland that the Americans do not keep their word. Their relatives, both here in the US and in China, will suffer if they talk. To a Chinese, family is everything. It would be shameful to put any family member at risk."

Boldt addressed the translator. "The people who took her money nearly killed her. They *did* kill three others. More will die. Maybe relatives of hers who follow in her footsteps. Doesn't that mean anything to her?" He hesitated, leaned forward and warned, "Tell her that we will arrest her as an accomplice to those deaths if she does not cooperate." This drew Daphne's attention as well. He continued, "Tell her that if convicted she will not be deported, but will spend the rest of her life in a prison with convicted murderers, drug addicts and thieves. Exactly that. Exactly those words, please."

The color had drained out of the translator's face; her eyes pleaded with Daphne for intervention.

But Daphne nodded at Boldt.

"You wouldn't do this," the interpreter objected.

"Not another word from you," Boldt fired back, "other than what comes from her or one of us. No more editorial. Three women are *dead*," he repeated loudly, now getting his earnestness across to the subject as well. "Now translate!"

The interpreter spoke to the woman, who subsequently blanched at the idea of a prison term. After a long and searching staring match with Boldt, this woman addressed her translator, who, upon hearing the words, suppressed a smirk.

"What?" Boldt asked impatiently. "And I want it word for word."

The translator did her job. The Chinese detainee smiled, for the first time without using her hand to shield her mouth. Her front teeth were missing.

"What?" Boldt repeated irritably.

The interpreter then reported, "She said you Americans must have big prisons."

CHAPTER 5

The following day, for five hundred dollars in cash, the state auditor supplied Melissa with the name Gwen Klein, and the Greenwood Licensing Service Office—in Washington State the equivalent of a Department of Motor Vehicles—where Klein worked. Melissa spent hours in the back of her van with a bulky broadcast-quality video camera and battery pack perpetually prepared to record. She shot tape of Klein leaving the LSO and running errands, tape of Klein picking up her kids from day care, tape of Klein grocery shopping. Her first "report card" was delivered in Stevie McNeal's sumptuous penthouse apartment over a pair of salads that Stevie had ordered by phone. The wine was an Archery Summit Pinot. Stevie drank liberally, Melissa hardly at all.

"About the only thing I have to report is that the husband is driving a brand new pickup truck and the house appears to have a new roof."

"Extra cash," Stevie suggested.

"Or a dead relative or a generous banker. The husband pounds nails. She's a state employee. That's a thirty-thousand-dollar truck he's driving, and new roofs aren't cheap."

"Let's find out how he paid for that truck," Stevie suggested.

"That would help us to pressure her."

"She's not going to talk to us," Stevie said. "Not without hard evidence of her involvement."

"Driver's licenses are small. She could make a drop anywhere."

"So you stay close to her," Stevie suggested.

"I can stay close, but I can't stick to her."

"Sure you can."

"Not and get tape. At least not with that camera. It's the size of a school bus."

"Let me look into getting you the digital," Stevie said. "There's a briefcase for it that we use on all the undercover stuff. You can go anywhere with it."

"That would certainly help."

"Not anywhere *dangerous*, mind you," Stevie informed her. "I want you to remember that." Melissa had been a risk-taker all her life.

"And if we don't get something more positive out of her in a day or two?" Melissa asked.

"Then our friend at the dim sum doesn't get his second payment."

"And the women in that container? We forget about them?"

"Don't do this to yourself," Stevie said.

"Do what?"

"Work yourself up. Go righteous on me."

"We have two options," Melissa said impatiently, brushing aside Stevie's concerns. "Journalism 101. The first is to confront her on-camera with what we know. The second is to make something happen."

"Journalism 101?" Stevie objected. "Since when? Confront her, sure. But entrapment?"

"If you can't break the news, make the news," Melissa quoted.

"That's not you and we both know it. Make the news? Fake the news? That's not you! Corwin maybe, but not you."

"Not make the news—*bait* the news. We solicit a fake ID," she suggested.

Stevie stood from the couch and paced the room. "That's dangerously close to entrapment."

Melissa reminded, "Who was it that said: 'Real news is never found, it's uncovered'?"

"Don't take what I say out of context."

"Three women died in that container. The others were stripped naked, de-loused, shaved head to toe and will be on a plane back to China in less than a week. If I approach Klein and she offers to sell me a driver's license, then we've got her by the thumbs. She's ours. She either leads us up the next rung of the ladder or—"

"We extort her?"

"We pressure her."

"What's gotten into you?" Stevie asked.

"You hired me to get a story."

"I hired you to pursue a lead. There's a big difference."

"Not to me."

"Since when?"

"Look at me. Look at my face. If not for you and your father, that could have been me in that container. Those women are my age and younger! Are you going to walk away from them because we have to work a little harder to get the story?"

"You see?" Stevie said. "You see what happens with you?"

"Me? What if it's a strong enough story to run nationally?" She raised her voice. "We may have different reasons, but we both want this story."

"Don't confuse the issue."

"The issue is three dead women and more coming in behind them every week. The issue is the deplorable conditions that allowed those women to die." Melissa added, "The police are investigating those deaths as homicides. *That's* the story I'm interested in: bringing down whoever's responsible. And I'll tell you what: I'm willing to bend the rules for the right cause. If Klein sells me a fake ID, that's her problem."

"It's our problem too if we handle it wrong, Little Sister. These people—"

"See? What people? Who? That's exactly my point!"

"Let's exercise a little patience, shall we? You've been on this a day and a half. Keep up the surveillance. If you want a partner, I'll—"

"No! This is our story, yours and mine. No one else!"

"And I'm in charge," Stevie asserted. "Keep an eye on her. One day is nothing."

"Try telling that to the women trapped in those containers."

"Patience."

"Yeah, sure," Melissa snorted.

"I'll work on getting the digital camera. That'll help, right?"

Melissa beamed. "Then you *do* want this!"

"Of course I want it, Little Sister. I brought it to you, remember? But we talk it out, work it out together. We've got to set aside our personal agendas. I want this as much—"

"Yeah, yeah," Melissa said interrupting. "You don't always have to mother me, you know?"

"Old habits die hard."

"Get me that camera."

"Work with me," Stevie said. "A team," she suggested.

"A team," Melissa echoed.

Through one day and into the next, Melissa Chow sat impatiently in her brown van, following and videotaping Gwen Klein's movements, from home to the grocery, and for the second time in three days, to a car wash.

Mid-morning, Melissa received a phone call from Stevie.

Stevie informed her, "A friend who works with a credit rating service says that there are no loans, no liens on the Dodge 4X4 registered to Joe Klein."

"Where's that camera you promised?"

"Are you listening?"

"They own it free and clear?" Melissa asked, her eyes on Klein's taillights as the van sat parked in the automatic car wash.

Stevie said sarcastically, "That's just a little unusual for a couple with a reported combined income of sixty-seven thousand a year."

"A little unusual?" Melissa exploded. "That's damn near impossible. That's a thirty-thousand-dollar truck."

"There's more. The Kleins' credit cards, which for seven years had maintained balances in the mid–four thousands, were all paid off over the last eighteen months."

"So, if nothing else shapes up we threaten to turn the Kleins over to the IRS."

"There you go again," Stevie said.

"Just trying to think ahead."

"Don't. Stay where we are."

"You're not the one chasing the All-American mom from the grocery store to the—"

When Melissa failed to complete her thought, Stevie checked that they still had a connection.

"I'm here," Melissa acknowledged. "Okay, so I missed the obvious."

"Little Sister?"

"You know those trick posters that are all color and pattern, and you stare at them long enough and suddenly this three-D image appears?"

"You missed what?" Stevie asked.

"She washed her car two days ago. I mean, what was I thinking? I sat right in this same spot! Talk about lame!"

"You missed what?" Stevie repeated.

"She's rolling. I gotta go," Melissa said. The phone went dead.

CHAPTER 6

Boldt sat on the back porch on a warm Friday night, the kids in bed, waiting for Liz, the slide projector at the ready, aimed at the only smooth white surface available, a door that had once led into what was now the kitchen pantry. Painted shut. Lately, he had felt pretty much the same way as that door: closed off, stuck.

He might have set up the projector in the living room; there was a wall there, pretty much of it white if the framed watercolors were removed, but the noise of the carousel's clicking was certain to wake Sarah, who was as light a sleeper as her father, and if she awakened it might be an hour or two before she could be coaxed toward slumber again. So the carousel sat out there on a wicker table, the yellow Kodak box alongside. Boldt blinked in an attempt to decipher the firefly mystery: He couldn't figure out whether he was actually seeing fireflies or if those spots of white light before his eyes were simply another sign of his total exhaustion.

"I think we have fireflies," he told Liz when she finally joined him.

"We'll need to cover Miles before we go to sleep. Remind me, would you?"

The wicker creaked as she sat into it. Boldt wanted her twenty pounds heavier. He wanted that wicker chair to cry when she took to it, not simply moan.

"I didn't think we had fireflies. Six years in this house, I can't remember ever seeing a firefly."

"I don't see any fireflies," she informed him.

"Give it a minute," he said. "Over toward the back fence."

She eyed the projector. "If we'd bought more carousels we wouldn't have to load it each time."

"Don't use it enough to justify two carousels."

"We should have the slides put onto video."

"Then what would we use the projector for?" he asked.

She stared out into the lawn. "I don't see them."

"That's what I was afraid of."

"What are we looking at?"

"On her seventy-fifth birthday my mother gave each of us slides of old family photos."

"I remember these."

"Right."

"Old, old family photographs."

"Right. That's what I said." He got the projector up and running and focused the image of a gray-haired lady onto the overpainted door.

"I love summer evenings," she said. "The charcoal in the air, the fresh-cut grass. Shouldn't ever take any of it for granted."

"My mother's mother," he said. "She died in her sleep. I remember her clothes smelled like mothballs. Hair like cotton candy. But what sticks in my mind is that she died in her sleep."

"That's the cop in you. You're always more concerned with how a person dies than how he lived."

He didn't like the comment. He sensed she might apologize for it, and he didn't want her doing that, and he wasn't sure why. "I think it's strange I'd remember that about her."

"How'd your grandfather die?"

"No idea. They never told me, I guess. He came over first. He was the one who brought us here." He fast-forwarded through a dozen slides. Liz wanted him to stop at a few, but he plowed through them with the determination of a man who knew where he was going.

He landed on a photograph, a sepia print, of a young boy of eighteen standing by the butt end of a huge fallen timber. He said, "We were Polish. My father called us Europeans."

"This is about the container," Liz stated. "This is about the women who died."

Boldt worked the projector through two more slides of his grandfather. "We all crossed an ocean at some point," he observed. "Your people came in the early 1800s. Mine, during the Great War. You think our people would make it in now? All the qualifications and requirements?"

"Don't do this to yourself."

"Technically they died of malnutrition, but Dixie says that some kind of flu was a contributing factor. If they had lived longer, the flu might have killed them. How's that for irony?"

She pointed. "I think I saw one!" She craned forward. "I didn't think we had fireflies!"

"Not over there. Those are those Christmas lights that they never take down." He pulled off the carousel, leaving a blinding white box on the old painted door. Liz jumped out of her chair with the enthusiasm of a little girl and made hand shadows of birds flying. She wore shorts. Her legs were tan but too thin. She made a duck's head and her voice changed to Donald Duck. Donald told him he worried too much. She wouldn't have jumped up like that two years ago before the illness. She'd become unpredictable that way. He didn't know what was coming next. She wouldn't deprive herself of a single moment of joy. She seized each and every one unabashedly. He envied her that freedom, that allowance of youth. She was no longer painted shut.

"Can you imagine leaving Christmas lights up all year?" she asked.

"There ought to be an ordinance."

"Always the cop."

He loaded the carousel with shots of a vacation they had taken years before.

"If your grandfather had never made the crossing, we wouldn't be here," she said.

"That's what's bugging me, I think. If those women had lived . . . At least for a while they would have had a legitimate chance at freedom."

"They found a different kind of freedom," she said.

He wasn't going to go there. He wasn't going to touch that one for anything.

CHAPTER 7

"What do we know?" Boldt asked LaMoia before the man ever sat down. Boldt's office had been transformed into an art gallery, the present exhibition finger painting and crayon coloring by daughter Sarah and son Miles. He treasured each and every drawing, had invented titles for most; the scientists were wrong about the world spinning on an axis—it revolved around his two kids.

"I been following up on that fabric. Spent the weekend with dockhands, Customs and my face in the Yellow Pages. That's the part of this job you forget, Sarge. When you went up to Lieutenant you got your weekends back."

"The polarfleece," Boldt said.

"Yeah, the bales we hauled out of that container along with the body bags," LaMoia answered.

Boldt spoke with great but unfounded confidence, for he was only guessing. "There's no bill of lading that can be connected to it. No record of the container number. No import company on record."

"Two out of three ain't bad, Sarge."

"Where'd I miss?"

"*Officially* there's no import company that we can tie to that container," LaMoia corrected. "No paperwork—true enough. But unofficially?" When LaMoia got something right, which was more often than not, he enjoyed dragging out the success like a kid retelling an old joke he's just heard for the first time. Bernie Lofgrin in the crime lab had the same bad habit of turning what could be a one-line answer into a ten-minute lecture. Boldt felt no obligation to egg him on by responding, so he waited him out. "After I struck out IDing that container, I decided to put the word out on the street. Nice and gentle like . . . nothing too severe. There's an art to working the street, you know?" he said, fishing for a compliment.

"Uh-huh," Boldt agreed.

"It's like lovemaking: You start slow and easy and let things develop of themselves."

"Try to get around to your point sometime today, if possible."

LaMoia didn't so much as flinch. He was on stage; he was performing. Nothing could rattle him. "So rather than make an issue out of this, I just let it be known that we would be interested in whosoever might be ordering polarfleece by the container load. Okay? I know it's not Eddie Bauer or REI 'cause I've already checked with them. Can't be a mom-and-pop with that kind of quantity. So what the fuck, chuck?"

"John!" Boldt raised his voice enough to send the two-minute warning.

"It wasn't a snitch, Sarge—wasn't no squirrel. The right snitch, and I coulda worked some Monopoly magic on him, you know? 'Get out of jail for free,' or something along those lines. Okay? Coulda come up with a name, a contact, something firm enough to squeeze by the neck and start choking. Okay?" He stopped talking. Stopped, and stood there, waiting to elicit some kind of response from his lieutenant, who sat impassively enough to allow another unsuspecting person to believe he had died there in the chair. Boldt would not, did not, move. He waited. LaMoia took this all in and finally understood that he was to blink first. "Part of me thinks we should contact I.I. before they contact us. Save 'em the trouble."

I.I.—Internal Investigation—a pair of initials that drove a heat rash to the back of the neck of even the most honest and upright soldier-in-blue. I.I. could stall careers, stop paychecks and cause months of consultation with overworked attorneys on retainer to the Police Officers' Benevolent Association—the union. LaMoia's suggestion meant that whatever he'd turned up could put one or both of them directly in harm's way. The implication was obvious—organized crime was involved.

Corruption swept through police departments and other government agencies like the flu, passed one person to the next, indiscriminate of rank, race or gender. Like any contagious disease, when its proportions became epidemic within the given population, measures were taken to eradicate or at least reduce its influence; a few scapegoats were found and hung out to dry while the others went more deeply underground.

Throughout the course of his twenty-odd years on the force, Lou Boldt had carefully avoided and had never succumbed to even a hint of impropriety, which occasionally amounted to a full-time job. He stood sentry at the gate, alert and watchful. He would not willingly rat out his fellow officer to Internal Investigations; likewise, he would not tolerate compromised police work. He purposely avoided any social contact with individuals known, or even suspected, to have ties to organized crime including certain politicians and even a few of his own superiors at SPD. If even a whiff of a rumor surfaced, Boldt mentally added the name to his list.

Professionally, he could not afford such luxury. Crimes Against Persons—CAPers—implicitly required fundamental knowledge of, and contact with, elements of organized crime, whether the Chinese Triad, the Russian Mafia, or any of a number of gangs that in recent years had begun to pick up the crumbs—the street level crimes—left behind by their larger counterparts: drugs, prostitution, auto theft and small-time gaming. While the Russian mob controlled the brothels, the gangs ran the street hookers; while the Chinese Triad imported the coke and heroin by the boatload, the gangs distributed them. Each group had cut out its own niche, and for the most part, left the other alone. Only at the street level, the gang level, was this not the case— where hotheaded loyalties and romantic notions gave way to the occasional street war leaving teenagers and twenty-five-year-olds dead in the streets.

To receive a request for a meeting with any person known to have association with such organizations could mean the kiss of death—an either/or offer that might include a threat to one's family or, to one's life, profession or aspirations. There were few police officers who could not be reached given the appropriate pressure point. Boldt knew that of all his possible vulnerabilities, his children presented the biggest target for such people. He would never accept money, nor improved station, but if the health and welfare of Miles and Sarah were brought into play, he knew he would be faced with one of two choices—strike back, or roll over. Each cop knew his own vulnerabilities; Boldt, whose daughter had once been threatened, guarded his carefully.

A cop's home number was never given out, never published in the phone books. Some lied to neighbors about their profession both to protect their families and to avoid being called into petty disagreements. The game of dodging compromise, of avoiding corruption, was never-ending and required great vigilance on the part of any police officer, Boldt included. When the call came from Mama Lu, he briefly gave pause. It was the day he had feared most of his professional career.

LaMoia was the messenger. They had moved to the fifth floor's coffee lounge. Boldt shut the doors and prepared himself a cup of tea.

"So there's this girl I went out with for a while name of Peggy Wan."

"Woman," Boldt corrected. "Let's hope so anyway."

"We hit if off pretty great. Not that it lasted."

"Not that that's news," Boldt said.

"But we stayed friends. Are you interested in this?" LaMoia asked.

"If it's going somewhere. If it's the Further Adventures of . . . I can do without it this morning. Your trail is littered with Peggy Wans, John. For your sake I hope someone comes along who actually means something to you."

"Just 'cause I'm altar-shy . . . Gosh, Sarge, I didn't know you cared."

Boldt hesitated a moment too long to keep things on a joking level. "Yes," he said, "I do care."

LaMoia stiffened while his smile softened and his eyes found a lint ball in the far corner of the room. His bottom lip twitched beneath his mustache.

Boldt said, "So tell me about Peggy Wan."

LaMoia took a second longer to recover, to regain the boyish enthusiasm and cocky independence that were his trademarks. "So Peggy is evidently the niece of Mama Lu—although Asians throw around this aunt and uncle business a little too often, if you know what I mean. And so maybe *that* explains why Peggy—God bless her silky smooth tush—went the way of other LaMoia conquests. A little too tight around the collar, you know what I mean. I hang with that piece of work and pretty soon I'm going to be doing the dance with Mama Lu herself—am I right? And then I'm jammed but good."

"So Peggy's name gets a line through it in Seattle's most famous black book."

"But evidently she does reciprocate the favor—"

"The legend lives on," Boldt said.

"—on account I hear from Peggy last night. She calls my crib, right? Which means she lifted my number off the home phone because I never gave it to her."

"Bedside phone, no doubt."

"And what does she want but to arrange a meet between you and her aunt?"

"Me?"

"That's what *I* said to her."

"Mama Lu?"

"Exactly."

"Oh, shit," the man cursed uncharacteristically. "Why me?" Boldt protested.

"I can't answer that. I imagine she can, and will."

"You're coming with me."

"I wasn't invited."

"Doesn't matter. Two of us in the room, it changes the approach." Boldt reconsidered. "Only if you're all right with it. No arm twisting here, John. I don't want to put you into something . . . you know."

"Yeah, I do know. But I'm cool with it. You want me to hang with you, I'll hang."

"We may both hang," Boldt warned ominously.

Two sinewy, lithe men stood outside the Korean grocery smoking non-filters that smelled like burning tires. Two men going nowhere. They both wore nylon gym pants that whistled as they moved to follow La-Moia and Boldt through the store's screen door. A seagull complained loudly, flying overhead, trapped by the buildings. The International District occupied a forty-block area south of the downtown core and just north of the industrial wastelands that gave way to Boeing Field. Of unremarkable architecture and few tax dollars, the District's only color was its energetic people.

"I'm LaMoia," the sergeant said, turning to greet the welcoming committee. "This is Boldt. She's expecting us."

The men's faces were placid and unresponsive until one of them nodded, his neck so stiff that the gesture ended up more of a bow.

Boldt bowed back to the man.

LaMoia mumbled, "That's only for the Japanese, Sarge. These two are Chinese."

The grocery smelled of ginger and hot oil. Its floor plan violated the fire code with not a spare inch of unused space: diapers and paper products kissing the century-old tin ceiling where a dust-encrusted paddle fan spun slowly, trailing broken lengths of spider web like bunting.

They were escorted through the impossibly cramped butcher department where a bone-thin grandmother wielded a Chinese knife like an axe into a side of beef. Wizened and otherwise frail looking, she had a smile that flooded them with kindness, and her eyes flirted.

"I think she likes you," LaMoia said as they climbed noisy wooden stairs through a dark hallway.

"I hope she does," Boldt replied, unprepared for what he saw next. Mama Lu was the size of Orson Welles. She wore a bright red housedress with gorgeous black hair braided down to her waist. Surrounded by piles of books and a single black rotary dial telephone, she occupied a wingback chair under the floral shade of a standing lamp that fit her more like a commercial hair dryer. Yellowing roller shades were pulled to block any sun, and a persistent air conditioner struggled in the one window that remained free of a covering, offering a limited view of Elliott Bay and the islands beyond.

Mama Lu reached into a glass of water with fingers as fast as a frog's tongue and had her teeth in before her guests had introduced themselves. When she spoke, the windy baritone emanated from somewhere beneath the substantial bosom that hung off her like the continental shelf. By the sound of her, she had smoked for a long, long time. Maybe still did, unless the green oxygen bottle standing in the corner was more than decoration.

"You honor me with this visit," she said in passable English.

"It is said," Boldt began, "that Miss Lu's family is very large indeed: mother to many, friend to all. You have made substantial contributions to our Police Athletic League, to the firemen and to the hospitals, and for this the city and its people are extremely grateful."

"We are all of one family, yes?"

"I wish more were as thoughtful of the family as you, Great Lady."

"Ya-Moia, you are friend to Peggy Wan."

"Yes, Miss Lu."

"She say you honest man. This man with you, Mr. Both, he honest man?"

"As honest and as good a man as any man I know."

"That says much, Ya-Moia."

LaMoia bowed slightly.

"Tell me about investigation, Mr. Both," she said. There was no mention of *which* investigation.

"Chinese immigrants are being treated like dogs, shipped here in huge metal boxes, like kennels, without water, without food. It is inhuman and it must stop."

"When a person runs from a monster, he is prepared to suffer."

"But these people pay for this."

"My grandfather and I rode in the bottom of a freighter without sunshine, without fresh air for over a month. My grandfather paid much money for this. Things not so different today. My people have been running from the Red Chinese for many generations now."

"People enter this great country in many ways, some legal, some not," Boldt said. "I am not here to judge that. But three women died in that container. Young women. Their lives ahead of them. Everyone involved is going to jail. *Everyone*. They will end up in metal boxes just like their victims. Those who cooperate with the police will receive the lightest sentences."

Mama Lu did not move, did not twitch. She sat like a piece of stone in her padded throne, all levity, all kindness gone from her face. "Yes," she said deliberately slowly, "I agree."

Boldt was surprised by this, and spoke what his mind had already prepared to say. "The young women who survived will not cooperate with us, will not share any information with us."

"They scared of you. With good reason, I might add. Police at home not like police here. But there are others. These children, their families, in both countries, will suffer if they cooperate."

"And *your* family."

"You give me far too much credit, Mr. Both," she said, her accent suddenly lessened, her voice softer yet more severe, her hard eyes fixed on Boldt and not releasing him. "I have no influence over these children." She struggled with a deep breath and said, "Three died. Yes. Very sad. But tell me this please: How many die if they stay behind?"

"I'm only responsible for Seattle, Great Lady," Boldt announced.

"I will make inquiries," she said, nodding her large head once again. "Let an old lady see what she can find out."

"The ship responsible," Boldt said, "the captain would be a good place to start."

"You travel in the dark, Mr. Both. Move slowly. The dark holds many unseen dangers."

"The dark eventually gives way to the light."

"Not always. Ask Officer Tidwell. But I will help you. In return, you will tell me of progress of investigation, will keep my good name out of press. So tired of the lies."

"We're all tired of the lies."

"Chinese blood moves in my veins, Mr. Both. These three were my sisters, my children."

"Your customers?" he dared to ask.

She grinned. "You bite hand that feeds you?"

"When I'm hungry enough," he answered.

She lifted her soft pudgy hand and held it for a moment as if expecting he might kiss it. Then she waved, dismissing them.

Boldt stood, and LaMoia along with him.

LaMoia said, "I thank you, Miss Lu."

"You be nice Peggy Wan, Ya-Moia. She my niece." Directing her attention back to Boldt, she said, "Move slowly. The dark holds many challenges. Maybe I offer some light."

"Thank you."

"You will visit whenever you like, whenever you have something to tell me. You always welcome."

Boldt caught himself in a bow, lifted his head and grinned at her.

Back on the street and well away from the Korean grocery LaMoia said, "Are you crazy, Sarge? You basically accused her."

"I communicated my suspicions."

"Oh, you communicated all right."

"If she's smart, she gives them up. They'll never bring her into it, not with her reach. They wouldn't last a week in lock-up. She gives us this operation, and she skates. What was that about Tidwell?"

LaMoia warned, "You remember Tidwell. Organized Crime?"

"Retired?"

"Retired! He went out for a morning jog, came back on a stretcher. Every damn bone broken. Claimed he'd been hit by a car. Car with four legs is more like it. Left the department on a medical disability 'cause he can't walk right."

"Mama Lu?"

"Remember that semi with the Mexicans in the back? Dead of fumes? Word was Mama Lu had a piece of that trucking company. That was Tidwell's baby until his unfortunate accident."

"Are you trying to warn me, John?"

"She was, that's for sure," he said emphatically, eyes wide. The leather soles of his ostrich boots slapped the sidewalk loudly with each long stride. He said to Boldt, "I'm just trying to tell you to listen up. Either that, or I'd up my Blue Cross if I was you."

CHAPTER 8

Melissa accepted the digital camera from Stevie along with two very small tape cartridges and an extra battery. They talked in the corner of KSTV's news studio while all around the crew prepared for the live broadcast of *News Four at Five*. As Stevie handed her the camera bag she felt compelled to caution Melissa. "This is not a license to take matters into your own hands."

"I understand."

"Don't be so glib about it."

"I understand that you have to say that. You have to protect yourself and the station."

"It's not that at all. It's you I'm trying to protect."

"Your nurturing instinct?" Melissa asked.

"You're to clear everything with me ahead of time."

"Of course I am."

"I'm not kidding, damn it!"

"Ms. McNeal?" the floor director called out. "Two minutes."

Stevie dismissed the person with a brutal wave. She looked at Melissa and saw trouble. "You've got something going, don't you? I know that look."

Melissa shook her head.

"What were you saying about the car wash?" Stevie asked.

"Nothing but a hunch. A picture's worth a thousand words, and I've got some good pictures. You'll see."

"When?" she persisted.

"At the pay phone, I overheard him mention the graveyard," Melissa whispered.

Stevie suffered a bout of chills. "Who him? What graveyard?"

"Ms. McNeal?" the floor director called out.

"I'm coming!" Stevie snapped. When she turned around, Melissa was already leaving the studio. Stevie knew that the thing to do was to go after her, to stop her. Melissa suffered from professional tunnel vision. "Wait!" she called out.

"Sixty seconds!" the floor director announced.

"I'll call you tonight," Melissa mouthed silently, holding her hand to her ear as to a telephone.

"You call me!" Stevie demanded, still tempted to abandon the anchor desk and stop her Little Sister. "I'm going to wait up for that call!"

An intern held the double doors open for Melissa, who looked back one final time and smiled at Stevie. Again she held her hand to her ear: She would call.

"Thirty seconds! Places, please."

Stevie moved reluctantly toward the anchor desk, the pit in her stomach growing ever deeper. If she hadn't had the interview with the head of the INS lined up, she might have bailed. As it was, she climbed into her anchor chair and reviewed the script while the sound-man wired her. She had a sinking feeling about Melissa that she couldn't shake: It felt more like a farewell than a good-bye.

The temperature of the studio hovered in the mid-fifties, a concession to the computerized electronics. The floor director reading the shoot-ing script was dressed in a cotton cardigan. Behind the anchor desk things were a little hotter because an intern had delivered Stevie's latté with a teaspoon of real sugar instead of sugar substitute. Stevie slid the mug aside combatively and studied her own script one last time. No matter how many times this team prepared for a broadcast, nerves were always taut. *News Four at Five*'s continuing efforts to keep the number one Nielsen rating in the race for local news viewers had a way of turning up the heat.

Stevie's male co-anchor, William Cutler, was more intent on his appearance in the monitor than on the script. Billy-Bob, as Stevie referred to him, spent his time at ribbon-cutting ceremonies and lunchtime speaker appearances—appreciating the fees for these extracurricular activities quite a bit more than the news.

She checked herself one last time in the monitor. At thirty-seven, she knew the camera still flattered her. Her hair was highlighted and cut shoulder length, her camisole cut a little low, a little bare, a little tasteless, but just right for the producers and their precious ratings. Those ratings justified a contract that included a Town Car and driver to shuttle her to and from her all-expenses-paid five-bedroom co-op apartment. A promotional arrangement with Nordstrom provided her with a wardrobe, all for a five-second credit in the closing scroll. The creamy pale skin of her surgically enhanced cleavage and the ease with which she carried herself had won her a description of "overtly sexual," by *Newsweek* in an article about the decline of standards in local news broadcasts. Whatever the criticism, the ratings remained superb. Only Billy-Bob's libido threatened to bring them down. There were rumors of high school girls, drugs and all-night parties. If Billy-Bob didn't keep it zipped, *N4@5* was in trouble.

"Fifteen seconds," announced the floor director standing between the two robotic cameras, headphone wires trailing. She held a hand-scrawled notice to remind both anchors of an insert—"page B-36"—that was not part of their preprinted scripts.

"Hair!" William Cutler shouted as he preened.

The studio coiffeuse bounded up on stage as the floor director continued the count. "Ten seconds!" The hairdresser, who carried a sheen of perspiration on her upper lip, dragged a brush carefully across Cutler's lacquered coif and toyed with an escaped lock.

"You idiot! What are you, a dog groomer? Give me that!" Cutler stole the brush away from her and laid the lock down.

"Nine . . . clear the set . . . eight . . ." the floor director droned, not the slightest hint of concern in her voice. Pros, every one of them.

The hairdresser stepped off camera as a snarling Cutler inspected himself in the monitor once again. He threw the brush off set at the young hairdresser.

"Four . . . three . . . two . . ."

Stevie's face lit up as she faced the camera. She typically lived for this moment: Hundreds of thousands of viewers hanging on her every word, but Melissa's earlier zealousness negated the usual thrill. The prerecorded voice said into her ear, "And now, Seattle's most watched news team, Stevie McNeal and William Cutler and *News Four at Five*."

Stevie read from the scrolling text, her smile picture perfect, her tone slightly hoarse and sensual, her eyes soft and locked onto camera two. Sadly, the news was "there to fill the time between the ads." A mentor had explained that to her when she had been coming up in New York, hoping to make the jump from on-camera reporter to anchor.

Sources close to the illegal alien investigation resulting from a shipping container being fished from Puget Sound say that detectives from the homicide squad of the Seattle Police Department have now questioned at least one of the detainees who survived the passage. The interrogation is said to have revolved around a failed attempt at a plea bargain agreement, that left police with few, if any leads.

File footage rolled of the container's recovery and the blanketed women being led to emergency vehicles.

In related news, the preliminary autopsy of the first of three women who died in the crossing is said to suggest that the victim died of natural causes, namely malnutrition and dehydration, though it appears uncertain these conditions were anything but the result of negligence on the part of the ship's captain. Identifying the ship involved in the transport of that container and the ship's captain are believed to now be the target of the ongoing investigation.

News Four at Five *will carry a live interview with Adam Talmadge, regional director of the Immigration and Naturalization Service, later in this broadcast.*

William Cutler and his brazen voice took over, reporting a homicide in Madrona that afternoon. Some poor kid's lights had been dimmed over a parking space dispute. They alternated the anchor work on the more gruesome and hopeless stories. She tried to leave the out-and-out bleeders for Billy-Bob. But when the illegals had washed ashore in a sewage-encrusted container, abandoned there by some greedy son-of-a-bitch, she held on to it. All the stations, radio and TV, were still leading with it. The nationals were interested, spurred on by the feed of Stevie's first reporting of the story. It was hot. *She* was hot because of it. And when something started burning hot, you fed the fire with any fuel available. If not exactly in execution, she and Melissa agreed in concept: This was one story that had to be told. And it had to be kept alive to be told. Pending a coup by the city's prosecuting attorney, who hoped to hold the detainees as material witnesses to a homicide, the illegals were rumored to be scheduled for deportation, to return to whatever lives they'd fled. Out of sight was out of mind. Stevie considered it her job to keep the story current and in front of viewers while Melissa sought out the possible connections to the people responsible. In the business of reporting corruption, disease and death, the opportunity to investigate and expose a criminal ring that exploited human beings was a rare opportunity. For once her work could count for something more than filling time between ads. But for that to happen she had to keep the public's attention riveted to this story. She embraced this as a personal challenge.

Following a lead by Billy-Bob, Stevie read six more lines from the TelePrompTer—a crack house catching fire—and then settled back into her swivel chair as a taped report took over.

The floor director signaled camera three, lifting a hand like a race car flagman. That hand dropped and Stevie recited from the scrolling script.

Stay with News Four at Five *for an exclusive interview with Adam Talmadge, Northwest regional director of the INS, based here in Seattle, as we continue our investigation into the trade*

*in illegal immigrants in High Seas, High Stakes. Back after
this break.*

The TV screen went to ads. Third-quarter revenues were up 31
percent. Stevie knew the numbers.

"Clear!" shouted the floor director. "Stevie, living room! William,
camera two in sixty."

Adam Talmadge wore a dark suit, a white button-down shirt and a
blue tie bearing red eagle heads. His wingtips were resoled but well
shined. He had most of his hair, a light gray curly nap cut close to his
scalp, dramatic black eyebrows and clear blue irises like fresh ice or
taxidermy glass. His face filled with a reserved but friendly caution as
he shook hands with Stevie. His eyes did not stray to her anatomy for
even an instant, as some men's did, and she ascertained immediately
that he was well versed in media performance. She had little doubt
that by agreeing to the interview, Talmadge brought his own agenda.
She had, in fact, requested that this interview be with Coughlie, who
presently occupied a formed-fiberglass seat off-camera, but Talmadge
had accepted for himself.

"All set?" Stevie asked her guest.

"My pleasure," he said.

The floor director's arm prepared to flag her, and chopped with
authority.

"*News Four at Five* is pleased to welcome Adam Talmadge, Northwest regional director of the Immigration and Naturalization Service
based here in Seattle. Welcome."

"Good to be here, Stevie."

"The INS is the gateway through which every legal immigrant
must enter this country," she said. "It also maintains its own, independent federal police force at our borders and ports of entry. You
detain how many individuals a year here in the Seattle area?"

Talmadge's tan spoke of a low golf handicap. He said, "We detained approximately twenty-two hundred individuals in the last calendar year—but let me just say—"

"That says plenty," Stevie interrupted, setting the tone for the interview. She would resist allowing Talmadge to stray and change the topic the way the media coaches taught. "And of those, approximately how many arrive by container or ship?"

"A third to one-half, perhaps." He glanced imperceptibly off camera toward Brian Coughlie.

She stated, "So, of those detained, seven hundred to one thousand illegal immigrants—political refugees—enter this city as stowaways or human cargo or slaves."

"Political refugees account for only about ten percent of all illegal entries," he corrected.

"And what percentage of all illegal entries are in fact detained by your service?"

"We have no way to measure that."

"An estimate?" she asked.

"If we were fifty percent successful we'd be pleased."

"Less than ten percent of drugs coming into this country are seized," she challenged, reading from her notes. "Why would your results be significantly higher?"

"Drugs can be hidden in a ski pole, can be left on the bottom of the ocean for a month, air-dropped into national forest. We're dealing with human beings," he reminded.

"So if your twenty-two hundred is fifty percent, there are roughly five thousand illegals entering via the Northwest each year. And yet the national number is more like three hundred thousand, isn't it?"

"The majority of which—some eighty percent—come across our southern border."

"Mexico."

"From Mexico, yes."

"And here, Asians account for most of the illegal immigration, do they not?"

"That's correct."

"Chinese?"

"A large percentage are from mainland China. Yes. Vietnam. Indonesia."

"Political refugees," she said, returning to her earlier point.

Talmadge pursed his lips and cocked his head. "We screen carefully for those individuals with legitimate claims to political persecution."

"And yet a recent ruling by Congress allows detained illegals only nine days to confirm their status as political refugees, isn't that right?"

"Six working days," he corrected.

She attempted to contain the gleam in her eyes from having purposely overstated the waiting period, luring him into the correction.

"After which they are deported and returned to their country of origin—whatever their fate there."

"That is generally the procedure, yes."

"And to qualify as a political refugee these individuals, these refugees, have to be able to prove they have been tortured."

"Tortured is a strong word. Either physically or mentally abused," he corrected. "Or at substantial physical risk if they remained in-country."

"As I understand it," she went on, "select INS agents are receiving special training that has itself come under fire from both Capitol Hill and the psychiatric community. Your department employs how many such specially trained interviewers?" she asked.

"Three," Talmadge replied with another glance to Coughlie. "Only a small percentage—ten percent perhaps—of all illegals claim political refugee status."

"Then you support the new policies?" she tested.

Talmadge returned quickly, "Congress has enacted one of the most far-reaching, sweeping overhauls to the Immigration Act this century, making our borders more welcoming than they have been in over seventy years, while *reducing* paperwork and increasing efficiency on the part of this agency. As to those people out there perpetrating these crimes against their fellow human beings, all I can say is that such behavior will not be condoned by this administration, nor by the Immigration and Naturalization Service. We *will* ferret out those responsible, and we *will* see them in prison for their actions. I should add that the Seattle police are currently conducting an active homicide investigation into the three deaths aboard that recent container. Let this serve as notice: The black market in human cargo is over. Immunity will be offered to the first few willing to expose this trade. The rest are going to prison."

Stevie then understood Talmadge's agenda. He had used the broadcast to soapbox for informants.

The floor director signaled Stevie, who wrapped the interview quickly.

"Clear!" the floor director shouted. "William, camera two, two minutes."

Talmadge stood and unclipped his mike. He brushed himself off as if he'd eaten a meal.

Brian Coughlie stepped up to Stevie. "Good questions."

"Vague answers," she replied.

Talmadge winced a smile and headed for the exit; he clearly expected Coughlie at his side.

"Dinner?" Coughlie asked her.

"No thank you," she answered.

"An off-camera interview? 'Source close to the investigation'?"

"You're getting warmer," she said.

"I can provide more specific stats," he offered.

Stevie told him, "I'll call you."

"Good," he said.

He reached out and they shook hands. Coughlie kept hold of hers a moment longer than necessary. She didn't like the feeling. She wouldn't flirt to get a story. She turned and walked toward the anchor desk, confident that Brian Coughlie was watching.

CHAPTER 9

Seven years had passed since Boldt had consulted Dr. Byron Rutledge at the University of Washington's—"the U-Dub's"—School of Oceanography. Rutledge, a physical oceanographer who had a long history in the department, was a leading authority on the tidal currents of Puget Sound and had once assisted Boldt with a homicide investigation involving a body washed ashore by those currents. As North America's largest estuary, Puget Sound experiences unusual but highly predictable tides and currents, including some of the fastest surface currents in the western United States.

Rutledge was of medium build and height. With his carefully trimmed Abraham Lincoln beard, his ice blue eyes and his smoker's pipe, he looked the part of salty dog. The office was cluttered with paperwork: graphs, charts and reports occupying most horizontal surfaces. Its walls were adorned with engravings of square-riggers, brigs and whalers, as well as a chalkboard and a rack of maps that retracted like window shades.

"You know," Rutledge said in a smoky voice, "about a year after we worked together, a prosecutor from Skagit County asked me up there to work another corpse. I had a hell of a good time with it. I'm almost ashamed to say so. A woman's remains were found in Bowmans Bay west of Deception Pass, pretty much like the one you had on the beach. This one turned out to have been thrown off Deception Pass bridge by the husband."

"A conviction, wasn't it?" Boldt asked, recalling the sensational trial.

Rutledge's teeth, discolored from the pipe smoking, looked like a rotting picket fence. "You're looking at the state's expert witness. That boy won himself a cell for thirty-one years. His people challenged my findings on appeal and lost again." The smile was contagious. "So this time," the man said, referring to the phone call that had arranged the meeting, "it's a shipping container." He nodded. "You wouldn't believe the number of lost containers drifting out there in open water. They're a primary cause of collision damage at sea. Ask the insurers."

Boldt said, "Your people had a chance to look over the container."

Rutledge nodded. "Did you bring the stats for me?"

Boldt slid a piece of paper across the man's desk. "Weight of the container, number of souls inside, weight and approximate volume of the bolts of fabric." He added, "The fabric was sealed inside six-millimeter visquine."

Rutledge peered over the top of reading glasses he had donned. "You want to be able to trace that container to its mother ship."

Boldt told him, "We need the ship if we're to get to the ship's manifest. Did your inspection tell you anything?" Boldt had arranged for Rutledge to visit the container.

"Smelling it did," Rutledge said. "No Porta-potty."

"No."

"You imagine living like that for a two-week Pacific crossing?"

Boldt repeated anxiously, "Anything at all?"

"Open water exerts its personality on anyone or anything it contacts. The waters of the Northern Pacific differ greatly from the more brackish estuary water we find in the Sound," began the professor. "This can be attributed to the presence of fresh water from the dozens of rivers and tributaries within its seven hundred square miles. The rivers empty into the estuary fast enough so the estuary refreshes despite the higher saline-content ocean water in the outer strait and west of Vancouver Island. For that reason, Puget Sound plays host to several hundred specific floral and fauna indigenous only to estuarine waters, microorganisms that won't be found a hundred miles north or forty miles west. You remember raising pollywogs in fifth grade science and how fast scum coated the walls of the aquarium? The same thing happens in the Sound or out in the ocean; it's real apparent if a vessel is left sitting a long time—the algae and barnacles take over quickly. That algae is preceded by bacteria and diatoms that begin affixing themselves within six hours of submersion. A puddle, a freshwater pond, an estuary, the ocean, it doesn't matter. There is a long food chain just waiting in the cafeteria line. And that gives marine biologists a trail to follow.

"The same way an entomologist can study a corpse for insects," Rutledge continued, "a marine biologist can study microorganisms and algae on the hull of a ship—or even a container—and estimate fairly accurately how long that surface material has been immersed, and in what kind of water."

"A clock?" Boldt asked apprehensively.

"Very much so. You gave our arriving students a very valuable field trip followed by equally valuable lab time. I'm grateful for that opportunity."

"And did we learn something?" Boldt said.

Rutledge answered, "One man's slime is another man's gold mine." He hesitated for effect, leaving Boldt hanging. "Several million small organisms adhering themselves in predictable progression to the immersed sides and bottom of your container. What these marine bacteria, diatoms and attached larvae tell us is that the container was immersed in brackish water—more precisely, the waters of the Sound's central basin—for between sixteen and twenty hours. No more, no less. The accumulation of hydrocarbons from the water's surface that adhered to the sides of the container tell us that it was at one pitch for maybe half that time—about fifteen degrees—and then took on additional water sometime around the eight-hour mark, changing the pitch closer to twenty-two degrees while increasing the depth of its draft by three feet."

"We can use that? Sixteen hours?"

"The presence of diatoms and barnacle larvae attached over the bacterial colonies confirms this, yes. All the work done by the students has been double-checked. Sixteen to twenty hours. That's your window of time."

"No more, no less," Boldt repeated while taking notes. "Just maybe, you've saved this investigation."

"We're not through."

"No?"

Rutledge challenged Boldt, "We've looked carefully at those bales of polarfleece fabric and the way that they were sealed, and it presents an interesting possibility."

"I'm listening."

Rutledge answered, "What if this particular container was never intended to reach a dock, but was supposed to be transferred at sea? Such a transfer is exceptionally dangerous. Your organizer planned for this, bought himself insurance by using those bales as internal flotation in case a container leaked water. Those bales are effectively huge balloons."

"He'd lost one before?" Boldt said, noting Rutledge's expression.

"Let me just say that even with enough flotation to keep it from sinking, even in calm waters, I wouldn't want to have been inside that container. If they attempted this in the storm we had the other night—" He didn't bother completing his thought.

"If they did attempt it during the storm," Boldt said, "could you tell me *where*?"

Indicating the paper Boldt had provided, Rutledge said, "These are the coordinates where it was found?"

"The first is approximate, noted by the plane that spotted it. The second was provided by the Coast Guard: exact time and GPS location of the intercept."

Rutledge approached his maps. He wore wrinkled khakis and leather deck shoes, the same as Boldt. An expert on the waters of Puget Sound, Rutledge pointed to a spot on the surface current map nearly instantly. "It was first spotted here, recovered here," he said, moving his fingertip an inch west. "Surface area exposure to wind, weight and the speed and direction of currents will all have affected its course. I can't give you a specific location, as we have a four-hour window of time within which to work. But what I can do is backtrack its probable drift route for a period of sixteen to twenty-four hours prior to its being spotted to estimate the transfer location. We have satellite images of that storm, weather station records of surface winds, tidal charts and current information for all depths. Plenty of data."

"So if I get a list of all container ships that docked twenty to forty-eight hours *after* this one was spotted—"

"And you can do that through Port Authority," Rutledge suggested.

Boldt followed the reasoning to its logical conclusion. "If you can give me a probable location where the transfer was attempted, then we might be able to predict which of the arriving container ships could have been in that area of the Sound during that window of time."

Nodding, Rutledge informed him, "Since we last worked together, we've computerized much of the data. Do you remember the model in the Science Center?"

Several years earlier, Boldt had spent an afternoon testing Rutledge's predictions on a working model of Puget Sound that accounted for tidal flow and water salinity. Rutledge's work had been proven flawless. "Of course I do."

"Gone. It's all done on computer now, and it's far more accurate. The computer analysis group should be able to give us the exact course that container traveled." He indicated a spot on the map of surface currents. "My guess is the transfer was attempted in here somewhere." He turned his attention to a stack of bound volumes by his desk and, referencing the map on the wall, selected the third in the stack. The volume contained pages upon pages of computerized maps marked by time and date and containing curving arrows and numbers that clearly indicated tidal current direction and speed. Several times Rutledge referenced the wall chart before leafing several more pages deeper into the images. Then, drawing a gentle curve with his crooked index finger with its long flat nail, and tugging with his lips on the unlit pipe so that it whistled, he concluded, "Somewhere in here, is my guess." He crossed to the wall chart and declared, "We'll have the computers work the real-time data so that wind conditions can be considered for greater accuracy." He stabbed the chart with authority. Rutledge was of an era and a mind to not leave everything to computers. "But whatever ship lost that container, whatever fool captain was insane enough to attempt a transfer on that, of all nights, he did so right in here." The man drew a small eyebrow of an arc on the map well away from where Boldt might have guessed. He said, "He was a mile or more out of the shipping lanes."

"Does that give me anything to work with?" Boldt wondered aloud.

"On-board radar," Rutledge said, suddenly brighter. "The Port Authority should have had him on radar, but on a night like that, the other ship captains *certainly* did. You talk to the watch officers of the transiting vessels. They'd have been watching him carefully, since the vessel was well outside the shipping lanes, that would have aroused curiosity. A night like that you remember, believe me. The bridge officers," he paused, drawing on the pipe again, "they'll be able to tell you who or what the hell was out there."

CHAPTER 10

An all-consuming darkness spread before Melissa so that she moved forward with the caution of the blind. This had developed into a mission, no longer a job, so that as she moved through this darkness quietly and slowly, a knot gripping the center of her chest, drenched in sweat driven to the surface by taut nerves, she also experienced a sense of righteousness.

A gray mouth of a windowlike opening appeared ahead of her, and she approached it cautiously, inching forward in tiny, thoughtful steps, the strap of the camera case slung over her neck and shoulder. This opening accessed a descending conveyor belt of cracked black rubber that smelled horribly sour and hadn't run in a decade or more. She tucked her five feet two, 103-pound frame into a ball and slipped through the opening and down the conveyor, the unnerving sound of machinery growing ever louder, ever closer, her fear manifested as a sharp pain at her temples, and pricking her searching eyes. The fear resulted not only from awareness of her predicament but also from the knowledge that she had directly ignored Stevie's instructions, had failed to call, and despite Melissa's seeming impatience with Stevie at the time, she trusted her older "sister's" instincts and experience. Somewhere not too far down inside her, she felt like a child disobeying her parent. She now knew she should have at least left Stevie a voice mail message to apprise her of her whereabouts and plans, this annoying sense of having done wrong continuing to plague her as the sounds of machinery grew ever louder, the area inside the conveyor more constricted, and the air more foul.

She attempted to stave off total panic through a series of deep breaths while she pulled out her cellphone, only to reconfirm that the signal had dropped off. She couldn't call out.

The far end of the conveyor offered her an elevated view of an enormous room where that roar of machinery became painful. Laid out below her, dozens of women—perhaps a hundred or more—toiled at huge industrial sewing machines. She prepared the camera, the poor lighting now her biggest concern. She recorded some images from that vantage point and was about to move on when it occurred to her to find a place to hide this tape for retrieval on her way out. If at any point she was forced to run, to abandon the camera and case, she would still have one of the two tapes to later collect as proof of the sweatshop's existence. Even as she worked to capture the story below, she couldn't entirely dismiss the thought that she could be caught. She had amplified that risk substantially by simply coming inside.

With the camera's viewfinder indicating too little light, Melissa nonetheless recorded the oppressive conditions below—emaciated women, their heads shaved bare, towering bales of fabric enclosing them like walls, the air clouded with a hazy dust, the room's only light coming from small, dim bulbs fixed to the sewing machines. The Asian women worked furiously, some sewing, others at cutting tables, still others gathering the finished product into bundles. Two Chinese males patrolled the floor carrying what looked like nightsticks—gang members probably. Another wave of fear overcame her: The Chinese gangs were notoriously ruthless.

She zoomed in, hoping that she could capture the feeling of the place. Exhausted faces drenched in sweat; the frantic pace; the tension of the guards' presence.

Through the lens she followed a leg chain from where it was bolted to a sewing machine which was in turn bolted to a blood-raw ankle. She moved station-to-station, woman-to-woman; not all were chained, but enough to know the lengths to which the guards went to prevent escapes or ensure discipline. Like slaves, she thought.

If they shackled their own seamstresses, what would they do to an uninvited nosy journalist? Perhaps she should turn back now. She already had some incredible images.

But she did not yet have the *story*. She wanted on-camera interviews with the illegals, pictures of the deplorable living conditions she felt certain she would find with a little more digging. She was a journalist not a cameraperson. And this was a career-defining moment.

She went ahead as planned and removed the camera's tape in order to hide it well enough so that no one would find it before she could come back and get it. She then worked her way farther along the catwalk that hung over the huge room, finally entering a long passageway that descended by steep metal stairs toward the sound of running water.

She felt her way to a steel door, its handle removed to prevent its use, to trap the inhabitants on the other side. But as she put her eye to the hole left behind by this missing hardware, she understood its other purpose as well—it offered the guards a peephole into a shower room.

She counted five women in all, naked and shaved of all body hair. The room might have once been used for storage—no drains or faucets, just garden hose and plastic showerheads secured to, and hanging from, the overhead pipes. The women—girls, really—stood clustered together, shivering under the limp stream of water, their faint whispers in the foreign tongue barely audible. Melissa craned to one side and spotted a sixth woman who stood sentry. Melissa's side of the metal door was fastened shut with two oversized dead bolts. One eye to the hole in the door, Melissa waited for her chance to enter. She could interview these women, thanks to her Chinese. And then a more devious thought occurred: What if she were to become one of them? Live with them? Work with them? What if she could spend a whole day and a night here? Who would notice one more Chinese woman among the hundreds? She grinned a grin of satisfaction, her attention no longer on the women showering but on a bar of soap and the pink plastic razor teetering on the ledge directly across from her, and the knowledge of what had to be done.

TUESDAY, AUGUST 18
1 DAY MISSING

CHAPTER 11

By midnight that Tuesday night Stevie McNeal began to worry. A late-night person, she often didn't go to bed until after the start of the new day, giving up the reruns and reading herself to sleep. Melissa, by contrast, was a morning person and, as such, went to bed early on all but the rarest occasions. Melissa had not called the night before as promised. She wasn't answering at the apartment, nor on her cellphone, which led Stevie to believe she was out conducting the surveillance, just the idea of which made Stevie anxious and worried.

She blamed the woman's silence on her own bossy attitude during the meeting with the state auditor, and the fact that with the two women knowing each other as well as they did, Melissa could easily have interpreted Stevie's attitude as a signal for her to deliver. For the past three years she had pushed her "little sister" to take the job offer she had arranged with the station, to take a regular paycheck rather than wallowing in misplaced pride and the unpaid bills of a freelancer. But Melissa declined the offered hand, in part because it came from Stevie and in part because of a refusal to compromise her work with a lot of worthless puff pieces ordered by an editor desperate to fill the time between ads. Stevie secretly admired the woman's nobility—in retrospect she had compromised her own career far too quickly by always taking the first job offered—but it did little to appease her present anxieties.

At one in the morning she called both numbers again, now taking to pacing while she thought this all out. Another aspect of Melissa's native pride was her professional secrecy; she had once worked on an independent environmental piece for three weeks before finally letting Stevie in on its subject matter—salmon poaching by Native Ameri-

65

cans—as if by being let in on it Stevie would have sent a camera crew out on the story. In the week since the auditor had leaked the LSO information, Stevie's only real knowledge of what Melissa was up to involved the surveillance of Gwen Klein. Beyond that and the financial information they had collected on the couple, she had few other leads to follow if needed.

Stevie finally fell asleep out of the exhaustion of being consumed in worry. When she awakened, she immediately called Melissa's numbers from bed, but only to hear that awful sound of endless ringing. She skipped the Nordic Trak, skipped the lazy morning routine of four newspaper subscriptions and the audio wallpaper of continuous CNN that typically occupied the first few hours of any day, and headed directly to Melissa's apartment in Pioneer Square, an apartment for which she had co-signed the lease, an apartment for which she held a spare set of keys warm in her hand.

The apartment offered nothing. She rang the buzzer on the ground floor, then let herself into the building, then knocked on the door to 5B and opened it when Melissa failed to answer. A modest one bedroom with a small living/dining area, it offered a poor view of a side alley and no cross-ventilation had the windows been open, which they weren't. It was, in fact, the slightly stale scent of the place that told Stevie Melissa hadn't been there recently. Melissa lived for fresh air; this contradiction spoke volumes. She found fresh food in the refrigerator and a garbage can filled to overflowing.

It felt dangerous all of a sudden, like realizing the noise downstairs is not the dog at all because the dog is lying by the bed. This was not merely an empty apartment, it was an apartment that had not been visited in recent hours. The bed was unmade—Melissa in her usual hurry. A toothbrush stood in the drinking glass on the sink and alarmed Stevie almost more than anything else about the empty apartment. Melissa was obsessed with clean teeth. The discovery of the toothbrush meant she had not taken a planned trip.

Her stomach clenched painfully in a combination of remorse and guilt, she left the apartment in something of a daze, her imagination running wild with possibility. At what point did she react publicly to the woman's silence? At what point did she go to the police or Brian Coughlie at the INS and seek help? At what point did she simply relax and take a deep breath, trusting that Melissa was on to a hot story and didn't have the opportunity to call? She left with that sickening feeling still plaguing her.

Stevie climbed back into the saddle, the anchor desk chair bouncing slightly as she sat. She scanned the pink pages of script for the *N4@5* news hour, but somehow she couldn't focus and she kept losing her place.

"Thirty seconds!" the floor director called out.

The daily ritual had grown so familiar to her as to be second nature, but on that day it felt entirely unnatural, all because of Melissa's ensuing silence. She felt simultaneously angry and worried. That call had never come. As independently as they both lived their lives, neither ever broke the promise of such a call. Not ever. Either Melissa was making a statement about her chosen lifestyle—or she was in trouble.

Of immediate concern to Stevie was Melissa's occasionally impatient ambition. She was competitive with Stevie's success, always hoping to ignite the spark that would accelerate her own career from occasionally employed to in demand. Stevie blamed herself for both encouraging Melissa to dig for the story, and for handing her that digital camera without a better understanding of what kind of undercover work she had planned. If Melissa was in fact on to the illegals story, Stevie didn't necessarily want to raise a red flag with authorities after just one undelivered phone call. She attempted to practice her own advice to exercise patience, but it didn't come naturally to her. She wanted control, and Melissa had taken that away from her.

"Fifteen seconds everyone! Ms. McNeal, you with us?"

Stevie twisted a professional smile across her face and once again studied the script.

"Ten . . . nine . . ."

Stevie would give Melissa one more night. After that, story or no story, the police had to be told.

"Four . . . three . . . two . . ."

A red light illuminated on top of the camera directly in front of her. Stevie heard herself speak as she read the lines, but she had no idea what she said.

CHAPTER 12

For the man in the back row of the smut film house, time seemed to slow down as the big Mexican next to him loudly blew his nose into a napkin and then threw the napkin onto the floor. Just being here with this man was a risk, and he'd come only because it had seemed unavoidable.

"So what's so important?" he asked Rodriguez.

"The count is off."

"An escape?" It wouldn't be the first.

"We're long by one."

"Long?"

"That's what I'm saying," said Rodriguez. "An escape I can handle, you know that. But this?"

"You counted wrong."

"I done this count six times. We're long." Rodriguez's voice was rough and scratchy. He kept sniffing back snot into his throat in a vulgar disgusting sound.

"Well it's off."

"It's *not* off," Rodriguez objected.

"You know what you're saying? Are they all Chinese?"

"Yes."

"Did you strip them?"

"Of course."

"And they're shaved."

"Every last snatch."

"So the count is off. It's the only explanation."

"It wasn't off last week. I done the count six times."

"So you said."

"Just so you know."

"Now I know." The idea disturbed him, but he didn't let Rodriguez know this. It was his job to worry—most of the time Rodriguez simply did as he was told. Inventory was off; it was as simple as that. "Maybe one of the ones in quarantine . . . maybe that threw the numbers off," he suggested.

"I got them into the count. I'm telling you—last week we done the count and the numbers was right."

"Use your squirrels, your snitches. See what you can find out."

"Got it."

"Tell your boys to keep their eyes open."

"Done already."

"Well, do it again," he snapped, regretting the tone. It wouldn't help matters to piss off Rodriguez.

The big man sneezed again. This time he forgot the napkin entirely.

THURSDAY, AUGUST 20

3 DAYS MISSING

CHAPTER 13

B oldt gripped the white rubber lip of the Boston Whaler, a flat-bottomed fiberglass skiff used as a Port Authority launch, as it tossed in the substantial wake of an arriving passenger ferry. LaMoia didn't react to the movement whatsoever, having grown up on the waters of Narragansett Bay.

Seagulls followed high above the ferry's foaming stern, diving into the prop wash after the pretzels and popcorn tossed there by unthinking tourists who were doing the shorebirds more harm than good. The captain of the *Visage* had refused to come ashore to be interviewed. His ship had been called back to port, and he was furious with authorities. With the political and legal Ping-Pong match continuing at a fevered pitch, Boldt instructed Port Authority to inform *Visage* that a pair of Seattle policemen were coming aboard to interview crew members.

Boldt correctly guessed that a shipping captain's greatest enemy was not the Coast Guard or the Port Authority, or a homicide cop, but time. He would not want to be delayed again from weighing anchor, and he would not want to leave any crew behind. By combining Rutledge's data with the Port Authority docking schedule and interviews with the Port Authority's radar station personnel, the *Visage* appeared to be the vessel in question. It had been well outside the shipping lanes the night of the storm, a night every navigator had been glued to his radar scope hoping to make it into port without incident. The *Visage* had gone radio dead for more than three hours—inexplicable in such traffic and high seas. The Port Authority radar controller distinctly recalled the ship's return to the southern shipping lane on scope but off the air, and how, predawn, it had slipped back into the lane, causing all ships behind it to give berth and thereby experience delays, forcing them to endure even more of the storm—something no one forgot.

Boldt and LaMoia climbed up a noisy steel ladder suspended from heavy chains, a crew member behind them, presumably, as a backstop should they slip. The pungent odors of a ship ripe with a three-week ocean crossing struck them—seaweed, diesel fuel and a tangy metallic rust that formed in the back of Boldt's mouth like the scent of blood at a crime scene. He gripped the chain, steadied himself and looked back toward shore and the noble city skyline that gave the Emerald City its jewels.

Nostalgia tightened his chest—he had devoted his life to service of this city, and was now considering plans to abandon it. At forty-four, with over twenty years on the force, the possibility of a job in the private sector insinuated itself. The unspoken evil of Liz's cancer treatment was the lingering debt, caused not by medical bills—all paid for by the bank's health care—but by loss of their double income for over a year. The bank had paid her full salary for three weeks of "vacation" and had then reduced her to one-quarter pay for her "leave of absence." But their lifestyle, which included day care and a house-cleaner, had left more going out than was coming in. Even Boldt's advancement to lieutenant had not made up the gap. He was seriously considering a private security position that paid nearly double his city salary. He had an interview scheduled, though he had not told Liz.

With the captain of the *Visage* on "shore leave," and therefore unavailable, the crew was all they had. A list of fifteen names was provided by the ship's first mate, an Asian with few teeth and a leath-ery face. Boldt and LaMoia divided their energies. Boldt was led below deck through cramped hallways, the gray steel reminding him of pris-ons, to a game room that contained an oversized projection TV and an enormous video library.

Thirty minutes of frustration left Boldt's patience brittle and his nerves raw. The first two crewmen had not spoken a word of English, replying to Boldt in some Balkan-sounding tongue. The third crewman listed as a deckhand, a young man with a stubble head and dark eyes that contained a tinge of fear, marched in wearily and, like his fellow seamen, spoke this same foreign language.

"English," Boldt instructed, knowing that at least someone on this ship spoke the language—the international language of the sea and a Coast Guard requirement. The young deckhand shook his head and prattled on in his native tongue again.

It was then that Boldt's eye landed on the wall of videos, and the titles there—all in English—included Super Bowls and NBA title games. He said to the deckhand, "Michael Jordan! Now there was a player!" He paused. "Even so, Sean Kemp is a better shooter."

"No way!" the young man protested.

Boldt did not so much as flinch. He said, "Kemp's jump shot?"

"Jordan was the best play—" the boy caught himself as Boldt's grin surfaced.

Boldt said, "Do you know that refusal to cooperate with police is a crime here? I could have you locked up."

The boy's eyes went wide and he shook his head as if not understanding.

"You think I'll tell the others? Is that it? Do you think I would say anything? How does it benefit me to expose a possible witness?"

"I witness nothing," the man returned.

"You are a deckhand. It says so right here. You spent the last three weeks up on deck. Hong Kong. Hawaii. Three weeks with that container. You know the one I'm talking about."

The boy's upper lip shone as he said, "The trip it takes longer to expected. The storming."

Boldt understood the malnutrition and dehydration then. "How much longer than expected?"

"Normal, ten days. This crossing, two times that."

"The people in the container?"

The boy shook his head.

"I can detain you here in Seattle. The ship leaves without you."

"There was nothing us people able to do. It was shut up."

"Locked."

"Yes, locked."

"But you heard them?"

The young man looked back suspiciously and shook his head again, a familiar response.

"We have laws about lying to police."

"We hear them. It bad, all the crying. Locked," he confirmed. He crossed himself.

"Food? Didn't you feed them?"

Again, the young man shook his head no.

"Water?"

Another.

"You heard them," Boldt pressed, remembering the shrill cries and haunting pounding. "And did nothing?"

The man's eyes glassed under a tightly knit brow exaggerated by his nearly shaved head. He mumbled, "The captain."

"Yes," Boldt said, seizing upon this. "The captain." The captain, who no doubt had taken the bribe; the captain, who had the connections to make the drop; the all-important captain. "You were paid extra because of this container."

The man appeared angry.

"How many times before?"

"No. Not me. The others, yes. Not me. This, my first crossing with *Visage*."

"No food, no water." Boldt hesitated. "People died. Three people died. You understand?"

A small nod, the man's first.

"Murder. You understand 'murder'?"

Terror-stricken eyes. Moist lips from a nervous tongue. A faint nod.

"I arrest *you*," Boldt said.

"No!" the man protested.

"The captain," Boldt suggested.

A reluctance in the eyes. A stiffening of the spine. Then the slumped shoulders of resignation. The man mumbled, "The captain not open the container. He said, 'The sea plays tricks on the ears.'"

"It's blood money," Boldt said. "You understand?"

A nod.

"Jail," Boldt stated.

A nod. "The captain, he is not talk to you."

"We'll see about that."

"He not talk. No. And I? I not talk against him. Jail?" he shrugged. "Better than to talk against this captain."

Boldt saw crew members "lost at sea." He saw bodies caught in the ocean's midnight swells fading into blackness, a hand crying from the waves. A crew kept loyal through fear. A silent captain. He saw a brick wall ahead of him.

"The transfer during the storm. Something went wrong. Tell me about it."

"Bad seas."

"Your people lost the container?"

"Us people? No way! The others on the barge. That tug captain, has brain of a baby. Not able to handle barge. Their tower, not ours! They lost that piece, not us!"

"Their crane?" Boldt asked. "Is that what you mean by tower?" He gestured to indicate a crane and finally resorted to demonstrating with his pen.

The deckhand nodded vigorously. "Crane on barge."

"Yes, of course." Boldt wondered how many crane-and-barge combinations there were available to such people. He saw a narrow opportunity for investigation. "Something went wrong with the crane?"

"Not so much crane's fault. Seas too high. Both captains are fools to make try. But we try."

"The crane dropped the container?"

"No. No. Not crane. Guy lines snapped." He moved his leathery hands in a circle as if shaping a sphere out of clay. "Container spin. Fall into water."

"And your captain tried to recover them?"

The man did not answer. He stared back through hollow eyes.

"He did *not* try," Boldt said.

The man sat stoically. The answers were not with him.

"Go," Boldt told him.

The man appeared stunned by the offer.

"Go," Boldt repeated, "before I change my mind."

The young man hurried from the room, pulling the steel door shut behind himself with the familiar hollow *thunk* of a jail cell door.

Boldt knew from earlier discussions with Port Authority that this investigation had become a question not only of jurisdiction but of whether any crime could be proven: The ship's manifest was unlikely to list the dumped container, and it certainly would not list humans as its cargo. Even if it could be confirmed that the *Visage* had been carrying the container, the captain could claim it had been lost to the storm, that its contents had never been known. A ship held hundreds of containers—hundreds of secrets—and it was usually the case that their contents were listed but never actually verified by captain or crew. Customs inspected less than 10 percent of arriving containers. Even so, with confirmation that the container had been aboard the *Visage*, Boldt had to try for the shipping manifest. If paperwork existed for the container, it would list the shipper.

Time, Boldt realized, remained his best weapon. If he threatened a delay, and thus prevented the ship from sailing, he might force the captain to cooperate. As backup, he had the INS's authority to impound any vessels involved in the transportation of illegals. They did this regularly, as did the DEA.

He collected his things and sent for LaMoia. Time was everything.

Boldt was halfway into his explanation to Talmadge when the man passed responsibility, and the call, to deputy director Brian Coughlie, and Boldt had to start his explanation all over again. It seemed Coughlie, in charge of field operations, investigations and processing the illegals, had more direct experience in impounding vessels, which was what Boldt hoped to set in motion.

"You'd like a chat with the captain," Coughlie summarized, "and you're willing to play hardball to get it."

"You have authority to impound or even confiscate the ship. You've done so before."

"All the time. But I'd need a smoking gun for that."

"How about the testimony of a crew member?"

"Good, but not great. The crew always holds some grudge against the captain. Anything else?"

"You could threaten him with impounding," Boldt encouraged.

"Sure I could," Coughlie agreed.

"And?"

"Maybe the captain is dumb enough to fall for it."

"You don't think so."

Coughlie said, "Listen, we could be more convincing if you guys picked him up on charges. That's a kind of pressure we can't apply. Some of them gamble, some of them whore, all of them drink. If this guy is facing criminal charges of some kind then there's no harassment involved, no intimidation. International law gets sticky." He hesitated on the other end, and when Boldt failed to respond, Coughlie said, "Listen, we used to cut deals with the detainees—they talk, we cut them some slack—but it's such a crapshoot, such a waste of time, we gave up trying. We just ship them back home now. Return to sender. There are too many protections, too many complications with international law."

Boldt realized that Coughlie knew the details of his own interrogation out at Fort Nolan. The interpreter? The detainee herself? The idea that Coughlie already had the line on one of Boldt's interrogations disturbed him. The feds were never up front about *anything*!

Coughlie offered, "Let me put the word out on this captain. I have plenty of contacts dockside, believe me. Someone has seen him. I get word on his location, your boys watch him and hope for a miscue. If you pounce, the only thing I ask is that you share any information you get."

"That works for me." But he wasn't sure why he said it.

CHAPTER 14

Stevie McNeal, accustomed to more attention than what she received from the Seattle Police Department, sat impatiently in an uncomfortable chair in the Crimes Against Persons reception area, next to a secretary pool of Hispanic, Asian and African-American women busy at computers.

She remembered LaMoia from the raising of the container. Flippant, cocky and a womanizer, if she was any judge of character. Adding to insult, she had the sinking feeling she was going to have to reintroduce herself.

"Stevie McNeal," she reminded him, as loath as she was to do so.

"I know," he said. "We met last week. You wouldn't remember."

"But I do remember." She won him over with that one comment, and congratulated herself on knowing how to play him. He traveled the length of her—head to toe with a few layovers—before offering her a chance to sit down. Across the room, a number of heads began turning. There were times celebrity had its benefits.

She said, "I'm working with a freelance reporter to assist me in my ongoing series. She does the footwork and the footage. I do the voice-overs. It's an investigative, expository piece. I've lost contact with her. I want you to find her."

"To say I'm a fan would not be fair, Ms. McNeal. Not always. But I'm familiar with your work. I've been taping this series on the illegals—both to see myself on TV," he offered a toothy smile, "and to pick up any leads you might have to offer."

"Her name's Melissa Chow. Chinese by birth. Five foot two. A hundred and five pounds. Oval face, small nose . . . I have pictures." She passed them to him.

LaMoia studied the snapshots. "She's just a colleague?"

"We're sisters. Legally. It's a long story. We grew up together. My father brought her over from China when she was little, and we adopted her. She's family, and now she's in the middle of doing this work for me, and she's gone missing."

"Missing for how long?" LaMoia asked.

"I don't know exactly. I last saw her on Monday."

"It's Thursday."

"Thank you for that," Stevie said. "I loaned her one of the station's digital cameras, and sent her off to get a story. I've lost touch with her."

"We can put a photograph of her into our radio cars. We can get her paperwork going," he conceded. "But most of the investigative work I suspect you've already done: contacting co-workers, family members, friends, neighbors. If you'd gotten anywhere, you wouldn't be here."

"And here I am."

He jotted down a note. "We'll check with pawnshops."

"You think she *sold* the camera?!" she asked, incredulous. "Do you have any idea what is going on here? Melissa stuck her nose into something she shouldn't have and she's gone missing. That's it. That's all. We need to find her, and we need to find her fast."

"Let's start again," he suggested. "She was working on your series? The illegals?"

"She was following a lead I got on this illegals story."

He bowed his head and gave her a telling look.

"I don't know exactly how far she had gotten, where she was going with it."

"We need to know exactly what she was working on," LaMoia prompted.

"There was a man who offered us some information," Stevie explained cautiously.

"His name?" LaMoia inquired.

"He wished to remain anonymous. I honored that. We met at a restaurant."

"His name," LaMoia repeated, a pen hovering above paper.

Calculating how much to tell him, Stevie said, "If I give you that, you'll track him down and then we'll both lose him. I don't see how that helps anyone."

LaMoia said, "And what if your 'source' is actually the one responsible for her disappearance? Have you thought of that?" He added, "Listen, Ms. McNeal, I see things that even as a reporter, you couldn't dream of. My job is to find her as quickly as possible. I need every scrap, every handout I can get."

Stevie placed a file folder onto the desk. "Photos, background, handwriting samples. Find my sister, goddamn it, or I warn you: Your incompetence will be my next story." With that she stood up and walked out. One way or another, she would get them to help.

FRIDAY, AUGUST 21
4 DAYS MISSING

CHAPTER 15

The call came an hour before sunrise, while the population at large, including Lou Boldt, remained fast asleep.

With two kids, the Boldt home looked alternately like a petting zoo or a toy factory, its floors and shelves cluttered with stuffed animals, pieces of Lego sets, dolls and action figures. Liz typically went to bed immediately after the kids; her energy sapped. Once in bed, she read from the Bible and a book she called her textbook, doing "her work." She no longer spoke of the lymphoma by name—she referred to it as her "challenge," relying on her role as God's creation to remain in remission. Boldt wasn't sure what he thought about any of it, but he kept his mouth shut. For whatever the reason, Liz did seem well. Whether temporarily or permanently, no one knew—though Liz fervently believed it was the latter. And as any cop knew, it wasn't worth it to fight City Hall. For now, he placed her continuing remission in the win column.

Boldt answered the bedside phone in a groggy voice and continued the call in the kitchen so as not to disturb Liz. On the other end of the phone, dispatch informed him of a floater found face down in the canal on the border of Fremont and Ballard, a one-mile stretch of protected waterway where working fishermen of five nations frequented sailor bars. The victim was Lo Wan Chang, the former captain of the freighter *Visage*.

Within ten minutes of hanging up the phone Boldt was in his Chevy Cavalier heading for the crime scene.

Boldt arrived ahead of the chuck wagon—the medical examiner's emerald green panel van that transported cadavers—and refilled his plastic tea mug before venturing out to join the two uniformed patrol officers who had responded to the original call and who had correctly established a crime scene perimeter in an effort to protect the scene. The sky was brighter now. The wharf area where the body had been found was within easy walking distance of a half dozen bars and rooms for rent by the hour. It was a decrepit stretch of sea-rotted piers, their tops stained white by seagulls, the air pungent with seaweed, engine oil and the exhaust of a patrol car left running to power headlights aimed onto the ugliness of the captain's soggy body stretched out on the cracked and weathered blacktop.

The patrolman pointed, "This big guy over here seen the body on his way to his boat. Says he was floating face down right about here," he said, walking over and indicating a space between pier and hull. "Side of his head all thumped in like that, looks like maybe he slipped. There's some blood smeared back here."

Sure enough, a foot-long streak of something dark brown was adhered to the hull of a wooden fishing boat. "Could be," Boldt agreed, not eager to rule the death an accident, nor to accept its timing as coincidental. If the captain had talked, if he'd cut a deal with either Boldt or Coughlie, if he'd tried to scapegoat the responsibility for the container and the deaths of the illegals, then any number of people might have wanted him dead. Boldt wondered if his own candor during the shipboard interviews had gotten the captain killed. "There's a Polaroid in my trunk. Make yourself useful and take a couple pictures," Boldt said to the patrolman. He handed him the car keys. "Canvass the neighborhood. See what we can come up with in terms of witnesses."

"People around here talk?" the young officer questioned sarcastically.

Frustration winning out, Boldt said, "Just do the job." The point wasn't so much the dead body, the loss of a possible witness, it was the decision behind the death, the swiftness with which someone had acted, and Boldt's realization that these people were a step ahead of him, knew his intentions. Outside of his own squad and the INS, only Mama Lu had been told of his intentions to interrogate the ship captain, although whoever had hired the man to transport the container would have foreseen the inevitability of his being questioned and might have acted not only to prevent it, but to send a signal to future ship captains to keep their mouths shut.

LaMoia's earlier mention of Tidwell, the detective who had retired on disability after investigating an illegals case, rang in Boldt's ears. These people played tough. He had only to look down at the captain's puffy face for a reminder. He thought of Sarah and Miles and Liz. Maybe this case wasn't worth the risk. Maybe that was the other purpose of this kill. Maybe he was supposed to see his own face lying there on the dock.

Forensic sciences—the responsibility of Bernie Lofgrin's Scientific Identification Division (SID)—had made so many advancements over the past twenty years that crime scene procedure had been reinvented to accommodate the painstakingly exact collection of evidence, including photography and videography, as well as the careful preservation of the physical environment on and around the cadaver. When coupled with careful documentation, thoroughly working a homicide crime scene could, and in this case did, easily consume two to three hours.

At the start of the third hour, Boldt was notified that the entire crew of the *Visage* had been found asleep in quarters aboard ship and was being held by the Coast Guard for SPD questioning. He expected they would back up each other's perfect alibis, but LaMoia would interrogate all of them nonetheless. If anyone could get a person to talk, it was John.

By seven o'clock, the local TV stations had cameras and crews on location, joining a half dozen other reporters, along with the morbidly curious that peopled any homicide crime scene. A zoo scene. A public spectacle. A political nightmare if reporters made the connection to the container and took the spin that police had lost control to organized crime. Boldt would be hearing about this one for days.

As if reading his thoughts, a voice said from behind, "I don't know about you, but for us, this is going to be a public relations nightmare."

Boldt turned and shook hands with Brian Coughlie.

"Once he's connected to the *Visage* it hits the fan," Boldt said. "The crew has been rounded up."

"I heard," Coughlie said, letting Boldt know he had some impressive contacts. LaMoia had grabbed the crew in near secrecy. "It's one of the things I wanted to talk to you about; we've got the interpreters—I thought we might share that work. We could handle it for you, if you'd rather."

"We're okay," Boldt said, refusing both offers.

"Could be my fault," Coughlie said, allowing the comment to hang in the air. "I put the word out on him like you asked. Maybe that was the wrong call."

The guy delivered it as if he'd rehearsed it, which bothered Boldt. The truth was: Coughlie bothered Boldt; the feds always had hidden agendas.

Looking down at the black body bag, Coughlie said, "Maybe he had a name to give us."

"Mama Lu?"

"Five years ago, maybe. Now? I don't think so, no. Not that she doesn't have serious pull. Of course she does. But control? Doubtful. We watched her closely for two, maybe three years. Your guys, too—OC." He meant Organized Crime. "Phone taps, audits, undercover work. We ate shit on that one. Tried twice with a grand jury; failed both times. We still look in that direction every now and again, but not very hard. She has made some serious friends downtown."

"I like her for this."

"Be careful."

"That's what they say," Boldt said.

"Do me a favor. After you've worked the crew, let me have a shot at them. Maybe we get lucky."

It was a compromise Boldt could live with.

The two men shook hands.

Coughlie avoided the press as he left, deftly ducking under the police tape and running quickly to his car, driving off as reporters chased him.

Boldt used the distraction to order the body bag into the chuck wagon. If the captain's death sent any message, it was a simple one—people involved with this one were going to die.

He hoped like hell he wasn't on the list himself.

CHAPTER 16

A little more than twenty-four hours after reporting Melissa missing, Stevie, her guilt and fear levels increasing exponentially, took matters into her own hands, deciding to return to Melissa's and search more carefully.

Pioneer Square on a Friday night teemed with a mixture of the college crowd, tourists, indigents and police. A person could buy anything from a microbrewery beer to a Persian rug. Stevie drove her 325i a dozen blocks and left it in a parking garage. During the short walk to the square, she allowed herself to wonder why Melissa had chosen such a noisy, crowded, touristy location in which to live. They were so different from one another, and yet so close. For Stevie, any stroll down the street meant the likelihood of contact with her viewing public—autograph-seeking strangers who would see her and want to meet her. She hated that part of her job.

In hopes of avoiding recognition, she dressed down in jeans and T-shirt and wore no make-up. She walked with her head down, threading her way through the crush of people, making her way to Melissa's apartment.

She climbed the steps, rang the buzzer and let herself in. She trudged up flights of stairs, unlocked the door and stepped inside the apartment. The door locked behind her, the only sounds the dull beat of a nearby rock club. She took her time feeding the fish. "Anyone here?" she called out, hopelessly. Again, the lived-in feel of the apartment got to her. The bedroom might have been left that morning the way it looked—clothes tossed around. That toothbrush standing sentry in the water glass still hurt her the most, and it struck her how odd it was that such a small, insignificant item could convey so much. The pain in her weighed as a numbness now, a sleep-deprived aching, a longing to start all over, to win a second chance. There was no one to hear her appeal, just a ringing in her ears and a hollow emptiness in the center of her chest like a bad case of butterflies. She roamed the small apartment, feverish with anxiety, finally resorting to pulling open cabinets and peering behind furniture. It was this last effort that won her a reward. She saw it piled behind the couch, utilizing the wall plugs—some of the station's electronic gear. It was the SVHS setup Melissa had used in the van, including two waist-belt battery packs. Stevie unplugged both packs and rummaged through the gear, discovering three videotapes, the first two marked "Klein," the third, "car wash." Just the sight of the handwriting stung Stevie with fear. At that moment she would have traded a dozen hot news stories for the chance to have Melissa back safely.

She glanced over at the bookshelf and saw a porcelain doll, its cheek cracked, its eyes staring directly at her. Her emotions overcame her.

The afternoon sunlight played off the walls and crown molding, blinding the man standing at attention in the oil painting that hung above the fireplace. The air in the room smelled of Father's tobacco, while outside the sun struggled through dust and automobile exhaust, always the same dull wheat straw, never brilliant like Switzerland. The Chinese seemed surrounded by dust, consumed by it.

The precocious young girl with the ring curls tied off with red satin ribbon clutched her porcelain doll with determination, alone in the lavishly decorated sitting room awaiting introductions. Stephanie didn't want this other girl living here. She wanted Su-Su and Father all to herself. Father had left the room only minutes before, accompanied by two of his deputies and an embassy aide, leaving the sweet smoke behind as a reminder. Father seemed always accompanied by someone.

She heard the front door open. Su-Su called her name from the hallway, but Stephanie did not answer. Let them find me, she thought.

"Miss Stephanie?" came another appeal, as the door to the room opened. Su-Su stood about half the height of Father. She walked in

short little steps and pursed her lips rather than smiled. She spoke softly with a thick Chinese accent. She could speak French as well, and read music. Stephanie had no idea what it was like to have a mother, but Su-Su was probably pretty close to the real thing. Father liked her, too. He touched her sometimes, lightly, quickly; it made her purse her lips and blush. Su-Su had a son of her own. This girl was said to be her niece, and in need of a home. Stephanie didn't like the sound of that. She wasn't big on sharing.

The large white door swung open in a lazy arc, and there at Su-Su's side, clutching her silken dress, was a tiny girl with jet black hair, bowl cut at her shoulders and bangs that hung to the sharp slashes of her eyebrows, bright red cheeks and wide eyes of wonder, as first she took in the splendid room, and then, a heartbeat later, Stephanie herself—her satin bows, her dress and doll. Everything changed in that instant.

"Miss Stephanie, allow me introduce to you my niece, Mi Chow. Your father say we will call her Melissa." Su-Su spoke to the little girl in Chinese and Stephanie understood every word. Su-Su was a good teacher. She said, "This is Stephanie, your big sister."

The girl's face lit up and filled the room with light.

"Welcome, Little Sister," Stephanie said in her best Mandarin. Both girls giggled in unison.

Stevie quickly collected the tapes and, eager to view them, hurried from the apartment and down into the chaos of Pioneer Square. She had no choice but to join the crowd, and it was only moments before she heard, "Hey, Tina! Look who it is!" Footsteps approached from behind and a man pulled roughly on her elbow. "Channel Four, right? We watch you every night!"

Stopped at a corner, she glanced over some heads, willing the pedestrian signal to change. "Channel Four, right?" the balding man repeated. "Right," she said, clutching the tapes tightly. Someone else was there, someone watching her. She could feel it.

The light changed.

Stevie fought her way quickly across the street—straight ahead.

She checked behind herself, paranoia working on her. Every face seemed as if it were looking directly at her. Panic rose inside her. She reminded herself that she had the tapes. Presumably they would tell her something.

The parking garage was two blocks away and closing. She picked up her pace.

With half a block to go she broke into a slow jog, again hearing footsteps behind her. The same fan? Someone else? She didn't want the answer.

Her car was at a pre-pay parking lot, and the booth had closed at 10 P.M., thirty minutes earlier. The entrance was now chained, the exit guarded by a set of outbound springed tire spikes.

She entered the dimly lit garage at a near run, the tapes held firmly under her arm, her mouth bitter and dry, her heart racing. She wanted to be home, behind the safety of a doorman, two dead bolts and a security system. She wanted to be anywhere but in an unattended downtown parking garage.

The trailing footsteps followed her into the garage, and then suddenly went silent—or was it only her imagination?

She dared a single glance backward, and nearly gasped at the sight of a silhouette of a man moving quickly toward her.

A mugging? she wondered.

"Wait!" The male voice echoed loudly off the cement walls. She reached her car and fumbled with the wireless remote, clicking the doors unlocked. She fished for the pepper spray she carried in her purse.

Behind her, shoes on cement like hands clapping.

She pulled the driver door open, tossed the tapes onto the passenger seat, and armed with the spray aimed outward, slipped into the front seat.

"Ms. McNeal!" Closer now, suddenly more familiar. "It's John LaMoia."

She looked up into the man's sweating face.

"I was watching the apartment," he explained. "The disappearance is at the top of our list."

"You scared me to death."

"I didn't want to shout your name in those crowds." His eyes found the passenger seat and the three tapes in their plastic boxes. "I didn't see you go into the apartment with those."

"I have a key. I feed her fish."

"The fish watch videos, do they?"

Melissa's tapes were hers and hers alone. She would view them first and pass them along, if pertinent. She felt the tapes burning a hole in the seat. She pulled the door shut, turned the key and lowered the window.

LaMoia spoke softly. "Listen, this is strictly off the record, but this illegals investigation is getting nasty."

"The ship captain," she said. "We got that right in spite of you."

"It'd be safer for everyone if you gave me those videos—they're hers, right? Melissa's? You don't want to fool around with these people."

"You want the tapes, you're going to run smack into the First Amendment. These are *news* tapes."

"I had hoped to run smack into cooperation. Don't we both want the same thing?" He added, "To find her?"

"Nice try."

He pleaded, "I need whatever's on those tapes. Melissa needs me to see those tapes."

"We'll talk," she said. She rolled up her window. LaMoia leaned to speak to her, but his words mumbled incoherently through the glass.

As she drove out of the garage, she reached over and touched the tapes. She picked them up and dropped them onto the backseat floor behind her. There wasn't anywhere safe for those tapes. There wasn't anywhere safe at all.

SATURDAY, AUGUST 22
5 DAYS MISSING

CHAPTER 17

Bobbie Gaynes entered Boldt's office mid–Saturday morning without knocking and pulled up a chair while her lieutenant placed a pencil mark in the margin of the report he was reading in order to mark his spot.

He looked up and saw his son's crayon artwork hung on the glass wall that looked out on the hallway. It hung there to add color, to relieve the monotony of gray that some interior designer had imposed on the place, and to remind him of his priorities. Liz did not like him working weekends. His son's self-portrait fluttered as a pair of detectives hurriedly passed the office door.

"Go ahead," Boldt said, knowing in advance that the topic of discussion was crane rentals. Having lost the *Visage* to a homicide likely to go down as an accident, Boldt had all but given up that leg of the investigation, assigning Gaynes to investigate crane rentals and possible links to the barge and tug that had attempted the failed transfer.

"You just don't own a crane. Okay?" Gaynes advised. "It's not something you keep in your garage. You rent them or lease them." She referred to her notes. "There are five outfits between here and Tacoma that rent or lease the kind of equipment capable of lifting a container."

Boldt had brought her up to Homicide single-handedly, breaking the gender barrier for the first time and landing her into a tough assignment. She had rallied behind the challenges, required to repeatedly prove herself, but never holding a grudge. She did some of the best police work on the fifth floor. The latest attack on her had her gay and in a relationship with an ousted detective. It was an invented story meant to smear her. The dust had yet to settle.

"A woman's gone missing. A reporter, no less."

She eyed him curiously. "You want to rent one of these cranes, you need bonding, all sorts of insurance, you name it."

"She was investigating something to do with the containers," he said. "The brass is having conniptions. It's all about how the press will tear us apart if something has happened to her and we don't find her first." He added, "For them, that is. For us: we've got a missing persons who may have busted open this investigation."

"You want this?"

Boldt said, "I need the short form. We do, or do not have record of a rental the night of that storm?"

"The paperwork to prove it? No. A rental? Maybe. I'm going to need some manpower."

"If you're pulling for OT, you've got it." He was not fond of his new role as administrator, guidance counselor and disciplinarian—all of which were required of a lieutenant. He often felt like little more than a file drawer between his captain, Sheila Hill, and the sergeants and squads that worked beneath him.

"Third place I try, a place called Geribaldi's Equipment, I make the guy behind the counter real nervous with mention of cash rentals that bypass the paperwork. He's sweating bullets by the time I'm through explaining how aiding and abetting works in the eyes of the law. Takes me outside for a smoke. Says how maybe a telescoping crane went out the morning of that storm that he knows for a fact it didn't make it into the books because when he tried to rent out the same crane, it didn't happen to exist in the yard. His manager blamed the screwup on him—but also told him not to worry about it. Said maybe the paperwork had been misplaced."

"So there's no proof a crane went out," Boldt pressed. "What's the good news?"

"I've got the manager's name: Zulia. I was thinking maybe we check the guy's bank accounts for an extra deposit or two." She added, "I'd like to sit on his crib, the yard, monitor his bank transactions. I could use a couple guys for surveillance. Maybe we have a little chat with him in the Box."

"Okay, let's do it."

"First we gotta find him. He has taken an unexpected vacation."

Boldt said, "Rental shops are easy targets for theft. All that equipment sitting outside. Protection makes sense."

Gaynes asked, "Mama Lu?" She knew what Boldt was thinking when others seldom had a clue.

Boldt said, "If she wants someone found, I imagine it's only a matter of time."

"In that case, you might mention our missing reporter."

"Point taken."

"You're looking for a world of hurt, you go opening that door," LaMoia said, interrupting from the doorway. He added, "McNeal lifted some videotapes from our girl's apartment last night. I'm thinking they gotta be relevant to my investigation. She's not in the mood to share and claims she'll hide behind first amendment privileges if we come after them."

"How do we know this?" Gaynes asked.

Boldt didn't answer her. Instead he said to LaMoia, "We go after the tapes anyway. Find a judge that's running for reelection. Let him figure it out."

"Waste of time," LaMoia said.

Boldt conceded. "Okay, so we work the cranes. Mama Lu's a businesswoman. She knows when to cut her losses. She doesn't want us dragging in every gang member for questioning. That makes her look weak."

"She also cuts throats, Sarge," LaMoia warned. "Or at least her soldiers do."

"Set up a meeting," Boldt requested.

"I don't think this is so smart," LaMoia complained.

"Set it up," Boldt repeated sharply.

The artwork rustled on LaMoia's way out.

"Surveillance of the rental place is approved," Boldt told Gaynes. "Work it out with Special Ops."

CHAPTER 18

Mama Lu occupied the same wingback throne as she had on his first visit. Only the dress had changed: teal with black embroidery. She wore it wrapped around herself like a towel. Her long black braid fell over her shoulder heavy like a horsetail.

LaMoia had asked to come along, but Boldt had refused, not wanting to give the impression of teaming up on her.

He kept his opening comment to the point. "Your influence both as a businesswoman and great friend to this city stretches far and wide. No, don't shake your head—we both know this to be true. Let us suppose that someone in this business of importing illegals decided not to risk unloading their cargo on shore but instead decided to make the transfer while still out at sea. To accomplish this effectively this person would need a tugboat, a barge and a crane. We, the police, have identified a company that looks good for this. Our problem is that the individual we believe responsible for renting that crane has failed to show up at work."

"I own a few humble groceries, Mr. Both—"

"And four Laundromats, a movie theater, a limousine company, a hotel—"

"A few investments is all! Who trusts the banks anymore?"

"Geribaldi Equipment. The rental company. The manager is named Zulia. If he were encouraged to cooperate with police—"

"As a good citizen," she said, testing.

"Yes—out of his generosity of spirit—it would certainly save us opening up his or the company's financial records. Cash flow. Payments."

Her brow tightened. She sat forward, however imperceptibly. She took hold of her braid with both pudgy hands as if it were a butler's pull.

Boldt said, "There would be no reason for our forensic accountants to examine any of their records."

"Only a fool stabs a dragon thinking he will kill it. To kill a dragon one must cut off its head."

He paused. "If forced to . . ."

She grinned, her eyes disappearing behind the folds of flesh. "How sharp is your sword, Mr. Both?"

"Zulia drops a name. He goes home." He paused. "Everybody's happy."

"Not whoever's name is mentioned."

Boldt grinned. The room felt suddenly hot to him. "The three women who died in that container were sick. They died of malnutrition and dehydration because the captain refused them food and water. Storms slowed down the crossing and the captain just let them die in there."

She said, "You reap what you sow," and Boldt added yet another name to his list of possible murder suspects. The captain of the *Visage* was not short of enemies.

She said, "Once on these shores, these girls are good for economy. Maids in hotels, waitress in bars."

"Sweatshops, prostitution," he added.

He sought out the person behind those dark eyes, eager to determine her level of involvement, but saw nothing revealed. She sat there as impassive as the best judges.

For a moment he felt convinced this woman had not been involved with the deaths. When she smiled, he lost hold of it, like chasing a wet bar of soap.

"They say ignorance is bliss, Mr. Both. Maybe true."

"If he'd given them food and water they would have lived. There was no reason for them to die."

"That man no longer with us. We must forgive him his sins."

"Him, perhaps. But not the others." He paused, having locked eyes with her. "Do you condone such treatment of your fellow Chinese?"

"A topic that bears much discussion."

He hesitated a moment and told her, "A Chinese-American has gone missing. A television reporter. She was investigating the container. If they harm her, they are fools. The power of the media is far greater than a single police department, believe me."

The woman's face scrunched up tight. If this wasn't news to her, she was a good actress. "You know this as true? Missing woman?"

He said, "If a person were to help us locate this missing woman, the city would smile upon her." He added, "The media, too."

She grinned and nodded and returned his determined gaze. "I understand." A silence fell between them. "Go carefully, Mr. Both. Accidents happen to the nicest people." She added, "And trust no one. Not even me." She smiled again, more widely. She had forgotten her teeth. He saw them then in a clear glass to her right, grinning all on their own.

MONDAY, AUGUST 24
7 DAYS MISSING

CHAPTER 19

On Monday morning—one week to the day since Melissa had last been seen—Ernest Zulia, the manager of Geribaldi's Equipment, made the morning news by exploding into several thousand pieces. The shock waves were felt at Public Safety.

Boldt met with Captain Sheila Hill in her office. Hill still turned heads at age forty. She understood how to dress for her athletic body and wasn't above using her legs as a distraction. She came down hard on Boldt over Zulia's death, but Boldt wouldn't be drawn into it.

"The Zulia surveillance was pulled, Captain," Boldt complained, reminding her of what he had been told only minutes before by his detective. "We had a crew watching Geribaldi's Equipment and they were removed from duty under orders." Hill had given that order. Bobbie Gaynes had been told to cancel the surveillance, pulling an end run on LaMoia and Boldt, neither of whom had been informed of the decision. It wasn't something for which he could out and out blame her, but they both knew the score. He understood perfectly well that she had called him to her office for damage repair. He also knew that although she could invent any number of excuses for her decision, she had probably canceled the surveillance out of a combination of budget considerations and politics. Knowing Sheila Hill, she resented LaMoia not consulting her on the original surveillance and so had exercised her authority as a means of proving who was in charge. But now she had another dead body on her hands and live newscasts tying this and the ship captain to the container—a political hot potato. Unfortunately, Boldt thought there was more at play than met the eye. LaMoia had bedded down Hill a year earlier in an act of poor judgment and primitive instincts that had left her calling the shots and nearly destroying the man's career. An odd relationship still existed between the two—LaMoia had suffered the breakup hard; Hill had eventually sought to reconcile. She tended to spoil him; he tended to ignore her, his captain. Only Boldt knew of the affair, though many on the squad suspected. When LaMoia slipped up, Boldt, as the man's lieutenant, heard about it—but lately Hill seemed to be using him more as a marriage counselor. She wanted LaMoia back. If there was hell to pay for the investigation's woes, it was for Boldt to sort out.

At the time of the "accident," Zulia had been in the seat of a propane-powered forklift, as he was every morning, according to his employees. The explosion caused flames to rise three hundred feet in the air, and total destruction to one-third of Geribaldi's inventory and most of its warehouse. For the first time since a string of arsons several years earlier, there was no physical evidence of the victim found by SID. Along with firemen, they searched the rubble hoping for bone fragments.

"You don't like John running operations without consulting you," Boldt stated, speaking plainly. "Point taken."

"We have to *deal* with this," she reminded, glancing at him sternly, but not wanting to invite discussion of the relationship. She left it up to him to offer some kind of way out of the mishap. At last, he saw a compromise position.

He said, "The missing television news reporter, Melissa Chow, is a far more pressing case than someone like Zulia. Once he returned to work, we could have picked up Zulia anytime."

"Go on," she encouraged.

"The reporter gets a lead on the illegals and then vanishes. Not only could any information she have be pertinent to the investigation, but there's a young woman's life at stake. It has been a week."

"So we shifted manpower," she stated as if it were fact. She liked where he was going with this.

Boldt kept silent. He'd fed her the bone; he didn't need to chew it with her. As a sergeant Boldt had rarely been privy to such negotiations. One more reason he hated his lieutenant's shield. Politics made him nauseous. The fieldwork—active investigations—was a much more pure environment.

Boldt offered, "Her disappearance may be tied to the deaths of two key witnesses in this investigation. She's of primary importance to us."

"She certainly is," Hill agreed. "We moved our resources to this missing persons case."

"I wouldn't mention this out of the house. We don't want to put her at any more risk."

"Point taken. So get on it," she said.

||||||||

Boldt, LaMoia and Gaynes met behind closed doors.

"Saturday I tell Mama Lu we'd like to chat up Zulia," Boldt said. "And look what Monday morning brings."

"I wouldn't go there, Sarge," LaMoia cautioned. "It's these video tapes McNeal lifted from the woman's apartment. That's *evidence*—if we can get a judge to agree."

"Good luck," Gaynes sniped.

"I'm not '*going*' there," Boldt complained. "I'm being led there."

"It was a pro hit," Gaynes reminded LaMoia. "Zulia climbed onto that same forklift every morning. They knew exactly what they were doing."

"Someone told him it was okay to return to work," Boldt suggested, still focused on Mama Lu's involvement.

"There are plenty of pros who have no association with Mama Lu," LaMoia said.

"Why are you constantly defending her?" Boldt complained.

"I'm not defending her," LaMoia objected. "I'm trying not to jump to conclusions. The guy I learned from," he said, meaning Boldt, "stressed the importance of following the evidence, of listening to the victim."

Boldt nodded. "Two potential witnesses killed in the last four days. They're cleaning house, taking care of loose ends. Maybe Mama

Lu is too easy, and maybe she's good for this, but you're right about following the evidence," he conceded. "I'm listening."

Gaynes said, "Maybe I made too much fuss at Geribaldi's. Anybody working there might have known we were interested in talking up Zulia."

"So we question the employees," Boldt said. "What else?" the teacher quizzed.

LaMoia answered, "Canvass the neighborhood."

Gaynes said, "Look for moving violations in the area."

LaMoia said, "And this missing woman?"

Boldt answered, "According to Hill, she's our top priority."

LaMoia said nothing. Message received: Boldt was playing shortstop.

Boldt said, "Let's work McNeal. We need her cooperation." The hum of Homicide continued on the other side of the glass, the way traffic noise was a permanent part of the urban backdrop. "If we find Chow while she's still alive," Boldt said hopefully, "then maybe we blow the illegals case wide open."

"She's alive," Gaynes stated, leaving a moment of silence for this to sink in. "Or we would have found her body already—same as the others. These guys aren't shy. They're making statements. They don't want anyone talking about any of this. But if she is alive, and they have her, and they know what she was up to, then God pity her. She might wish she was dead."

"I'm telling you," LaMoia said. "We want a look at those videotapes. If we can't get a judge, then we sweet-talk McNeal—"

"Daffy," Boldt said. Matthews could sweet-talk a pet viper.

"But we get a look at those videotapes one way or the other."

CHAPTER 20

Stevie viewed the tapes she had taken from Melissa's apartment, the ordeal painful, even excruciating at times. Her fourth time all the way through. Melissa's narration rose with her enthusiasm and sank into cautious whispers despite her seclusion inside the van. The early surveillance footage documented the LSO and its location. Melissa had driven the entire block and had shot the building from all four sides, where in the back parking lot and for the first time, the camera recorded Gwen Klein leaving work—a short, stocky woman of average looks.

Klein walked stiffly and without a hint of grace. Melissa and her camera followed her to the supermarket, and to Shoreside School, a day-care center where she picked up a young boy and slightly older girl. With Melissa's van following, they drove to a clapboard home with a postage-stamp front lawn and a Direct TV satellite installed on the recently shingled roof.

On the video, the time stamp changed hours—18:37—approaching the hour of seven o'clock, providing the tape's clock was correct. It suggested Melissa had killed nearly two hours sitting parked waiting for activity. A pickup truck arrived and parked—the same pickup truck that Stevie already knew belonged to the husband and had been bought with cash. At 20:21, nearing eighty-thirty on the tape, the minivan left with Gwen Klein behind the wheel. With each start and stop of the video Stevie felt a little more uncomfortable, a voyeur, a spy. The subsequent sequence showed a run-down car wash, but no shot of any sign out front, any name. The van's taillights shined at her like a pair of squinting red eyes, Klein's foot on the brakes. The vehicle remained inside the automatic wash for the full cycle and then drove off, returning home. Melissa followed and captured the van parked at 21:07. The tape changed to gray fuzz. Stevie fast-forwarded through to the end, once again making sure she hadn't missed anything.

She poured herself a glass of juice, loaded the second tape, rewound and started it running. Eavesdropping on Melissa's monologue with the camera, Stevie felt as if she were reading from someone's private diary. Melissa would have edited the tapes down to a few brief shots, writing copy to accompany it—copy that Stevie wished she had, copy that might explain the significance or give continuity to the various shots. As a journalist, Melissa had recorded the footage in hopes of editing together a story sometime in the future. Stevie wanted that story now, but instead took away only the occasional grunt or groan from the camerawoman, the rare comment: "That's the husband's truck." "She wasn't in the grocery store long. But I suppose she could have passed someone the counterfeit licenses in there."

The second videotape showed Klein arriving by morning to the LSO. She carried a coffee in hand as she crossed the parking lot. There were shots of the public coming and going, first taken from a considerable distance, and then more footage with the camera zoomed and concentrating on faces. Melissa had either been bored and burning footage or had focused on the people coming and going out of a significance Stevie did not yet understand. Tempted to fast-forward, she nonetheless stuck it out as she had before, not knowing if one of the faces might be recognizable—the auditor who had contacted them? a politician or public official? She wasn't sure who or what she was looking for; she only knew that these were the tapes Melissa had shot prior to her borrowing the smaller digital camera, that these same images had more than likely led Melissa to take one step too many.

Convinced that time was working against her, Stevie needed that connection to her little sister. She fast-forwarded to the end of tape two and inserted the third and final tape she had liberated from the apartment.

Tape three began with familiar footage: again Klein left the LSO, this time amid a late afternoon drizzle strong enough to percussively pelt the top of the van and be picked up on the tape; the errands were different only in location—off to the vet's for a large bag of pet food, a drugstore stop tied to a dry cleaner next door, the same day-care center and retrieval of the kids. Melissa remained silent throughout all the recording, her enthusiasm of a day earlier muted, the sound of her breathing strangely present on the tape as background noise, like hearing a lover softly snoring. She returned to the same small house, the pickup truck having beaten her home on this day. The screen jerked as Melissa moved inside the van to shut the camera off.

This cut on the tape led into darkness, rain falling hard. The camera had been switched off and back on again. A darkened figure clad in rain gear, Klein's height, hurried to the van and climbed inside. Melissa's voice spoke softly and intimately, and Stevie could picture her peering into the camera's viewfinder while wrapped around its bulk. "I thought that might shake you up," she said, delivering the non sequitur. The van started up. "Show time," she said. The van backed up. The screen flickered and went black.

This scene immediately fed into a location with a view of the same car wash Stevie had witnessed on the earlier tape. Shot from a different angle, the tape showed the near side of the automatic wash's cement bunker, only a single taillight showing. Overheard through the van's one-way window and the constant scratching of the rain on its roof, came the angry honking of a car horn. Stevie associated the honking with the van, though reminding herself there was no way to be sure of that.

Only as Klein—or whoever was wearing that hooded rain gear—emerged from the cement bunker, that taillight still glowing, only as that person marched through the rain and the camera followed to focus on a dilapidated construction trailer on the back half of the lot, did it occur to Stevie that Klein had driven to a car wash *in the rain*. Hadn't Melissa mentioned something about a car wash? The figure approached the trailer and beat on the door relentlessly, finally raising her voice loud enough to be picked up by the camera inside the van.

Melissa whispered faintly, "That a girl . . . Come on home to Mama."

After battling the rain and the trailer's door, the figure retreated back to the van and drove away, aiming toward and passing immediately in front of the van and the camera. Stevie stopped the tape and rewound it several times, reaching out for her glass of juice only to find she had drained it. She finally resorted to advancing the footage frame by frame: the approaching van, its windshield glinting a reflection of an overhead street light, a face behind the wheel, just barely glimpsed: Gwen Klein. She zeroed the footage counter—she wanted to be able to return to that image. Then she let the tape run.

Melissa had stayed with the trailer in an act of investigative journalism that confirmed her nose for a story. According to the video's time stamp, twenty minutes passed before that trailer door came open. A large figure of a man, too dark to see clearly, ran through the rain. The camera panned down the block, passing darkened stores too obscured by the weather and the darkness to identify. And there in the corner of the frame appeared Melissa's profile as she rushed to the window to peer outside and follow the man. Stevie gasped at the sight.

"A bar," Melissa said for the benefit of the camera. She passed in front of the lens, this time moving to the rear of the van, the camera still running. A moment later another break in the recording was signaled by gray fuzz and waving colorful squiggles.

A brief shot of that same man running through the rain, back to the trailer, the time stamp indicating a passage of five minutes. Another cut. The van was moving now, the camera aimed out the windshield. "He boarded a bus," Melissa said for the benefit of her tape. The van swung a full U-turn, blurring the identifying lights and buildings and annoying Stevie as it bounced so violently as to be nothing but blurred and jerky imagery. Then she identified a city bus up ahead and realized moments later that Melissa was in pursuit. The chase led out and down a street still too jerky to recognize, past an I-5 on-ramp that Stevie felt certain she could find. The bus took a series of turns, made stops and continued on, the camera running tape all the while. Twenty minutes of this pursuit passed until the city's downtown landmarks were easily identified. The bus traveled north on Third Avenue, the van immediately behind, Melissa jerking the vehicle to the curb at every stop in search of that same figure disembarking from the bus. "No . . ." she said, "I don't see him."

The bus started back up. The van followed.

One block passed, then another. Stevie felt the tension in her chest and a bubble stuck in her throat, Melissa's determination palpable even across the videotape. At last the bus veered and sank into the bus tunnel, with the van following until Melissa realized she could not enter. She swore aloud and the picture went dark.

This was the last image on the tape: that city bus dropping down into a tunnel reserved for buses only, and the camera falling as it briefly caught a shot of a frustrated Melissa behind the wheel. "Damn camera's too big . . ." she mumbled to herself, her last words recorded on tape.

Her request for the digital camera made sense then—something light and portable, easily carried. That request had been met on Monday. Perhaps she had intended to follow this same man again. Perhaps she had even boarded a bus or entered the bus tunnel as a pedestrian.

Perhaps . . . perhaps . . . perhaps . . . Stevie caught herself tempted to toss the juice glass across the room, but placed it back down and poured a refill. As with any good lead, the tapes presented as many questions as they offered answers. She could look up the locations of car washes in the Yellow Pages and drive to them one by one. She hoped that particular car wash was listed, but there was no saying it was. She could try any number of wild attempts like that, or she could act like a journalist and get down to business. Suffering under a headache and the pressure of time passing much too quickly, aching over Melissa's disappearance and the tape's implication that she had aggressively gone after the story, Stevie resorted to what she knew best: journalism. The story started with Gwen Klein. It was as simple as that.

The LSO was crowded, its fiberglass seats filled with a cross section of the city's diverse population. She wore a baseball cap and kept her head down, not wanting to be recognized as she wandered the enormous room. Of the seven teller windows, four were in use. Stevie drew glares as she avoided the lines and headed straight to the front where small name plaques identified the tellers. In front of the third teller the sign read: Hello! I'm: G W E N. Stevie memorized that face, the Irish nose, the square-cut bangs that cantilevered out in a frosted blonde cascade. She went heavy on both the brown lipstick and the pale purple eye shadow. Klein delivered a self-important attitude via a demeaning, intolerant impatience. She was of average height with slouched shoulders. Stevie remained in line just long enough to take all this in, then feigned discouragement and walked back outside.

At 4:07 P.M., the building's rear door opened and several employees including Klein walked to their cars and drove off. This event eerily matched what Stevie had seen on Melissa's tape. Klein collected her kids from day care and led Stevie to 118th Street NW, a congested neighborhood of small clapboard houses. The van pulled in to #1186. Mom and the two kids left the car and headed inside the home.

With *News Four at Five* rapidly approaching, Stevie had no choice but to drive quickly to the studio and perform her on-camera duties, but her mind remained on #1186 118th NW, to which she returned immediately following the broadcast.

At seven o'clock, running low on patience, she left her car and headed to the front door. Answers could no longer wait.

Stevie hoped that the sharp attack of her knuckles on the front door might telegraph her attitude, her intentions, to the occupants, especially given that both a doorbell and a brass knocker were available.

To her relief it was Gwen Klein herself who answered the door. Klein recognized Stevie immediately, her face lighting up at first—the flush of a glimpse of celebrity—and then tightened in reaction to the association with news media. She stepped back and grabbed the edge of the door.

"Please . . . it's a personal matter," Stevie said.

"I have nothing to say to the press!"

The door began to swing shut. Stevie unleashed her only weapon. "You shut that door and I'll have a camera crew camped on your front lawn for the next two weeks."

The door stopped, partially open. A moment later Gwen Klein stepped outside, out of earshot, and pulled the door to within an inch of closing. She crossed her arms at her waist as if fending off a chill.

"Ms. Klein, I'm not here to make accusations, nor can I afford the luxury of wasting time." She did not want to mention Melissa's disappearance, not to someone like Klein, who if involved with supplying counterfeit licenses probably knew little of the overall operation. But Klein was the place to start, Stevie felt sure; Melissa had started with this woman. So would she.

"I don't know what you—"

"And let's dispense with the protestations of innocence or ignorance. I have no time for it. We both know *exactly* why I'm here, and if you play this otherwise, I'll turn and walk away and you'll have lost your chance."

"Chance at what?" Blank-faced and suddenly silent, Gwen Klein waited nervously.

"Do you follow the news?" Stevie asked, met only by that same blank stare. "Are you aware of the ship captain who drowned? The ship captain responsible for transporting the container of illegals? The man's death was not an accident, Ms. Klein." She lowered her voice for effect and said, "You have to come to grips with the fact that he was murdered. Killed, because someone didn't want him questioned by the police . . . the INS . . . whoever. Are you listening?" Klein's eyes went glassy and distant, as if looking right through Stevie.

"How long until whoever is paying you for those driver's licenses decides you too are a liability?"

Klein's mouth sagged open. As her jaw jutted out to speak, Stevie cut her off.

"I want the whole story. The truth, start to finish. Who contacted you, what they offered, how it worked, how long it's been going on. *If,*" she said strongly, "you are willing to share this with me openly and honestly, I'm willing to forget all about your sad little life and your bad decisions. You have children." The woman winced. "I'm not here to expose your behavior to your children, your neighbors, your employer."

"But how did you—"

"Never mind how. What matters is the truth. It's *all* that matters. I need the truth. You give me the truth, I go away. I can't remember your name. Do you understand what I'm offering you? I can use the First Amendment to protect you. What do you think *they* will offer you? What do you think they offered the ship captain?"

The woman's head snapped up. She looked left and right, as if afraid of the neighbors or someone else watching her. She met eyes with Stevie. Hers were hard and cold as she said, "Not here. Not now. You've *got* to leave." She stepped backward into the house, her hand blindly searching out the door.

"I need answers," Stevie cautioned, "or I'll tear your life open on your front lawn." She warned her, "Don't underestimate me."

"Not here."

"We'll talk."

The door closed further.

Stevie rushed her words. "We *have* to talk. You have to choose sides. Me or them?"

The door slammed shut. A full minute later, Gwen Klein pulled back a drape and peered out at Stevie, who remained on the front steps. Klein would want to discuss Stevie's offer with her husband, Stevie thought, so she would give her the night. One night. In the meantime, Stevie decided to make as if she were leaving. She climbed into her car and drove off. She came around the block, switched off her lights and parked. It was going to be a long night.

CHAPTER 21

"I tell you, this girl, she stupid and she scared." The Mexican kept his congested voice intentionally low despite the loud groaning of pleasure from the big screen. He spoke in a clipped Hispanic mix of thick accent and misplaced grammar. He'd been sick for a while now. In the pulsing flicker of light, six silhouettes could be seen in the various rows of the theater, all sitting well apart from one another and none anywhere near the two men who occupied the center of the back row.

The reflected light from the screen caught the other man's profile as he unstuck his right sole from whatever glue was down there, spilled soda or otherwise. He averted his face from both the brightness of the screen and the unspeakable acts portrayed by the two naked women in the grainy film. He understood the necessity of choosing such places for their meetings—the choice had been his, after all—but it didn't mean he had to like it. He kept his voice calm and quiet, negating any remote possibility of being overheard. "I can handle the reporter. Our friend will settle down." He never mentioned names, not ever. He knew all the tricks available to law enforcement. He trusted nobody. "Let's keep cool heads. This too shall pass."

"It's coming apart on you."

"Nothing is coming apart on anyone. A few speed bumps is all. It's to be expected with something this size. Shit happens. It's no reason to lose our cool."

"What do you mean, you handle reporter?" the Mexican asked.

"Not like that. Let's just keep cool about this, okay?" the other man encouraged.

"I do the girl?"

117

"Absolutely not. She'll be fine."

"I tell you, she not fine. Very upset. Last week it was the car wash in the middle of rainstorm. No brains at all." He pointed to the screen. "This? This is the only thing girls do right."

He felt knots in his jaw muscles form like hard nuts. He told himself to settle down. "Admittedly, it's not a perfect situation. She made a poor decision by coming to you. That's regrettable. But she'll stay on schedule with the deliveries. You watch. When she comes back, you tell her that we're taking care of the reporter, that everything's fine."

"And if she don't come back? If she misses the delivery?"

There was no silence in the theater, the pale-skinned teenagers on the screen filling every moment with either excited panting, exaggerated licking, or pleasure-ridden cooing. The other man rode out a particularly frantic climax before whispering to the Mexican, "If we have problems with her, we'll go looking to resolve them."

"That sounds better. I tell you what . . . in the middle of a goddamn rainstorm!"

"But we talk first, you and me. She's not the only one making poor decisions. No more fork lift fires. *Comprendo?*"

The Mexican pursed his lips. The man shaved infrequently, bathed infrequently and had the teeth of an old horse. "Speed bumps . . . like for the automobile? This kind of speed bump?"

"It's an expression. That's all."

"No, I get it. Speed bumps. I get it." Proud of himself, he plunged his meaty hand into the cold popcorn and stuffed his mouth with it. He offered the bag to the other. Speaking through the mouthful, he said, "You stay for next show?"

He glanced to his right. The seat was empty. Brian Coughlie was gone.

TUESDAY, AUGUST 25
8 DAYS MISSING

CHAPTER 22

When INS Field Operations Director Brian Coughlie was announced by the building's doorman, Stevie McNeal was wearing only a terrycloth robe, her hair wet and freshly combed out. She had dragged herself out of bed an hour later than usual, having kept the Klein home under surveillance until two in the morning. She studied Coughlie on the apartment's small black-and-white security monitor: He stood talking to the doorman as if they were old friends. Just the way he carried himself bothered her—overly comfortable, chatty, casual; but with the underhandedness of a card shark. Coughlie was part actor. A large part, if she were the judge. His unannounced visit bothered her, bordered on invasion of privacy or some form of harassment—the feds muscling their way into the media's business. Then it occurred to her that if she played this right, she might turn the tables and milk him for information.

To do so, she would have to play part actor herself—she would have to pretend not to be repulsed by him. She told the doorman that she would call down for him when she was ready, enjoying a renewed sense of control.

She slipped into a pair of jeans, pulled on a camisole top and a white T-shirt, making sure she wasn't advertising herself. She didn't want him getting any ideas.

A few minutes later Coughlie was standing in the middle of her substantial living room enjoying the view. She wondered how a public servant on a government paycheck felt surrounded by such opulence, how much envy and anger played for his emotions, how much of the long-established discord between the press and law enforcement stemmed not from ideology but paycheck envy. She could imagine his attitude: The container deaths and Melissa's safe return meant little or nothing, another file to close.

What drove a person to sign up with the INS in the first place, she wondered. What kind of person volunteered to be a glorified border guard?

"Nice view," he said, as if expected to compliment.

"The nature of your visit, Agent Coughlie?"

"Brian." He fingered a carved piece of black stone a friend had brought back from Egypt. He held it upside down and admired its base. He offered her a small pamphlet that she accepted. "You asked Adam Talmadge about this: investigative techniques used in our preliminary interviews."

"I asked him about the training to identify political prisoners and victims of torture."

"Political refugee interviews," he corrected. "We're not the bad guys, Ms. McNeal."

"You're part of the system . . . *Brian*. And the system is part of the problem."

"My trouble with this view," he said, his inflection implying a question. "Looking down on something is not the same thing as looking it in the eye."

"Lessons in perspective?"

He offered: "How would you and your cameras like to pay a visit to Fo-No, our Fort Nolan detention facility? A chance to see our operation firsthand?"

"Look it in the eye. Gain a little perspective?"

"You got it."

"And what do I offer you in return?" she asked suspiciously.

"Nothing."

"I'm supposed to buy that?"

"Does it sound like I'm selling? Are you always so skeptical?"

"You came here to drop off a pamphlet and offer me access to your detention facility? I'm supposed to accept the Santa Claus routine?"

"We have to be enemies on this? Tell me why."

"You can't buy cooperation from me," she warned. "A pamphlet

and a visit of Fort Nolan and I'm supposed to give something back—
withhold a story, supply you with sources—what is it your boss is
after?"

"We could discuss Melissa Chow."

"They shared that with you?"

"A missing persons case believed tied to illegal aliens?" he asked
rhetorically. "You want SPD including us, believe me. And the FBI
and the King County Police. There is talk of a task force. It's our job
to find this woman."

"A job? I suppose so," she said, mulling this over.

"Let's talk about this whistle-blower."

"Oh . . . okay. I get it," she said sarcastically. "Terrific."

"Do you?"

"They couldn't get the name out of me, so now it's your turn to
try."

"You want to find her, don't you?" He didn't deny her accusation.
"We need to question this guy. He could help clarify the details, give
us the specifics you're unable to give us."

"Or is it the videos?" she asked. "That's it, isn't it? They've sent
you to try to talk me out of the videos. Well, forget it." She immediately regretted mention of the videos because his florid skin and tightened expression informed her that he'd never heard of them, though
he recovered quickly.

He said, "The videos are especially important to us."

"I just bet they are," she said.

"They show what? People? Buildings? The container? The ship?"

"Nice try."

"How much are you willing to gamble?" he interrupted. "Your
friend has disappeared. The ship captain has been killed. Do you want
to be next in line?"

"Are you threatening me?"

"Just trying to scare you," he said. "Listen, I do this for a living—
investigate illegal alien rings, the Chinese mob, the gangs. It may be
hard to conceive of, but just maybe I've had a little more experience
at it than you. And as for your paranoia . . . I don't operate the way

the cops do. There's *no reason* for me to expose your sources or what's on that video. I work a network of informants and snitches. I probably get ninety percent of my information from them. Would it make sense for me to expose my sources? Your sources? My guys wouldn't trust me after that. Think about it! Do you have any idea what it is you're investigating? No, you don't. They made your friend disappear, Ms. McNeal. Think about it! Where's that leave you, you go nosing around?"

"I'll read the pamphlet. Thanks for stopping by."

He was not to be deterred. He apparently felt obliged to educate her. She wanted him out of there. "The vast majority of illegals come across the Mexican border—and that *includes* Asians and East Europeans. Most arrive owing at least half the fee charged to smuggle them into the country—five to ten thousand dollars. The men are shipped off to migrant labor camps, the girls to brothels and sweatshops. They're kept in service until they earn out the balance owed. It's not pretty."

Was that where Melissa was, she wondered. In some brothel or sweatshop? She cringed. "Are you trying to tell me someone's turned Melissa into a sex slave?"

"These container ships go both ways, Ms. McNeal. You go poking around, you go stirring things up . . . With your looks you'd probably end up in Syria, the property of some prince. Is that hair natural? Blondes command a premium."

"You're threatening me?" she asked, astonished.

"What is it with you?" he asked. "Am I the enemy?"

"Are you?"

Outside the huge plate-glass windows, a jet sank in the vast expanse of sky. It flew behind Brian Coughlie and out the other side of him, like some kind of magic trick.

She said, "As a reporter you wonder what kind of person signs up to be an INS agent."

"Is that right?" he said. "That's funny, because as a federal agent you kinda wonder about people who make a business out of sabotaging your investigations and turning them into sound bites."

"No one's sabotaging you."

"You went after Adam Talmadge like he was the enemy," he reminded. "You seem to forget it's our job to save these people."

"Save them or deport them?"

"I didn't invent the system," he pointed out.

"Just doing your job?" she asked sarcastically.

His face burned red and he looked away angrily. He spoke to the back lights of the jet descending toward Boeing Field. "A pragmatist says my job is to offer people a chance at a new life; a pessimist says that I'm in the business of wrecking other people's dreams. I live with it. Same as you. The press tears apart more lives than I ever will."

"And where's all that leave Melissa?"

"I can help with that."

She cautioned him again, "I won't reveal my sources. Neither would you—you just said so yourself."

"Trust me," he said.

She nodded faintly and whispered privately, "I'm working on that."

CHAPTER 23

Lou Boldt and John LaMoia stood over the black, open mouth of the cemetery grave, looked down inside and took in the sight. The victim was an Asian female—Chinese. She was naked. Her toes, breasts and dirt-covered face protruded from the mud and sand that had been washed away by overnight downpours that continued intermittently. Her head was shaved. Boldt felt the familiar twinge that any contact with death delivered.

She had been deposited into a hole in the ground that had been dug for a casket. Someone had hoped that casket would be lowered down on top of this woman, burying her forever in anonymity.

LaMoia won every officer's attention as he shouted orders. Boldt couldn't take his eyes off the woman in the grave. "Where the hell is SID? Enlarge the perimeter tape to include the entire cemetery. I want the statement of the gravedigger who found her. I want somebody to get Stevie McNeal up here nice and quiet like. And I don't want another word of this going out over the radio. Got it?" Boldt turned to face LaMoia, and said in a normal voice, "Why is she so pale? Does she look right to you?"

LaMoia called out sharply to a pair of uniforms, "Somebody find a tarp! Let's get a curtain up that the cameras can't see past. Anyone not wearing gloves is going to be writing traffic tickets 'til Christmas." That sent them scurrying.

When Doc Dixon arrived a few minutes later, he was helped down into the hole. Boldt gave him only a matter of seconds before asking, "How long has she been dead?"

Dixon's low, sullen voice did not transmit well outside. "Give me a minute, would you?"

"Does she look right to you?" Boldt asked.

Dixon wore a windbreaker, gray flannels damp from the knees down, and a pair of "lab walkers"—leather shoes with overly thick rubber soles. "They never look right to me. Give me a minute," he repeated.

"She's too pale," Boldt repeated for his colleagues. "And her breasts are all black around the nipple—What's that about?"

Dixon was rarely terse with Boldt, but he snapped, "If you don't mind?"

He let Dixon work the victim until he finally called up out of the hole, "Soles of her feet like elephant skin. I'm guessing she's early twenties. Left ankle shows signs of ligatures."

Daphne Matthews arrived. The team . . . Boldt thought. She wore an ankle-length trench coat and carried an open umbrella. She came and stood alongside Boldt, and as always, he noticed how strikingly handsome she was.

"Zoo's here!" a patrolman shouted from the distance, warning of the arrival of the media. The rain fell harder.

"Maintain that crime line!" LaMoia shouted. "No one crosses except McNeal."

Down in the hole, Dixon talked into a dictation device held in his meaty right hand to screen the rain.

LaMoia asked Boldt quietly, "What's she doing buried here like this?"

Boldt answered, "Hiding." He looked up at the sea of headstones.

Daphne picked up on this. "If there's one, there may be others."

LaMoia gasped, "More of 'em?"

"Visitor!" a patrolman shouted, indicating an umbrella approaching.

"McNeal," LaMoia said.

Daphne complained, "Since when is graveside identification procedure? This is hardly fair to her. Did anyone think about *her*?"

"This was my call," Boldt said.

She reminded them, "The corpse should be cleaned up and presented on the other side of the glass in the morgue. *That* is procedure. A body found down in a muddy hole?"

"She's a reporter," LaMoia said. "She can handle it."

"Punish the press? Is that the idea?"

"The idea," Boldt said, "is to know what and whom we are dealing with, just as quickly as we can."

Daphne hurried to intercept the approaching woman. "Listen," she said, unable to slow down McNeal, "we can do this downtown in a couple of hours. It doesn't have to be now . . . like this. There's a lot of mud. The face . . . it's not that visible anyway."

McNeal nodded, but kept walking toward the grave.

"You're protecting me?" Stevie asked. "From what?"

"It's an awful sight. If it is your friend . . . this reporter . . . "

"Then I've got to know," Stevie said. She stopped short of the others and crossed her arms. "Thank you," Stevie whispered to Daphne. They met eyes and Daphne understood she was going to go through with it.

Stevie stepped up to the grave. LaMoia introduced her to Boldt who said, "Sorry for any inconvenience caused by the location."

Stevie glanced at him, as yet unable to face the body down in that grave.

"I've heard about you for years," she said from under the umbrella.

"Not all bad, I hope," Boldt returned.

She hesitated and said, "No, not all." She then inched toward the grave's edge, her shoes sinking into the mud, dirt and gravel. She looked straight ahead for a moment, her eyes brimming with tears. She pinched her eyes shut, hung her head, and then opened her eyes slowly, her expression controlled and impassive.

"It's not her," she said, exhaling in a long sigh. She turned and walked away. "Not her," she repeated for all to hear.

CHAPTER 24

B rian Coughlie answered his office phone, annoyed by the inter-
ruption until he identified the voice.

"It's me," Stevie McNeal announced into the receiver.

Coughlie felt a boyish flutter in the center of his chest. "Hello,"
he said.

"Did I interrupt you?"

"No, no," he lied—a way of life for him.

"The police found a Jane Doe up on Hilltop. Shaved head and
eyebrows. I thought maybe you'd want to know."

He was shocked by her call. He couldn't think what to say.

Stevie said, "She was meant to be buried underneath the casket.
Maybe Melissa had caught on to this burial thing."

Coughlie recalled Rodriguez's warning that Stevie was a threat to
them. He didn't want to see her this way. A necessary distraction was
more like it—someone he could use to their benefit, confirmed by this
call.

"We agreed to share," she reminded. "The cops aren't giving us
anything. Whatever details you can find out . . . I'd appreciate it."

"Sure thing." He had no intention of trading in a vacuum. "You
were going to consider sharing those videos with me." If she didn't
share them soon, then Rodriguez was going to have to perform a
break-in.

"We might be able to arrange something," she said.

"I'll get back to you," he said.

"I'll be waiting."

CHAPTER 25

Although procedure required an investigating officer to attend a victim's autopsy, this requirement often amounted to cruel and unusual punishment. For Boldt, who understood perfectly well the need to protect the evidence's chain of custody, it still seemed a waste of the officer's time, because the surgical procedure could drag on for hours. He and his squad, like every other homicide squad in the country, had found ways around the requirement—attending the autopsy, but not start to finish, leaving the bulk of the cutting and sawing to the people in the white coats. But no matter what duration of time was actually spent in the tile room with the ME or one of his assistants, the assignment required a strong stomach—there was no way of avoiding at least a brief encounter with the pale and naked corpse of the bloated victim, whether bludgeoned, bullet-ridden or burned. Technically, it was LaMoia's investigation and therefore his autopsy, but Boldt filled in both to free up his sergeant who was busy with an unusual assignment and to gain firsthand knowledge for himself.

The cadaver lay on the stainless steel table, drains beneath her feet and head, a hospital band around her ankle, the chalky discoloration of her bloodless skin, sickening. Her bald skull and shaved pubis held a dull smudge of growth and reminded Boldt of his wife during her chemotherapy. The two men in lab coats cleaned up the ligature marks, removed most of the mud, sand, and grass, the bugs, worms and weeds, bagging, labeling and indexing. All such physical evidence was destined for Bernie Lofgrin's SID forensics lab back at Public Safety.

Preliminary exterior examination of the cadaver continued for thirty minutes. While Boldt made phone calls from a wall phone,

Dixon spent equal amounts of time inspecting the cadaver's head, genitals, hands and feet. It was ascertained that her chest showed an inflamed skin rash, that her extremities showed signs of postmortem frost burn—explaining the darkened skin on her breasts and toes. Her hands and fingers held lacerations and puncture wounds.

A few minutes later she looked like something from *Gray's Anatomy* as Dixon used a scalpel to unzip her from collarbone to crotch with a sure and steady hand. There were cop stories about medical examiners using poultry scissors and chain saws, Skilsaws and power drills, not all of which were exaggeration. The procedure could run anywhere from forty-five minutes to several hours. Dry land jumpers, floaters and burns occupied the Worst of All Time list. Jane Doe, for all the tragedy of her young death, was not too bad in terms of the autopsy.

Dixon opened her up like a frog in biology class, tucking one breast under the left armpit, the other under the right, calling out his observations for the sake of the video that captured the cadaver and the spoken dialogue for use in court if needed. He worked his trade—he took a liver plug, inspected her heart, emptied her stomach contents, manipulated her kidneys and finally cut open a lung—he called it "looking under the hood," and sometimes slipped in other automotive analogies.

Time crawled. Dixon mentioned bronchial occlusion, edema and renal failure.

An hour and ten minutes later the video recorder was shut off and the two men adjourned to Dixon's office for "the postgame show." An assistant was left behind to sew her up and "get her back in the cooler."

Despite the use of surgical gloves, Dixon used a jeweler's screwdriver to clean under each fingernail. Some things never changed. On his desk were laid out a number of sealed plastic bags from the autopsy.

"You're an obsessive-compulsive," Boldt said.

"Yeah? Well catch this." Dixon flicked a discolored spec toward Boldt, but missed. "The gloves rip more often than not."

"A lovely thought. I hope you disinfect your floors."

"Only when it starts to smell."

"I'm never bringing the kids down here again."

"Autopsy day care," Dixon said with a smile. "Another Boldt concept that never quite caught on."

Boldt asked, "Any surprises in your prelim?"

Dixon studied from some of the notes his assistant had kept during the autopsy and then set the papers back down on his desk. He began the process of cataloguing the samples laid out before him. "Technically, she died as a result of pneumonia caused by pulmonary infection. To you, she drowned in her own mucus—not unlike what we saw in the three victims from that container."

"Okay. You've won my attention."

"Couple things set her apart. One is that she'd been violently raped. We picked up semen samples, vaginally and in the esophagus. We'll run DNA. The other is a skin irritation. I'll get back to that. Of primary importance to you is the unusual hemorrhaging in both the intestines and lungs. That's your bridge between the container victims and this woman. Microscopically, the kidneys show inflammatory changes and infectious changes, but I keep coming back to the intestines, because that's what sets these women apart from other flu-related deaths. It's the same etiology as your container victims, Lou. In my lingo, this cause of death is not unlike the earlier cases we saw. Right now, your best shot would be to make a case for depraved indifference."

"We can connect her to the container victims," Boldt stated hopefully.

"Circumstantially. Our samples will go to CDC in Atlanta who already have similar samples from the container vics. Two to three weeks, minimum."

"That's too long," Boldt complained. "I've got the three dead in the container, two possible suspects murdered, and a journalist missing for over a week now."

"You do, or LaMoia does?"

"I'm his errand boy."

"Uh-huh."

"It's his case," Boldt stated to deaf ears. He asked, "Was she in this same container?"

"It's the same etiology," he repeated, "but unlikely the same container. This one had been frozen."

"What?"

"We see this often enough with cruise ships. Someone dies out at sea. Captain orders her into the deep freeze. What he doesn't realize is that the fridge would be a hell of a lot easier on us. When you defrost frozen tissue it decomposes quickly, the cells actually break as they thaw. Looks different. Behaves differently."

"Frozen?"

"That's what I'm saying."

"For how long?"

"No way to know."

"Guesses?"

"A couple weeks to a month or more. If we took it out past six weeks we'd be likely to see more freezer burn than this." He added, "That's only *opinion*, Lou."

"That rash?" Boldt asked.

"No, not freezer burn. It's chemical or allergy. Stay tuned."

"So she was here well ahead of the container," Boldt said.

"In my opinion, yes."

"But died of a similar illness."

"In my opinion, yes." Dixon suggested, "They could all come from the same village, something like that."

"I need that freezer. I need the location of wherever that container was headed. We're thinking sweatshop. The fabric inside the container—"

"I can support that with two needle marks on this one's fingers."

"*Not* a cruise ship."

"If it's a sweatshop, Lou, then it's near a wharf, the fishing docks, something like that."

"Why do you say that?" Boldt asked.

"Or inside an old cannery," Dixon continued. "The canneries all had freezers."

"You found something on her, didn't you?" Boldt said expectantly. He knew the man well. Like the lab's Bernie Lofgrin, Dixon held the best for last. "What the hell's going on, Dixon?"

"Not going on," Dixon corrected, "coming off. Her feet were covered with them. Got to be either a cannery or a ship."

"Her . . . feet . . . were . . . covered . . . with . . . what?" Boldt asked.

Dixon searched through the half dozen plastic bags and held one up for Boldt to see. "Fish scales," he said. "Her feet were covered in fish scales."

CHAPTER 26

Stevie and the mobile news crew entered through the front doors of the Greenwood LSO, cameras rolling, lights glaring, and parted the sea of those waiting in line.

She had left the graveyard only hours earlier, relieved that the body wasn't Melissa's but pained and haunted by the sight of that poor girl lying down there in the mud, all breath gone from her body. Such finality drove Stevie to take immediate action, her grief and terror overtaking her. Any fate could have befallen Melissa—death, captivity, white slavery. It had been over a week. A lifetime? The combination of the dead body in the grave and Melissa's sparse but haunting narration of the videos pushed Stevie beyond any professional capacity to handle her situation. Guilt ridden and obsessed with finding the woman, she succumbed to her spent emotions and heightened anxiety. At first bit by bit, this internal decay now crossed a threshold that left her in a constant state of panic.

Typically the public would never tolerate an individual cutting into the line, might even respond violently, but add the possibility of a TV appearance and smiles appeared on their otherwise impatient faces.

"Ms. Gwen Klein!" Stevie shouted out, her voice commanding such authority that her target froze behind the teller window. It took Klein a moment, at which point she headed for an Employees Only door behind the counter.

"Ms. Klein! You are KSTV's state employee of the week!" Stevie glanced to her left, toward the managing supervisor's office and the man in the button-down shirt and tie who occupied the doorway.

"Gwen!" the supervisor shouted. He nodded toward her teller window, indicating for her to return.

Klein stopped, looking first to the supervisor and then to the waiting room with its seventy citizens and McNeal with her team. She had a weighty decision to make.

If the woman ran, Stevie was prepared to turn her interview hostile. She too held her breath. "Let's hear it for Ms. Klein," Stevie prodded.

The room broke into applause.

The supervisor once again indicated the teller window.

Klein, distraught and churning, offered Stevie a mean-spirited look and returned to her window where Stevie and her crew waited.

The supervisor licked his fingers and spit-combed a few strands of hair off his shining forehead.

Klein and Stevie stepped face to face.

"Ms. Klein," Stevie began in a voice of seeming adulation for her subject. "Gwen! It has come to the attention of this reporter, and KSTV viewers and staff, that you approach your job not only with diligence, but with enthusiasm, joy and efficiency." She paused just long enough for her gallery to sparsely applaud. "In a world that moves too fast for most of us, and a job where the lines move too slowly . . ." another pause for the requisite laughter ". . . you are an inspiration to all of us. KSTV would like to present you with . . ." she vamped for an appropriate-sounding gift, since nothing had been arranged, "dinner for two at the Palomino restaurant in City Center, and two tickets to the musical *Rent,* now playing at the Fifth Avenue Theater." The crowd lit up with applause. "Here is our IOU, which you can redeem—later on," she emphasized, "at the KSTV studios." She slipped a folded three-by-five card across the stone countertop. Klein made the mistake of opening the card.

On it was written: *I know about the car wash.*

Klein paled.

Stevie said, "Can you share with our viewers the secret to keeping your customers so satisfied, so impressed with you as a person?"

"I ahh . . . No . . . No . . ."

"Well . . . Thank you, Gwen Klein, for setting such a fine example. KSTV hopes you enjoy the gift." She signaled the cameraman and the lights faded and the camera went off his shoulder, and the small crowd dispersed as people regained their places in line.

Stevie leaned across the counter and whispered through a faked smile, "I'll air this footage unless you meet with me."

"I can't."

"I'll be expecting a call." Stevie stepped away from the window.

Klein glanced once again at the three-by-five card, all blood gone from her face.

The cameraman, gathering his gear, asked skeptically, "Since when do we feature an Employee of the Week?"

"Since now," Stevie said, hurrying toward the door, her public gawking from a distance.

CHAPTER 27

B oldt and LaMoia walked a couple blocks to the Public Library and took a seat on a recently added bench out front. They took a moment to scan the area around them, alert for anyone eavesdropping. Boldt nodded his okay. He felt badly about the need for secrecy, about the games within games, but LaMoia had started this, and for the moment Boldt did not see a way out.

LaMoia spoke softly, looking straight ahead. "I was tempted to put Gaynes on her, so we didn't miss anything."

"Forget it! You know this is suicide if anyone finds out," Boldt reminded. "We'll be chalking tires. We can get away with me filling in for you, just as long as no one gets wise as to what you're up to."

"She watched a house up on 118th Northwest last night until two A.M. Name of Klein. Late morning I follow her from Hilltop back to the station. She and a film crew take off to an LSO on Greenwood a half hour later. This interesting you yet?"

"I'm not comfortable with any of this."

"It wasn't your idea!" LaMoia reminded.

"Maybe that's why I'm not comfortable with it."

"So I check the name on the house she's watching against state payroll. What else connects the two, right?" He said sarcastically, "She's bringing a film crew in to renew her license, I suppose." He lost the attitude and said, "There's an LSO employee name of Gwendolyn Klein. The connection has got to be driver's licenses." He pointed out, "Illegals need documents."

"If it proves good, we'll have to find some other way to connect the dots," Boldt reminded. "If McNeal ever found out we had her under surveillance and that we stole her sources . . . she'd not only have us in court, but we'd lose our suspect."

"You worry too much," LaMoia said. "What about a random credit check on a handful of LSO workers that just happens to turn up Klein. She has got to have some unexplained money in her pockets if she's good for this. "

"But what made us run the check of LSO employees in the first place?" Boldt asked.

"I see what you mean."

"It has to be a believable trail. Then we never mention McNeal." Boldt asked, "What about Coughlie? Maybe his people already have suspicions that there's documentation coming out of the LSOs. Something like that could make the connection for us."

"Not a good idea. I wouldn't go there. He paid her a visit first thing this morning."

"*Before* we found the body at Hilltop?"

"Right. Was with McNeal for the better part of an hour."

"She *has* been busy."

"We gotta figure they're working together somehow."

"Information exchange," Boldt suggested. "He promises her an exclusive to the story as long as there's a two-way flow of information."

"And they're cutting us out?" an exasperated LaMoia cried out. He added, "I hate that shit!"

"Just because he got to her first?" Boldt teased.

"Exactly!" LaMoia added, "But *he* didn't think to put her under surveillance."

"Let's hope not anyway."

LaMoia grimaced.

"What if we asked Daphne to try to open her up for us?" Boldt suggested. "She seeds some doubts about Coughlie's integrity, offers exclusivity with us?"

"End run the feds? That would be sweet! You want me to pull the surveillance? Is that what I'm hearing?"

"You're hearing me concerned about the police getting caught for having the press under surveillance. It's dangerous for all concerned, John. We've been over this."

"McNeal is withholding key information to this case. She admitted that to my face. If she wasn't press—"

"She *is* press. If we want her sources we go to court, not surveillance."

"We gonna do this dance again?" LaMoia whined. "We go to court, it'll be Christmas. This missing woman, and our case along with it, will be long gone. We're *protecting* McNeal," LaMoia reminded. "Her associate went missing with this same information. We believe those videotapes—and remember, I saw her leave the apartment with them—are pertinent to the case. We've got our bases covered on this, Sarge."

"We've got Klein. Maybe we *should* stop while we're still ahead."

"But we aren't ahead," LaMoia reminded. "We're still playing catch up."

"Well let's play catch-up at a distance. Shall we? And let's close the gap as quickly as possible. This thing makes me nervous."

"It's a way of life for you. If you weren't worried *I'd* be worried.

Boldt said, "That would be a first."

They studied the area once more before breaking up and leaving the bench. They walked in opposite directions without ever having talked about a plan. It seemed symbolic to Boldt—LaMoia, two years into his sergeant's stripes, was increasingly difficult to control.

CHAPTER 28

Stevie was applying the last touches of blush when her name was called over KSTV's public address system. She called reception as requested, one eye fixed on herself in the large mirror surrounded by dazzlingly bright lights that mimicked the brightness of the set. Her guest was identified as Daphne Matthews—Seattle Police. The woman from the cemetery who had tried to protect her.

An intern delivered the woman to Makeup. Without the raincoat and hood, Matthews came off as quite pretty. Dark features on olive skin. Her presence put Stevie on guard. She was conditioned not to trust the cops.

Daphne had a job to do. She lived for the fieldwork the way Boldt did, and the fact that he had asked her to do this made it all the more important to her to succeed. He still had this effect on her, this unintentional yet underhanded control that for years she had fought to overcome. Struggled, was more like it. She could point her life this way or that, redirecting it as far away from him as possible—her on-again, off-again engagement to Owen Adler the most overt example—but inevitably her emotions returned to him. Comfort. Home.

She saw in his eyes that these feelings were reciprocated, though it went unmentioned between them. No hot glances. No teasing. Those days were behind them. He with his family and his wife, as passionate a father and husband as one could ask for; she, like a sailboat without its keel, pointing strongly into the wind but endlessly sideslipping and losing her course.

It was some kind of horrific joke, the way she tried to throw it away only to have it come boomeranging back at her. Those emotions for him. The desire that wormed hot like an infection deeply within her. If she heard his voice, she turned to look. If his name was spoken, she listened in—all the while wearing the mask of indifference. She understood that she had to move on. She believed it. But accomplishing it was something altogether different. All the education in the world could not explain this to her. Nothing seemed to help.

And so when he asked her to see McNeal for him, she responded immediately like a child eager to please the teacher—and she hated herself for it.

▐▐▐▐▐▐▐

"I'm on the set in a minute," Stevie said, giving herself a way out.

"This won't take long."

"We met at the cemetery, right?"

"Yes." Daphne took a seat in one of the two padded swivel chairs that faced the bright mirror, but she turned to face Stevie, who in profile continued working with the blush. "I wanted to talk about Melissa. Anything you can provide us . . . It's all a help to the investigation."

"Such as the videotapes?"

"Evidence is LaMoia's department. I'm more interested in her habits, lifestyle, friends, relationships—that sort of thing."

"You're a shrink?"

"A psychologist."

Stevie nodded, congratulating herself. "I didn't have you pegged as a cop. This is making a lot more sense to me."

"The thing about a missing persons case, Ms. McNeal, is that there are often leads that don't get pursued for one reason or another. We know this from hindsight. From the—"

"—cases where they don't come back . . . are never found," Stevie completed.

"We believe Melissa is still alive. That she's either in hiding, or has been abducted, but that she's alive."

"And you base this on?"

"The fact that we haven't found her body," Daphne said bluntly, stunning the other woman. "They're using violence to make statements. Why would they treat Melissa any differently?"

"Because she's a reporter."

"Is that what you think?" Daphne questioned. "You think it's a passport of some sort? Don't believe it, Ms. McNeal. They don't make those kinds of distinctions. They're sending messages. The easiest way to send *you* a message is to deliver Melissa's body."

"Maybe they know me better than that," she said, leaning back and turning her face to the mirror. "It would only incite my wrath."

"It's not incited already?" Daphne said, suspiciously. "I don't believe that. You know what I think? I think you're not sleeping, not eating well. I think you've probably been looking long and hard at a bottle of wine, maybe drinking a little more than usual. You lie awake thinking about all the 'what ifs.' You blame yourself. You blame her. You blame us. And none of it goes away."

Stevie blinked furiously, trying to discourage the tears that threatened. She took a deep breath trying to contain herself. "You'll excuse me," she said, "I have to be on the set." She averted her face while she returned the blush brush to the Formica countertop.

"Tell me I'm wrong."

"What is it you *want*?" Stevie said, stopped at the door, her back to Daphne.

"You'll blame yourself even more if you withhold information from us. I can help you deal with the grief, Ms. McNeal. It's what I do. You may be convincing yourself otherwise at the moment—the police are incompetent; the police don't play fair—all the arguments neatly worked out. Professional ethics. Or maybe you think the case isn't ours to give away, that it's the INS, only the INS, who can help you. So you put your eggs in that basket." She paused. "How am I doing?"

"You think too much."

"Professional liability. What'd you have for dinner last night? Breakfast, this morning? When was your last glass of wine? It's red wine, isn't it? Expensive, I bet. But you're drinking alone. And how's that feel? Not very good, I bet."

"We're done here." She couldn't will her arm to open the door. She stood there, her back to the woman. Frozen.

"You find yourself missing people—not just Melissa, but your family, your last relationship, anyone and everyone who's gotten close . . . who *is* close."

Stevie shook her head violently.

Daphne continued, unrelenting. "The INS oversees illegal immigration—no question about it. But a missing persons investigation? That's us. Would I hand you a sports story? And what about the INS? If you're the one running illegal aliens into this country, into this port, who's the first person you need on your payroll, the first person you must compromise? Do you think we missed that? Do you think we're sharing every lead with Coughlie and Talmadge? Why should we do that until we know more about them? And that takes a while, believe me."

"Turf wars? This is supposed to be news to me? You people fight your petty games while the investigation stagnates. I've seen it a hundred times from the other side of that anchor desk. That adoption ring last year—same thing happened there, right? One hand not washing the other. Same old story."

"Not turf wars, Ms. McNeal. Cautious is all. We're careful about to whom we go volunteering information. Are you?"

Stevie turned then and faced her. "I'll tell you what—let's just do our jobs: You find Melissa; I'll report it as news when you do. End of discussion."

"We have a solid lead we're pursuing," Daphne said. "The woman in the grave. In death, she told us something."

As tortured as Stevie felt, she remained alert, hanging on Daphne's every word. The lack of sleep . . . the loss of appetite . . . she knew too much, this woman. It felt invasive—a violation. And yet it also made her feel like someone actually understood what she was going through. Finally someone who understood. Tricks? It had to be a trick. The cops were full of them.

Daphne said, "Our first hard evidence. We think we've established a time line that suggests this woman is an earlier victim—a first victim. Do you know the significance of a first victim in a crime,

Ms. McNeal? The first victim is generally the one who is handled carelessly. It's only later the criminal mind thinks to start making better preparations, thinks to plan more carefully. This was sloppy. Hasty. This woman was handled poorly. That's in our favor."

"What evidence?"

"The thing is, we can work with you. We would *like* to work with you. But it would have to be in an exclusive relationship—we would have to trust each other to the point that you would not air nor share certain information, and that we, likewise, would not work with other reporters or news agencies until giving you first dibs on what we have."

"And if we work this out?" Stevie inquired.

"We'd want to see the videotapes—yes, of course. We'd want you to name your sources. We, in turn, would open up the autopsy prelim on Jane Doe to you. We'd share, Ms. McNeal. We'd give Melissa the best shot at coming home. The way we're working now—well, it's not working . . . that's just the point."

A knock came on the door. Stevie jumped. "Ms. McNeal?" a voice said from the other side. "You're wanted on the set."

Daphne offered, "I can help you find sleep. I can work with you on the loss of appetite. That offer comes without precondition."

"Who said I can't sleep?" Stevie barked defensively.

"No strings attached."

"I'm wanted on the set."

"You can't do this alone." She added, "And the INS can't clear a missing persons case. If they've represented themselves otherwise, it's unfair to you."

Stevie felt and looked paralyzed.

"The name is Matthews," Daphne reminded. "The switchboard will put you through. My voice mail has my pager number. I'm available to you around the clock." Daphne placed one of her cards next to the cosmetics. "I'm hoping you'll call."

"I'm wanted on the set," she repeated. She pulled open the door and left.

But when Daphne looked down, she noticed her business card was gone.

WEDNESDAY, AUGUST 26
9 DAYS MISSING

CHAPTER 29

The Seattle Aquarium was located out on a pier in the heart of the heavily touristed waterfront, a collection of crab and chowder houses and ferry traffic servicing the outlying islands. Seagulls swarmed fallen crumbs, picking the wide sidewalk clean. The familiar smell of suntan lotion hung in the air along with the choke of diesel fumes, a taste of salt spray and the permanent musty tang of rotting wood, indelible and almost sugary on the tongue.

Boldt walked quickly, not because he was late, but because he was driven by a mounting fear that the investigation itself was late, that Melissa Chow had run out of time. Nine days—far too long. He did not accept that there was a mortal power greater than that of the Seattle Police, that whoever was behind the container shipments and the recent murders could remain a step ahead, could murder their way into silencing the sources that might open up the case. But privately, his own fear of these people was wearing him down. The ruthlessness and daring of killing the potential witnesses and leaving them for police to find reminded everyone involved that no one was safe. Not even police.

Gwen Klein, the LSO employee, appeared to be the most recent statistic. She had failed to show up for work. She had gone missing right at the moment that LaMoia's team had found out about her and had decided, in a failed attempt, to put her under surveillance. McNeal had run an "Employee of the Week" piece on *News Four at Five* that Boldt blamed on the woman's disappearance. The stupidity of the press never ceased to amaze him.

The pressure on all involved had intensified, especially on Boldt and LaMoia. Too many dead bodies. A reporter missing. Television news turning the screws and making inroads ahead of police. There was talk of creating a task force to include SPD and the INS, although both sides were resisting. For Boldt, as he quickened his pace yet again, all of it took a backseat to locating Melissa Chow, who appeared to be not only a possible victim but also a key witness. To find this woman was to simultaneously bring down the people behind both the murders and the importing of human beings—he felt certain of it.

Dr. Virginia Ammond was a tomboy in her mid-forties with a freckled Irish complexion, callused hands and a Ph.D. in marine sciences. She dressed in faded jeans rolled at the cuff and an immodestly tight T-shirt that bore the aquarium's logo.

"The medical examiner's request to identify the fish scales went first to the university, but was passed on to me for confirmation."

Boldt visited the aquarium regularly with his kids, the floor plan familiar to him. Ammond walked him down the descending ramp that led deeper underground and into the heart of the facility—a 360-degree viewing room completely surrounded by glass and water, where fish circulated freely, lending the visitor the feeling of being submerged.

She led Boldt to a door marked EMPLOYEES ONLY and into a room where a stereoscopic microscope awaited them.

She explained, "I know it's an inconvenience for you to come down here, but phone calls just don't do it for me. Now this first plate is one of the less common fish scales in the sample your people provided our department. Notice the more pointed area where the scale actually attaches to the fish, like shingles on a roof. Of particular interest to us, to you, is the more heartlike shape of this scale, along with that serrated edge. Okay?"

Ammond switched plates and moved him to a comparison microscope.

"This is a side-by-side comparison," she told him. "Look carefully at both scales."

Boldt brought his eyes to the scope. "Okay."

"Recognize our friend?"

"On the left."

"Very good. Yes. And to the right?"

"A smoother edge. Less of a point. It's clearer. This may sound stupid, but the one on the right looks newer."

"Gold star, Lieutenant. You didn't minor in marine biology, did you? Yes, the scale to the right is from a live silver salmon in our back tanks. The sample we received from you consisted primarily of scales from both king and silver salmon."

"But not our friend?" he asked, using her term.

"No. We found two such scales in the sample. They're from a variety of Snake River coho. What's of interest is that this particular species has been extinct for over two decades."

"Run that by me again," Boldt said.

"The Snake River coho disappeared twenty-two years ago. Tens of millions of coho used to make the annual journey up the Columbia and into Idaho, the Snake River species among them."

"Extinct," Boldt repeated, withdrawing his police pad and making a note.

"Exactly."

She grinned. The white of her teeth gleamed against the freckled face. "Your explanation over the phone intrigues me. You collected these off a dead woman's feet. You mentioned shipping containers, and I'd have to question that. A container in service twenty-two years? Not likely. A ship is more like it."

"A cannery?"

"Could be. Yes. Why not? This way," Ammond said, showing Boldt out of the lab.

They walked back into the main galleries. She spoke loudly to be heard above the crowd noise.

"Have you seen our fisheries display?"

"I imagine," Boldt answered.

"The trawlers?" she asked, pointing.

An entire wall had been devoted to the history of commercial fishing. It traced the earliest Native American settlements to the contemporary five-mile gill nets used by the Russians and Japanese as well as the enormous floating canneries. Text and illustrations were complimented by cutaway models of the various vessels, and it was to one of these that Dr. Ammond led Boldt.

"Commercial trawler, fairly common to Pacific fleets for the last twenty to fifty years with few modifications. Bigger now." She pointed out the aft hold. "The catch is stored here, as it comes in. The crew then sorts, cleans and washes the catch, discarding the unwanted or undesirables, and the gutted, finished product is moved by conveyors to the forward hold." She indicated a huge room that occupied most of the front of the ship. "This hold is one giant freezer. These trawlers are able to stay out to sea days, weeks or months." She took a deep breath, the tomboy in her replaced by the expert. "Now given your mention of illegals, I'm inclined to see this trawler in a whole new light. Maybe the catch isn't so good this year. Maybe I'm putting Chinese illegals in my forward hull. Maybe this is quite an old ship—a *very old* ship—and despite the regular cleanings the crew gives these holds, a few scales remain behind, indicating a species of fish we haven't seen for over two decades."

"And if it's a cannery?"

"That works for me. The canneries go back further than the processing trawlers. This aquarium was a cannery in its former life. Any number of structures along the shoreline in this city have been, or once were, associated with commercial fishing. From Harbor Island to Interbay, Salmon Bay to Lake Union."

"You're saying I have my work cut out for me," he stated. "I can't narrow down the old canneries by the fish scales you've identified."

"The university has catalogued the history of commercial fisheries. That would include canneries. This industry dates back over a hundred and fifty years."

Boldt said, "Twenty-two years is all we care about."

Her face erupted into a smile. "Let me make a few calls."

CHAPTER 30

Lacey Delgato had thick calves, no waist and a nose that cast a long shadow—behind her back, cops called her "the Sun Dial." She wore an unfashionably long black skirt zipped too tightly across her seat so that a labyrinth of intersecting folds and seams showed in an unsightly display. She had a voice like a squeeze toy, a trial attorney's tendency to act out her words and an abrasive laugh that warned of her cynicism. Her one extravagance was Italian shoes. Her tall heels tapped out her quickened pace against the Justice Building's marble corridor. "This individual has offered to sell the camera back to KSTV."

"A digital camera?" LaMoia clarified. "You're sure about that?" he asked the assistant prosecuting attorney.

"I'm only repeating what was said to me," Delgato replied. "It's your case, Sergeant. You worry about what kind of camera it is."

"Do we foresee any problems with our involvement in this?" he asked.

"There are some issues need clearing up," she informed him. He struggled to keep up with her. "Possession issues. If you monitor the drop for them as they're asking you to do, then who gets the camera? Little things like that."

"And our position on this is . . . ?" he asked.

"Stolen evidence? You retain the confiscated property until such time it is no longer needed by us as evidence in a trial. No different than any other case." She snapped her head in his direction, but never broke her stride. "Mind you, they have a slightly different interpretation. They'll let us keep the camera, but they're claiming that if there's a tape in that camera then they retain the tape for themselves. Intellectual property laws are sticky. I've got to warn you up front about that."

SPD was under tremendous pressure to clear the container case. McNeal's nightly broadcasts kept the story not only in front of the public, but on the political front burner as well. Election years were always the worst.

"No mention of the missing woman? Just the camera? We're clear that the ransom demanded is for the camera alone?"

"I'm just repeating what I was told," she offered. "You heard the Asian community is going to march on the mayor's office?"

He said, "Thanks. I needed to be reminded."

"They're expecting a big crowd."

"Only because the press will be there," he said. "Take away the cameras, ten people show up."

She looked at him strangely, still at a near run. "You busy for dinner?"

"What dinner?" he asked. "I haven't had dinner in three days. I slept an hour and a half last night."

"We could skip dinner, I suppose."

The corridor's long wooden benches were occupied by attorneys, witnesses, detectives and distraught family members. For LaMoia, it was not so much a courthouse as a processing center, the law reduced to a series of appearances, negotiations and compromises. As a cop, he couldn't think about it without growing discouraged or even depressed. He didn't see Delgato as a woman, only as an attorney. He didn't know how to break it to her.

"I called Robbery figuring they would watch the drop," Delgato explained. "The minute I mentioned KSTV they put me on to you. They said anything to do with the television station went to you. . . . I told them I only wanted to do this once. I'm saying the same thing to you." She was clearly angry with him for not picking up on her passes. She wasn't going to take a third swing at the ball. She knocked on the door to a jury room and led him into where police and lawyer work ended and justice began.

Despite hundreds of court appearances, LaMoia had rarely been inside a deliberation room. It smelled of pine disinfectant. The long oval table's edge had been victim to jurors nervously doodling. He could almost hear the deliberations—angry voices ringing off the walls. Among the ballpoint graffiti he noticed a hangman's noose. He sat down into one of the chairs and ran his fingernail around the cartoon character's neck. He said, "Do we know this information is good?"

"The station engraves its initials on its gear. The caller described that correctly."

"The ransom?"

"He started at three thousand. The station settled at one—the amount of the deductible on their policy."

"And he went for it?"

"Apparently."

"That's not a junkie, that's a businessman."

"A junkie would have hocked it," she said.

"Which may be what happened," LaMoia concurred. "Who knows where this bozo got it from?"

"He demanded that anchor, Stevie McNeal, take the drop."

"No way!"

"Wants a face he can recognize."

"Can't do it."

"Nonnegotiable. The station already accepted the condition. That's why they came to us. Their security firm wanted us aware of it, and you on board."

"Prime Time Live? I don't think so!"

"It's nonnegotiable," she repeated. "You're there to protect and serve." She continued, "It gets worse."

"Not possible," he said.

"They claim anything recovered is theirs."

"You've got to be kidding! They ask for our help retrieving stolen property and then make demands on us if we agree?"

"I don't think that's exactly how they would put it," she said.

"This is *not* an episode of *Cops*!"

"They haven't shared the time and place of the drop. We could, if and when they move without us, file obstruction of justice, but to be honest with you, it would never reach court and we'd lose. The press is one slippery eel. You would never see that tape."

"If there *is* a tape," he muttered. Lives were decided in this room by grocery clerks, housewives and CEOs. He rarely struggled over his career choice, but that hangman's noose carved into the table twisted his gut.

"There are still some unanswered questions," she agreed. "How much do you want to be involved?"

"If there's something useful to us on that tape—if there even is a tape—I can't have it broadcast to the world. There's a woman missing. I have a life to protect—maybe hundreds of lives."

"If there's a tape in the camera, we can certainly take physical possession until trial. If they press for possession, they're likely to win. It's going to come down to timing. But the gloves-off attitude is you'll get a look at anything that's there."

"Set up the drop," he ordered.

"It's the right call," she encouraged.

"Then why don't I feel better about it?"

She walked out, seams and folds of fabric and skin in a shifting blur of whistling fabric. She stopped at the door. "I'm different when the lawyer hat comes off." She spared him any reply by hurrying out the door. Her quickened footsteps reminded him of horses' hooves.

LaMoia's eye fell back to that hangman's noose. The lines of the noose had been gone over repeatedly, the ink dark and saturated and leaving little doubt in his mind how the artist had voted.

CHAPTER 31

The man offering to sell the camera back to KSTV chose the Wednesday lunch hour and a granite bench alongside the water shower at the old Nordstrom's terrace for the drop. It was a sunny day, the last week of August, that brought out joggers and tourists, panhandlers and skateboarders. Office workers sought out sun-worshipping perches for a peaceful sandwich and a twenty-minute tan. Women hiked their skirts up over their knees. Men loosened their ties and rolled up their sleeves. Summertime in the Emerald City. At the other end of town a group of three hundred Asians were gathered to march on City Hall. Fifty off-duty officers had been called up.

Mixed into the crowd by the water fountain, eleven undercover cops kept their eyes on Stevie McNeal, who carried a thousand dollars cash, a KSTV tote bag, and a severe expression that contradicted the TV personality. McNeal wore a lavaliere microphone clipped to her bra, its wire taped down her back. LaMoia, as the Command Officer— the CO—wore a headset in a refitted steam cleaning van, forfeited years earlier in a drug conviction, and currently used as Mobile Communications Dispatch—or MoCom for short. He had an unobstructed view of the water shower fountain and bench out a mirrored side window of one-way glass. The loud noise of the fountain's falling water bothered the audio technician, a diminutive man with a silver stud in his left ear who by job definition could remain level and calm through the bloodiest of firestorms.

"That fountain is loud. She's wearing a condenser, which is a problem. We're not going to hear her so good."

"Well at least there's some justice," LaMoia said. "Maybe it won't make such good TV." The KSTV crew occupied an unmarked blue step van in front of GapKids. They too were monitoring Stevie's wireless.

"Stand by," the tech said, addressing all the undercover officers. "It's show time."

As Stevie sat down onto the stone bench she exhaled calmly in an attempt to settle herself. The water shower sculpture was a fifteen-foot L that a person could walk through without getting wet, curtains of water falling on both sides of its narrow aisle. Kids loved it, squealing with delight as they hurried through. Downwind of the sculpture, a cooling mist prevailed.

She missed the man's approach. He sat down next to her, a Seattle Seahawks bag held by the straps. He said, "You look different on TV."

"So they say."

He was mid-forties, balding, wearing clothes that had been popular a decade earlier and with a nose that begged for rhinoplasty. His oily hair shined wetly in the sunlight. He smoked a filter cigarette that attached itself to his lower lip wet with spit. He engaged in a perpetual squint to avoid the stinging spiral of smoke and the bright sunshine.

He did not look at her, his head up, eyes alert. A careful man. A planner. The cops had warned her that any man willing to take such a risk was either dumb, greedy, or both. Violent, maybe. Not to be trusted, for certain. She kept close tabs on him.

"How do you want to do this?" she asked.

"You hand me the envelope," he said looking straight ahead, "and I leave the bag behind."

"I have to see it first," she corrected.

"We can do that," he agreed, shoving the bag toward her. "Go ahead."

Stevie dragged the bag over to her. She carefully unzipped it and peered inside. Brushed aluminum casing, the brand name, SONY. She felt choked. She had handed this camera to Melissa. She hated herself for it. Worse, the camera's tape indicator was blank. No tape inside. Stung with disappointment, she reached inside. "I have to see that it's our call letters on it."

"They're on there," he said. "Have a look."

She turned the camera so that the call letters were visible. She said, "There's no tape."

He said, "If there's more you want, then we gotta talk."

"You talk," she offered. "I'll listen."

"You're interested in what was inside," he suggested.

Her heart beat frantically. "Am I?"

"You gotta come up with another five large."

"You should have mentioned this."

He said, "I didn't realize the thing was loaded until *after* we had us a deal."

The demand of five hundred dollars seemed so cheap to her.

"What's on the tape?" she asked.

"No clue," he answered.

"Five hundred dollars for a blank tape?"

"Not my problem. You want the tape or not?"

"Do you have it on you?"

"Five hundred dollars gets you the tape," he said. He tossed the cigarette. Sparks flew and the butt wandered in a lazy arc on the pavers. "You want it or not? I haven't got all day."

"We had a deal," she persisted. "I give you a thousand dollars and you give me the camera. The tape comes with the camera."

"The tape does *not* come with the camera," he said vehemently. "You got yourself an ATM card?" he asked.

"I'm listening," Stevie answered.

The man said, "You give me the thousand now and take the camera. Then you withdraw the five hun out of the ATM and meet me back here in ten minutes."

"We go together," she objected.

"No way. Meet me back here, ten minutes."

"You'll have the tape on you," she said, trying to sound definite.

"Ten minutes," he repeated.

Stevie stared off at the water fountain.

"What are you doing?"

"I'm thinking," she answered.

In the MoCom van LaMoia debated the offer made by the extortionist. The dispatcher awaited his decision, knowing better than to press. "Did you get all that?" he asked Boldt.

"Copy," Boldt replied. McNeal's wire transmissions were carried over a set of Walkman headphones he wore. He had declined LaMoia's offer to be in the MoCom van. As the day shift sergeant who had taken the complaint, the missing persons case was LaMoia's lead. Despite his own desire to take over, Boldt understood the necessity of the lead officer having full authority. A surveillance could turn in a matter of seconds. "It's your call," he reminded.

Boldt's Chevy Cavalier was parked only a few yards away in a tow-away zone. With his cellphone pressed to his ear, he was enjoying a cup of Earl Grey tea at a Seattle's Best Coffee in a plastic lawn chair out front of the Westlake Center from where he owned a slightly elevated and somewhat distant view of the occupied bench alongside the water shower. The SONY Walkman was actually a police-band radio monitor, its yellow all-weather headphones still in his ears despite the use of the cellphone.

LaMoia asked, "What the hell's he up to?"

"You have to make the call, John. She's waiting."

"It's a go!" LaMoia confirmed to the dispatcher, who threw a switch on his console and gave the go-ahead.

LaMoia leaned back nervously and said, "I hate this shit."

Not twenty feet away from the granite bench where Stevie and her visitor sat, a street bum suddenly spilled an entire garbage bag of crushed aluminum cans out onto the pavers. Her visitor jumped, a fresh cigarette bobbing in his lips and spraying embers that he batted off his lap. With the man distracted, Stevie quickly looked over her

left shoulder as coached. A woman not ten feet away—Detective Bobbie Gaynes, although she didn't remember the name—signaled a
thumbs-up, giving approval for the second ransom. Gaynes continued
on, skirting her way past Andy Milner, the undercover cop in the role
of the street bum who was busy collecting the spilled cans.

Stevie handed the man on the bench the envelope with the thousand dollars knowing that every serial number on every bill was accounted for. "Okay," she said, "we've got a deal."

Stevie took her time walking to the ATM assuming that the police
would need every minute to regroup and follow her. She recognized a
few of the detectives—though the introductions had been fast and
furious during her briefing and she didn't remember a single name.

She strolled casually up the slight rise of Fourth Avenue, approaching the ATM where she thought she recognized one of the detectives. The man met eyes with her and quickly indicated his
wristwatch. The signal was obvious: They wanted more time.

The detective stepped away from the ATM. She suddenly appreciated the police in a way she never had before. The surveillance team
was keeping up with her despite the change in plans. Their presence
lent her a feeling of safety. Nonetheless, she stepped up to the ATM
with adrenaline charging her system.

She inserted her card and punched in her PIN. Twenty seconds
later her money was delivered, followed by her card. She turned in
time to see two punk kids coming directly at her, their intentions fore-
cast in their determined eyes. She'd been set up. Tape or no tape, they
were going to mug her for the five hundred in broad daylight. Stevie
stepped back toward the ATM machine.

At that same moment, a blur of activity erupted to her right. A
homeless man collided with a woman and stole her two shopping bags,
violently shoving her to the sidewalk. He sprinted away from her heading directly toward the two youths approaching Stevie.

The downed woman shouted for help. Two uniformed police charged around the corner of the building shouting at the homeless man, and finally tackling him. At the sight of cops, the two punks scattered, one heading down Fourth Avenue, the other east on Olive.

Stevie stepped away from the ATM and collected herself. They were all cops, she realized—the street person, the assaulted woman—the event staged to scare off the punks. Guardian angels took on the strangest forms.

Halfway back down the street a hand gripped her elbow firmly. "Walk" . . . the man said.

"Let go of my arm," Stevie demanded.

Still holding her, the man placed a claim check in her hand. "The art museum," he said. She glanced down at the claim check.

"A woman was mugged," she said.

"It's a dangerous city."

"You think I'll give you five hundred dollars for a worthless claim check?"

He answered, "If you don't, you'll never know what was on that tape."

"You're not getting the money until I have the tape in hand."

"That's not how this works."

"That's exactly how it works," Stevie said.

"If you don't want to play," the man declared, "then we got nothing to discuss." He pulled her to the side out of the flow of pedestrians.

"Just to remind you: I have five hundred dollars here that has your name on it."

"Gimme the five," the man said anxiously.

"Let's take a walk," she suggested. "Ten minutes and you're five hundred dollars richer."

"That ain't the way it's gonna work," he said.

"Then it's not going to work," she declared. She reached into the bag and offered the claim check, wondering if he noticed her trembling fingers.

"Keep it. Just give me the money," he pleaded.

"Let's take a walk," she said cheerily. Retaining the claim check, she walked away from him, realizing he had no choice but to follow. She counted to herself—one thousand one, one thousand two—her anticipation mounting as she reached the pedestrian crossing where the light changed instantly. She crossed with the light.

"I ain't got no time for this," the man's voice complained over her left shoulder.

"Sure you do," she replied, looking straight ahead. "This is the easiest five hundred you've ever made." She kept walking, not knowing if he was following or not, but never so much as checking her stride.

"The woman has got nerve," LaMoia remarked in back of the van, his cellphone clutched to his ear. "What-do-ya say we pop the lid on this thing? You farting in here or what?" he asked the dispatcher.

"No sir." The dispatcher got up and slowly cranked open the van's skylight.

"Smells like a dog let loose in here," LaMoia commented, fanning the air.

"I'm going on foot," Boldt announced into the phone.

"We got her covered," LaMoia said somewhat arrogantly.

"Just the same, I'm going on foot."

LaMoia said, "We'll relocate the team to the museum. We got four on foot. They're your back-up."

Boldt said, "If he puts another hand on her, John, if he gets an idea to liberate that five hundred, we're all over him."

"Understood." He added, "We screw this up, hell, it'll make Brokaw."

Outside the art museum there stood on enormously tall steel plate sculpture of a man pounding an equally huge hammer. To Stevie, it looked Russian, a holdover of Stalinism, a dedication to the might of the worker. Her escort grew increasingly nervous with their approach, perhaps sensing the trap that was laid for him. Her own anxiety increased with each step, and she worried that the police didn't have anyone in place yet.

A group of Japanese tourists had collected in the courtyard awaiting their tour guide. She felt several of the men staring. Others shot pictures of the Russian worker.

"You don't need me for this," the man complained to her.

"I don't trust you," she said, spinning and confronting.

"You take picture us?" a Japanese man asked Stevie, extending his camera toward her and indicating his smiling friends. Stevie hesitantly accepted the camera.

"I don't have time for this," her escort objected again.

"Settle down," she whispered. Focusing the camera she spun the zoom by mistake. Behind the group of grinning tourists, she saw the steam-cleaning van turn left, cross traffic and pull to the side of the street. She clicked the shutter, capturing only the tourists' heads. The Cavalry had arrived.

Boldt approached the museum's sunken courtyard wishing McNeal would lower the camera and get a look at him. He slowed but did not stop, passing within a yard or two of the man at her side. Detective Mulgrave appeared to his left and entered the museum ahead of him. It would all move quickly now even if it felt like slow motion.

He paused at the museum's glass doors and studied the reflection as McNeal handed the camera back to the Japanese tourist. As she turned toward the entrance, he wondered if she would recognize him from the back, deciding that she probably would.

Stevie McNeal didn't seem like she missed much.

In the back of the van, LaMoia spoke into the radio handset, "If this goes south, if our boy makes tracks, Mulgrave stays on him. MoCom will follow. Lynch, you put your body in front of McNeal if needed."

"Roger that," Lynch confirmed.

"If we have to move on him, I want it down and dirty," he ordered. "We got civilians in there. Copy?"

The radio sparked with several distinct pops as undercover detectives tripped their radios. This told LaMoia plenty. His operatives were in place. No one could speak. It was going down.

Stevie stepped up to the coat check and handed the colored tag to the Asian behind the counter. She wondered if this woman had once been an illegal, and realized she had a stereotype to overcome. Her escort had stopped ten feet back in the midst of museum foot traffic coming and going, reminding her of a dog poised on a street curb considering crossing traffic. His face florid and feverish, he had broken into a sweat out in the courtyard.

She too was sweating. It seemed her chance to save Melissa—if there still was a chance—came down to these next few minutes and the tape promised. Boldt stepped up to the counter alongside of her and spoke clearly to one of the coat check attendants.

"What if I lost my claim check?" he asked. He was buying time.

The girl had turned to face the array of cubbyholes, looking for the match to Stevie's claim check. "You gotta have your tag," the other man informed Boldt.

Boldt patted his pockets. "But if I don't?" he asked. Stevie's confidence gained with his being so close.

The girl plunked down the camera bag in front of Stevie. Her heart fluttered; she had handed this bag to Melissa the last time she'd seen her.

Stevie turned. The man said, "Okay, we're outta here."

"Not yet."

"Bullshit," he hissed, leaning in close with his tobacco breath. "This sucker's done. Gimme the five."

She wanted to confirm the existence of the tape before surrendering the cash.

A fist tightened around her upper arm.

"Outside," the man ordered. "We're done here." His sideburns leaked pearls of sweat.

Stevie hesitated briefly, her fingers hovering on the camera bag's zipper. She moved toward the wall, a water fountain, forcing him to release her. He let go and pursued her to the wall; her arm tingled with relief.

She pulled the zipper, realizing that despite her intentions to stay calm, her anticipation had won the moment. Her heart felt ready to explode. She opened the bag and peered inside: a pair of black slippers with red roses embroidered on the toes. Her throat tightened— they were Melissa's. She moved them aside. The small tape was there as well. She didn't understand the next few seconds when blood chemistry and emotions overcame all rational thought, when memories of Melissa and those slippers were all that mattered. Tears erupting from her eyes, she took the man by his sport coat, pulled her face to his and shook him, crying, "Where *is* she? What have you done to her?"

The stunned man plunged his hand into the shopping bag and came out with her wallet. "The money!" he said, his head lifting, his dark eyes flashing as he saw one of the detectives reaching for a weapon.

The man pocketed the wallet, turned Stevie, and shoved her into Boldt. He dodged across the entrance lobby, weaving through tourists, using them as protection. Stevie stumbled into Boldt's arms. He stood her up and took off at a run.

Detective Mulgrave shouted loudly, "Police! Everyone stay where you are!" The English-speaking visitors dove to the carpet. The Japanese smiled and took a moment longer to react. Shouts and cries followed. A uniformed museum guard stepped forward to block one of the exit doors.

Boldt and Mulgrave ran toward the entrance as the suspect

dropped his shoulder into the guard driving him through the glass door. The guard went down hard. The suspect fled outside, Boldt and Mulgrave immediately behind.

Boldt shouted at the suspect. Mulgrave called into his handheld for backup. The man crossed through traffic stopped at the light and ran hard, heading south on First Avenue.

Boldt caught a glimpse of LaMoia and a uniform out of the corner of his eye and, at the same time, a cameraman trailing black wires as he leaped out of KSTV's large blue panel truck which was stopped in traffic. The cameraman hit the sidewalk running. LaMoia and the uniform hit the cameraman's wires and all three went down.

Boldt dodged through the traffic and took off after the suspect, Mulgrave still shouting orders into his radio.

The suspect ran left at the next corner and disappeared from view.

His lungs burning, his right knee tightening, Boldt lost ground to Mulgrave and called out, "Backup?"

"On route!" the detective answered.

They needed this man in custody. To lose the suspect was not an option. Both cops turned left at the corner, Mulgrave already breaking across the street, the suspect nowhere in sight.

Sirens approached. The street rose up a hill. No suspect. Mulgrave headed across the street and down an alley.

Boldt stopped and spun in a circle. Their boy had either entered one of the buildings or had gone down that alley. Faced with a tough decision—await the radio cars and the uniforms so that they sealed off any chance of the suspect sneaking past, or pick one of the buildings to search before the suspect had time to escape—Boldt studied the wall of brick buildings that lined the northern side of the street, his eyes darting window to window, one building to the next.

It appeared first as a shadow, then an image: a woman in a third-floor window, one hand spread open on the glass. Descending a stairway, she had clearly stepped aside for someone. It was that spread hand that convinced him—the fear it implied. Boldt took the chance.

His police shield displayed in his coat's breast pocket, Boldt took two stairs at a time, passing the middle-aged woman on the second floor's landing. She pointed up. Boldt kept moving, never breaking stride. He had the advantage of surprise now. He had to move fast before he lost it.

By the fourth floor he was severely winded but still climbing. The movement came from his right as he turned left toward the final flight of stairs. It came as a change of color, of lighting, as if someone had dropped a curtain or waved a flag. It came as a flash of heat up his spine, his right arm climbing instinctively but opening him to the blow to his ribs. His momentum moved him away from the blow rather than into it; he was thrown off balance, careening into a chair that sat alongside a standing ashtray. He grabbed hold of a leg of that chair and hurled it in the general direction of his assailant, simultaneously reaching for his gun. The chair's four metal feet screeched like fingers on a blackboard, then traveled toward the stairs and, as if planned, as if calculated, flew off the top edge, rebounded off the far wall and headed end over end as if aimed at the unfortunate soul in its path.

The suspect, after shoving Boldt and then starting back down the stairs, never saw that chair. It came after him as if it were tethered to him, jumping and springing into the air and crashing only to lift again, gaining velocity. Boldt was back to his feet by the time the chair impacted, not only tripping up the man but sending him down the subsequent flight of stairs following the same route the chair had traveled. A tumbler, a circus act gone awry, the dull snapping of bone on stone.

Despite the fall, the man clamored to his feet but then sagged under the pain and Boldt was upon him. A handcuff snapped around the wrist in a ritual all too familiar to both men. Boldt patted him down for weapons while reciting the Miranda like a man talking in his sleep. He arrested the suspect on charges of trafficking in stolen goods and assaulting a police officer.

"I didn't steal nothing!" he complained as he was led down the stairs.

"You've got some thinking to do between here and downtown,"

Boldt cautioned the man. "If you've got half a brain in there, you'll trade a walk for the talk."

"Yeah, yeah . . . but I'm telling you, I didn't steal nothing!"

"If you're smart, you'll lose the broken record," Boldt advised. "Then again," he reconsidered, "if you were smart, we wouldn't be here, would we?"

CHAPTER 32

Gaylord Riley dragged his fingers against his sweating cheek as if rubbing a lantern for good luck, stoically proud of his refusal to talk to police and patiently awaiting his attorney. His stained polyester shirt stuck to him like cellophane so that his chest hairs rose like tree roots struggling up through old asphalt. The Box had warmed behind LaMoia's mounting frustration to where both men were panting and in need of a glass of water.

"The thing a prick like you doesn't understand, Riley, is that this is the wrong time to lawyer-up."

"As if there's ever a right time as far as you're concerned."

"I got a PA outside who will repeat to you everything I've been saying. You're a known fence. Fraud has you on file."

"Never been convicted of nothing!"

"You give up whoever laid this gear on you and you walk out of here, no harm, no foul."

"That's bullshit and we both know it. That big guy . . . he said assaulting an officer. He fell down is all—a shoelace or something. I didn't assault no officer!"

"You want me to get him in here? Hang on a second!" LaMoia went to the door. Boldt, who had been looking on through the one-way glass was already at the door by the time LaMoia opened it.

Boldt stepped inside. Old times: he and LaMoia working a suspect. All they needed was Daphne in the room for the picture to be complete. Boldt said, "You talk, you walk. I told you that."

"I'd rather hear it from a lawyer," the suspect said.

"By which time, you won't hear it," Boldt answered.

LaMoia sat back down in the chair facing the man. "Stupid is one thing. You were stupid to get into this—to call the station, set up the meet. But don't be dumb. Don't be an asshole, who thinks he knows more about how this works than we do. We've got jails filled with those numb-nuts, I'm telling you. You lawyer-up, you start things in motion that we're helpless to stop. You bring in the college boys and you, me and the lieutenant are in chairs over in the corner watching the suits do the dance. Is that what you want? Honestly?" He felt he was getting through to the guy. Gaylord Riley looked ready to pop a blood vessel.

"All we want is to start a dialogue here," Boldt encouraged. "Get some words going back and forth. Work through the attitude down to the truth. If we do that in a timely fashion, there's no reason lawyers have to be any part of this. Your little ransom attempt never happened."

"I didn't ransom nothing!"

"That's what I'm saying," Boldt agreed. "It never happened."

LaMoia cautioned, "We got you on videotape, audiotape and stills. We got maybe a dozen witnesses to this thing, pal—law enforcement officers, every one of them. What do you think you and your lawyer are going to use against that?"

The man looked back and forth between the two detectives, the epitome of a scared little boy. LaMoia loved every minute of it. He didn't have the degrees for it, but he thought maybe he should be a hostage negotiator, some guy who looks the bomber in the eye and dares the slob to push the button. He felt good all over, like after sex.

The suspect said, "He was Chinese. Twenty-one, twenty-two. Strong. Small. Never seen him before. Not since. Didn't know what he had—thought it was a camcorder."

"Gang kid?" Boldt asked, wiping any surprise off his face. Business as usual. Inside he was reeling with excitement. He knew better than to ask if he'd given a name.

"Are there any that aren't?" he quipped. "No clue."

"He speak English?" LaMoia asked.

"Pidgin shit," the man answered. "Marble mouth."

"Tattoos? Marks?" Boldt asked.

"Just a kid looking to cash in. A little scared of the whole thing, you know?"

"Scared of making the deal," LaMoia clarified.

"Right."

"So you thought it was hot," Boldt said.

"Of course it was hot," the man declared. "Do I look like a buyer for Macy's?"

"He called it a camcorder," LaMoia repeated.

"Yeah, right. Didn't know shit about it. I'm telling you: He came in, wanted some money for it. I give him two bills and he books. Whole thing, maybe a minute or two."

"Two bills for a twelve-thousand-dollar camera," LaMoia said.

"Hey, the station's call letters are engraved on the bottom. What can I tell you? He must'a never seen it. Didn't know how expensive this digital shit is. I'm telling you: He didn't know what he had, that kid. And the way he was nervous and all: He was either a junkie, or worried about making the deal somehow. That kind of build, that strength, I'm not thinking he was a junkie. More like a kid who stole his own mother's car stereo."

"He found it," Boldt said to LaMoia. "He found it, or he took it from her—"

"But he didn't tell no one," LaMoia completed.

"Who?" the suspect asked. "I didn't take nothing from nobody!"

"Shut up!" LaMoia barked. "We're talking here!"

Boldt said, "He found it and figured he'd make himself a couple extra bucks."

"So he hocks it with this bozo," LaMoia said.

Boldt informed the man, "We're going to ask you to look at photo arrays."

"Mug shots."

"Right," the lieutenant said. "You point him out, you walk out of here—"

"Hey! That weren't no part of the deal! That's bullshit."

LaMoia stood abruptly, startling the man. He leaned across the table. "Don't interrupt the lieutenant, asshole! The man's talking to you."

Boldt repeated, "You'll look at the photos. You point him out, you walk out of here tonight. You don't find him, you do a night in lockup for the assault, and you look at more photos tomorrow. You give us a face, we give you a passport."

"This is bullshit!"

"This is your way out of here," LaMoia corrected. "Or would you rather *we* call the attorneys, and tell them you won't cooperate?"

"But I *did* cooperate!" he protested.

LaMoia turned to Boldt. "Do you think he's cooperating, Sarge?"

"I think he's making up stories," Boldt said.

"I'm telling you the way it went down!" the man shouted.

"And he's yelling at us," LaMoia observed.

Boldt said, "You give us a face that checks out, and you walk."

LaMoia cautioned, "If you're making this shit up, you're toast."

"He was just some kid! Some Chinese kid. How am I supposed to know the difference?"

"They all look alike?" LaMoia challenged in a threatening tone. "Don't go there, pal." He lied to pressure the man: "You don't want to get within a few miles of that, given that the lieutenant here is married to a lovely Chinese woman and has five little daughters to prove it."

The suspect looked as if he'd swallowed an ice cube or was choking on unchewed meat.

Boldt had to turn to the door so the man wouldn't catch his grin. "Let's get it started," he said to his sergeant, wondering where LaMoia came up with such stuff.

CHAPTER 33

As a reporter, Stevie had perfected the art of using people, and although her last several years as a news anchor had clearly dulled those talents, they were not altogether lost. She understood the powerful effect that her body and looks had upon men, as well as the envy they incited in women—how to harness and exploit those attributes as needed. She needed them now. Brian Coughlie had access to SPD that she did not. She had picked the best restaurant in the city. She wore a low scooped teal dress that turned heads. She was ready.

Her body ached with fatigue and exhaustion after the police sting, but she wasn't going to surrender to it until she made it through the dinner and had accomplished what she had come to accomplish. Judge Milton Abrams was blocking KSTV's viewing of the videotape that she had personally recovered. Boldt, Abrams and others had burned her, and her only chance to return the favor lay with the man who now sat across the table from her.

Campagne was indeed one of the city's finest restaurants. Brian Coughlie, there at her invitation, looked slightly out of place, but she didn't let that bother her. Her celebrity had created a buzz in the restaurant the moment she'd arrived. She played it up, hoping to intimidate Coughlie, who was nothing but a government worker bee with a bad tailor. It was an odd alliance at best, and she intended to milk him for everything she could get. She would stop short of sleeping with him, but he certainly didn't know that.

A hint of sexual suggestion, an occasional compliment, a well-timed wiggle in her chair—she had the full arsenal at her disposal. Ready, indeed.

Coughlie was not about to turn down an invitation from this one. He'd been trying to think of a way to get her alone, to find out as much about her missing friend as possible. One man's ceiling was another man's floor. As a media source she had contacts and resources that he did not. Following her late afternoon piece that police had allegedly confiscated evidence belonging to the station, her invitation to dinner had come as a godsend. She needed him—the beginning of any negotiation.

If he got laid in the process, so much the better. Judging by the look of her, it would make for an unforgettable evening. The way she kept moving her butt in the chair was making him excited. But his interest in her was for what she knew, not what kind of ride she was. SPD was stonewalling the INS, and vice versa—business as usual. He stuck to the food and wine. Women loved to talk if you gave them half the chance. The way she was hitting the wine, she'd be giving a goddamn keynote address in a few minutes. Not to be outdone, he took a sip himself. Decent stuff. Archery Something. A yuppie wine—*peanut noir* was what he'd nicknamed it. He'd take a Chablis any day. At sixty bucks a bottle, he thought she was trying to impress him. *Nice try,* he said to himself. It took more than a chest and an attitude to fix his game.

|||||||||

"Why does a person join the INS?" she asked, meeting eyes with him.

"Why does a person put her face in front of a million people every afternoon?"

"It's four hundred thousand," she corrected, "and it's not a fair comparison. The public image of the INS is gatekeepers, border guards."

"Flattery will get you everywhere."

"Tell me I'm wrong."

"Power hungry ex-football players?" he asked, stabbing a piece of thin ham off the appetizer plate that had some kind of Italian name. Cheap bastards cutting it that thin. "We have our fair share of those. It's a fair shot to take."

"And you?"

"If I'd wanted to be a hero I'd have been a fireman."

She laughed at the comment.

He continued. "I suppose you start out thinking you're part of the group that gives people a shot at this country, its freedom, its opportunity. That's the underlying charter, don't forget. You find a lot of patriots in the Service. And in the job interviews, that's what they play up: the opportunity you're giving these people. The power that comes with it? Sure. Racism? Probably right. Some of the guys who sign up want nothing more than to smack some Mexican across the face with a nightstick. I've seen it. But they're ferreted out pretty quickly, those guys, believe me. No one wants them around. The flip side is that we also protect what's left of this country for those who have a legal right to it. Illegals dilute the status quo. They sponge off social programs that they've never paid into. You don't charge at the gate, you go broke."

"But there's paying and then there's paying. What about the detainees?" she asked. "Three or four weeks in a container with dead bodies. How badly do they want it? Haven't they paid a high enough price for their freedom?"

"We both know where those women were headed," he reminded. "Sweatshops? Brothels? Is that the dream you're selling?"

"I need a favor," she stated bluntly, reaching for the wine bottle and pouring them both more.

"Should I be surprised? A dinner like this? And I thought it was because you found me so irresistible."

"The cops used me."

"Welcome aboard."

"Confiscated evidence."

"I saw the piece."

"You watch the broadcast?"

"Every day," he answered.

"I'm flattered. What the broadcast didn't tell you: They recovered a tape. Not VHS, but digital. Footage she shot *after* I gave her that camera."

He took this all in along with another sip of wine and said, "You want me to get the digital tape for you."

"They double-crossed me. That tape is rightfully mine."

"Let's just say that the idea interests me."

"If the tape contains anything, it has to do with the illegals—that was the story we were working. Melissa wanted the digital camera because it was small and easy to carry. As in surveillance. Judging by the VHS tapes she shot before I got her the digital, I'm thinking she boarded a bus maybe. A car wash. I'm not sure. But whatever she shot, it has to do with illegals. And that's your turf."

He felt like the wind had been knocked out of him. *Car wash?* Where the hell had that come from? Time to give Rodriguez a call and close it down. He felt like bailing on dinner and making the call immediately.

He said, "So I press for the right to view this digital tape. Let's say they grant me that. What then? I give you a book report?"

The dress was a pleasure to look at. She knew about packaging, this one. She knew how to move to distract a man's attention.

"Yes. Exactly. You tell me what you saw," she answered.

"And in return?"

"I show you the VHS tapes: the first three tapes that Melissa shot. Quid pro quo."

"This car wash . . ." he tested. He had to know the extent of what she knew. If she knew too much, then he had some tough decisions to make.

She teased, "I'll show you mine if you'll show me yours."

He couldn't stop himself from grinning. She was good this one. Extremely good. "You're okay," he said.

"I'm a hell of a lot better than okay, Brian. You just have to trust me."

"I'm working on that," he said, echoing her words of their last meeting. He boldly winked at her and won a wide smile. He loved the dance more than anything. And this one knew how to dance.

THURSDAY, AUGUST 27
10 DAYS MISSING

CHAPTER 34

Boldt elected to view the contents of the digital videotape against the recommendations of every attorney consulted. Chow's disappearance mandated action, as did the larger implication of her possible connection to the dead illegals, the two murdered witnesses and Klein's having vanished. He had no choice in the matter. If a court eventually ruled against him, throwing out whatever the tape might reveal and whatever case they had built along with it, he would need a different way to that same evidence, something he would have to work out when needed. He wasn't going to allow attorneys to set his agenda.

"Why the suit?" LaMoia asked. "You going to a funeral?"

"Lot 17," Boldt answered. Lot 17 was King County's Tomb of the Unknown Victim—a five-acre piece of forest land where all the Jane and John Does were put to rest. The Doe family now numbered over two hundred. "The women from the container."

"Seriously?" LaMoia answered. "I'd rather we hold on to them."

"If I want to wear a suit, I'll wear a suit."

"You're making up that shit about Lot 17."

"Yes." He didn't tell him the real reason, despite their friendship. Rumor spread too quickly on the fifth floor.

Both men moved quickly down the stairs, Boldt feeling more agile than he had in years. Liz's illness had cost him twenty-five pounds in what Dixon called "a grief diet." The pounds had not come back, and he was glad for it.

"What do you make of the camera and slippers?"

"I don't like it."

"Me neither. A woman without her shoes is kinda like a car without its tires. Know what I mean?"

"No."

"Sure you do."

"She's dead?" Boldt asked.

"I'm leaning that way."

"Don't."

"Based on?"

"Just don't," Boldt said. "I want her alive."

"It has been like ten days since anyone's seen her, Sarge."

"I'm a lieutenant now. You've got to stop calling me that."

"I call you 'Lieu' and everyone's gonna think I'm using your first name. I gotta call you Sarge. Otherwise it's 'Lieutenant' and that's just way too long. You know?"

"Get used to it."

"Look who's talking."

Boldt stopped on a landing and looked LaMoia in the eye. Both men knew he was going to say something, but he didn't.

"Lofgrin called," LaMoia stated, referring to the head of the forensics lab. "Said he picked up fish scales on the bottom of those slippers. Wants me to stop by when we're done with Tech Services."

Although the discovery of the fish scales intrigued Boldt for their apparent connection to Jane Doe, Boldt felt a stab of envy and misgiving. He wanted SID calling him, not his sergeants. But given his advancement to lieutenant, it wasn't going to be that way. The lab and the ME's office notified the lead officer first, and a lieutenant was rarely, if ever, a lead officer. Supervisor, yes. Consultant, yes. But not lead. Boldt wasn't sure why this mattered so much to him, but it did. He didn't want to be the second to know, he didn't want to be the bridesmaid. He wanted it to be his pager to go off—even though he hated the things; his phone to ring; his decision. When a case went bad he was now called to the office rather than the crime scene. It just wasn't right. This, in part, explained the suit he was wearing. He had a job interview lined up for later in the day. Not even Liz knew about it. He was in turmoil over the decision to take the interview, much less the job if it were offered.

They stopped at the fire door to the basement floor. It had been painted with so many coats that it had a leathery look. "If anything decent comes out of this video," Boldt cautioned, "we need to be thinking about how else we might obtain it in case some judge shuts us down."

LaMoia's resources were legendary. He had friends who had friends who had access to the most sensitive and privately guarded information—financial and otherwise. Some said it was all those past girlfriends; others claimed he'd once been military intelligence. He never said a word about it, extending the legend and keeping his sources protected. "You got it," he said.

Boldt told him, "It's a job interview, but I don't want anyone to know." That sobered LaMoia.

"Yeah? Well I hope for all our sakes it goes really bad." He hesitated a moment and then added warmly, "Thanks . . . Lieutenant."

Boldt pulled open the door.

The geek in Tech Services said something about dubbing the digital down to an SVHS master and handed LaMoia the remote wand—yet another sign of who was lead officer—and told him to summon him if they needed anything, or when they were through. He left the two men by themselves in a small darkened room in front of a twenty-seven-inch color television.

"A private showing," LaMoia said, starting the tape rolling. "Who's buying the popcorn?"

Boldt wasn't in a joking mood.

The sound and picture were of a city street by day, the camera held about waist height. The video title stamp was set incorrectly to January 3. The time was 6:19 P.M. Boldt didn't trust that either. The two discernible background conversations were of a couple discussing a Native American festival and another two or three men all complaining about their jobs.

"The camera's concealed," Boldt said softly.

"In a briefcase, maybe."

"Agreed."

The scenery suddenly blurred and a city bus was seen approaching.

"It's a bus stop," LaMoia said.

"Yup."

"That make sense to you?"

"Let's watch," Boldt suggested.

The air brakes hissed and the bus pulled to a stop. Shot from the hip, as the video was, the scene played out from a child's height and perspective. Boldt thought about his own kids, Miles and Sarah, and worried that he wasn't seeing enough of them. He was barely seeing Liz either, for that matter—unless he counted the hours she was sleeping. With his insomnia back in full swing, he saw a lot of Liz while she slept. He lay there and worried—it didn't seem to matter about what; his kind of worry was a world unto itself.

They caught their first glimpse of Melissa in a shiny piece of steel or aluminum, or maybe even a mirror inside the bus. It happened so quickly that it was hard to tell. But there she was—twenty-something, almost pretty, blue jeans and a Wazoo sweatshirt—climbing the stairs of the bus. There was too much noise to pick out any particular conversation, but the camera seemed intent on the left side of the bus. It was obvious that she had worked at maintaining that angle as long as she did, given that she was walking the center aisle the whole time.

"What do you think?" LaMoia asked.

"I don't know," Boldt answered. He didn't like the man interrupting every few seconds. He wanted to watch the video, to get inside the images, not be constantly yanked back into the viewing room with his sergeant.

"Someone on the left side interests her."

"Let's just watch it one time through. You think?"

"Yeah, sure."

Melissa took a seat about two-thirds of the way down the bus, across from the vehicle's rear door, but the lens remained aimed on the same side of the bus. Images streamed by outside the windows.

LaMoia said immediately, "She wants to be able to leave in a hurry."

Boldt said nothing. Lead by example, he was thinking.

After only a few more seconds there was an abrupt jerk in the image, and the time stamp advanced eleven minutes. She had stopped and then restarted the recording. Boldt made note in the dark of the eleven-minute break.

"You trying to intimidate me, Sarge? Should I be taking notes?"

"I'll take the notes," Boldt said.

The bus turned and lumbered up a downtown street. The change in architecture said as much. It was noticeably darker outside— twilight. The nose of the bus lowered, all the passengers thrown slightly forward in their seats.

"Third Avenue bus tunnel," LaMoia said.

"Yup."

"She's following someone. What do you want to bet?"

"Let's watch."

LaMoia snorted, excited by what he saw and disappointed in Boldt's stubborn silence.

The bus pulled to a stop inside the tunnel and a dozen passengers stood to disembark. The camera continued to record as one waist and torso after another passed by. It then swung and Melissa carried it off the bus and into the bus stop where some passengers headed for exits and others awaited connections. For the first time, the camera clearly singled out one man in particular.

"There he is," LaMoia said anxiously. "Whoever he is."

The man grew increasingly larger as the camera approached. For an instant, he was held in profile, but an overhead ceiling lamp burned a bright white hole into the image and erased the man's face.

"Damn!" LaMoia gasped. "We *had* him."

"She had him," Boldt corrected. "The question that has to be asked: Did he have her?"

"You think he made her?"

"We know he made her, John," Boldt reminded. "We just don't know when."

"This shit gets on my nerves."

"I can tell."

"Film, I'm talking about."

"Yes," Boldt said.

She stopped at a city map, turned and sat down, presumably on a bench. The camera turned ever so slightly and held the man's back in frame.

"She's good at this, you know? A good aim."

The image jumped. In the lower right-hand corner, seven minutes had elapsed. The man's back was still on the screen. He wore an old moth-holed sweatshirt with a hood, black jeans and waffle-soled boots. The man's black wavy hair and build suggested ethnic blood—a big Hispanic or South Pacific man. It meant nothing without a better look.

"Why this guy?" LaMoia spoke aloud.

"That's the relevant question," Boldt agreed.

"Klein? Did she connect the missing skirt with this Frito Bandito?"

"That's a racial slur, John. You're a sergeant now."

"This rice and beans gentleman," he said, correcting himself. "Tommy Taco?"

"Way to go."

"Thank you."

A bus pulled to a stop. Passengers disembarked. The suspect boarded, followed a moment later by the camera and the woman carrying it. The image didn't last long. She established the man's location on the bus. Another cut. Elapsed time, seventeen minutes.

Boldt was thinking about timing specific bus routes. He wondered how many they would have to deal with.

"Exit, Tommy, stage right," LaMoia said, as if directing the film.

The broad-shouldered sweatshirt descended the steps. The camera moved toward the door, but then abruptly stopped. Only the sweatshirt disembarked. Melissa had apparently thought better than to join him out on a darkened stretch of sidewalk in the middle of nowhere.

"Well, she's not completely stupid," LaMoia said, picking up on the obvious.

"Recognize the area? The location?"

"You kidding? Those doors were open for maybe five seconds," LaMoia complained.

"Rewind," Boldt instructed.

Imitating a sports announcer, LaMoia said, "Our bus-cam will now perform instant replay as the star of our show descends the rear steps." He was as nervous outside as Boldt was on the inside. The missing woman had followed a man—a big man, a laborer perhaps, maybe not Caucasian. She had followed him for the better part of an hour, at night, on two different buses while carrying a briefcase concealing a camera.

They made three successive attempts to identify any landmark or piece of skyline when the bus doors opened, but to no avail.

The next cut was equally as abrupt as the others.

"We're a day later," Boldt observed. "That last shot. Rewind . . . Yes. See?"

The camera panned left to right. Small white lights glowed in the darkness. As the aperture adjusted, both men rocked forward at the same moment. Dozens of Chinese women—all with shaved heads, all wearing jeans and T-shirts—sat behind large industrial sewing machines, frantic with work. Others manned cutting tables, busy with razor knives and scissors chained to the tables. Melissa's rapid breathing mixed with the roar of machinery and played loudly from the television's stereo speakers.

"Jesus," LaMoia muttered.

The screen zoomed and the lighting improved as a few of the women seamstresses were captured in close-up. They appeared bruised and beaten. "Oh my God," Melissa remarked in a dry whisper. The next shot was of a chained ankle, blood raw. She gasped as the camera focused. Then another shackled ankle, and another. "The graveyard," the woman's voice whispered hoarsely.

"Hilltop?" LaMoia asked.

Boldt shot him a look. Had Melissa made a connection to their Jane Doe? How? When?

Another edit jump. The screen stole his attention.

The ominous groan of machinery continued throughout, grating and annoying. The camera closed in on a black surface, where there suddenly appeared a small hole the size of a silver dollar. The lens approached that hole and then focused automatically. It was a small room, poorly lit by a construction light. The sound of running water. Naked women—their heads and genitals shaved—hose water running down over them. They whispered amongst themselves. It sounded Chinese.

For once, LaMoia knew to keep his quick-witted adolescent comments to himself.

Another edit. A woman—Melissa?—stood in a dark bathroom working a razor on her scalp. The scene was only seconds long. She turned to face the camera and smiled. She said in a whisper, "This is Melissa Chow for KSTV News. I'm going undercover now. I will join the sweatshop's general population. This is where I become one of them."

"Oh, shit," LaMoia said.

The woman reached out and turned off the camera. The screen flashed black.

"The sound is so hollow," Boldt remarked, his musician's ears ever sensitive.

The sounds were of women's voices speaking Chinese. The camera faded in from black to an extreme close-up of a woman's face. She was bald. She spoke in whispered Chinese. The interview lasted close to a minute, the camera cropped at the crown of her head and the peak of her chin, the close-up dramatizing her words. Even without a translator, her message was of horrid conditions and fear; the tears told that much. Another fade to black, and then faded back in at yet another close-up of a different woman. There were three interviews in all. All done in whisper. All in Chinese, not a word of English spoken. The third was interrupted by a woman's voice speaking harshly. A warning perhaps. The camera aimed down to show a dormitory of woven mats and polarfleece blankets. Several women slept. Most of the mats went empty. The screen went black and then fuzzy.

LaMoia and Boldt sat watching a gray sparkled screen. LaMoia turned down the sound. He fast-forwarded the tape, making sure they missed nothing. "You feel sick to your stomach?" he asked.

"Did you ever play with Chinese handcuffs when you were a kid?" Boldt asked. "The woven tubes? You stuck your fingers inside?"

"Sure. I remember those. What about them?"

"The tube constricted. You could slip your fingers in, but you couldn't pull them back out."

"Those were chains on those ankles, Sarge."

"It's what happened to her," Boldt said. "She got herself inside, but she couldn't get back out."

"Like Chinese handcuffs."

Boldt nodded. He felt better than he had in days. "The good news is, she can speak the language, and with her head shaved, she looks like everyone else."

"You're thinking she's still alive," LaMoia said, his troubled voice barely rising above a whisper. The tape had set a mood, had captured them.

"I think she is, yes," Boldt said, equally softly. "The camera surfacing challenges that, I know. But the reason we haven't found her?" he asked rhetorically. "Is because they haven't found her, either." He turned to LaMoia in the dark, his silhouette captured by the light from the sparkling gray screen, making him look sickly and pallid. "Who knows?" Boldt said. "They may not even know she's in there."

CHAPTER 35

"Can get you nice suit cheap," Mama Lu told Boldt. She occupied most of the doorway of a building marked only in Chinese characters. She wore a red cotton tent dress, and leather sandals and she carried a rubber-tipped bamboo cane that didn't look right on her. In the daylight, out of her dim lair, Boldt saw her as much younger, mid-fifties perhaps.

"You don't like this one?" Boldt complained.

"It okay. A little big on you I think. Bad color. Too dark for skin tone. I have cousin."

"Skin tone?" He had bought the suit on sale too many years ago to remember. Her comments made him self-conscious. He worried about how his suit might play in his later appointment.

She struck Boldt as something of a Chinese Winston Churchill the way she held the cane and faintly bowed to him as he spoke.

Boldt had sandwiched the stop between the conclusion of the video session with LaMoia and his upcoming job interview, intending to work the woman for information on the location of sweatshops. But she had other ideas.

Sensing his impatience and urgency, Mama Lu demanded they meet at a location of her choosing: a nondescript building on a busy street in the heart of the International District.

"I have an appointment," he continued.

"This not take long," she told him. Mama Lu set her own pace, her own tempo. In the world of jazz, she was a ballad, not bebop. "You will be so kind," she said, indicating the door.

Boldt opened the door for her, stepping close enough to smell a faint trace of jasmine and was reminded of her gender, something easily forgotten when enveloped by her commanding presence. As she passed, he said softly, "Another woman was found dead. Another Chinese. Head shaved. Bad shape." He caught himself slipping into her clipped mode of speech.

"Chinese, or Chinese-American? You see, to us there is much difference, Mr. Both. I show you." She led Boldt down a short red hallway and through a bright pink door into a large, open room filled with fifty or more Asian children. They sat at low tables in groups of five or six. Finger paintings hung from the fabric-covered walls; a hand-drawn English alphabet was draped above the blackboard like a banner. There were beanbags, dollhouses, plastic forts and a wall of books. It was busy but not loud. Xylophones hammered out halftone Chinese melodies.

Boldt read a modest plastic sign mounted to the wall and understood immediately that she was playing politics. Beneath the prominent Chinese characters on the sign were the words Hongyang Lu Child Center and Woman's Shelter. Mama Lu was sole proprietor.

As if on cue—and he had to wonder about that—several adorable children ran to greet the great lady, clutching to her tent dress and jumping for her arms. Little dolls. Boldt thought of his own Sarah, and how quickly her childhood was slipping away. He was working long hours again, a pattern he had broken during Liz's illness, and though there were a million justifications for it, he suddenly wondered if he was working or running from something. Daphne had put these thoughts in him, and he couldn't get away from them.

Mama Lu interrupted his thoughts. "These my children: American citizens. They born here, live here. Grow up, make money, pay taxes." She spoke in Chinese to the half dozen children crowding her and they ran back to their stations. "Older girls upstairs," she said, pointing to the ceiling. "Different problems."

Boldt counted ten young adult women supervisors, far more per child than at his own children's day care. One of these young women approached and spoke softly and cordially, welcoming them. Unless a well-conceived act, Mama Lu was no stranger here. The woman shook

Boldt's hand and asked if the police would ever consider coming and talking to the students. He offered to do so himself.

Mama Lu glowed with his offer. The woman headed back to her kids and Mama Lu said to Boldt, "This girl once part of shelter. Now teacher, give back to community. This free day care. Anyone welcome."

"You're a very generous woman."

"Not point! Pay attention! Children *American*. No illegal. Born here means American citizens."

"Whether or not their parents were or are legals, yes, I understand the way the laws work."

"The laws not work," she countered. "Pay attention. These children are alive, Mr. Both. They grow up, pay taxes. American citizens."

"I understand," Boldt replied.

In a menacing tone she hissed, "You understand nothing."

Boldt told her, "We have evidence. A videotape. Other evidence as well. There's a sweatshop. . . . The people doing this will be caught and punished." He allowed that to hang in the air along with the clanging xylophones and the joyous squeals. "Those who cooperate with us," Boldt told her, "are treated differently in the eyes of the law."

"Law does not have eyes. Law is blind. Law does not see parents, only children." She swept her pudgy hand across the room.

"Lady Justice is blind," Boldt corrected.

She squinted up at him like a person looking into the sun. "Why you make so much trouble?"

"These people did nothing to help these women when they became sick. You don't need laws to tell you that is a crime! If one of these children became sick with the flu, would you simply allow the child to die?"

"You not sure of this," she tested.

"Oh yes, we're sure." He leaned in closely to her and whispered faintly. "The woman in the graveyard—buried without a casket, without a service, dumped into the mud—had been violently raped." He added reluctantly, "Every cavity."

This news clearly struck her. Red-hot anger flashed behind her dark eyes.

"Starved to death, raped and buried," Boldt repeated before leaning farther away. "They froze her body—we're not sure for how long, or why. We know she was a part of a sweatshop. Her fingers . . ."

Mama Lu stood, leaning on the cane in stunned silence, the gleeful sounds of children swirling about them.

"A sweatshop could not operate in this city without your knowledge," Boldt said boldly. "I'm not suggesting your participation, only your awareness." He added, "Can you continue to condone such behavior? Help me stop them, Great Lady. You will be a hero, a great friend to this city."

"People arrive from overseas," she said, equally softly. "They have no place find work. Government no allow them work. Much need this work, Mr. Both. What to do? Make lady favors? This kind of work? Die of disease? This not fair. Very much not fair."

"They starved her and they raped her." Boldt was struck by the severity of their discussion, especially when contrasted to the gleeful enthusiasm that surrounded them. "This is fair?"

"Horrible," the lady gasped. "Your visit much appreciated."

"No, no, no!" Boldt corrected. "We believe this sweatshop is in a cannery—an old cannery perhaps. We have evidence to support this."

"Many canneries, once upon a time. Big city. Big area."

"Exactly," he said. "Help me, Great Lady. We find the sweatshop, we stop looking," he suggested. This won her attention. He nodded his insistence. "If we don't find the right sweatshop, we're going to be conducting a lot of raids. Bottom line: The people who did this are going down for it."

"And these children?" she asked. "Their mothers once made the clothing you speak of. This is how they survived. What of them?"

"Four women are dead. Medical Examiner says three had given birth. Their children have no mothers. Is that what you want?"

"You have two children," she said, surprising Boldt with her knowledge. "One boy, Miles. Daughter, Sa-ra," she mispronounced. "You love your daughter, Mr. Both?"

He didn't answer. He glared at her, his heart racing, suddenly wishing he'd never met her. He swallowed hard, recalling the time Sarah had been kidnapped. He understood that hell firsthand; he relived it almost every night, the unspoken source of his insomnia.

"You see child?" she asked, pointing out a small girl no older than two. "Her mother give birth this child, yes? In China—one child only. If boy, he grow up, keep family home, take care parents. Girl moves away with husband. Girl child no good. Many daughters born, but left in street, never seen again. Yes?"

Boldt could think only of Sarah and Miles. Why had she mentioned them? How had she known?

"Many daughter sent to cousins in America. Here, Seattle. Yes? Mother pay much money for this. Mother come later, in bottom of ship. In container. Yes? American government say she not political refugee, has no right live in America. You, Mr. Both? You refuse her chance to be with own daughter? She work hard many years, no papers. Earn much money. Find green card. Citizen now." She added with a faint smile, "This America. Everything for sale."

Boldt held his tongue, still thinking about Sarah and the idea of daughters abandoned at birth, or shipped away to a distant land. He felt cold. Sick to his stomach.

"We don't know her name," he finally said. "The woman we found in the grave. Raped, starved. No name. She won't be buying her freedom. She won't be buying anything." He tried once again to get his point across. "There are people who say there's no way a sweatshop can operate in this city without your knowledge."

She craned forward ominously. "You believe such things?"

"A woman is missing. I must find her. I must stop these people who treat these women this way. It's going to stop, Great Lady, with or without you. I would be most grateful for any guidance you could give me in where to look for this sweatshop. Believe me, no one need ever know my source for such information."

"Leave this alone, Mr. Both," she said. "This dangerous, everyone involved. Yourself too. You help me very much coming here, tell me these things."

"I didn't come here to help you. I came here to ask you to help me."

She pointed to the door. "Of course I help you. No problem. But you must listen, yes? This woman who make the news on the TV, she make wrong people mad. Your name too get mentioned. You make her listen—no make so much trouble. Bad for everyone." She warned ominously, "You watch for shadows, Mr. Both—shadows not cast by you. Wrong people make mad."

Boldt felt his throat go dry as he restated, "Our evidence is growing. We *will* find the people responsible. We will put them out of business." He caught himself reducing his sentences to clipped English, pandering to her in ways he did with few others. For all he knew she spoke fluent English. "They, and anyone associated with them, are going to prison."

She said, "Go home your children, your wife, Mr. Both."

"It doesn't work like that," Boldt objected. "Lady Justice may be blind, Great Lady. The police are not. We are the law, no one else. Not you, not anyone else."

"We both idealists. Yes?" When she grinned her dentures showed, as perfect as a picket fence. Those teeth didn't belong in such a face. They robbed her of character. "Too bad for both of us."

CHAPTER 36

Boldt waited ten minutes outside the offices of Boeing's vice president of human resources, alone with his battered briefcase, his ten-year-old suit and a stomach churning with raw nerves. He was always in the role of the one doing the questioning, never the object of it. The idea of some corporate executive, with a title so long that it couldn't possibly fit on a business card, quizzing him about his life, his family, his dreams, struck him as deeply disturbing. How did he explain that he didn't want the job, only that he needed the added income? How did he explain that if Sheila Hill confined him to a desk, he'd just as soon the desk be across town for twice the pay? That sitting at that desk while others were at the game was a cruel form of torture? How did he tell another human being that in a way not morbid at all, he lived for the fieldwork, the dead bodies, if only because they kept his mind alive, his imagination active, and his raison d'être intact?

The thick glass of the coffee table was littered with aviation and golf magazines. Across the fairly antiseptic reception room, a matronly secretary stayed busy at her phone and computer, though she didn't appear too absorbed by the work, finding enough time to repeatedly sneak glimpses of Boldt and his nervous demeanor. He brushed the shoulders of the dark suit clean, inspected the hang of his tie. His hand darted into his crotch quickly to ensure his fly was up; the secretary caught that movement and taking it for a signal, lifted her head slightly, peered above a set of half glasses and said, "Shouldn't be much longer."

Melissa Chow hadn't been seen in ten days. This was the only clock running in his head.

"No, it shouldn't," Boldt agreed, forcing a moment of paralysis onto her otherwise expressionless face.

He checked his watch. Instead of seeing the minute or hour hand again, he saw the date. Ten days. The rule book would say she was dead. Boldt had the video—he believed otherwise. With the sweatshop now a matter of record, he had evidence to follow. He glanced at the aviation magazines, his head reeling.

LaMoia, who continued to keep McNeal under surveillance despite the risks, would keep Gaynes on researching polarfleece imports and manufacture; others would canvas discount houses, retail outlets, and street vendors, supplying Lofgrin and the lab with samples of every blue polarfleece garment available in King County. They needed a list of every vacant structure in the county, from canneries to former schools to airplane hangars. They needed that sweatshop. The work seemed endless. Suddenly the idea of babysitting a Fortune 500 corporation and spying on its employees lost its shine. Even sitting there waiting for the vice president of human resources to get off the phone seemed a futile act.

He glanced up at a black-and-white photo on the wall and saw three grave mounds, only to realize it was in fact the gray curving roofs of airplane hangars, not freshly dug graves. But the image served to remind him of the digital tape and Melissa's mention of "the graveyard." Were there other women buried at Hilltop Cemetery? Had they missed that?

He grabbed the phone and dialed his own pager number. Ten seconds after he hung up, the pager sounded loudly. Glancing at it, he stood and took hold of his old ratty briefcase. "Something's come up," he informed the secretary. "I've got to get back to the office."

"He'll be done with the call any minute," she pleaded. Boldt sensed it was her job to hold him, her problem to fix.

"It's urgent."

The woman nodded, seemingly relieved. Official police business would let her off the hook. "May I reschedule?"

"I'll call."

"We can do it now. I've got his Day-Timer right here." She flipped some pages.

"Mine's back at the office," he said.

"He'll be terribly disappointed to have missed you." She glanced toward the phone, clearly hoping to see the phone's line light extinguished. She resolved to stall him. No one would walk out on conversation. "There's a good buzz about you."

"A buzz?" he said. "I'm glad." He cringed. He didn't want to be the topic of buzzing.

Her index finger with its half-inch plastic nail roamed the man's schedule. "How's your golf game?"

Boldt returned a puzzled look and glanced down at the coffee table magazines. He had tried the game in another life, back when Liz had been whole and the kids only an idea discussed at the end of lovemaking.

"They need a fourth on Friday," she said. Keeping her voice low she informed him, "All the big deals are done out there. I imagine you'll be seeing quite a bit of the golf course."

"A bit rusty," he said. The closest he had come in recent years was mini-golf with Miles.

"I can pencil you in."

"I don't think so, no. I really had better check my schedule." He broke with etiquette and headed for the doors.

"You'll call?" she fired off somewhat desperately.

He winced. He wouldn't call. Not for some time. First he would run things by Liz in order to include her in the decision. She planned to return to full-time work by Thanksgiving. She would interpret this job change of his as a stubborn refusal to see her as healed, as his way of financially protecting his future.

His days of running the family alone, running things without her, were over. They had been over for several months, though he was loath to accept it. In a strange way he had become dependent on her illness, had adjusted his life to meet it head on, had focused on nothing but that for the last sixteen months, had learned well the role of single father, orphaned husband and head of household, had become dependent on her dependence on him. Her return to the family was difficult to take; his decisions were challenged again; his monarchy once more a democracy.

At the elevators, he caught a glimpse of himself in a wall mirror. Mama Lu's offer of a better suit teased him. More than a bad fit, its mood was wrong. LaMoia was right: He only wore a suit at funerals and award dinners.

If he returned for the job interview he was wearing khakis and a blazer. But he wasn't coming back, not any time soon. He knew Liz's vote before ever hearing it. He wondered if he could get used to that kind of participation again, and if not, what he was supposed to do about it.

CHAPTER 37

Boldt arrived alone at Hilltop Cemetery, struck immediately by the finality of death. Melissa had mentioned "the graveyard" on the digital tape. It was time to review that evidence. Hence the visit.

As a homicide cop he was surrounded by death, but not quite like this, the granite and marble headstones rising out of the lush green lawn, names rubbed illegible by decades of salt air so that the stones were nothing more than anonymous testimonies to death itself. The solitude overwhelmed him. He expected either LaMoia or Daphne to join him, having left voice mail for both, and he hoped it might be sooner than later. Visiting a graveyard seemed too close to home; he couldn't get Liz's illness out of his thoughts, and suddenly grief and fear overcame him. He stepped forward and leaned his weight against someone named Lillian Grace Rogers who had been in residence in that spongy earth some seventy-three years.

"Do you believe in God?" It was Daphne standing incredibly close, just behind him. He'd called her and asked her to meet him. He thought he had found the missing link, but would need support within the department. He didn't turn around because of his tears. But Daphne always seemed able to read his mind.

"Yes. Of course," he answered.

"Do you have faith in God?" she asked.

"Maybe not," he admitted. "Not after twenty years in this job."

A light rain, a mist, began falling. Boldt pulled himself off Lillian Grace Rogers and stood erect.

"Liz has faith in God," Daphne said. "A deep penetrating trust. A reliance. I'm not qualifying that. It's foreign to me, too. But until you understand the difference between your belief and her faith—until you bridge that gap—you can't possibly hope to understand her."

"I have to understand her," he said into the light rain.

"Yes, you do."

"So it's incumbent on me to do this?" She didn't answer. "You think?"

"She's not the one struggling, Lou."

A jet passed overhead, its lights flashing, its turbines grinding. The air seemed to shake. Boldt hoped it was the air and not him.

Daphne asked, "What's with the suit?"

"I interviewed with Boeing," he said. To him it felt like a confession; Daphne, of all people, should have heard ahead of time. "Actually, I didn't. But I was scheduled to."

"I see." She added, "Whose idea?"

"Liz doesn't know."

"Okay."

"You think I'm running. From work, or from Liz?"

"I didn't say anything."

"I don't understand her spirituality. Her reliance upon it. Okay?"

"But you've tried," she said questioningly.

He turned around. She had been smart enough to wear a Gore-Tex jacket. It was green and complemented her eyes. "How does a person get there? How does a person cross that bridge?"

"You don't have to cross a bridge. You simply have to acknowledge the other side, allow the other side to exist as equally valid as your own."

"But it's not equally valid!"

"So you have your work cut out for you."

"I'm supposed to start reading the Bible or something," he said sarcastically.

"Maybe just talk to her about it," Daphne suggested. "That's the best bridge of all." She tugged on the hood and a rivulet of water streamed down to her shoulder and cascaded off her elbow. "Why are we here, anyway?"

"I'm beginning to wonder," Boldt admitted. "I thought I came here to find more graves, more bodies." He added, "Maybe it was just to find what's buried."

"More bodies?"

"If they buried one, why not others? I'm sitting there in a waiting room at Boeing, and I'm seeing graves in photos of airplane hangars and I'm thinking Jane Doe wasn't alone up here."

"Isn't it pretty tricky to exhume?"

"Extremely difficult, especially given we don't know where to look. But if there are other women buried up here, they may hold information we need. This missing reporter mentions 'the graveyard' on her video. I'm thinking that's the connection we're missing."

"She followed someone here?" Daphne suggested. "Followed someone *from* here?"

"The gravedigger maybe. Someone who could tell them when a fresh grave came available. They keep the women frozen until they have an opening."

"Melissa made the connection."

"Maybe. But if the gravedigger was on the take . . ."

"He'd have to have a way to contact them," she said, completing his thought.

"My job is to find Melissa before she ends up here."

The rain slackened off and Daphne drew the hood away. She fluffed her hair and shook her head side to side. She said, "Has it occurred to you how complex an operation this is? The ships, the containers, the cargo, the rendezvous, transportation, fake IDs, graveyards, brothels, sweatshops."

"At thirty thousand dollars a passenger, the margins are pretty good."

"But who could pull off something like this? And with the INS out there, how long could they get away with it?"

"Big players," he said. "Has to be. On that end, the Chinese Triad would know about it or control it. On this end, people like Mama Lu. That's why I'm so interested in her. You're right: It's huge. It's no mom-and-pop affair, that's for sure."

"But to get away with it . . ." she said, coming back to her original thought. "My job in all this is to come up with a psych profile, a personality sketch of our suspect. I built a model. Closest thing I could come up with was a beehive. Lots of worker bees following orders. They handle the day-to-day."

"The gangs."

"Exactly. Then come the drones. They can give orders, but they take orders, too. You work your way up this succession of power, and the thing I kept coming back to, the bee in my bonnet—if you will—is that in the upper ranks, up near the very top, it requires, even necessitates, someone in a position of strength. Not power, not physical might; I don't mean that. But strength: connections, knowledge, insight." She added, "No matter what model you use, they don't get away with this without someone in that position. Luck only lasts so long. The way you win in a game this big is not to rely on luck at all."

"Stack the deck," Boldt said.

"Yes. Stack the deck."

"They've bought someone off," Boldt said. "That's what you're saying."

"I don't like it, either."

It started raining again. Daphne jerked the hood up over her head. Boldt stood in the rain. "Imaging systems."

"What?"

"I saw it on the Discover Channel with Miles. Archeologist, using technologies developed by oil companies. They found dinosaur bones without digging."

"Dinosaurs?"

"So why not humans?" he asked, looking up and indicating all the headstones.

FRIDAY, AUGUST 28
11 DAYS MISSING

CHAPTER 38

With police refusing to share the video, and no word from Brian Coughlie, with it being a Friday and another long, long weekend looming before her, Stevie elected to turn to viewers for help, knowing full well it would entail an enormous risk. Now in the eleventh day of Melissa's disappearance, she felt she had no choice. She had never experienced the bright burning glare of the studio lights quite like this—they felt more like those used in interrogations in old black-and-white films, blinding and intimidating, meant to extract the truth.

With her own words spread out on the news desk before her and echoed on the TelePrompTers, with these words hers and not some news writer's as they typically were, she found the anchor desk, the wireless microphones and the penetrating stare of the clear glass camera lenses suddenly terrifying. Jimmy Corwin looked on from behind the thick glass of the control booth, his agitated expression a mixture of stunned amazement, twisting curiosity and deep concern. It wasn't every Friday morning that Stevie McNeal showed up at the station at 5:30 A.M. demanding a two-minute segment on the *Wake-up News* and another one-minute piece on the Seattle Today cutaways that frequented the national morning show. He had negotiated such appearances by her as part of their deal when he gave Stevie the container assignment, but he had never expected her to deliver.

An eerie silence enveloped the set; the morning crew were on pins and needles because they didn't have down the peculiarities of how to manage the afternoon talent. Or so Stevie surmised. That along with her tired appearance and her lack of makeup. She wore only some lipstick. She had sent both the hair girl and powder boy packing—

there would be no touch-ups between shots. She wore a dark cotton turtleneck that did not emphasize her curves. In fact, all of this, along with having her hair pulled back, meant that there was nothing suggestive about her whatsoever. The sexploitation of the news would have to wait for the next fresh face to come along. She was done with it.

Now, as the floor director's fingers rhythmically counted down five . . . four . . . three . . . Stevie turned inside herself searching for that sense of calm that she knew had always been there when she most needed it. The cameras were aimed on *her,* she reminded herself; the lights aimed on *her;* the hundreds of thousands of viewers hanging on *her* every phrase, every syllable, every nuance. Nothing compared with live television.

She was not thinking of the container series, she was not aiming to impress New York or Atlanta, she was making an effort to save a friend, a sister. Her Little Sister.

Mi Chow she had been called back then, for the name Melissa had not yet been given to her. Stephanie didn't recall exactly how old they had been at the time; but she did remember that they'd been small enough that she had needed to stand to see out the side window of the chauffeur-driven Chrysler as it passed an open-air market, the craggy faces of the Chinese women and men hiding beneath the enormous straw hats, worn as protection against the unbearably hot sun.

Mi had occupied the center of the backseat flanked by Father and a beautiful English woman that Stevie had seen at Father's parties. Stevie could still see this woman's hat and black veil, her bright lipstick and dark blue dress. Shiny blue leather shoes with spike heels.

Stephanie saw bicycles and dust, heard the sound of chickens and smelled a noodle shop. This ride thrilled her to her core, for there was much whispering, much secrecy surrounding it, though this was something Stephanie only sensed.

Her aunt Su-Su was crying softly from the passenger side of the front seat, one hand stretched back but not quite touching Mi Chow. Tears ran down her cheeks.

"Not to cry, Su-Su," Stephanie said, but she cried all the harder

with that. She glanced back at Father, whose enormous height, white skin, golden hair and broad brown mustache had once frightened Mi Chow to the point of hiding.

The open-air market passed in a blur of activity, bamboo crates and brilliant green vegetables. The lucky ones wore sandals, the rest went barefoot. The olive tunics were the same that everyone wore. Everyone everywhere. Only in the gigantic posters of the Great and Beloved Leader, and in the city, did people dress differently. Father wore a pin-striped suit, a white shirt, gold cufflinks and a broad red necktie bearing golden crowns. He wore wire-rimmed glasses and smoked a cigarette. He had a low commanding voice as he warned Stephanie to hold on tight.

The buildings streamed by in a colorful blur with the speed of the car. Stephanie let go of trying to fix to any particular image—shanties, corner markets, the bicyclists flowing like water around the car. Su-Su's soft cries occupied her every thought—something was terribly wrong.

Father spoke aloud, and all at once Su-Su spun, leaned over the seat and took hold of Mi Chow's hands. She whispered in Chinese, and Stephanie heard her say that Mi was not to be afraid, that Su-Su and Steph and Uncle Patrick loved her very much, and that Uncle Patrick was a great man, and that Mi should listen and obey this English woman who was to accompany her.

Father was too busy looking out the car window to take in any of this. He shouted frantically at the driver, who constantly checked with him in the rearview mirror. All at once the car swerved sharply and nearly struck a man on a bicycle. The tires ground to a stop, enveloping them in a cloud of swirling brown dust. The English woman lifted Mi to her lap as Father threw open the back door and climbed out. Together, the three of them, Mi clutching tightly to Father, disappeared into the dust caused by a second car that had pulled up behind them. This car had been the source of Father's earlier distraction. There was much shouting and confusion.

Su-Su called out to her niece, "Be brave, child. Steffie and Uncle Patrick will be with you later tonight."

A car door shut loudly, the dust swirling around Father, who sud-denly stood alone among the curious peasants.

"I will see Little Sister tonight?" Stephanie asked Su-Su in Chinese.

"You take long trip," she replied. "A long, long trip across the ocean."

"And you?" Stephanie asked.

The woman, already in tears, broke down and hid her face. "My child . . ." she said, "my child."

Stevie thought of television cameras as the most powerful weapons in the world—they affected far more people than any bomb. It had taken her thirteen years to fully understand and take advantage of that power. She believed fervently that with just two minutes of the right air time, a person could change the world.

For her there were to be no more tedious interviews with INS directors, shipping company executives and politicians. Melissa's early surveillance footage was both potent and incriminating. Coughlie had encouraged her to use the power at her disposal, and he was right. Klein had gone into hiding. Leads were running out. If she teased the police while calling on the public to help, she felt she could bring the police back to the bargaining table. She wanted that digital tape. She wanted Melissa back.

The floor director signaled her. The camera's red light illuminated. She was live.

Good morning. Eleven days ago a reporter from this station, Melissa Chow, went missing. This is a clip of her shot two months ago that some of you may recall.

On the screen, Melissa stood high on a bluff, the Sound's green waters in the background, her jet black hair tossed by the wind. A white passenger ferry slid into view as she said into the camera, "The state's passenger ferry system has never carried more people more miles than it has over the past twelve months. But what of postponed maintenance schedules, hiring practices, rumors of embezzlement and drunken pilots . . . ?"

The television screens across the state returned to a picture of Stevie at the anchor desk.

That is Melissa Chow. She is twenty-six years old. She is Chinese by birth. She speaks English with little or no accent. She stands five feet two inches and is approximately one hundred and five pounds. She is believed to have been investigating illegal immigrants at the time of her disappearance and is feared to be in grave danger. On the screen you are now seeing images she recorded prior to her disappearance. The first is of a licensing service office worker, Gwen Klein, who is presently wanted by police for questioning. This next shot is of an unknown male, in whom Melissa was clearly interested prior to her going missing. The dire circumstances of her disappearance speak for themselves. Police have few, if any, clues. Anyone having any information leading to her recovery will be rewarded ten thousand dollars cash by this station . . .

Jimmy Corwin jumped out of his chair on the other side of the soundproof glass and threw his arms in the air, waving frantically. He then pulled at what little hair he had left and mouthed a series of shouted orders at his team. Stevie hoped they weren't cutting her off and going to ad.

Any such information will be treated confidentially by the police. Your coming forward will never be made public, not ever— whether an innocent observer who happened to see something, or one of the very people responsible for Melissa's disappearance. We want her back.

You, the people of Washington State, are the finest anywhere. We at KSTV have lost one of our own. We appeal to you, our community, for information—any information—that may help us bring Melissa home safely. The number on your television screen is a toll-free number that connects you directly to the police. It can be called from any phone, anywhere, twenty-four hours a day.

Please *help us find our friend.*

Thank you for your concern.

"Clear!" the floor director shouted.

The hush that followed Stevie's announcement was shattered by Corwin hollering over the intercom, his voice booming into the room.

"Who the hell authorized that? That script wasn't in the booth! McNeal, my office, this minute!"

For the benefit of the microphone still clipped to her turtleneck, Stevie said calmly, "If the money's a problem, Jimmy, don't worry— I'm prepared to pay the reward myself. And if you want to talk to me, it will be in *my* office, but you'll have to get in line. I have a hunch my phone is about to start ringing."

CHAPTER 39

Boldt had just stepped out of the shower when he heard his pager's annoying beep. The bedside phone rang nearly simultaneously, and Boldt knew immediately there was either a dead body or trouble. He felt leashed to these devices, no longer ever truly alone, the idea of public service taken to a level of absurdity that left him without a private moment—not even a few minutes in the shower.

Liz climbed out of bed naked, and Boldt winced to acknowledge that the body that had once sparked so much desire in him was now mostly a reminder of his wife's battle with cancer. Her ribs showed. She answered the phone. "Hello? Yes it is, Captain. He's in the shower." She listened carefully before signing off by saying, "Yes, I'll be sure to tell him."

"I'm turning the TV on for you," she announced. "That was Sheila Hill. You know I really resent having to call her by her rank. Why does it bother me so much that my husband reports to a woman with half his experience, half his brains and more than half again his paycheck? She wants you tuned in to Channel Four right away. You're supposed to be interested."

Boldt entered the living room dripping wet with a towel wrapped around his waist. Ten minutes later he was creating his own lane and passing traffic behind the incessant strobe of the dash-mounted-bubble gum light while talking on the cellular.

"We're going to be flooded with calls," Boldt warned LaMoia. "We burned her and she burned us back. She just sank us and the investigation."

"Options?" a groggy LaMoia asked.

"We move ahead of the tidal wave that's certain to come. If we don't, it'll trap us and drown us. Call Coughlie over at INS. We want a list of any and every possible sweatshop location in the city."

"That's all I tell him?"

"Tell him we're going to start kicking some doors in, and that we want—no, we *need*—his foot to lead the way. That ought to get a rise out of him."

CHAPTER 40

Vacant structures were a scourge to any city because they ended up crack houses, gang lairs and arson targets. It was their designation within this last category that made them of interest to the Seattle Fire Department. SFD tracked all structures vacant more than one calendar year. Boldt knew this from his involvement with an arson investigation two years earlier.

Within half an hour of his request, Boldt had on his desk a ten-page list of every known vacant structure in King County. He faxed this to Dr. Virginia Ammond, who had been compiling her own list of former canneries for him. Cross-referencing this list against her own, Ammond pinpointed two possible structures—both vacant, both former canneries.

When Brian Coughlie called and offered a federal search warrant to help speed up the process, Boldt accepted. Without any formal mention of it, they had formed a task force, and although their superiors—Hill and Talmadge, respectively—might fight over the concept, Boldt and Coughlie were determined to get down to business.

The only glimpse of the structure's interior came as a huge garage door lifted to admit a Ford minivan, so new that it still carried a dealer's paper permit taped to its rear window. One of Boldt's squad pulled the permit number using a pair of binoculars and called it downtown in order to run it. Boldt sat in the passenger seat of Coughlie's Buick, a considerable step up from his own Chevy.

"This video you guys got hold of? You thinking about sharing that?" Coughlie asked.

"That could probably be arranged. The PA's office might have a thing or two to say about it."

"I'm not asking the PA's office," Coughlie said.

"You probably should," Boldt said. He didn't fully trust Coughlie for the same reasons Daphne had cited. Other than Mama Lu, Coughlie had been the only one outside of SPD to whom Boldt had mentioned the freighter's ship captain. A few hours later the captain had been found dead. His frustration with the INS, his suspicions of Coughlie and Talmadge, in particular, had started then. Regardless of how far-fetched it had seemed at the time, millions of dollars were at stake, and no one could be counted out. If Coughlie hadn't produced the search and seizure warrant as he had, he wouldn't have been part of this operation. Law enforcement made for strange bedfellows.

When the temporary dealer permit came back stolen, Boldt asked Coughlie, "Can you give me any reason a sweatshop would need a hot minivan?"

"To transport their workers," the INS man stated matter-of-factly. "I can't think of a vehicular bust we've made in the last three years that didn't involve either a stolen vehicle or stolen plates. The thing about what we do?" he asked rhetorically. "None of these people exist. Can you imagine? They don't exist. There is no paperwork on them: no birth certificates, credit information, tax records—no nothing. That's what we're up against: phantoms. We pull 'em over; they scatter into the streets and we have nothing to follow . . . because they *are* nothing. A confirmed stolen vehicle? In terms of probable cause this bust just got a whole lot easier."

"Agreed," Boldt said.

"Have you been shot at lately?"

"Only by my captain," Boldt said, causing Coughlie to laugh.

"I'm from the George Patton school," Coughlie told him, reaching into the backseat for a Kevlar vest. "I don't believe in sending my guys into any battle that I don't engage in myself."

"You don't have kids," Boldt observed.

"No kids, no family, no no one," Coughlie replied dryly. He strapped on a throat-mounted microphone that straddled his voice box, and he then inserted an earpiece. The device allowed hands-free conversation between team members. He toyed with a small black box that he then clipped to his belt. "You guys with me?" he spoke for the benefit of his team. "Yeah, we're going in."

The bullet-resistant vest was not physically heavy, but its presence was. It meant battle; it meant risk. For Boldt a vest was a symbol of youth. It had been well over a year since he had worn one. Ironically, as he approached the hangar's north door at a run behind his own four heavily armored Emergency Response Team (ERT) personnel, he caught himself worrying about his hands, not his life. He didn't want to smash up his piano hands in some close quarters skirmish. One of his few selfish pleasures in life was the piano—his evening practice and the occasional happy hour performance at Joke's On You. To break a finger or a wrist was to dislocate more than bone and ligament, it was to sever him from personal expression.

Unlike a typical SPD covert operation, Boldt had no way to monitor communications. His own ERT officers were outfitted with hands-free radios, but they were short sets for both LaMoia and Boldt, who were to rely on hand signals. Absurdly, in the name of government secrecy, the feds used their own protected radio frequencies, meaning that even though they wanted to, the two teams, INS and ERT, could not hear the other's radio traffic: hand signals were used to communicate between the two digitally equipped units. Well aware that they had thrown this together a little too quickly, perhaps hastily, and that he was relying on men he'd never met, Boldt kept pace with the ERT operative in front of him, eyes ever vigilant for the hand signals that controlled his movement and thought process. When that hand reached up, fingers open, and then closed firmly, cementing into a fist, Boldt stopped and squatted down. When it made numbers—four and four—Boldt paired up with another of the ERT operatives and stepped to the left of the door.

The eight men crouched. The door was knocked in with a ram, and they streamed into the building, the line dividing in two. Boldt followed the yellow letters POLICE printed onto the black nylon vest in front of him.

It was a chop shop, not a sweatshop, the enormous area littered with automotive parts and vehicles in various stages of disassembly, the air reeking of welding torch and burning paint. Boldt's team took shelter behind the disembodied shell of a gutted pickup truck. Coughlie's team ducked behind a pile of automobile doors.

The first shot to ring out came from the far side of the room. Men scattered in all directions. Once provoked, law enforcement returned fire. Some of their targets dove to the floor, arms spread. The rest fled like rats.

A few hand signals and the weapons went quiet, gray smoke lofting into the air.

Two of the opposition were down, but squirming. Alive, but wounded. In all, nine men were cuffed and read their rights. SPD officers caught two more suspects fleeing on foot. The remainder escaped.

Within the hour, the scene began to sort itself out, the suspects having been transported downtown and run through booking. A computer was seized. A thorough inventory began.

Bernie Lofgrin's SID technicians went to work—photographing, cataloguing, developing prints, accounting for the wounded— attempting to ensure that the charges would stick. Surfaces were swept, evidence bagged and collected.

Finding a free moment, Boldt stepped aside and called Liz just to hear her voice.

"If it hadn't been early in the alphabet we might not have caught it for a couple weeks," the Robbery detective, Chuck Bandelli, explained to Boldt from the other side of Boldt's desk back at Public Safety. Bandelli had a crude look to him, like a horse left out in the rain. "But as it is, two of us got given the job of notifying all them people whose vehicles were chopped, and we divided up the list by threes, you know?—A through C, D through F, this kinda thing—to make things faster. So I'm the one got stuck with the Cs. And when I seen that girl's name right there on the list, I figured I better clue you in."

CHOW, M. / VIN:3678-90-8754C65E7/613 1ST AVE. #2C SO./SEA

Boldt stared at that line on the computer printout for the longest time. A world of confusion. Her car—it was a van—had been stolen and gutted for export. Boldt did not want to believe that she had met a similar fate, but the cop in him had his doubts.

"Listen, Bandelli," Boldt said, "I'd appreciate it if this didn't get around the house. The press gets a whiff of this and we're going to be in the middle of a big stink."

"Sure thing, Lieutenant."

Boldt knew it would leak. The question was when.

CHAPTER 41

The gravedigger was not the man Boldt expected. Others had interviewed him the first time around, and so his slight frame, his aged gaunt face and hollow, ice-blue eyes came as a surprise. Boldt had envisioned a thick, burly man with dirt under his nails and a cold distance in his eyes. The one major requirement of the job, as it turned out, was to operate a backhoe.

Boldt stood on the far side of the observation glass, hoping that this man might connect them to whoever had buried Jane Doe. Melissa's mention of the graveyard and Boldt's subsequent visit to Hilltop had sparked a thought: they had been intentionally misled. It was LaMoia's interrogation. Friday afternoon. Everyone wanted to get home.

The detective kicked his two-thousand-dollar boots up onto the Formica table and leaned his head back. "You know why you're here?"

"More questions." His voice was as thin as he was.

"You're right about that." LaMoia waited a moment. "What do you think we want to ask you about?"

"That girl?"

"Which one?"

"The one I found. That Chinese girl."

"That's something we need to clear up," LaMoia informed him. "That's a good place to start."

"What's that?"

"We're thinking it wasn't you who found her."

"Of course it was. I called the police. You people must have recorded—"

"Yeah, you called the police. And you played it out real well. But someone else found that body. Isn't that right, Mr. Caldwell? Someone visiting Hilltop early that morning. An old lady maybe? An old man? This person reported it to you, and you made the call to us. I mean if you make the call, why should we look at you very hard? And of course that's what happened."

Caldwell blinked rapidly, jutted out his jaw and said, "That's not true."

"Which part isn't true?" LaMoia asked. "And I should warn you that you want to be careful here. This is an incredibly important moment for you, Mr. Caldwell. You cooperate with me, and I can see the possibility of your walking out of this building a free man. But if you try blowing smoke up my ass, you're going to be wearing denim courtesy of the state for a few years. Got it? So I'd think my answers through if I was you, and I wouldn't go making nothing up, on account you don't know what I know and that puts you at a distinct disadvantage."

The man furrowed his brow and blinked some more.

"So let's try it again," LaMoia said. "You knew that body was there all along."

The old man shook his head faintly. "I knew something was in there."

LaMoia glanced over his shoulder at the one-way glass and Boldt on the other side. It was a gesture meant to compliment Boldt on his suspicions.

"Did you bury that woman?"

"No!" he barked sharply.

"But you knew there was a body there because you'd done this before. A little side money to help with the rent. Cash, I imagine." He waited. "Now is not a good time to be inventing the truth."

"A Mexican. Big guy. Offered me five hundred bucks if I'd dig the graves the night before instead of the morning of, like I usually do." Melissa's video had showed a big guy on the bus. Mexican, maybe. LaMoia compartmentalized this.

"You called him? Paged him? What?"

"No, nothing like that. I only seen him that once. The first time. After that I start digging at night. That's all. A couple times, there's an envelope in the tool box the next morning. That's all."

"How many times?"

"A couple."

"How many?"

"Twice. That's all."

"A thousand bucks all together."

"Right," the old man said.

"This Mexican? Can you describe him?"

He shook his thin head again. "It was raining. Didn't get a very good look at him. He was wearing this . . ." the man stroked his chest, "apron, sort of thing. Rubber. Black rubber."

"Like a fisherman?"

"I don't know no fisherman. A big son-of-a-bitch. That's all I remember about him. Mean-looking, you know? Like that."

"Who found the body?" LaMoia asked.

"An old lady. A dingy old bird. Said someone had stolen a casket and left the body. She didn't get it. I told her I'd handle it." He looked up at LaMoia. "I called you guys 'cause I wasn't sure what she'd do about it." He added, "And maybe 'cause I wasn't feeling so right about it anyway."

"Don't try to sell me the good citizen thing," LaMoia cautioned. "Quit while you're ahead."

"I'm telling you: I wasn't feeling right about it."

"We want you to look at some photographs for us."

"Mug shots?"

"Like that, yeah. You'll do that for us?"

"Do I need me a lawyer?"

LaMoia glanced over his shoulder again toward the glass. He hesitated a moment and said, "No. You're gonna walk out of here today. But we're gonna want you to stick around. And no more night graves."

"Someplace I can take a piss?"

"Down the hall. I'll get the photos ready."

CHAPTER 42

At 11:00 P.M. Friday night, under the glare of halogen floodlights powered by a noisy and smelly generator, a woman researcher from the university's archeology department gestured toward Boldt. Unheard, and unseen, radio waves penetrated the earth and returned signals to her computers via a pair of antennae atop small boxes. This was the third grave site she had tested. Red and black wires ran from the antennae back to an aluminum table hosting the array of computer gear.

Boldt took the signal and walked the boxes two feet apart. He looked up, awaiting his next command.

LaMoia nudged Boldt and said in a whisper, "We're losing the world to geeks. You realize that? Think about it. The geeks run the computers and the computers run everything from long distance phones to ICBM missiles. I'm telling ya: We're not safe no more with these people behind the dials."

"We can't exhume without evidence of an unexplained body. That's the way the warrant reads."

"I understand that," LaMoia complained. "I'm just saying . . . anyone who knows how this shit works . . . especially a woman! I mean, anyone who could think this stuff up . . . Who wants them in charge?"

"You've been watching too much TV."

"In all my free time," LaMoia quipped.

The woman called out to Boldt, "Okay, Lieutenant. Let's try four feet."

Boldt approached the two boxes and moved them farther apart, LaMoia following him like a trained dog. Boldt said, "Her name is

Heidi Mack. She was recommended by Necrosearch out of Denver."
Boldt moved the two antennae a few feet apart and looked up. Mack
lifted onto tiptoes to see over the computer gear, and gave Boldt another thumbs-up.

"She's cute," LaMoia said.

"Keep it on the job, Sergeant." After several more "sets," Boldt
led LaMoia over to the woman.

He was right, of course. LaMoia could spot the good-looking
women from any distance. In a heartbeat. He could love them and
leave them just about as quickly. Heidi Mack had warm dark eyes, a
strong face, and a runner's body. Boldt found her eyes and mouth
captivating to where he caught himself staring. He averted his attention, looking at the equipment instead. On the computer screen he saw
a color image that vaguely resembled a sonogram.

"The stuff in Jurassic Park?" she said, in a voice smooth and
sensual. "The movie, I'm talking about, not the book . . . It can't be
done. Not yet, anyway. Maybe one of these days. In the meantime, this
is the best we've got." She worked the computer mouse, sharpening
the image. "We call it forensic tomography. Ground Penetrating Radar
is a geophysical method which is an outgrowth of technologies developed for the petroleum industry. We can determine depth of ground
disturbance. But actual contents is way trickier. And we're lucky we're
up here on a hill, because any saline-saturated soil wreaks havoc on
GPR. This program we're using is in Beta phase. It's all in the software, okay? Sure it's experimental, but it's also cutting edge."

"What'd I tell you?" LaMoia whispered to Boldt, nudging him.

Boldt pointed to the screen. "This?"

"Good eye, Detective. Yes."

"My wife had sonograms with both children."

"Are you married?" LaMoia asked her.

Both Mack and Boldt looked over at him at the same time. Mack
replied, "I have a girl, six, and a boy, three."

"Why don't you call SID, Sergeant?" Boldt ordered. "Will we be
digging?" he bluntly asked Heidi Mack.

LaMoia stood his ground. Mack pointed to the screen where squiggles and loops of different colors were grouped in three distinct lumps. They reminded Boldt of Sarah's crayon drawings back on his office wall. "We've got a good read, a good look at all three grave sites you indicated." Her finger directed them to a rough yellow green at the bottom of the middle of the three. "This area is deeper and badly disturbed, especially when compared to these other two. It could possibly be explained by hand digging—shoveling, rather than a backhoe. You see how these other two are less busy? The backhoe doesn't disturb the walls nearly as much as hand shoveling."

"Bones?" Boldt asked.

"Necrosearch has been burying pigs for years."

"Pigs!" LaMoia blurted out.

"Pigs," she answered. "And working on imaging systems to identify bone mass. They're still a long way off from anything close to perfect. About the best we can do is make educated guesses based on some of these trial experiments." She waited for another LaMoia exclamation, but he withheld his comments. She continued, "Typically, bodies are buried about two feet down, and that's the depth of the experiments. This is much trickier—six to eight feet in depth. But these shadings here, and these returns here," she said, fingertip to the screen, "are your best bets. The coffin registers here: This sharp straight line and these unexplained returns are most certainly below that line. They're not rock. Sticks, maybe. Bone, maybe."

"Am I picking up reservations?" Boldt asked.

LaMoia fired off, "You don't need reservations to book this room!" The joke fell flat.

Heidi Mack answered Boldt. "Yes, I suppose you are. Definite reservations. My problem is this. I've seen dozens, maybe hundreds of GPR returns on all sorts of experimental burials. You learn to spot the anomalies." Again, she indicated the screen. "The problem here? The problem you've got? We've got way too many returns, and they're layered. You see this? One . . . two . . . maybe three different strata."

"Three?" Boldt whispered.

"What the hell's going on?" LaMoia blurted out.

Boldt turned to him and said, "Ms. Mack?"

"If I'm right," Heidi Mack explained to LaMoia, "you don't have one, you have three other bodies buried down there."

"We have indications the tissue has been frozen!" Doc Dixon called up from the bottom of the open grave. 2:00 A.M., Saturday morning. Day twelve. Another bank of halogens to combat the multiple shadows so deep. Heidi Mack had stuck around at Boldt's invitation—every piece of data collected would be added to the Necrosearch database in Denver. "Moderate decomposition. When was this grave dug?"

"Five weeks ago," LaMoia answered.

"That fits."

"The bottom of their feet?" Boldt asked.

"What feet? There's little to nothing left," Dixon replied. "SID will have to sift this soil for debris. You're hoping for fish scales?"

"Be nice to find," Boldt admitted.

"Fish scales?" Mack asked.

"You didn't hear that," Boldt told her, having warned her that some of what they would discover would be off-limits for a while. She nodded.

"Can we have someone dig at this end?" Mack said, pointing on her screen to the area that lay away from the headstone. "Into that dirt wall there?"

"What's up?" Boldt asked her.

"Another anomaly I'd like to verify for the sake of the software. Could be anything."

"Dixie? You mind working a shovel for a minute?"

"It's not in the job description!" the medical examiner complained from the bottom of the hole.

Boldt handed him down a shovel.

"Where?" Dixon asked.

Mack returned to her equipment, walked over to the open hole and pointed out an area in the very corner. "It should only be a few inches lower than the grade where you're standing. A foot at most."

Dixon planted the shovel into the mud and began digging. He

stuck something on his second attempt. "You're good!" he called up to Mack, his gloved hand reaching down and extricating the treasure. "It's a rope," he called out. "Check that," he said, studying it more closely. "It's a chain!" He knocked off some of the dirt and held it up for all to see.

But Boldt didn't need to look. He'd seen it already in the digital videotape—a chain used to bind an ankle to a sewing machine.

"Might have been attached to the bottommost victim," Dixon hollered up, fighting the roar of the generator. "Know what I think?"

"What?" Boldt called down, excitement pulsing through him with the find. The three bodies were most certainly linked to both Jane Doe and the importation of illegals. Coughlie would have to be notified. SID were already on their way.

"I think we were wrong before."

"Wrong?" Boldt shouted back down.

Dixon looked up, still holding the chain. "I'd say we have a new candidate for our first victim."

SATURDAY, AUGUST 29

12 DAYS MISSING

CHAPTER 43

"M s. McNeal?" a woman's trembling voice inquired.

Stevie recognized that voice immediately. "Ms. Klein?"

"I saw you on TV. The reward and all."

Klein sounded nervous. Stevie took that to be in her favor.

"I didn't have anything to do with a woman going missing. I want you to know that. But . . . what I was wondering . . . about that reward. If I could help you out, where would that leave me in terms of that reward?"

"If you—"

Klein interrupted. "You're gonna get me killed. You understand? Those people would kill me in a heartbeat." She added, "So we gotta work this out, you and me."

"I've tried to work this out—"

"I know, I know. My husband says I'm gonna bring a world of hurt down on this family, and my family's everything to me, absolutely everything, and if there's ten thousand dollars in it for me, then maybe I'm better off talking to you, on account I'm already involved with these people and all and they've got me scared half to death."

Stevie felt as if she'd swallowed a bubble of air, or eaten ice cream too fast. She spoke a little too quickly for the professional she was trying to be. "My sources are protected by the First Amendment. Better you talk to me than call the police. We can work this out. I think we should talk, Ms. Klein. Why don't you start at the beginning and tell me *everything* you know?"

"I'm standing at a pay phone in a mobile home park. You want to talk, you gotta come to me, on account I don't want to be seen in my car."

"Who is it you're afraid of? Give me a name, Ms. . . . Gwen. I need something, *anything*, in order to know you're telling the truth. You understand?" *You could be setting a trap,* she was thinking.

"Forget it. I'm not doing this over the phone."

"Then where?" Stevie asked. "Tell me where you are."

Klein described a mobile home park east of Avondale. She would be waiting.

Just before cradling the receiver, Stevie heard a click on the line. At the time, she thought it was nothing more than Klein hanging up.

One of the sports teams had played. The traffic was bumper-to-bumper at a complete standstill. Stevie took the floating bridge to Bellevue, a fifteen-minute drive that took forty-five. She drove north toward Redmond, home of the Microsoft campus, still caught in traffic. Well over an hour since Klein had called. Residential communities had popped up everywhere in an area once predominantly second-growth forest. Condominiums, co-ops, single-family homes—cul-de-sac neighborhoods where dinner conversations centered around "bandwidth" and "port speed." She drove through the surviving forest on Avondale Road, twilight glimpses of Bear Creek to her right, consternation mounting as she became suspicious of the constant stream of headlights behind her. An hour and a half. Any of these cars might have been following her. She pushed against her own paranoia and stuck to the job at hand: The key witness in the case had just agreed to talk. An hour forty-five.

With less than a mile to go, Stevie turned right and finally lost all the headlights.

Blood drumming in her ears from excitement, she licked her lips and spoke a few words to clear her throat.

She rechecked her note to be sure she wanted number seven, where lights burned. She climbed out. Conflicting television shows battled their laugh tracks across the asphalt, past the propane tanks and the mildewed laundry lines. A telephone rang down a ways and a woman's voice cried out, "I'll get it."

The aluminum screen door on number seven had been hung incorrectly. It was pocked and blackened with corrosion. She banged on the frame and called out hello. The trailer's redwood steps were slick and treacherous. The air smelled loamy, wet and dark with rot. This was a place that did not know sunlight.

She caught a whiff of propane gas coming from the trailer itself. She pressed her nose closer and confirmed this. The blinds were pulled, but the smell leaked from the slatted windows as well. Her heart lodged in her throat.

Still on tiptoe, she leaned heavily to her right and pushed her eye to a crack between the interior blinds. Two legs. A woman sitting, perhaps. She knocked again, checked back: Those legs had not moved. The surge of adrenaline seemed to start in her toes and race up toward her face, which became hot with panic.

She tested the door. Locked. Pounded on the door in frustration.

She jumped off the steps and hurried around the trailer, leaping to steal looks inside. On the far side of the trailer another, smaller door. Also locked. She pushed against the door, creating a gap between the cheap molding and the door itself. She used a credit card to open the latch. The door swung into the trailer, unleashing a sickening stink of propane. Her stomach wretched as she leaned away and gulped for fresh air.

"Hurry!" she pleaded with herself.

She charged inside, aware that the slightest spark would ignite the gas. The quarters were small and cramped. Her eyes stung, her lungs ached. Klein sat in a chair, head slumped, eyes shut, her swollen tongue a black-violet rage. Stevie wretched bile, coughed and staggered. Her head swooned. She took hold of the woman's body and pulled her violently from the chair. The body thumped onto the floor. She weighed several tons. Stevie shoved the woman out the door, got caught up with her and somersaulted down the steps, buried under the dead weight. Stevie grunted, heaved and thrust the corpse off her, that bloated tongue aimed at her cheek as if asking for a kiss.

Stevie vomited again, frantically extracting herself from the mud, the cold, the ooze. She struggled for her cellphone and dialed 911.

CHAPTER 44

LaMoia found it difficult to fit his tall frame into the front seat of her 325i. All that money and so little room! The car was running, its heater going, the windows fogged. LaMoia opened his window a crack.

"You stuck around," he said. "We appreciate that."

"I . . . I've never touched one before. You know? All my reporting, you just look. You never touch them."

"You said she had something to tell you."

"*She* said she had something to tell me," Stevie corrected.

"She was claiming the reward?"

"Trying to. Yes."

"You told her you'd protect her as a source," he guessed.

"Of course."

"Who else did you tell about it?"

"No one!"

"An editor? A cameraman?"

"No one!"

"Coincidental timing?" he asked. "Boldt won't like that."

"No, I won't," Boldt said. He carried a hot tea, handed them each a coffee, apologizing if it wasn't still hot, but it was. After a few needed sips, LaMoia switched places with his lieutenant. Boldt rolled up the window and LaMoia headed back to the crime scene.

"She panicked and killed herself," Boldt said.

"You believe that?"

"No."

"She knew they'd get her. Said as much. If I hadn't gotten stuck in traffic. If I'd come right here instead . . ."

"Who else did you tell?"

"No one." She paused and blurted out, "You don't *believe* me?" Her lips found the edge of the Styrofoam cup.

"Doesn't matter."

"It does to me."

"It isn't relevant," he said.

"It is to me."

"You've been sharing information with Agent Coughlie." He answered her dumbfounded expression, "We hear things."

"I didn't share this!"

"You sure?"

"You suspect Coughlie?" she blurted out.

"I didn't say that."

"You didn't have to."

"When there's a lot of money at stake, we suspect everyone."

"The INS? My god . . ."

"Coast guard. Our own people. The list is pretty long, I'm afraid."

"You're wrong about Coughlie," she warned.

"I didn't say anything about Coughlie. It's just that his attorneys—the federal prosecutor's office—tried to get hold of that video today. And since I'd heard you'd seen him . . . I thought maybe—"

"Well you thought wrong!"

"How can I help if I don't know what's going on?" Boldt asked.

"You stole that tape from me."

"I made a bad decision," Boldt said. "Let's say I'd be willing to reverse that decision?"

"In return for?"

"A look at the videos you took from her apartment." He cautioned, "And *don't* tell me you didn't. Being a reporter doesn't allow you to lie to a cop."

"I'm cold," she complained, knowing when to cut bait.

"We'll get you home," he offered. "Our officers will see you home."

She said, "So if it wasn't coincidence, someone knew I was coming here."

"Is that so impossible? Do you use a walk-around phone by any chance?"

"Not at the office. She called me at the office."

"Cellphone?"

"It was my office phone."

"No one in the room? No other calls? Cancel a dinner, something like that?"

"Nothing!"

"So maybe it was coincidence," Boldt said. He added, "But it wasn't suicide. Wasn't even a good try at it." He informed her, "Broken blood vessels in the eyes—manual strangulation. We think he may have raped her. If he did, it was postmortem."

She sat paralyzed behind the wheel. "You're trying to *scare* me into cooperating."

"Not at all. I'm just reporting. Funny, isn't it? I'm reporting. You're here investigating."

"It's not funny at all."

"We can protect witnesses," he said.

"They're not coming after me, Lieutenant. I got here too late."

"But she contacted you," Boldt reminded. "They may know that. How often do they sweep the station for surveillance devices?"

"That's ridiculous."

"I'm willing to trade tapes, Ms. McNeal," Boldt repeated, hand on the door handle. "Offer stands. The offer of protection stands as well."

"Someone to drive me home would be nice. I'll take you up on that."

"Well, that's a start," he said. "You think about the rest."

CHAPTER 45

Stevie arrived at her apartment exhausted and afraid. Melissa had gone missing, Klein had been found dead, and the link between them was obvious, and worse, a link that Stevie herself had pursued despite warnings. She locked her apartment's front door behind her and armed the security system. She drank Armagnac from a snifter, the bottle clutched under an arm, as she first locked and checked her bedroom door, then the door to the bathroom suite, before finally running bath water and undressing. The drink did nothing to quell the image of Klein's body slumped in the chair. She could still feel the woman atop her in the mud, lukewarm and stiff, her own sense of helplessness trapped beneath *it*—not a person, not any longer. She had known this woman, she had spoken to her. It was no longer an image, but something warm and visceral.

She stayed in the tub for a long, long time, running the warm water continuously and allowing it to spill out the overflow drain. She scrubbed and soaked but never felt clean, the alcohol as warm inside her as the water on her skin. She refilled the snifter with slippery fingers hoping to purge her demons, but each time she closed her eyes she felt Klein on top of her. She caught herself wishing that she lived with somebody, wishing for a roommate or lover or husband, some companion to pamper or comfort her. Her aloneness caught up to her and caused an ache that nothing could reach, nothing could numb.

At last she dragged herself out and toweled off, surrounding herself in a sumptuous terrycloth robe, wondering why she allowed herself to feel so vulnerable and threatened. She let herself out of her sanctuary to where she had a commanding view of the Sound and the city's night skyline. She could tell it was the weekend by the number of

237

small boats out there. She longed to be tired, but this was not a night for granted wishes. She thought of all that shipping traffic coming and going, of all the thousands of containers en route from one place to another, the body bags hauled out of the recovered container, the families of the victims, the chain of events begun by that discovery. She wanted them all back; she didn't give a damn about the power or impact of the story; she wanted Melissa safe and warm and sharing this view. She ached for her return. She cried about it, cried hard, finishing up the contents of the snifter and looking around for the bottle that she had left by the tub. She heard voices and wondered if they were in her head or far below on the street. She cried some more.

Feeling chilled, she checked to see if she'd left any windows open, walking around the darkened apartment in a state of shock and remorse. The night air that blew off the Sound was her favorite part of the apartment, though on this night she sought warmth. She found nothing open, except the front of the robe. She tied the robe shut, checked the lock on the balcony—something she never bothered to do, being she was the penthouse—and headed to bed.

She saw a shadow out there and jumped, only to realize it was one of her tropical plants in the sea breeze.

The walk back to the bedroom seemed to take too long and included a stop at the front door just to make sure. She wished she had something more than a keyed entry, dead bolt or not, but the building regulations specifically prohibited any such extravagance. (The building's old-timers claimed this resulted from a lawsuit brought by the family of a man who had died of a heart attack. Though he had called 911, he had left his apartment door chained from the inside, delaying the response time of the emergency service.) The hallway to the master bedroom stretched impossibly long past a coat closet, a linen closet, a guest suite and a half bath. Never before had it seemed so far away. She locked her bedroom door, slipped out of the robe and into a pair of cotton pajamas. The pajamas held their own significance for her—she usually slept with no clothes on. She refilled the snifter and took it to bed with her, knowing she must be drunk, or close to it, but not feeling anything. This she also took as a signal because Armagnac typically flattened her. Afraid to make the room dark, she watched TV, surfing from one channel to the next, in what turned out to be an endless parade of commercials. In the black screen pulses and pauses between her switching channels she saw only Klein's discolored face and swollen tongue. She saw death. Time seemed to be both moving slowly and running out at the same time. She caught her heart racing and thought maybe the booze was having some effect. She drank some more and decided it was not.

The phone became her enemy for it teased her, taunted her. Anyone she called would respond—she felt certain of it—from friends who lived nearby, to half the Seattle Police force; but she wouldn't pick it up, she wouldn't admit to her own fear, much less speak it to another. She could imagine the resulting laughter behind her back, the jokes that would circulate in the industry. There was no way she was going to subject herself to that. Boldt had given her his card—she could invent something she had remembered from Klein's, she could drag him into a hopelessly long visit until his presence convinced her she was safe or the booze finally wore her down.

As it happened, she simply fell asleep, the television remote cupped in her hand, one of the independent stations airing a colorized film. She slept half sitting up, her neck bent awkwardly, her head arched as if falling. She slept with the snifter half empty and her mind half full, the bedside light ablaze, the television's volume muted—for a string of ads during which she had passed out—a cotton blanket pulled up to her waist, the bedside clock counting the passing minutes. She slept half in, half out of consciousness, a deadly combination of visions of Klein and an alcohol-induced coma. The dreams, vivid and dangerous, leaving her only partially asleep and very much in the grips of an endless nightmare.

Held down by the wine, she awoke to the vague but distinctive rumble of the building's elevator, believing it at first to be the growl of a ship's horn, and wondering why either would awaken her. The clock: 3:20, a small light indicating A.M. She shook her head gently awake. Her

penthouse was on a controlled floor; the elevator required an electronic key to access the floor, and only she and the building's doorman
or night watchman had access. Not even maintenance. But why would
Edwardo, the night watchman, come up unannounced at this hour? It
seemed inconceivable to her. Unexplainable.

The digital display switched to 3:21, and to her it was as if
someone had winked at her. Slowly her mind came into focus, the
sounds sharpening. It was just plain wrong: the wrong hour, the wrong
floor—everything wrong. Her ears pricked, suddenly able to hear everything: the ventilation, the city hum, her own breathing, her heart
pounding in her chest. She found herself out of bed and moving
wraithlike across the floor, a specter of fluid pajama and flailing limb
dimly lit by ambient light that slipped in through shuttered blinds.

Her fingers deftly turned and unlocked the dead bolt to the bedroom door, no thought to the added security this extra door provided.
If that corridor had seemed long before, it seemed twice as long now,
extending from her toward the front of the apartment like a tunnel.
Her bare feet captured the raised nap of the carpet. She remembered
fighting the decorator over this carpet—the station didn't want to go
the extra nine dollars a yard, but the decorator's job was to please her.
She scoffed at such notions—self-serving importance, the struggle for
absolute control. What did any of it matter—the quality of the carpet
included—as she hurried down the hallway fearing for her safety?

Other thoughts entered her head: the telephone, which was now
an equal distance from her in either direction; the handgun, which
resided in the drawer of her bedside table but which she had left the
room without; her father; Melissa; Gwen Klein's swollen tongue. A
parade of thoughts and images that came down Main Street and
walked right over her, trampled her, stealing her from her single-
minded intention to determine what the hell was going on out in the
hall.

And then she was the yo-yo at the bottom of the string, stuck
between climbing back up that tether or lying down and giving in—in
her case, giving up—for the next thing she heard was a key attempting
to open her lock. The sound paralyzed her, froze her, claimed her, at

first because it was so utterly impossible a notion than anyone should try to break into her apartment, and then, only fractions of a second later, from the realization and understanding that that was exactly what was going on. Mixed into her confusion, images of that swollen tongue flashed before her eyes, and she knew beyond a doubt what fate lay in store for her: rape, strangulation, the oven's gas turned on high. It was the wrong story to pursue, a story that consumed anyone and everyone involved. She felt like shouting, "Okay, I quit!" as if she could stop the momentum that had brought this visitor to her door, but he wasn't a decision maker, only the messenger.

What drove her feet toward that door, she did not know, only that she found herself immediately on the other side of this person's efforts, separated by a two-inch-thick slab of wood. She dragged over a straight-backed-chair and wedged it under the doorknob as she'd seen done in films. It seemed so pathetically fragile, cocked at an angle like that.

Her eyes found the small security monitor, a five-inch TV screen that alternated shots between the entrance lobby, the inside of the elevator, and the hallway outside her door.

The lobby appeared empty. At two in the morning, Edwardo should have been at the desk, the only possible excuse a cigarette or bathroom break. Or was it him on the other side of the door? Did she dare call out? Was this some kind of a mix-up? Did he believe she was in trouble? Was he coming to help? Had she pressed the wrong button in setting the security device? Edwardo possessed the only other key to her elevator. It made sense, in the way any reasonable explanation satisfies panic. For that instant she felt relief—a mix-up was all. The tension that held her nearly paralyzed subsided. She could move again.

The next image that appeared on the small security monitor was of the empty elevator. This made sense as well. Edwardo had ridden the elevator up to her floor.

The scratching sound continued on the other side of the door, at which point her theory went all to hell. *Edwardo knew which key to use.*

The next video image showed the back of a man standing at her door. The man was big. He wore a hooded sweatshirt. It was not Edwardo.

The lock opened, the alarm sounded, and the chair buckled.

Stevie ran down the hallway. It stretched away from her, growing longer with each stride.

The station had run a piece on home security alarms. Stevie knew much more than she wanted to know about them. Average police response time was twenty to thirty minutes. First the alarm signaled the security company of a breach; then the security company telephoned the resident to check if it was a false alarm or to verify its authenticity; then the company dispatched its own security officers to the scene and, if needed, it was only then the police were summoned. In her case, because of the stalking, any breach was to be treated as a home invasion—the police were to be called immediately. This change reportedly would cut at least ten minutes off the response time. But that would hardly help her. The alarm was meant as a deterrent, something to send a low-life burglar running. It would do nothing to discourage a determined rapist or killer.

The hallway stretched on.

The chair creaked and made popping sounds as its joints gave way. Her feet would not carry her fast enough. The door at the end of the hall seemed to grow no bigger, to draw no closer—an unkind illusion born of panic.

When the chair broke and splintered it sounded like gunshots. She did not look back, did not waste a single movement until she made it through that door and turned to slam it and to lock it. She looked back. He was a big son-of-a-bitch, the sweatshirt hood obscuring his face; he ran like a water buffalo, head down and charging. She bumped the door shut and pushed the button locking it.

As he hit the door running, the entire frame, jamb and all, popped out of the wall as the plasterboard cracked, giving way. Stevie dove for the bedside phone, trying for the gun in the drawer at the same time she attempted to dial 911. The phone was dead. She squeezed off a round; it went through the ceiling above the door. Another. It shot out her TV screen, eight feet from the door where she thought she had aimed.

She heard another shot—this one from the far side of the door—and threw her gun down instinctively, tossing it away as if it did not belong to her. She looked at it then and, wondering what the hell she was doing, fell to her knees and lunged for it.

From the other side of the door came sounds of a fight.

Stevie huddled by the door, one hand on the weapon, the other preparing to unlock the bedroom door, driven by an innate curiosity and an instinct that she was needed. When she heard one of the plate-glass windows break, she turned the doorknob. Someone was out there defending her. The button popped out. The sounds of breaking furniture and the dull wet slap of flesh grew louder and more easily distinguished.

The alarm deafening, she hurried down the hallway, the gun extended.

The big man with the hood crawled across the carpet in an attempt to reach the apartment's open door. Blood ran from his nose and marked his progress along the carpet.

Another man, tall and lean, struggled across the carpet and delivered what was left of her six-thousand-dollar Hondel lamp over the back of the first man's head. The victim erupted, turning and kicking this other man in the face, throwing him off to the side and stealing the lamp himself. But his target rolled and kicked sharply, catching the man in the shoulder.

She saw the blue glint of steel—a gun on the kitchen floor—and this inspired her to aim her own gun overhead and pull the trigger. The blast shot a hole through the ceiling and rained down grains of sheetrock, briefly winning the attention of the two. In that millisecond, the hooded man lunged for the other, caught him by the jacket, stood and put him between Stevie and himself. Then he spun the man, threw him across the living room and ran for the apartment door—all before Stevie understood any of what was happening.

The thrown man struck yet another plate-glass window and it shattered, the sound deafening. He staggered and collapsed into the debris out on the balcony. The intruder fled out the door, so fast as to be only a blur of size and color.

Stevie stood there, the gun gripped in both hands, trembling—bone-numbing cold. She took two steps to her right, aimed at the alarm's ceiling siren from just a few feet below and shot it out, silencing the room. Not knowing herself.

In the resulting stillness she heard the fire door at the end of the hallway thump shut, the heavy winded breathing of the stranger who had gone out the plate-glass window, the panic of blood pounding in her ears. Not a single siren anywhere to be heard.

"Who are you?" she asked, keeping the gun in front of her defensively, stepping forward but stopping short of the broken glass. "I'll shoot," she warned.

"You'll miss . . ." he groaned. The man raised his head. It was John LaMoia.

CHAPTER 46

O
n the flickering screen two naked women without tan lines showed acute dexterity with their tongues.

Brian Coughlie watched them go at each other for the better part of a minute. It wasn't lovemaking; it wasn't even sex; it was a series of savage, desperate acts, meant to justify the ten-dollar ticket. He felt sick to his stomach. His mouth was dry and tasteless. Clearly these girls had not even reached age twenty. They were Korean and not eating well. Their lives were over. They'd be statistics in a year or two.

Rodriguez held the paper cup of soda and ice to his right eye. "He was a cop."

"You don't know that. He got there way too fast. He wasn't a cop. A friend of hers maybe." Coughlie had grown to hate even these brief encounters with Rodriguez. Having busted him for illegal entry, he had later found out the man was wanted by Mexican authorities for a variety of crimes including assault and murder. They had struck an uncomfortable alliance that had grown increasingly worse. The man was obviously into some hard drugs, and Coughlie had watched him degenerate. It was only a matter of time until something would have to be done. What, where and by whom, Coughlie wasn't sure.

For a long time Coughlie had been the one with all the leverage— threatened deportation or incarceration for the crimes committed. But now, if anything, the roles were reversed: Rodriguez had been part of it nearly from the start; he knew too much.

"Guy can take a punch, I tell you what," he complained.

"You'll live."

"We got to handle her."

"No."

"She trouble, dis lady."

"I said no. Scare was all. Get the tapes. And as badly as you handled it, I'd say you accomplished at least that much."

"He was a cop, I'm tell you." Rodriguez pointed to the screen. "Watch dis. You see dat? Can you believe dey show dat? Damn!"

"Forget her. You got it? She's handled."

"You think?"

"She saw Klein. Count on it."

"She got plenty of nerve, that one. Too bad I didn't get to—"

"Enough!" He didn't want any association with Rodriguez. Whenever he met with him, their conversations deteriorated into monosyllabic thug speak. Coughlie reminded himself he needed to keep his distance. "Forget her," he repeated.

"You give the word, everyone forget her."

"Nothing on your own," Coughlie reminded, beginning to warm under the collar both out of anger and because his eye kept straying to the screen. "No more like that forklift. That was stupid! We stay on track for the next delivery. No choice, or I'll be the one having an unexplained accident. Got it? We've got a break after this next one. I can use that time to get us through this. Nothing more from you unless it comes from me."

Coughlie resorted to the one anesthetic he knew would work, at least temporarily: He slipped the man a two-hundred-dollar bonus for the attack at the apartment. He knew Rodriguez would use it to self-medicate. If Coughlie was lucky, it would get him through the weekend.

CHAPTER 47

"I don't remember all that much. It happened so quickly." Stevie McNeal wore a T-shirt over her pajamas. The T-shirt promoted a five-mile run to benefit cancer, with KSTV as a sponsor. Teams of police had been inside her apartment for nearly two hours. The Sunday morning sun was trying to steal the night from the sky. The apartment still smelled of weapons fire.

Detective Bobbie Gaynes, looking as tired as the rest, nodded sympathetically.

LaMoia, cupping a disposable blue ice pack to the side of his face, directed traffic in the living room where SID shot photographs and dusted for prints.

She thought that the police were worse than the press when it came to turning a place into a zoo.

Lou Boldt sat in a chair facing the news anchor. He looked older. "When you're dressed," Boldt informed her, "we'll move you to a hotel. Detective Gaynes will stay in your room with you, if that's okay. We'll post a uniform in the hall, outside a room next door, a room that will be empty."

"What about Edwardo?" she asked to blank expressions. "The night watchman."

"Emergency room. Concussion," Boldt answered. "We'll question him in the morning."

"I didn't mean *that*," Stevie said.

"They knew what they were doing," Gaynes explained. "Clubbed him, took his keys, killed the building's phone system, removed the security video. Without you, we've got nothing."

"I've provided you as much detail as I can."

"I'm sure you have," Boldt said patiently, though he was clearly disappointed.

"So it was . . . professional?" she asked them both tentatively.

Gaynes looked to Boldt and then back to McNeal. "They . . . he? . . . knew what to do. Knew the building. Your location. The elevator pass. We're assuming it wasn't blind luck that got him up here, and it certainly was not a random act."

"Was *not*," Stevie clarified, needing to hear the words again.

"They'd scouted the building," Boldt stated. "That's how it looks to us."

Stevie knew she should say something, but she couldn't think what. She couldn't think hardly at all. "So they meant to—"

"We don't know what they had in mind," Boldt corrected, intentionally interrupting and preventing the words from being spoken. Maybe he was superstitious about that.

"Klein . . ."

"We don't know that," Gaynes echoed her lieutenant.

Boldt retreated to an earlier subject. "We'd just as soon get you out of here, Ms. McNeal. When you're ready. When you're up to it."

"Are you going to show me photos?" she asked. "Maybe I can recognize the guy."

"We can try that—later today, or Monday morning—if you like," Boldt said, but it was clear he didn't believe she'd make identification.

"A hotel," Stevie muttered.

"When you're up to it."

"I hate this."

"Yes," Boldt agreed. "We'd like to work *with* you," he added, reminding her of his earlier offer.

"About the sergeant," she said, nodding toward the bedroom's open door. "How the hell did he respond so quickly?"

"We were lucky this time," Boldt answered.

"That doesn't answer my question," Stevie said. Boldt remained impassive. He wasn't going to answer the question. "Was he *following* me?" she asked indignantly. "Do you have me under surveillance?"

Boldt noticed the three gray boxes by her television set and was drawn to them. He said, "Are these the tapes?"

"Those are private property."

"Who knew about these tapes? We did, yes. But who else? A producer, an editor?"

"No one!"

Thinking aloud, he stated, "We've been assuming whoever broke in here was coming after you. But what if we're mistaken? Or maybe it was supposed to be a two-for-one: look like a robbery gone bad. A VCR, some jewels, these tapes. You're killed or injured in the process."

Stevie paled, hesitated a long time, looked directly at Boldt and finally offered, "I mentioned the tapes to Brian Coughlie. Both the VHS and the digital. I asked him for help with the digital tape. You should have allowed me to view that tape!"

"When was this?"

"Wednesday night. The meeting you knew about. Dinner. Coughlie knew I had the VHS tapes up here. The first ones she shot. I as much as told him so." She waited for some reaction from him. "You don't think—?"

"I heard you," he snapped.

The dull drone of city traffic filled the room, barely audible, competing with the gentle hush of the ventilation system. A ship's horn far in the distance, followed by a police siren like a wounded cat. These sounds were as much a part of this city as its weather.

She objected, "But it doesn't necessarily mean that Coughlie —"

"No, it doesn't," Boldt said, interrupting her. He looked around, closed the bedroom door firmly and said, "Okay. Now, let's start all over."

MONDAY, AUGUST 31
14 DAYS MISSING

CHAPTER 48

S he signed off the same way each day: "This is Stevie McNeal for
William Cutler and all of the *News Four at Five* team. Have a good
evening. Thanks for joining us. Stay safe." By the end of any broadcast
Studio A's initial chill was tempered by the heat thrown from the dozens of overhead lights and the staggering assemblage of sophisticated
electronics. The weather in the fake skyline behind the anchor desk
never changed, nor did the time of day, suspending viewers in the rare
Seattle sunset that sustained thirty miles visibility. The news repeated
itself, the 3 Ds: death, disease, disaster. On that day the lead story
concerned Klein's death—her "questionable suicide," as told by
Stevie McNeal, who had witnessed the incident first-hand. Billy-Bob
Cutler, with his upright, Eagle Scout look, covered a scandal at the
convention center concerning catering overcharges.

Two weeks since she'd seen Melissa alive.

"Clear!" the floor director called out sharply. "We're black in five,
four, three . . . We're out. Thank you everyone!"

Two weeks. In some ways it felt like yesterday; it felt like years.

Billy-Bob jumped up from his chair like a quarterback breaking
from the huddle. He removed his audio gear and headed straight for
the exit—for a beer with his public—pats on the back on his way out.

Stevie could have removed her mike herself, but in no hurry to go
anywhere, she waited for the soundman. Two weeks. Where? Why?
She hadn't left the studio all day, in part out of a concern for security,
in part because of the endless meetings. Management—hoping to protect their investment, no doubt—wanted two bodyguards assigned.
Stevie wanted her independence, arguing that the break-in had been
coincidental and was unrelated to Klein's death and the events sur-

rounding her investigation; arguments that fell on deaf ears. A compromise was struck: Because she had already moved to the Four Seasons under a different name, hotel security would be provided. The police had called off the hallway guard. The station would beef up its security, something already built into the business plan, so that while she was inside KSTV she and everyone in the facility would be well protected. She was free to come and go of her own choosing—they encouraged use of the Town Car—as long as she notified security of her movements; she would carry a small GPS transmitter in her purse to identify her location at all times. In the unlikely event anything should happen to her, they would, at the very least, have a way to track her down.

These negotiations complete, the broadcast over, an entire day exhausted, she briefly settled into her office, intent to be out of there as quickly as possible and to a much needed sleep. She reviewed e-mail and phone messages. Her world crumbling, she looked around and wondered how long all this could last, how long her thirty-seven-year-old face would hold, how long her public and the station would want her. It was a vicious business. Careers were canceled with overnight ratings. Another new face was always waiting. And whereas men would work broadcasts well into their fifties and sixties, women rarely stayed in front of the camera past forty.

When she caught sight of Brian Coughlie in the control room talking to Corwin, her heart fluttered, and her first childish instinct was to hide so that he couldn't find her. Next, terror struck her. Following her questioning by Boldt, she suspected Coughlie's involvement, either with the importation of illegals or even possibly the deaths and Melissa's disappearance. It had not occurred to her that with his credentials he could gain access to the station without question. She didn't want him here. She wanted nothing to do with him!

A moment later, he stepped into her office.

|||||||||

Coughlie arrived at the unscheduled meeting with McNeal hoping either to scare her into seclusion and force her to withdraw from her story, or to convince her to share the VHS videotapes that Melissa had shot from the van. Her disappearance or murder would bring the national media spotlight onto the case, and he couldn't bear up under that kind of scrutiny. He would be discovered. He hoped at the very least to reinforce his authority and stay on top of her and of what she knew.

As directed, he sat down onto a colorful chintz couch while she lightly sponged off her cosmetics in a brightly lit mirror.

"I heard about the break-in," he said.

"I don't appreciate unannounced visitors. At my apartment, or here at the station."

"I'm not here as a visitor. I'm here as a federal agent," he announced. "I'm here to warn you who you're playing with."

"To warn me? First Klein, then my own apartment, and you're going to warn me?" she asked incredulously.

"Offering the reward was a mistake. Maybe you meant to punish the police by flooding them with calls—you were upset over this digital tape. But instead, you put *yourself* at the center of it."

"The gloves are off."

"I hear the first officer on the scene was LaMoia," he said, restructuring his line of attack. "Let me ask you this: How does a sergeant end up the first cop on the scene at that hour of the night?"

"Meaning?"

"He should have been home in bed or downtown writing up paperwork on Klein. The police have you under surveillance. What else explains a sergeant being the first officer?"

She processed all this and felt a sickening twist to her stomach, but she recovered quickly and maintained the offensive. She lied convincingly. "Of course they did. Following Klein, I requested twenty-four-hour protection. In a minute you're going to tell me that you've been following me as well—and tapping my phones and bugging my apartment."

He tried to remain calm through this, but she took his blinking eyes as an indication of strained nerves. "It's all one big conspiracy, right? The Chinese mob, or whoever's behind this, has paid off everyone in law enforcement, and only the press is in the way of all this quietly disappearing from the public conscience. Is that about right?"

"You shouldn't joke about such things," he cautioned. "These people play tough."

"Firsthand knowledge?"

"Absolutely."

"Not hands-on knowledge, I hope."

"You're still joking? Are you aware of the size of the rock you're attempting to roll over?"

"I'll roll over any rock that I think is on top of Melissa. It's too bad you don't work for these people, because if you did I'd tell you to pass along to them to simply return Melissa. Give her back to me. She shows up alive on my doorstep and this story will tank so fast you wouldn't believe it!" It seemed to her like a valid bargaining chip, one that he might even mistakenly believe.

"Did they tell you about the raid on the chop shop?" he asked.

She stumbled. "Of course," she lied again, working too long on her face. Her voice broke as she asked, "Does that mean what I think it means?"

"On the surface, it means her van was stolen and recovered, that's all. In this city that would normally not constitute any kind of event. But given the rest of what we know, it holds all sorts of significance. I led that raid. The arrests were ours—federal. Chinese gang members, every last one. Connected to the illegals? Not that we'll ever prove. But why did a gang-run chop shop have your friend's van? Any guesses?"

She couldn't catch her breath. She tried brushing the spray out of her hair to cover her moment of paralysis. Two weeks . . .

"We won't get squat out of any of them—guaranteed. In their world you rat, you die. Inside or out, it doesn't matter. Rules are rules."

She swiveled in her chair and faced him. "Suggestions?"

"We need to join forces," he suggested, not answering her. "SPD can't help you with an illegals investigation. Have you figured that out yet? This chop shop? That was ours! They couldn't get a warrant fast enough. That's my point. We can move way faster than they can. We can and do take all sorts of liberties they can't. You want to tap a pay phone? That's us. Take them weeks to get a warrant like that. You want to raid a sweatshop? Where do you think they'll turn? Right here," he said. "We've got the probable cause and they don't. Night and day, I'm telling you. You know what I think?" he asked, not allowing her a reply. "I think you and me should go into business together. We start with these videotapes and we work backward. I know that you probably think you've already done that, but we do this for a living! You want your friend back? We start there. That's where we start."

Now she was without her usual stage makeup, and she felt that she looked much older. Her grim expression wedded with her exhaustion and grief to paint a picture of pain and impatience. She tore off the paper bib that protected her dress and crunched it into a ball that she held on to, so that her fist was tight and bloodless.

He announced, "I think you should turn the VHS tapes over to me and take a vacation. I'll push to gain access to the digital tapes as well. You leave town for a while. Long enough for us to make it *safe for you around here*." This, she decided, was an intentional emphasis. He was threatening her. He, too, had taken the gloves off.

"And if I stay?"

"After what you've been through?" he asked. "Who can protect someone that well? You don't know these people like I do. These gang members are worthless excuses for human beings. Ask Boldt . . . LaMoia . . . they'll tell you the same thing. One mistake, a bullet through the back of the head. Pop!" He clapped his hands loudly, jangling her nerves. "That's all. No explanation. No remorse. You want to challenge those kind of people?"

"Comes with the turf. You challenge them on a daily basis, right? You look healthy to me." She met eyes with him and would not let him go. "How's that work?"

"They smoke a federal agent and they'll never sleep. A reporter? Your friend Melissa knows how they feel about reporters."

"So why not use me as bait?" she suggested.

"It isn't done. You're a civilian. We don't put civilians at risk. Not ever."

"Do you think she's dead?" she asked bluntly. "If it was *you* running things, for instance . . . Would you have killed her by now? What would you do with her?"

"Me?" he blurted out.

"Hypothetically," she acknowledged unflinchingly.

He stared back at her, trying to read in her face what she knew.

She said, "If anything has kept her alive, it's that they haven't found the second digital tape. Without it firmly in hand, they'd be stupid to kill her. She's the only one who knows where it is."

"If there's anything they want from her, they'll simply torture her and get it," he said flatly. "These people do not play fairly."

Not taking her eyes off him, "But they don't know her, do they?"

"Don't they?"

"Her parents were great heroes in China. They survived seven months of torture by the Mao regime. Seven months of it! They're legends. Melissa's family honor is at stake. Do you understand? To the Chinese, family honor is everything. She won't talk. And then they'll have to make a decision. Kill her, and risk never finding that tape, or wait her out. What do you think?"

"I know all about the Chinese and their families," he said a little too defensively.

"So if she doesn't talk?" Stevie asked.

"You should take a vacation, a leave of absence. The only thing they would want from you is silence. I'd think about that if I were you."

Coughlie dragged himself forward to the edge of the couch. "If you stay, you're making a mistake," he warned.

"If they let her go, then that's the end of it," she repeated.

"You need to tell them, not me," he said.

"You have sources," she pressed. "Connections. You said so. You told me you did."

He stood and paused at the door. "It doesn't work like that," he told her.

She spun back around to catch his reflection in the mirror. "Help me," she pleaded. "I'll keep my word on this."

"If that break-in taught you anything, it should have been that it's too late to negotiate. Just ask Klein." He paused there at the door. "You take care of yourself," he advised, turning his back on her and walking away.

When the receptionist rang almost immediately, Stevie was convinced that Coughlie wanted another chance at her. The announcement that Boldt was in the lobby surprised her. She asked that he be shown back to the set because she wanted to meet him on her turf for a change. A minute later, her head still spinning, he entered the enormous studio, taking in every detail as if a student.

"Did you cross paths with him?" Stevie asked Boldt.

"Who?" Boldt asked.

"Brian Coughlie. He came to tell me I should leave town."

"Did he?" Boldt pondered this. "Not the worst advice. We can hardly arrest him for that."

"I offered my silence for Melissa's safe return." She kept Boldt standing because she didn't want him to stay long. They talked between two of the large robotic cameras facing the backdrop of the Seattle sunrise that needed a few thousand watts to look realistic.

He said, "When a victim lives through what you went through, we call her a material witness."

"Is Melissa dead, Lieutenant?" The only question that mattered. The one that haunted her.

"We need to work together. To trust each other. You need it for the sake of your safety. I need it if we're to find Melissa. I have reason to believe that they may not have found her yet."

"But you found her van," she said flatly, surprising him with her knowledge. "Why the hell didn't I hear about that?"

"Coughlie?" he asked, wondering about her source.

She fumed. "I should have been told."

Boldt shook his head. "Not without ground rules laid. He's playing us against each other. You see that? I need to know everything you two have shared. We could be way off base with him."

She studied him. "I can go along with that." She added, "So what is it you want from me, Lieutenant? Why the visit?"

He met eyes with her. "Police pressure isn't always the most effective. The press has powers that we don't."

"You see? You hate us until you need us."

"Are you so different?" he asked.

"You ask around about Lou Boldt," she said, "and you get back this guy larger than life. As a reporter you don't trust those myths. Those guys don't exist anymore. They lived in another era. White walls and wide lapels."

"And if you ask around about Stevie McNeal," he said, "you hear that she's much more than a pretty face, that she's one of the few anchors in this town who's capable of reporting a story, not just reading into a camera."

"What is it I have to do?" she asked.

"You have to use that anchor chair to force someone's hand."

She debated this long and hard. She looked at him curiously, cocking her head as if getting a better view. "I'll do whatever it takes."

Boldt reached into his pocket and pulled out the digital tape confiscated in the sting. "Let's get to work," he said.

CHAPTER 49

"This is out of order." Boldt pointed to the screen. They had reviewed all the tapes together. They were taking their second look at the digital tape.

McNeal's expression was grave, her reaction time delayed like a person working off a translator. From his experience when his own Sarah had been abducted, Boldt knew this horror firsthand: the hollow resonance of people's voices as they spoke to you; the way the clock hand refused to creep forward; the insomnia.

"I beg your pardon?" Stevie said, finally responding to him.

"You're the reporter here—don't get me wrong. But the outside of the bus on the VHS looks dirty to me, like it has been raining, whereas the bus on the digital tape, the one she boards, is clean. We get just a glimpse of it, but it's not the same bus, believe me. And if that's right, then there may be as much as a day or two between the VHS and this digital tape being shot. If *that's* true, as thorough as she is in her reporting, then maybe there's another tape. Maybe there's one still missing. And if there is, who knows what's on it? Maybe that's the tape that establishes the location of the sweatshop—or even the people responsible."

She studied the two screens—one showing the back of the dirty bus as it descended into the bus tunnel; the other, the opening shot on the digital tape. She said, "I told Brian Coughlie there was a tape missing, but at the time I was just making it up—trying to buy Melissa some time. I just assumed the remaining tape I gave her was blank, but you're right about the dirt."

"So she may have shot yet another tape."

"It's possible." Her voice was fragile and did not carry. "She may have simply had nothing to shoot for a day. It happens. You know surveillance work."

He proposed, "Let's assume that when the camera was confiscated it contained the second of the two digital tapes, not the first. Let's say the first had already been shot and put aside, and whoever got the camera only got the second tape."

She said hoarsely, "So maybe there is a second tape."

"We have to explain that camera showing up. If whoever's behind this found it, would they hock it? Not likely! Destroy it, yes, but hock it? We have Riley's statement—the man you met at the water shower fountain—that it was a gang kid who brought the camera to him in the first place. So maybe this kid simply found the camera, or stole it, or maybe she hid it. That would make it a random discovery. He doesn't tell anyone about it—he simply hocks it to cash in on his discovery. But conversely, maybe she used it to buy this kid's silence, or to help her to escape—"

"And if that was all she had to trade, what happens next time they come looking?"

"Or maybe someone in the sweatshop—one of the leaders—took it, traded it, used it. It doesn't mean they've found *her*," he reminded.

"I aired her photo," Stevie whispered. "They've identified her."

"We can't confirm that."

"The papers ran it . . . the other stations. You'd have to live in a vacuum to have missed that photo." Equally softly she said, "I screwed this up." She added, "All because you bastards were moving too slowly." He'd been waiting for that. Blame followed on anger's coattails.

Boldt allowed a moment for the air to clear and held to the high ground. "We'll pull a picture of the car wash and distribute it to every radio car on patrol. Someone will recognize it. You . . . you have two assignments. One is to go back over this digital tape and translate. I don't mean the spoken language—what the women are saying—we've already had that done. She gets their histories, the conditions aboard ship—"

"I speak Mandarin," she reminded. "We've seen the tape twice."

"What I need—*we* need—is to be inside Melissa's head. Her

thoughts. Emotions. Why is it she dwells so much on the ship's conditions, when we're assuming all they saw was the inside of that container? She mentions the ship over and over. We need all that subtext."

"The second?"

"I need you to craft a smear piece. I need you make someone look pretty damn bad."

"I don't know how I can get by putting something on the air that's pure fantasy."

He hesitated, needing her, and said, "Nothing libelous, but bad enough that she'll squirm." He asked, "How long does something like that take?"

She considered all this, her face a mixture of curiosity and concern. She answered reluctantly, "Anywhere from a couple of hours to a couple of days. Depends on who the subject is, what kind of existing footage we have."

"It doesn't have to be long, just powerful."

"You're sounding more like a producer than a cop." She tried to smile, but her face only found a grimace.

"You know a woman called Mama Lu?" Boldt asked.

She arched her back, opened her eyes and said sarcastically, "The crime lord? You really *do* want me killed."

"Former crime lord," he corrected. "More of a politician these days. She's the one. She has the answers."

"She's behind the disappearance?" Stevie asked. "She's who Coughlie's protecting?"

"We don't know anything for certain. My gut says Mama Lu has the answers. Some of the answers? All of the answers? I don't know. But I'll never get any of them without some way to open her up. She's getting older. She wants acceptance in the community. That's her pressure point."

"Let me check the clip files," Stevie said, committing to helping him. "How soon do you need it?"

TUESDAY, SEPTEMBER 1
15 DAYS MISSING

CHAPTER 50

Mama Lu's empire included the largest Asian food distributorship in King County and partial ownership in Asian restaurants in the city, one of which was the unmarked noodle shop where Boldt found her engaged with a bowl of brown broth, shrimp, green onion and ginger, the smell of which encouraged him to accept her offer of a bowl for himself, though he made it clear he was required to pay for this out of pocket, a condition she tolerated.

Dressed in a blue cavalcade of cotton, her flesh inflated from joint to joint, wrist to elbow, so that if he reached out and touched her, the skin would feel taut and ready to burst. When she smiled, her eyes fell into shadow, elongating to thin black slivers like chips of coal in the face of a snowman; her lips, too, grew long and thin, stretched like a rubber band across her false teeth.

The soup was delicious.

"How is your wife's health, Mr. Both?"

Boldt considered the number of times he'd been asked this question over the past eighteen months and the hundreds of variations and forms it took, from sympathetic expressions to probing curiosity. But from the mouth of this woman, the inquiry sent a chill through him.

"Do the Chinese have any sayings about coincidence?" Boldt asked, attempting to change the subject.

"I not Confucius, Mr. Both. Humble businesswoman. You no want talk of wife? How about the children?"

"It's not a social visit, I'm afraid," he answered, his skin prickling. He would not put his family at risk; he had been through that, had learned the hard way. But he thought back to her day-care center and his children as something they had in common. "My children are the light of my life. There is so much wonder through their eyes, so much is new. I learn something from them every day."

"Children are windows to past and future. Much to learn."

"And your children?" he asked. "The ones I met?"

"Yes . . ." she said, sipping grotesquely from the Chinese spoon and spreading her smile onto the table.

They ate in silence then, for Boldt could not salvage any more common ground between them; they ate like lovers, talking only with their eyes. By the end of the brief meal Boldt felt oddly confident.

She pushed the bowl aside with her forearm, dabbed her large mouth with a paper napkin and burped softly. "Good enough to savor twice," she said.

Boldt finished and placed his bowl aside as well, perceiving correctly that so placed the bowls could no longer capture the words spoken between them and thus business could now be discussed. She supported this notion with her inquiry.

"Now, what accounts for your visit?" she asked.

Collecting his thoughts, he bowed his head. "We—the police, that is—investigate the ship's captain and he drowns; we inquire after the manager of the equipment rental, and his forklift explodes; we hear of a government worker selling counterfeit driver's licenses and she sucks oven gas—all convenient coincidences to whoever is profiting from the transportation of illegals."

She said only, "Trouble comes in threes."

"It doesn't require a great leap of faith to suspect that someone with inside knowledge is remaining one step ahead of us."

"Change begins in our own house," she said. She touched her enormous chest. "Inside ourselves."

"We, the police, that is, have shared each step of our investigation with Immigration and Naturalization."

Her eyes became darker, if that were possible.

"And only them," he continued.

"You have shared much with me as well," she offered, testing to see where his suspicions lay.

"The government does not pay its workers well," he said. "One can easily imagine a dissatisfaction with the system, an openness to the persuasion of corrupting influences." He continued cautiously. "You, Great Lady, might have heard of such a government employee, and whereas I would understand, even respect your reluctance to mention any names, I thought perhaps were I to speak the names, you might be able to show some indication, make some sign to me that might prevent me from wasting my time."

"You overestimate me, Mr. Both. I humble businesswoman. A few investments here and there."

With the carrot failing, he decided to try the stick. "A certain television station intends to run a series on power and influence within the International District and the Asian community and its relationship to the flow of illegal immigrants into the city." Boldt pulled the VCR cassette from his coat pocket and set it on the table. "You may want to see some of the footage they intend to use. Arrests that didn't need to happen. Courtroom trials that ended in hung juries." He met eyes with her and said, "It's so unfair the way the press can air our dirty laundry, trials that have long since been forgotten by most."

"You have influence with this station," she suggested calmly.

"Influence might be too strong a word. They are as hard on the police as they are on the innocent businesswoman. In their search for the guilty they stop at nothing. The rules are so different for the police."

Mama Lu kept quiet, mulling over what Boldt had told her. When she spoke, she sounded happy, as if not bothered by any of it.

"Do you take any pride in a knowledge of astrology, Mr. Both?"

"As ignorant as a babe," he confessed.

"Do you pay any attention to the calendar, professionally, personally?"

"Only in terms of pay days." He smiled at this mountain, whose features began to melt like wax too close to the fire.

"You see, the Chinese pay particular attention to the calendar. Take the phases of the moon for instance. Important to crops, the cycle of the woman, the seas. Extremely important in warfare. No? The darkness of the *new moon* is every general's ally." Her emphasis was not missed on him.

He searched her eyes. "I'm listening."

She frowned, not wanting to be so direct. "These people delivering the new citizens, they consider themselves *at war* with the government. No? Do not forget, Mr. Both, the storm they call Mary caused much delay at sea. You said so yourself. Run out of food and water."

Then Boldt saw it: The arrival of the *Visage* had been targeted to coincide with a new moon when the resulting darkness would help hide the transfer between the crane and the barge. It was at once both simple and convincing. "A time schedule," the cop suggested optimistically.

"There you have it," she agreed, opening her huge, rubber hand as if offering its invisible contents.

"The new moon."

"I believe you find it upon us shortly," she said. She rummaged in a purse at her feet and withdrew a complex wheel of Chinese characters, numbers and windows. She spun the various elements of the wheel to the desired setting and said, "Thursday, two days from now."

He glanced at his watch, every passing minute carried weight. "Just like that?" he asked, surprised by her cooperation. Or was she intentionally misleading him?

Anticipating his suspicions she said, "No want TV story. True. But more than that, Mr. Both. A woman's body is God's treasure. Its magic makes children, bears milk, delivers life. To violate this . . . to enter a woman unwanted is the most unforgivable sin in all God's creation. I would rather be killed than succumb to this fate. You tell me on last visit about violation of woman found buried. I find out what you tell me is true. No food, water, even illness, is regrettable but understandable conditions of any such a war. This other violation, unforgivable. Must stop."

He suggested, "Two days is not much time."

"Ship sail from Hong Kong in time to reach Seattle on new moon. How many ship can there be?" She stared at him like a disapproving teacher. "Police make much trouble about rental of crane," she observed, intriguing him. "Your doing, Mr. Both. If no crane rented, what option left?"

Boldt digested her message. "The container will have to make shore."

"You good listener."

Boldt pulled out five dollars to leave for the soup. She waved him off, but he left it anyway.

She said, "I make exception, watch television news tonight." She shoved the video back toward him. "The past have no place in present. Keep the past where it belongs."

"I'll see what I can do," Boldt said. He caught himself as he bowed slightly.

"And as to that other matter you raised, Mr. Both," she called out after him, stopping him. "You have good instincts. The Chinese never trust anyone in government."

He hurried, feeling crushed by time. Another shipment of illegals was due. What that meant for Melissa was anybody's guess.

CHAPTER 51

Had Boldt not requested Stevie to repeatedly review Melissa's digital tape, perhaps she would not have done so, too upset at those darkened images of the sweatshop and the horrid conditions described in the close-up interviews. But his suggestion that Melissa might be not only alive but undiscovered by the enemy charged her with a renewed hope that sputtered and flickered inside her, giving off light like a lamp with a bad wire.

She attempted to deal with her mood swings, for the dryness in her throat and the stinging in her eyes. She could not recall her last meal. She found it impossible to sleep, the hotel room offering her no feeling of safety despite the presence of hotel security. Nor did she understand why it was so difficult for her to remain focused. She constantly caught herself stuck in some memory of Melissa, her vision clouded by it, her senses stolen from her. She had been robbed of her existence, denied it. She needed out of this—no longer simply for Melissa's sake, but for her own. If she failed, she would fail completely, would crumble, unable to work, unable to live; she felt absolutely certain of this.

In one of her wanderings, her immediate task dissolving behind this curtain of regret and anger, her eye fell onto the frozen image of a city bus on the video. Not the bus in particular, but its route number, posted electronically on its side. The route number, glimpsed briefly as Melissa boarded the bus in her attempt to follow the big man wearing the hooded sweatshirt. Mexican? Chinese? She couldn't be sure. But that route number! The man's destination was somewhere along that bus route. A quick review of the other video confirmed that he had changed buses at least once. Melissa had followed him into the bus on her second try. Had he transferred to the same route both times? What if he'd ridden the bus to the sweatshop? What if she compared that particular bus route to the list of vacant structures that Boldt had confirmed the police were investigating? What if they could follow the rat to the nest?

She trembled with excitement, suddenly feeling fully awake and invigorated. It seemed so obvious to her. So overlooked. What could it hurt if she checked it out on her own? What damage could be done by a simple bus ride around town? What if she could bring Boldt the location of the sweatshop?

She clicked off the monitors, removed the tapes and hurried to lock them in her office despite the fact they were only copies—the originals safe with Boldt.

She had a bus to ride.

CHAPTER 52

Fall was a time of dying, the annual ritual of transition from summer's lush wealth to winter's bleak bankruptcy. Volunteer Park sat poised behind an affluent neighborhood's three-story colonial homes. The park housed the Asian art museum and a stone water tower. At night it played host to hard-core drug use. All walks of society appreciated a good view.

Boldt met his wife in the museum's parking lot from where the hill spilled down and away from them toward the intrusion of high-rises and the gray-green wash of the Sound. Late afternoon, the first day of September, it was busy with in-line skaters and baby strollers. Boldt smelled fall in the air. It brought a pang of anxiety. He didn't need any more change right now. Liz's invitation to meet away from downtown implied trouble. She knew it was more difficult for him, especially midday.

"Everything okay?" he asked.

She made every effort to return the weight savaged by the chemotherapy, but all these months later, she still looked the same—a piece of dried fruit, the juice of life sucked out. He loved her, appreciated her, and yet did not accept her as fully healthy in part because of her appearance, in part a resistance to the idea of sharing management of the family with her. Her sickness had put Boldt in charge of the kids, the schedule, even the meals and menus. And though he welcomed the relief from his duties, he also felt a bit like a dictator, unwilling to recognize the democracy.

"Where are you?" she asked accusingly.

"I'm here."

"You were off somewhere else."

"I'm right here, Liz."

"You're slipping back into it, you know? The twelve-hour days. The leaving before they're up and coming home after they're asleep."

She had brought him to Volunteer Park to lecture him on old habits dying hard?

"I'm working on stuff," he confessed. "Trying to work things out."

"Living with my being healthy," she stated. "It's hard for you."

"I'm working stuff out," he repeated.

She took his hand. Hers was icy. There was never any warmth in any of her extremities, as if she'd just gone for a swim in a cold lake.

"Dr. Woods' office called," she said.

Boldt swooned. The world seemed to slow to a stop, all sound replaced by a whining in his ears, his vision shrinking. He managed only a guttural, "What?"

"The tests. My annual. There's evidently a newer, more sensitive test they can run. They want me to book an appointment. You're a part of that decision."

"I appreciate that," he said.

She stared out at the water.

"It's not that I don't respect your faith. It's that I don't understand it."

She explained, "They say they want me in for an early flu shot. They say they're worried about me getting the flu. But I know Katherine. It's about the tests."

"Which is it? Flu shots or the tests?" Something teased his thoughts: the container victims had been exposed to a flu. Could he use that now?

"They mentioned both. The excuse to get me in there is the flu shots."

"It's your decision, Liz: You want to skip the tests," he said, "I'm with you." But he wasn't with her; he felt distracted.

She offered, "You have to be fully behind this. I need—"

"My faith?"

She smiled. "I don't expect miracles."

CHAPTER 53

Boldt caught Dixon in the middle of an autopsy. An eighty-five-year-old widow had fallen off a ladder while changing a light bulb and had broken her neck. The law required Dixon to cut her up and take his samples, and though typically an assistant would have handled such a case, the late summer vacation schedule put the burden on the boss. He went about it with all the enthusiasm of a parking lot cashier.

The room smelled foul despite the ventilation system. Boldt hated the taste it left in his mouth.

"Flu shots?" Dixon asked.

Boldt said, "What if the illegals aren't the only ones sick? These Hilltop women were raped—that's close contact. What if the skin irritation on Jane Doe was from industrial detergent, as in a *car wash?*"

Clearly impressed, Dixon said, "Not so far-fetched."

"Close physical contact," Boldt repeated. "You said yourself it was highly contagious. What if it spread? What if a couple guys are real sick? What if the evening news happened to report that a flu shot and an antibiotic had just come available? That both were specific to what authorities were calling the 'container flu'?"

"The antibiotic wouldn't be specific to the flu," Dixon advised.

"So they issue a retraction? The point being that we could use it as bait. We've seen guards on the videos. People have been around these women. Close contact. Someone has buried them. Handled them."

The doctor's gloved hands made sucking noises inside the cadaver. He said, "This is no Ebola, or something—it's a very bad flu. It's treatable."

"But if the news plays it up, if there's a treatment available at a clinic, if our people are at that clinic, and if it requires them to fill out a form that includes an exposure date—"

"That's completely unnecessary!"

"But they don't know that! The average guy doesn't know that! *I* wouldn't know that. Jill Doe was in the ground weeks ahead of Jane Doe. Jane Doe was dead before the container. The point being that if we can trick someone into naming a date *ahead* of the container's arrival, then that person will have to explain his exposure."

"No one would ever run such a story. It's medically unsound. They fact check, you know? Your only hope is with the tabloids, believe me."

"My hope is that this office will issue a press release," Boldt stated bluntly.

Dixon's hands stopped, submerged in the corpse. "Well then, you just lost all hope." He said firmly, "I understand what you're going for, Lou. In a warped kind of way, it even makes sense. It's a pretty good idea. But I cannot put this department in the position you're asking me to. If we lose integrity and trust, if the public believes we're willing to manipulate the truth for the good of SPD . . . It just doesn't work. We're a team of medical professionals. Believe me, we have image problems enough without this kind of thing: 'second-rate doctors'; 'surgeons whose only patients are dead.' Can't do it, Lou."

"But it might work," Boldt suggested, looking for encouragement.

"I'd give it a qualified yes—a *highly* qualified yes." He repeated, "But it doesn't matter. You'll never get anyone to run the story."

Boldt said, "I wouldn't be so sure about that."

CHAPTER 54

Between the chauffeur-driven Town Cars and her own 325i, Stevie realized she had not ridden a Seattle city bus until then, surprised by the diversity of its riders and the unexpected neighborliness of its passengers. She had thought the bus system a place for poor people, the homeless and indigent, "The Unseen Minority" as they had been called in a feature piece on *N4@5*. Instead, on that Tuesday afternoon she found teenagers, college kids, moms and children, even a businessman or two. They read books, newspapers, knitted, listened to Walkmans, shared a conversation, or stared out the windows, which was what Stevie did, ever alert for landmarks that might signal the location where Melissa's subject had disembarked. In her right hand, Stevie carried a printout from the digital video for comparison.

The bus stops came and went. People switched seats. The doors hissed shut. The bell line buzzed the driver.

She marked a tourist map as she went, indicating the running time of the trip. With the video time-stamped, it seemed one possible way to identify the bus stop this man had taken.

The bus route dragged on, her broadcast nearing. After ten more minutes, as they approached the Fremont Bridge, she realized the bus trip would have to wait. She had a meeting scheduled with Boldt to determine if they should air the clips of Mama Lu. Frustrated with the idea of giving up she nonetheless disembarked, crossed the street and rode another bus back into town. As it turned out, Boldt was waiting for her.

CHAPTER 55

Brian Coughlie felt obsessed with her. Aware that following the botched attack in her apartment, the police or the other security were more than likely to keep her under protection, Coughlie nonetheless assigned two of his own INS agents to also watch her from a distance, to report not only her every movement but who else was keeping tabs. When his people reported her boarding a city bus Coughlie became perplexed. Try as he did, he couldn't make sense of her riding public transportation out to Fremont Bridge and then back into the city again. Was it something she had gleaned from one of the videos? A tip from an informer from the hotline? What? Worse: How did he stop her?

He had gone without sleep, compensating for this additional fatigue through a liberal dose of amphetamines and as much espresso as he could force down. He lived broadcast to broadcast, terrified at what she might come up with next, debating his options and not liking any of them. To watch her broadcasts felt to him like professional leprosy: watching the slow rotting of his own career as bits and chunks sloughed off.

Two days more. His focus remained this last shipment of illegals yet to arrive, although he felt plagued by the police's recent discovery of three more buried bodies in Hilltop Cemetery and what those cadavers might reveal to the experts. Rodriguez was a liability—his solutions only created additional problems.

More terrifying to him personally was that his request for police to share this Hilltop information had gone without any acknowledgment or reciprocity. LaMoia hadn't even returned the call. What was *that* about?

He couldn't pick up and run even if he'd wanted to; it wasn't the police he was worried about, but the Chinese "businessmen" who owned him. A person didn't run from such people, not ever. You stood and faced the music. You implicated others in the failure; you framed people if necessary.

The more he thought about it all, the sharper the pain behind his eyes, the drier his tongue. He had work to do. If he got this next shipment in without incidence, he felt reasonably confident he could wrestle control back from SPD and contain the damage.

The success of the next shipment was everything.

CHAPTER 56

Stevie McNeal sat up straight in her anchor chair facing the three robotic cameras, a barrage of lights pouring color and heat down onto her.

At Boldt's request, she prepared herself to lie, to use her anchor chair for her own good, to willfully manipulate her trusting public in an effort to rescue her Little Sister. It was professional suicide if it ever came out, but she felt bound to pursue anything that increased Melissa's chances. *Anything*.

She would break from the prepared text of the news hour and read from her own cards. There would be hell to pay, especially if the station managers ever found out she had known in advance that the information was inaccurate, a construct of a police department desperate for a break. In the next few seconds she was going to put her entire career on the line. She wouldn't find work in a fourth-tier city if this ever came out.

Her director's voice came through the earpiece she wore. "You okay, Stevie?"

She raised her hand to signal him, though she did not open her eyes, her full concentration on Melissa and putting her needs first.

Surprisingly, she thought of her father, alone and unloved in some veteran's hospital, courtesy of the federal government. Melissa had mentioned his poor health. Stevie blamed her father for her years in New York, for feeding her to a skirt-chasing producer whose idea of educating the fresh recruits was getting their clothes off. She hadn't spoken to her father since her departure from New York—her ending the affair had also ended her network career. But faced with compromising her career, she suddenly thought of him and how she would be letting him down, would be damaging the McNeal name, and she realized he still held power over her, even off wherever he was, battling whatever it was. She could break the communication but not the connection.

Five . . . four . . . three . . . two . . .

She opened her eyes. The floor director's finger pointed ominously at her. She felt cold despite the glare of lights.

Good evening. You're live, with News Four at Five. *I'm Stevie McNeal.*

She broke from the prepared text.

Local health authorities announced just moments ago that the flu-like virus that may have been responsible for the deaths of several illegal aliens including three found dead in a shipping container last month is a far more serious threat to local health than previously imagined.

Corwin stood up from behind the console in the soundproofed booth and waved frantically at her, pointing to the thin pink sheet of text he held in his hand, the yellow copy of which lay before her on the anchor desk, and the text to which scrolled on the prompting screen below the camera lens. She saw him only peripherally, her attention primarily directed to the cards but divided between the cards and the camera with the red light, his angry voice carrying through her flesh-colored earpiece and attempting to distract her as she continued to read her cards. But Stevie McNeal was a pro: She never broke her cadence.

News Four at Five *has learned that this contagion, which produces flu-like symptoms of high fever, congestion and can result in bronchial infection, stomach cramps and diarrhea, is also believed responsible for the deaths of the Jane Doe and three other corpses found improperly buried at Hilltop Cemetery in the past week. There are unconfirmed rumors that the virus is spreading rapidly through the detainee population at the INS facility at Fort Nolan.*

Health officials, responding to the public's needs, have estab-
lished a free inoculation program at New Care Health Clinic
across from Harborview Medical Center. Any persons having
confirmed direct contact with anyone known to be carrying this
virus are strongly encouraged to seek immunization and/or a
series of specially created antibiotics at New Care between the
hours of twelve and one P.M. and eight and ten P.M, daily, until
further notice or the limited supply runs out. Health care offi-
cials stress the severity of the problem, the systemic nature of
the contagion and the importance of this preventive treatment
program. For further information, interested viewers can call
this toll-free number twenty-four hours a day.

She read the 888 number that Boldt had provided her, a number
that ran directly to the fifth floor of the Public Safety building and had
both caller-ID and trap-and-trace functions enabled.

"In other news . . ." She returned to the top of the prepared broadcast. As she read from her sheet the TelePrompTer scrolled backward
and caught up with her. Corwin would have to edit during the first
break and cut a story or shorten weather or sports to accommodate
Stevie's unexpected announcement. He would never drop an ad—the
station had its priorities set.

An amazing sense of relief pulsed through her. Any effort to save
Melissa was worth the price. Boldt's trap was properly set. She had
joined forces with the police and they with her, and she thought that
if anything, this was a lesson for both sides. She wondered if she had
a year to keep her anchor chair, or a week, or a day. Truthfully, she
didn't care. If Melissa came home because of this one sixty-second
manipulation of the truth . . .

Then, in what she considered a moment of brilliance, as she finished reading the lead story and the camera bearing the red light
switched to Billy-Bob Cutler, she stood from her anchor chair,
stripped off the microphone and earpiece, distracting but not interrupting her co-anchor, and marched off the set. When she turned not
toward her dressing room and the bathroom there but toward the studio
exit, the floor director rushed away from the set and caught up.

"Ms. McNeal?" she hissed, stopping Stevie and turning her. "Anything wrong?"

Jimmy Corwin's lean frame appeared through the door to the control booth and froze, understanding her intentions from the expression on her face. Surprisingly, he spoke calmly. "If this story is sound, then why not include it in the script?" Corwin was a newsman. Corwin knew before making a single phone call. "Who's your contact on this?"

Stevie met eyes with him. "Billy-Bob will have to take my remaining segments. He'll do fine."

"Mr. Cutler? The whole broadcast?" the floor director inquired.

Corwin said, "Tell me this story is going to check out. What the hell is going on here?"

She liked Corwin. She hated to do this to him—to the station. She took a deep breath and said, "I have a bus to catch."

CHAPTER 57

"I need you. *Pronto.* She split the station early. I'm in trouble here." Coughlie had paged Rodriguez to call him back, taking a huge risk by using his cellphone but seeing no way around it. The call had been returned nearly instantly. He heard the barroom noise in the background and knew that Rodriguez was in some happy hour haunt watching *News Four at Five.* They both had made a regular diet of it.

He followed the BMW toward downtown, wondering what she was up to. First the story about a flu vaccine, then the sudden departure. He knew how Rodriguez would react to that lead story. He had to involve the man in McNeal's surveillance in order to keep him from going to that health clinic. Coming from her mouth as it had, the story had sounded plausible, even legitimate, but for a variety of reasons Coughlie was deeply suspicious: The INS would have been told if Fort Nolan's population was at any kind of health risk. It was a glitch in her story that he couldn't see past. Fearing some kind of trap, some kind of sting, he needed to keep Rodriguez clear of the clinic. The guy had been pretty damn sick for the last several weeks, had buried women who had died with similar symptoms and had repeatedly complained about his health. Coughlie feared that the man would take the bait. If Rodriguez had any love, it was for any kind of medication.

Rodriguez said, "Forget it. No can do. Got me an appointment." The big man sniffled snot back into the back of his throat. It sounded grotesque.

"This health clinic? Forget about it. It's a trap."

"I'm busy."

"It's a trap. The cops tricked her into this. Listen, I'm following her right at this very moment," Coughlie said. "I need help with this."

"Busy."

"Listen to me—"

Rodriguez interrupted, "Try me later." The line clicked.

"Hello?" Coughlie said into the receiver, astonished the man would hang up on him. A first. "Hey!" he shouted. He held out the cellphone and stared at it, placed it back to his ear and repeated, "Hey!" Nothing.

McNeal parked the BMW.

Coughlie pulled over, fearing he might have to follow her on foot.

McNeal approached a bus stop and stood there waiting. A bus stop? She had mentioned to him that one of Melissa's surveillance videos had shown a bus. Rodriguez regularly used the bus to reach the sweatshop. Brian Coughlie went numb with the thought.

He tried the pager again. But this time, his cellphone never rang with the return call.

A city bus pulled to a stop. People shoved for position. Stevie McNeal climbed aboard.

CHAPTER 58

As Stevie sat across from the rear door of the city bus watching the landscape parade past, she reminded herself of the big man with the hooded sweatshirt, consulting a color printout—a freeze-frame—from the video. She tracked the exact second the bus arrived and departed each of its stops, looking for an elapsed time of twenty-two minutes and seventeen seconds as recorded on the digital video. Believing she was onto something, she wanted to test her theory before taking up SPD's time with it. Adding to her excitement was the realization that she might have lost her tail—as unintentional as it was—by leaving the station through a back exit during a time she was anticipated to be on-air. She assumed, quite rightly, that if there was any time her guards ran for a bite to eat, or took a break, it was during the two-hour period that *N4@5* typically occupied. As much as she appreciated the reassurance of their presence she preferred her independence, especially on the eve of what she believed was to be a major discovery. This way she could savor the moment of delivering news of her discovery to Boldt or LaMoia—or better yet, both at the same time. If she found the sweatshop, or even the general neighborhood where the man had left the bus route, she would be doing something positive to help Melissa, not just sitting back and being a target of these people. Playing the victim was not her idea of taking part.

Her eye constantly referenced the printout she held in her lap, the eerie dark image of the big man a blur at the bus door, but the stair-step pattern of the skyline seen through the bus windows distinct, if not distinctive. Looking outside again, she intentionally blurred her eyes to recapture the vague image on the printout. Still nothing; the background offered not a hint of the footage Melissa had shot. Melissa needed her and she was not delivering.

The bus pulled to yet another stop. Fremont Bridge—the same place she had turned around her last time out. She checked the print-out and glanced up, her eyes stinging, her head ringing with defeat and grief. If only Melissa knew how much she cared, how much she loved her; if only she had taken the time to be with her, to involve her in her life—maybe even then things would be different, she would feel differently somehow, but she had not done these things. She deeply regretted it now.

Stevie had little time to think about such things. She looked up as Brian Coughlie climbed onto the bus.

He moved down the aisle deliberately, self-confident and strong, look-ing directly at her and never taking his eyes off her, and for an instant a spike of fear raced through her. Where the hell had he come from? What the hell did he want?

The seat next to her was vacant. She would have gladly had it occupied by the smelliest street person at that moment, although the determination in Coughlie's eyes indicated nothing would stop him from taking that seat. The bus rolling, Coughlie sat down next to her and looked straight ahead.

"I caught your act," he said, still looking toward the front of the bus. "A Watchman," he explained. "Nifty little gadget. I keep one with me everywhere I go now. Addicted to the news, I guess you could say."

"What a coincidence," Stevie said, "both of us on the same bus and all."

"In your dreams," he replied. "SPD dropped the ball when you took off from the station. Not my boys. No sir. Right there is the differ-ence between local and federal, I'm telling you. Be glad we're on your side."

"You've been following me," she said with disgust.

"Hell, you've so many people watching your ass you might as

well be leading a parade. You're a regular majorette!" His arrogance disturbed her—a different man from the one previously seeking partnership.

The bus bounced. All the passengers' heads rose and fell in unison. Stevie's teeth chattered, but that had nothing to do with the bus's jerky movements.

"Tell me about that little stunt of yours."

"Stunt?" Her legs shook she was so nervous.

"Your idea or Boldt's? This flu thing . . . It's a simple enough question." He waited for her, but she couldn't find a defendable answer, couldn't find her voice at all. "You reported this flu was spreading out at Fo-No—Fort Nolan. who gave you that? Who's your source on that? Or did you make it up? Does the news simply make things up? This is *my turf* we're talking about here." His crimson face took on a greenish purple under the tube lights. "I'll catch hell for this. You know that? Health inspectors. ACLU. You buried us with that piece." He pursed his lips and edged forward on the seat. "This story is bullshit."

"The CDC issued—"

"Oh, that's bullshit! We'd have seen it before anyone else! Don't you get it? It's *our* detention facility we're talking about. We'd have been the first notified. Our population would have been the first immunized. Did they *use* you?" he asked incredulously. "Or are you part of it?"

They met eyes. His were bloodshot and half-blind with anger. She wanted off that bus. It stopped, but she didn't look up. "Whatever it takes to save her," she said.

"It was Boldt's idea," Coughlie said.

"I'm telling you: The CDC issued a health bulletin."

"And I'm telling you, it's not possible. They used you." He looked around. "And what's this about? You don't mind me saying so, you and a city bus have got nothing in common. Is it the videos?"

"The police found a bus ticket," she lied. "It was worth a gamble."

"If they'd found a bus ticket, it would be them riding the bus, not you. What's going on with you? Why are you lying to me?"

"Why are you having me followed? Protection? From what? From whom? Or do you want me to do your work for you? A federal agency keeping a reporter under surveillance—"

"A witness."

"No, Brian. Not me. You want to deal with all this, or are you going to call off your people?"

"You're making a mistake—a *big* mistake."

"It's mine to make," she said.

"Yes, it is," he answered. His smile turned her stomach. "So have it your way. But remember: Some mistakes are costly."

The bus pulled to another stop. Coughlie stood and disembarked. He didn't look back.

CHAPTER 59

A woman detective from vice named Laura Stowle was dressed in nursing whites to play the role of clinic receptionist. LaMoia commented on how a tightly packed white uniform had irresistible effects upon him, and how, based on this rare opportunity to see Stowle's darkly handsome face and "well-rounded personality" in such a tantalizing costume, he needed to ask her out.

Boldt told him to keep it in his pants.

The clinic had gone along with the substitution because the receptionist required no medical training and until a doctor or paramedic became involved in the process there was no legal expectation of privacy.

"The only problem with Stowle in this assignment, Sarge, is that even with her hair pulled back, she's a little too cute, a little too much like a soap opera star instead of the minimum wage ethnic receptionist we've all come to expect."

"One of these days that mouth of yours is going to get you into more trouble than it can talk itself back out of," Boldt warned.

"This mouth of mine ought to be registered as a weapon, what it can do to a woman."

"You're not scoring any points, John. Go inside and take a chair. You want to stare at Stowle? Permission granted. At least I won't have to listen to you."

LaMoia occupied the chair in the far corner for two hours, wondering why it was that waiting rooms offered only grossly out-of-date magazines and wall clocks the size of pizzas. He was bothered by how young the people using the free clinic were, and how much of its traffic seemed involved, one way or another, with drugs and addiction. Only seven people had arrived as a result of Stevie McNeal's broadcast.

Each of the seven times, Stowle had signaled all four of the undercover cops inside, and Boldt in the control van. The lavaliere microphone was hidden in her dark hair, its wire running down the back neck of her dress. Seven different people, all seeking the RH-340 flu shot—all health care workers or dockhands who had been on the scene of the container recovery.

The eighth time Laura Stowle signaled LaMoia it was for a tall Hispanic male wearing a dark sweatshirt with a hood. LaMoia buried his face into a six-week-old copy of *People*; the janitor with the bucket and mop kneeled down to work a piece of gum from the stone floor; a wiry-looking woman in hot pants and platform shoes pulled out her lipstick and used the mirror of her compact to get a good look at the door behind her; a woman in civilian clothes, typing at a station behind Stowle, took her fingers off the keyboard and took hold of her weapon, beneath the table.

The big man was told to wait. He took a seat two chairs away from LaMoia, who had the audacity to turn to the man and say, "How ya doing?"

"Feel like shit, man," the other said, his nose running, his voice rough.

"I hear that," LaMoia said, returning to his magazine.

After five minutes the Hispanic male was handed a form to fill out. He looked at it with contempt. Standing in front of him, Stowle explained in a bored voice, "We need your name, place of employment, if any, and relevant phone numbers for notification of follow-up. They're very important. If you need the Spanish form—"

"Yeah," he grunted.

She returned with a different clipboard and spoke Spanish. "You can skip the insurance part because the treatment you've requested is free. Fourth line, date of exposure, is *extremely* important because it will determine the extent of treatment you receive and therefore the effectiveness of that treatment. Repeated exposures don't matter to the physician. It's the *initial* exposure that is critical to proper diagnosis and subsequent treatment. If there's anything I can help you with—"

"You could speed things up a little," LaMoia said, interrupting in English. "Or maybe a drink after you're through here."

Stowle glared at him.

The Hispanic sniffled, coughed and scribbled his name onto the top of the form in crude but legible handwriting: Guermo Rodriguez.

Stowle returned to her place behind the counter.

LaMoia was called a few minutes later under the name Romanello. " 'Bout time," he said, placing the magazine down. "Good luck, man," he said to the other. "You'll be a couple years older by the time they call you."

Rodriguez stood simultaneously and returned the clipboard and form to the receptionist, who passed it on to the officer at the keyboard station behind her, the woman's loaded weapon still available on the shelf by her knees.

LaMoia passed into the back and took up a position in the examination room adjacent to the room where Rodriguez would be examined, effectively blocking any use of the building's back exit. They had him cornered now. LaMoia waited impatiently for information back from downtown. The keyboard operator's input of the outpatient form was not headed for the clinic's medical records but instead was connected by modem to the department's criminal records bureau. The name Guermo Rodriguez came back negative: no criminal arrests or convictions. The system also failed to kick a driver's license or a registered vehicle. Guermo Rodriguez did not exist. He was, however, a man who might ride the city buses. Rodriguez had more than likely listed a bogus address on the clinic's form, as well as a bogus phone number. Rodriguez was probably himself an illegal, a connection that could easily put him into service for a corrupt INS official.

"He's gotta be our guy," Boldt announced over the radio. "The sweatshirt matches what we saw on the videos. We go with it."

A few minutes later Rodriguez was given an injection of a placebo, told to take aspirin and drink plenty of water, and released.

By the time Guermo Rodriguez left the clinic, SPD had fifteen officers in ten vehicles assigned to his surveillance—the largest surveillance operation conducted by the department in the past eleven months.

CHAPTER 60

With SPD monitoring his every footstep, nearly his every breath, Rodriguez was carefully followed, first to an all-night pharmacy where he bought a bottle of aspirin, some cough syrup and a head cold decongestant, and subsequently to "A place on Military Road in Federal Way," as LaMoia explained to Boldt, who had returned to the office to oversee and direct the surveillance from the situation room. "He climbs up into an eighteen-wheeler cab—a flatbed—and takes a two-hour nap. I got a hunch that truck's his home for the time being. But then he fires it up and drives off. What's that say to you, Sarge?"

"Mama Lu was right about the new moon," Boldt answered. "There's a shipment coming in. Tomorrow? The next day? *Soon!*" The truck was intended to move a container.

"So then he drives a couple miles, parks it and takes a lawyer's lunch at a greasy spoon—only it's after midnight. He's in no sign of being in any hurry."

"We know for certain he's in there?" Boldt pressed.

"Cranshaw is getting his fill of cherry pie and coffee. We got a visual."

"Waiting for a meet?" Boldt proposed.

"That or a call. Got to be. You want I should bring him in for a chat?"

"Negative," Boldt stated. The evidence they had against Rodriguez was entirely circumstantial. "I could try for a trap-and-trace on the diner's pay phone—"

"Now there's a long shot."

"Never get it," Boldt admitted.

"Let's hope this guy's girlfriend doesn't have a thing for the inside of truck cabs or something. I hope to hell we're not wasting our time here."

"Is sex the only thing you think about?" Boldt asked.

"No way!" LaMoia answered without missing a beat. "I'm pretty fond of money, too."

At 3:00 A.M. Wednesday morning the flatbed semi with Rodriguez behind the wheel finally left the diner's gravel lot. Boldt was awakened from a nap in a storage room where a bunk bed offered detectives a chance to lie down. Surveillance was tricky at that hour, and with Boldt's request for a phone warrant denied, all the police could do was guess at the call Rodriguez had been seen making from the diner and to follow him at a comfortable distance.

Thirty minutes later he used a bolt cutter to enter the gates of a naval storage depot that proved to have been part of the 1988 base closures that had caused a brief downward blip in King County's otherwise stellar economy. Rodriguez pulled the flatbed down to a dock area where a pair of towering cranes pointed up toward the night sky. It was those cranes that caught everyone's attention.

Fifteen minutes later, as LaMoia and two other detectives made their move to get a better vantage point, Rodriguez was spotted crossing through the navy yard's side gates on foot. A moment later he dragged a motorcycle out of the weeds and took off without lights, catching the surveillance team by surprise and LaMoia in the midst of cutting a chained gate accessing a dark spit of land that looked directly across a small thumb of water at the navy yard. Detectives pursued in unmarked cars, but Rodriguez took the cycle off-road and disappeared.

"Eluded?" Boldt roared into the phone.

"We screwed up, Sarge."

"And then some," Boldt said.

"Didn't expect the bike."

"Don't try for sympathy from me. You lost our prime suspect."

"We still have the flatbed," LaMoia reminded, attempting to salvage something from his loss, "and the two cranes. Gaynes is still on Coughlie. He paid a visit to KSTV. He took a brief ride on a city bus. You got that, Sarge? A city bus!" He added cautiously, "This navy yard has got to be the place. It's perfect. The cranes, for Christ's sake! I'm gonna issue a Be on Lookout for Rodriguez. We'll set up out here. If we're right about this drop, Sarge, we had better be prepared for an all-out war. I'm thinking Mulwright and Special Ops."

"I've got to report it to Hill, John."

"I understand."

"Hang in there."

"Right."

As the sun crawled into a slate gray sky looking like a bug light held behind a curtain, three men pushed a step van out onto their surveillance point to avoid having to run the van's motor and risk its being overheard. LaMoia and two technicians climbed into the back of that van, dog-tired, hungry and humiliated. They took turns with twenty-minute catnaps, but nothing helped LaMoia. Failure was the worst kind of fatigue.

The barren spit of land with its rough gravel and broken glass was littered with the skeletons of commercial fishing equipment: buoys, engine parts, booms, cranks, winches and miles of coiled and damaged fishing net wound onto enormous spools. Water slapped against a sea wall of boulders, chunks of former roadway and the rusting carcasses of dead automobiles and railroad boxcars. The seawater, a murky green, moved like mercury. A light but steady breeze colored the air with a salty ocean spray.

At 6:00 A.M. that Wednesday morning, LaMoia received word over the radio that they had trouble at the gate. He slipped out the back of the van wondering when the trouble would stop. Every time he turned around there was a screwup or a problem.

The problem this time was a rent-a-cop with a company called Collier Security. He wore a gray-blue uniform with a can of pepper spray where on a cop the gun would have been. The Collier logo on the arm patch tried too hard to look like SPD's. The name badge pinned over the right pocket read Stilwill.

"Mr. Stilwill, what's the problem?" an exhausted and agitated La-Moia inquired.

"What I'm telling the officer here is that I got me a job to do, Lieutenant."

"Sergeant," LaMoia corrected.

"Cops or not, you can't be here on this property without the owners knowing about it."

"We will handle notification," LaMoia assured him. "For the time being it would be whole lot better for everyone if you just continued your rounds. Forget about us. We aren't here. That would save us all a trip downtown and a lot of lawyering."

"Yeah, but like, you can't be in here. See? It's private property. And the equipment on it is private property. You got a warrant?"

"I've got probable cause. This is an active investigation," LaMoia said dryly, his patience running thin. "You have a clear choice here, Stilwill. It's your call to make, right or wrong."

Detective Heiman crossed the road from an unmarked car and hurried over to LaMoia. Out of breath, he spoke a little too loudly for the situation. "Port Authority has six freighters scheduled for arrival over the next twenty-four hours. Three of them listing Hong Kong last port of call."

"Give me a minute here, Detective," LaMoia said, well aware the security man had overheard.

Stilwill looked out over the water and clearly took note of the cranes. "That container thing?" he asked. "You're on that container thing?"

"It's an undercover surveillance operation, Mr. Stilwill," LaMoia explained, avoiding a direct answer. "You want me to say good things about you, you'll just pick up and move on. 'Cause otherwise I'm gonna rain down shit on your parade so deep you'll drown in it."

Stilwill glanced around nervously, outnumbered.

"What you need to do," LaMoia repeated, "is move on and forget about this. Are you listening, Mr. Stilwill?"

"I hear ya," he said, his attention remaining on the view of the naval yard. "That over there has been deserted for years. Ain't never seen nothing over there. Where'd that flatbed come from anyway?"

"You need to think about our little situation here."

"What situation?" Stilwill asked, intentionally naive, offering La-Moia a shit-eating grin.

"That's better," LaMoia said, but inside he didn't trust the man.

WEDNESDAY, SEPTEMBER 2
16 DAYS MISSING

CHAPTER 61

Early Wednesday morning, *Live-7*, second in ratings to Channel Four news, led off its Morning Report quoting a "reliable source" that "police are involved in a massive surveillance operation directly linked to the illegals investigation."

The report infuriated everyone from Sheila Hill, upset over the apparent leak, to Jimmy Corwin, annoyed that KSTV had been scooped by the competition. Adam Talmadge complained vehemently through legal channels that the INS had not been informed of, nor included in, any such surveillance.

By 8:30 that morning, the trailing network affiliate identified security guard Clarence Stilwill as the source of the information. On the "advice of attorneys" Stilwill was in hiding, and unavailable for comment.

KVOW, public radio, reported not only that a possible suspect had been lost during the surveillance but that the King County medical examiner's preliminary autopsy report on the most recent Hilltop Cemetery cadaver, "Jill Doe," was due out that same day and was said to contain additional information pertaining to the illegals investigation.

Political shock waves ran through the system as denial upon denial was issued, no-comment upon no-comment echoed through the media and filtered down to coffee shops and the office copy room. Melissa Chow's disappearance and possible abduction had become an emotionally charged issue stumped by would-be politicians running for office in November, and as word spread that police were possibly closing in on the people behind it, the radio talk shows buzzed with various leaks.

Boldt and LaMoia felt this pressure on both professional and personal levels. They were told to stop the leaks and solve the case. Sheila Hill summed it up for them both, "Get us something in time for the six o'clock news that will make both the mayor and the PA look good, something to feed the beast and satiate it. If you can't come up with something, I'm going to feed them your reassignments, gentlemen, so don't take this lightly."

Their pagers sounding, Boldt and LaMoia left Hill's office and headed directly to the ME's basement offices in the Harborview Medical Clinic. The bear of a man led them with huge, hurried strides into his office and closed the doors.

"I don't know where that leak came from," he apologized, "but if I find out, that person will never work again. Not ever! Not anywhere!" Not a man to lose his temper, this particular Ronald Dixon was a rare sight.

"I thought you said it was the leaks you wanted to talk to us about," Boldt complained. Although LaMoia was scheduled to return to the naval yard surveillance, there had been no activity at the location since Rodriguez's escape. "As you can imagine, John and I are a little busy this morning, Dixie."

"No, not leaks like that . . ." Dixon corrected, losing his anger to a smile. "Leeks!" he said. "The kind you *eat*."

"Leeks," LaMoia repeated.

"Exactly," said the medical examiner.

"Exactly what?" Boldt asked.

"Jill Doe," Dixon answered. "It's always the first victim," he ruminated. "The mistakes, the haste."

"What mistakes?" Boldt answered.

Pointing to Boldt, Dixon said to LaMoia, "Take lessons from him. He's the best there is. Knows when to interrupt and what to ask. Knows when to keep his mouth shut and let a man talk." He looked at Boldt. "So let me talk." He moved to behind the security of his large gunmetal gray desk. "They froze her, same as Jane. But they had more time. They froze her hard . . . solid, and I'm guessing they forgot to take that chain off ahead of time, so that by the time they realized, if they realized, it was still attached, they had little choice but to leave it there. They then buried her over ten feet deep in relatively cool soil, a week, maybe even two or three ahead of Jane Doe. You see where I'm going with this?"

"She stayed frozen," Boldt guessed.

"Gold star. For a while. Yes. And that helped not only preserve her, but severely retard her decomposition."

"She stayed frozen down there?" LaMoia asked.

"Are you listening? No, she didn't. But she was in forty-degree soil. Her extremities thawed first, followed by the epidermis in general. The heat moved from both ends toward the center like defrosting a leg of lamb. But you know how long that takes: You put a twenty-pound turkey or a six-pound leg of lamb on a seventy-degree kitchen counter and it takes all day—sometimes longer—to defrost. Try putting it inside a forty-degree refrigerator! You pull it out the next day, the thing has barely begun to thaw. Now try it with a hundred-and-seventeen pound human being—"

"Pass," LaMoia said. "Do we learn anything from all this fascinating detail?" he quipped.

Dixon said sadly, "In other ways, you're more like him every day."

"The Cliff Notes, Dixie," Boldt said.

"Stomach contents relatively intact. Plenty of organic matter to work with."

Boldt wondered if he'd wasted his morning.

Dixon continued. "Did it occur to either of you brilliant investigators that if these people have a hundred women locked up sewing polarfleece pullovers for a dime a day, they still need some way to feed them?" He grinned widely. "Ah, ha! I can see it did not! No, you overlooked the obvious, did you not? So locked, like me, into the dead—the dead evidence, the dead witnesses, the dead ends, that you never extrapolated the situation out to the obvious: These women have to eat. And this woman, Jill Doe, did eat. Not only did she eat, but she ate a tuberous root, an edible bulb, similar to our own leek. She also apparently consumed brown rice. But it's this leek that interests you, this leek that's the best evidence you've had in this case. Asian, and not sold in your typical Safeway if the few phone calls we've made are any indication. We can't find one for comparison."

"Asian groceries," Boldt muttered, stung by this information.

LaMoia followed suit. "Mama Lu is the Asian grocery queen. What do you want to bet that she has the contract to provide the food for these people? That's how she knows so much about it and yet isn't directly involved to where she has to fear us."

"A humble businesswoman," Boldt repeated at a whisper. "She kept flaunting it right under my nose."

CHAPTER 62

"Ms. McNeal, it's Roy," a familiar but unidentifiable voice said over her cellphone. Stevie was more interested in the ice cream she had ordered from room service than the phone call.

"Roy?"

"Traffic?" the man inquired, identifying himself.

Chopper Roy they called him. Drive-time traffic reports for both the morning news and *N4@5*. Once she made the connection, the voice was all the more recognizable.

"Yes, Roy."

"Station gave me your cell number. Hope you don't mind. I thought you'd want to hear this."

"Hear what?" She sat forward on the couch and pushed the ice cream aside, her heart beginning to beat more strongly in her chest. What was the traffic guy calling about?

"Friend of mine, Sam Haber, works over to the FBO, handles Seven's SkyCam."

Channel Seven, he meant. The competition. She didn't like this already.

"Their chopper. Yeah. Sam does their maintenance. Also does their outfitting. Calls about canceling a Mariners game we had planned on account Seven has him outfitting their bird with some high-tech infrared shit that has something to do with hunting down a ship. Tonight, we're talking about. He overhears one of the guys with the gear saying they're going to scoop us on our story on account the cops have been asking all sorts of questions at Port Authority. Thought you ought to know."

"A ship," she repeated, scribbling down notes on a white linen napkin. "Our own story."

"Scooping our own story. Yeah."

"Know anything about this gear?"

"Only that it's not standard issue. Ultrasensitive infrared. Sam said some professor type from the university was the one installing it. They had to black out the hangar to even pull the lens cap and test the gear—it's that sensitive. Daylight will fry the thing. Guy blew up at Sam over opening a door because of the light. Pissed Sam off, I'll tell you what. If he hadn't, maybe Sam wouldn't have told me. Sam's kinda like that: doesn't like someone shouting at him, you know?"

"They're hunting down a container ship," she stated. "Is there any way we can mess them up on this?"

"Does the Pope shit in the woods?" the helicopter pilot replied.

"Get the bird ready."

"She's being refueled as we speak."

As Stevie was about to hang up she was trying to think of some way to lose her various guards and surveillance. "Roy," she asked, "are there any downtown buildings where you can land on the roof?"

"Can you get over to Columbia SeaFirst?"

"Give me a number where I can reach you," she said. "I'll call from there."

CHAPTER 63

LaMoia was not above circumventing existing law to get what he needed, but he did so only by working with detectives willing to forgo overtime pay and to keep silent about their actions. Chief among these was Bobbie Gaynes, so fiercely loyal to Boldt that she had no problem with the assignment to place a federal agent under round-the-clock surveillance despite the fact that any such surveillance required special notification. It was nothing new for LaMoia—coming up through the ranks his nickname had been Stretch, for how he dealt with the law. Everyone wanted what LaMoia could get for them—snitches, bank accounts, tax records—but not one of them wanted to know the details. It was okay with him; it helped perpetuate the myth, and the myth was now what defined him. The Myth. It controlled him as well, dictating his actions, and he knew that couldn't last forever. He moved through women like a drunk through booze—in part to maintain that image. He drove fast and lived that way, too. But the wax, melting from both ends, shrank ever smaller, and John LaMoia identified with it more clearly every day.

LaMoia had no physical evidence against Brian Coughlie, only a deep-rooted suspicion prompted by a number of unexplained coincidences. Without evidence, he had no case to build. But as a point of law, it was not explicitly illegal for any person to follow or watch any other person, so long as the person being watched did not feel threatened or have his or her expectation of privacy violated. Washington State did have a tough stalker law in place, but it required certain criteria to be met that Gaynes and LaMoia avoided without any effort whatsoever.

Gaynes called from a pay phone in order to avoid the open air-
waves of cellular telephones and the lurid intentions of police radio-
band scanners. LaMoia and Gaynes maintained a relationship of
respect-at-a-distance, his womanizing so legendary that she skillfully
avoided him; her investigative abilities and position in Boldt's inner
circle crucial to his squad's all-important high clearance rate. They
rarely played politics with each other and never socialized.

"Go ahead," LaMoia acknowledged, having moved into the passenger seat of the surveillance van still parked with a view of the naval
yard. Despite the media blitz earlier in the day, as far as LaMoia and
others could determine, the press had yet to cotton on to the actual
physical location of the naval yard surveillance.

"I think I lost him."

"Lost him?"

"That's what I said," she fired back angrily. "He parked it and
went into City Hall," she reported.

"City Hall?"

"That's what I said," she repeated. "It's been half an hour. I'm
thinking he burned me. Must have gone out a different door. Left his
car."

"You tell Sarge?"

"You're lead," she reminded.

LaMoia didn't feel like the lead detective. He wasn't sure he ever
would. And he didn't know if that was because of Boldt, or his own
personality. He had followed in the man's footsteps for too long to give
it up. Only that past year when Boldt had worked Intelligence had
LaMoia felt like his own man. But now, the two reunited at Crimes
Against Persons, title or not, rank or not, the Sarge ran the show and
no one was complaining, least of all LaMoia. Never heavy-handed
about it, Boldt simply had an instinct to lead, a nose for the next
avenue to pursue. The man owned an eighty-eight—a ten-year clearance rate that seemed likely to stand for all time. LaMoia was a sixty-
four, and proud of it; there were guys down in the mid-forties. Gaynes

was a seventy, though she didn't flaunt it. As the one and only woman wearing a gold badge on the fifth floor, she was smart enough not to flaunt any of her assets. She dressed to hide her body, had a tongue on her that could keep up with anyone, and could drink as much beer as the next dick. LaMoia liked her, though he hoped it didn't show. When it came to investigations he didn't always feel like the lead, but in terms of his squad, he was the sergeant, the one in charge, in command. In this regard, he was unflinching.

Thinking aloud, he said, "Half an hour in City Hall is nothing. Those drones? He could easily still be in there."

"Could be. Could also be that he took this morning's news to mean we might have him under surveillance. Could be guilt working him, making him take precautions. You want me to look around?"

"Nah, don't move. Keep an eye on his wheels. I'll be there in a few. We'll double. I'll check inside. What's your location?"

She told him.

LaMoia sneaked out of the surveillance van and was on his way back into town.

LaMoia started with Vital Statistics, thinking death certificates offered the most direct route to forge a new identity and that perhaps Coughlie was hoping to reinvent himself and get the hell out of Dodge.

The description of the man failed to register with the Asian woman behind the desk, and only then, upon hearing her thickly laced accent, did it occur to him that any one of these minimum wagers could be in cahoots with an INS agent.

He tried state property tax records next, only because it was the next door down the hall. One door to another: the workers behind the counters Asian, Hispanic, Black; not many whites. LaMoia had no problem with the melting pot, so long as everyone working City Hall spoke English, drove fifty-five, and paid their taxes same as him. He didn't support the concept of welfare and frowned at food stamps—too much corruption for anything like that to work. You took your shovel or your pen and you went to work, same as the next Joe. That was the America he wore his badge for. A trip down the halls of city government could shake a person up.

Coughlie was nowhere to be seen.

The next floor held five more doors—all the same thing. Too much paperwork, too many stamps of approval, too many hands under the table grabbing for the same cash. It depressed him.

Another flight up the polished marble stairs. Who the hell could afford marble anyway?

Permits. The idea did not jump out at him; he heard no trumpets or voices guiding him.

The door to Permits was blocked only by a rubber wedge. A matronly black woman who knitted her own sweaters and chose not to color her vaguely gray hair stood behind the long counter. She had the cheerful air of a first grade teacher or public librarian.

"Police," he introduced himself, displaying his badge. He began his description of Brian Coughlie only to be interrupted.

"The INS agent who was just here," she said.

"Yes." Coughlie had made his INS identity known to the woman. LaMoia took this as a bad sign, for it supported the man's innocence. He wanted Coughlie defined—on or off his list of suspects—he didn't want to keep guessing.

"His interest here?" LaMoia asked.

"Building permits," she said. "Must have spent a half hour going over them."

"Current? Past?"

"Current. Said that construction sites often employed illegals— illegal immigrants, you know?—for the manual labor, the 'grunt jobs,' I think he called them. Said construction permits were a great resource for the INS."

This made sense. LaMoia sank a little lower, his suspicions dashed. "Then you'd seen him before?" he inquired, thinking to ask.

"Me? Oh, no. Never once. Not ever."

"You're new to this department?"

"Aren't you the one for compliments!" she said. "Eighteen years I've worked here behind this counter."

"Other INS agents?"

"Here? Never. Not so as they identified themselves, anyway."

LaMoia considered all this carefully as he asked to be shown the same material Coughlie had viewed.

LaMoia spent twenty minutes reviewing the exact same construction permits as had Brian Coughlie but failed to connect any importance to his case. He considered every angle: location of the sites; any possible connection to Mama Lu. He found nothing.

He asked a dozen questions, including if Coughlie had focused on any particular permit, if he had asked for any specific qualification. The woman couldn't help him.

He could feel the connection staring back at him but could not see it. He decided to let it go, hoping it might make sense to him later, the way that sometimes happened.

"Where to from here?" Gaynes asked.

"I gotta get back to the surveillance," LaMoia replied from the passenger seat of her Chevy. He didn't see the point in wheels like this. No style. Nothing to offer.

He'd brought her a cup of mocha coffee, and she had seemed touched that he knew the way she took it.

"Me?" she asked.

"Try his crib. Try his office. Make up some bullshit if you have to. Try to find him. Keep me up to speed. If you strike out, when you get back to PS check with the lab. The Doc said he passed the Jill Doe evidence on to Lofgrin. Where's it at? How come we don't have it?"

"The Sarge?"

"He's doing the dance with Mama Lu. He may have something— providing we ever see him again."

"Don't joke around like that," she chastised him. "That shit bothers me."

"Who's joking?" LaMoia replied, taking one last noisy sip from the cup's plastic lid before venturing back outside.

CHAPTER 64

"We're working together, right?" McNeal asked Boldt from the other end of a cellular call.

"Far as I'm concerned." His mind was on Mama Lu—the location of that sweatshop. If the Great Lady wouldn't cooperate, then, as far as he was concerned, their one and only chance of finding Melissa, of busting the sweatshop, came down to the shipment expected that same night. Stevie McNeal, and her world of problems, was far from his thoughts.

"Together as in: Whatever I have, you have and *vice versa*."

"As in," Boldt confirmed, his attention still drifting.

"This surveillance that was reported," she said, waking him up some. "What are your chances of making this bust?"

"Until they reported it, our chances were pretty good, I think."

"And now?"

"Not so good," he answered.

"There's something going down," she stated. "A container shipment?"

His mind sprang fully awake. Where had she gotten that? "It's possible," he admitted. "We don't know exactly when, although any time around the new moon makes strategic sense for them." He added, "We thought the drop was going to be at a naval yard—that is, until things leaked this morning. That hurt us. Now, quite honestly, we're not so sure."

"Your plan?"

His mind briefly prevented him from discussing it—*do not share this with the press!* But his tongue overruled. "Had been to intercept the drop fully cloaked and to follow the shipment wherever it led. We believed that would include not only the sweatshop and those people responsible, but quite possibly Ms. Chow as well."

"And now that it has leaked?" she inquired.

"One step forward, two steps back. We're still watching our location, but I'm guessing we've been sandbagged by the leak."

"So you're tracking all arriving freighters," she stated. Reporters and cops thought the same way.

"Freighters, tankers, trawlers." He hesitated. "Any ship making port in the next thirty-six hours. Of special interest are any that made port in Hong Kong. I'll be down at Port Authority. We'll be tracking every ship closely," he confirmed, though his jaw was tight and his voice sounded foreign even to him. "Three in particular, due in later tonight, all made port in Kowloon. That matches with the *Visage*. None due in from Hong Kong scheduled for tomorrow or Friday, so we're leaning on tonight. We play the high-percentage hunches."

"So do I, and my hunch is you're about to be sandbagged again," she warned. She explained what she had found out about Channel Seven's SkyCam crew.

Boldt remained silent trying to clear his thoughts, suddenly a tangle of confusion and outright anger. The press no longer reported cases, they intervened and destroyed them.

"We haven't much time," she warned.

"I'm listening." His throat dry and scratchy, his temper flaring.

"No one—not you, not the mayor—can stop a news crew from reporting."

"Believe me, I'm aware of that," he said.

"Competition is a wonderful thing. The infrared technology has its limits: It doesn't like light. If we—my team, I'm talking about—were to aim enough light toward that infrared camera, we'd blind the equipment. We'd piss them off, sure—but we wouldn't be breaking any laws, just one news crew out to scoop the other. You see how this works?"

"You're going to sabotage a live news feed?"

The open line hissed with static. "I'm going to improve Melissa's chances," she said. "They expose this freighter, and who knows what happens? When people panic, they make poor choices."

"Agreed."

"If you're going to be at Port Authority, then that helps. I need you to provide me the exact locations of these three freighters," she suggested. "Maybe we can mislead Seven's chopper."

Boldt paused, his mind whirring.

She asked, "You've got to trust me on this."

A week earlier he might not have, but they were two pieces of the same puzzle now. Boldt said, "Let me have your number again. I'll call you from Port Authority."

CHAPTER 65

LaMoia pulled up to a red light. A dozen ways existed that he might have made the connection between Coughlie and the purpose behind the man's stop at City Hall. He might have used a detective's cunning or logic or some complex strategy born of his years of experience. Instead it was simply that red light. The Camaro idled alongside a high-rise construction site. LaMoia, ever on the lookout for a nice set of legs or a chest to fix his eyes upon, noticed a construction crane in the process of hoisting a pallet of steel beams. The light changed. He pulled to the side of the street, set his flashers to blinking and thought it through. What if they were right about Coughlie being involved? What if the man suspected the reported police surveillance was on his drop point, the naval yard? With only hours to go before the arrival of the container ships, a new container of illegals, with crane rentals being carefully watched by SPD—information to which Coughlie was privy—how would he select a backup location? The answer was now obvious to him: Look for a waterfront construction site that had a permit to operate a crane, and therefore, a crane on-site. He popped open his cellphone and dialed: They could have surveillance in place on any such sites in a matter of minutes.

CHAPTER 66

Light rain struck the traffic helicopter's plastic bubble sounding like pebbles on tin, heard even over the ferocious roar of the chopper's blades. Stevie McNeal could not get used to the empty space of the clear plastic beneath her feet. She floated high above the white chop of the water and the wickedly fast gray wisps of cloud that raced past underfoot, half nauseous, half adrenaline rush.

Boldt stood over the Port Authority radar, its circular black scope fully refreshed every seventeen seconds, returning images of any vessel with a deck taller than six feet above the waterline or carrying a radar reflector, as most pleasure craft did. Radar installations rimmed Puget Sound's coastline, all feeding data into this one facility, two miles south of downtown. There were four such scopes in all, covering every shipping lane from the Strait of Juan de Fuca to the Elliott Bay waterfront. The six men and women in this darkened room tracked the movement of commercial ships into the Port of Seattle "twenty-four, seven." Twenty-four hours a day, seven days a week.

"As they enter the system," the man with the military haircut explained to Boldt, "they identify themselves and we tag them, much the same way air-traffic control would with an aircraft. The only difference here—these ships move a lot slower," he said, trying but failing to evoke a response from the lieutenant. "But being as they're tens of thousands of tons set in motion, tens of thousands of tons that take anywhere from one to three miles to come to a complete stop, they bear our attention. Most, if not all, have contracts with tugs to be picked up and moved into port. We track where and when that is to happen to remove any possibility of collision or bottle-necking. On top of the commercial shipping lanes we have over two dozen commercial ferries on regular schedules through these waters, an impossible number of cruise ships, military craft, Coast Guard and tens of thousands of registered pleasure craft. It keeps us busy."

"The SS *Hana, Zeffer* and *Danske*," Boldt quoted, cocking his notepad to catch some of the limited light in the windowless and blackened room. "They're all in the system. The reason I'm here—"

The military cut nodded. "Yes. The SS *Hana* is reporting equipment failure and has requested to leave the lanes and hold closer to shore."

"Is that common?"

"It happens, sure."

"But it's not common," Boldt pressed.

"Listen, with you guys breathing down our necks, we take everything just a little more seriously, okay? Anything you can name, it has happened out there: fires, explosions, collisions, you name it. If an equipment failure threatens to slow down traffic or bottle us up, we're only too happy to get that ship out of traffic."

"The *Hana* stopped in Hong Kong," Boldt verified.

"All three: *Hana, Zeffer* and *Danske*, just as we reported to you." He pointed to a small blip on the screen, below which was a six-digit number. "*Hana* was the first of the three into the system. She's number six thousand, four hundred and twelve this year. She's done everything by the book, and we've got no complaints against her. Some of these captains can be real assholes, believe me. Double-hulled egos, I'm telling you. She wants out of the lane, she's got it."

"She's a container ship."

"That's correct."

"And once she's out, what then?" Boldt asked.

"To be honest? Our concern is with the lanes: keep the traffic moving. On a typical night, we'd pay little or no attention to her once she's down in speed and picked up by a tug and out of our way."

"But she's on your screen," Boldt reminded.

"Of course she's on the screen! But all I'm saying is, out of sight out of mind. You know?"

"And if she made an unscheduled stop? Would you guys spot that?"

"Why the hell would she make an unscheduled stop?" the man asked.

"I need an exact location. A GPS fix, if you've got it."

"You learn quick," the man said, clearly impressed. He grabbed a piece of paper and scribbled down a string of numbers. Like a bat, he was used to working in the dark. Boldt couldn't see a thing.

When the dim but visible lights of SS *Hana* appeared off the chopper's port side as a faint cluster of pale color in an otherwise blackened backdrop, the pilot banked the chopper left, rendering his passengers briefly weightless. "Contact," he said with confidence. Channel Seven's SkyCam, heard occasionally over the air-traffic control radio, became visible for the first time—a set of blinking lights pointed out by the pilot. He deftly brought the tail around to give him a better view and then sideslipped his craft through the rain, down and to the right, a kite lost to the wind, falling, falling, falling.

"Will they see us?" she asked into her headset. "The freighter mustn't see us! We mustn't spook them."

The KSTV technician, who had crowded the chopper's backseat with gear, reported, "I've got their feed." He passed Stevie a small color screen the size of a paperback book, a single wire running from it. On the tiny monitor Stevie saw the ship's shape as a collage of iridescent colors—a yellow-orange wake spilling away from the stern of the ship like a paper fan set afire. She couldn't look at the screen very long without added nausea.

Below her the freighter grew in size from a child's toy to something large and menacing as the rain fell harder and the collapsing ceiling of thick clouds swirled like water headed down a drain.

Fully loaded, the SS *Hana* carried twelve hundred containers the size of railroad boxcars. Stacked five high on deck, a few hundred of these were secured by chain with links as wide as a man's leg and leveraged turnbuckles that required two strong men to set or remove them. With containers rising fifty feet from its deck, the ship looked ready to capsize.

The technician warned, "They're getting ready to go live, or they wouldn't be transmitting images."

Stevie asked the pilot, "Can we get between them and the ship, and still avoid being seen?"

"Not with our lights on," he said, flipping a switch and making them dark. No strobes whatsoever.

"Is this legal?" she asked.

"Hell no."

"Could you lose your license?"

"Hell yes."

"Is it safe?"

The helicopter dove so quickly that Stevie reached out for a grip.

"Depends," the pilot answered, talking loudly into the headset.

"On what?' she asked nervously.

"On what they do," he answered, indicating the neighboring helicopter as they passed below it.

"Stand by," the technician said, "I think they're going to broadcast."

"Get between them!" Stevie instructed. She could not have Seven revealing the ship and spoiling Boldt's efforts. Melissa! she thought. "Oh my God!" she hollered. "Hurry!"

The screen in her lap showed the water as a dark green, the ship's outline boldly as black, its wake, a flaming orange roil, its onboard lights pale yellow and tiny.

She asked her technician, "What's that red blob at the stern?"

"I'm thinking engine room," he answered. "Those engines will be cooking. The bright yellow dots are probably some of the crew out on deck. Same with the darker yellow just forward of that—most likely the pilothouse."

"And this?" she asked, indicating another much larger mass of pale yellow slightly forward of midship.

"That's coming from a container," he confirmed.

"As in people inside a container?" she asked.

"Warmth," he answered. "The source? We don't know." He touched his headset. "Hang on! They've gone live. Listen up!" He threw a switch and Stevie's headphones filled with a reporter's introduction. On the screen, the ship appeared against the blackness of the water, a large rectangular shape of unexplained color. Sparkles filled the screen.

"That interference is us," the technician said proudly.

"Blind them!" Stevie ordered the pilot. The helicopter slowly turned to the right and aimed up toward the flashing strobe lights just below the layer of clouds. Both helicopters remained to the stern of the SS *Hana*, less likely to be heard or spotted by the crew.

The reporter said on-air, "Without infrared, you can barely see the stacked containers aboard this ship . . . but in a moment we'll show you what the eye cannot see! It is this reporter's contention that the heat inside a forward container represents body heat from illegal immigrants. What you will see next is an infrared image of this same ship, with yellow and red representing heat sources. It is *Live-7*'s intention over the next hour to follow this ship to port."

The video screen switched to the infrared color images.

"Now!" Stevie shouted.

The pilot brought the chopper's nose up. He tripped a bright spotlight that flooded the other helicopter white. On the screen, this appeared as a blinding bolt of fire-engine red that interrupted the view of the ship.

"Direct hit!" shouted the technician.

"You're brilliant," Stevie said. "Pun intended."

The image on the screen appeared to burn and melt from the edges until completely white.

The fraught and anxious voice of the news reporter complained like some old lady with her garden torn up by a neighbor's dog. Channel Seven had caught a few seconds of the infrared image and it reappeared on their live broadcast. The reporter delivered a voice-over narrating the events below.

Stevie asked the pilot if it was possible to contact the other helicopter by radio. He warned her it would have to be quick, threw a switch on the console and indicated for her to depress a button when she wished to speak, and to release to listen.

"Now?" she asked.

He nodded.

"Julia?" Stevie spoke, naming the Channel Seven reporter. "It's Stevie McNeal. Do you realize what you've just done? What you're *doing*? There are human lives involved here. An active police investigation! Do you understand the consequences of these images?"

"Was that you who just fried our gear? You competitive bitch!"

"You can't stay on the radio," the pilot warned as air-traffic control began to call out to the aircraft.

The reporter screamed into the radio, "We'll sue you!"

The pilot mumbled, "They'll ground me."

Stevie moved her hand away from the talk button rather reluctantly.

"Check it out!" the technician shouted, handing a set of night-vision binoculars forward to Stevie.

"I think they've made us!"

Through the binoculars, Stevie watched in the eerie green-and-black environment of night vision as the crew ran forward toward the stacked containers.

"They're working the chains!"

Below, a half dozen deckhands looked like ants as they hurried to free that top container.

The technician announced, "They're going to dump it overboard!"

The winch jammed with only forty feet of cable deployed as crewmen worked furiously to fix it. Nothing on *Hana* worked anymore; it was amazing that she even floated.

A crew of four sprang into action, carrying a fifteen-foot, twelve-inch-thick plank atop their shoulders as they climbed the adjacent stack of containers and then shoved the plank beneath the topmost container and hung their weight from it in an attempt to leverage the container up and over the side.

At the first considerable tilt of the container, the ship rocked and the loosened boxcar swiveled, cantilevered over the dark water below. One of the planks snapped and men fell forty feet to the steel deck. The ship rocked to port and the container miraculously pivoted most of the way back.

One lone figure scrambled up the stack and went at the huge door with a bolt cutter as the rain fell harder.

"He's letting 'em out!" the technician exclaimed.

"We've got to *do* something," Stevie cried helplessly.

"What's done is done," the pilot said.

Far below, the huge container doors swung open. Massive bundles of fabric sealed in plastic cascaded down to the ship's deck. Dark figures fled from that container, the first two falling forty feet to the deck below. A woman jumped into the dark water.

"Follow her!" Stevie said. "Call the Coast Guard! Goddamn it, if only they hadn't . . ." She caught herself about to chastise the press as she and her team had so often been chastised. That mirror was not one she wanted to look into. Several more illegals scurried down the walls of the containers, wild with their escape. Frightened. Terrified. The outnumbered crew was helpless to stop them.

The *Live-7* chopper dove toward the black water and hovered over the ship. Stevie and her crew remained behind, staying with the woman who had gone overboard. The radio came alive with requests for the Coast Guard. The *Hana* would never make port, would never lead the police anywhere. Not to the sweatshop, not to Melissa. The press had ruined everything.

CHAPTER 67

Reports from the covert surveillance teams established at both construction sites identified by LaMoia's visit to City Hall had already suggested that Delancy Avenue Wharf was the container delivery's backup location. For the last hour, three cars of Asian males had been observed driving the area, circling like hungry buzzards. Fifteen minutes earlier, two of those men had jumped the fence at the site and had hot-wired and fired up the crane, breaking any number of laws in the process. Boldt allowed himself the faint hope that his team still had a chance.

Boldt had been inside the Port Authority radar facility when LaMoia had called with word of the live news story and how the illegals had fled the container. Not only was the idea of following the SS *Hana* a bust, but there had been not a twitch of action at the naval yard. Despite these glaring setbacks, Delancy Avenue Wharf seemed their best bet to stay with the importers—the coyotes. One final chance for Boldt and his team.

Boldt ordered LaMoia to abandon the naval yard and to head downtown. "Get hold of someone at the INS," he instructed. "Call Talmadge at home if you have to. Tell him we're making arrests at Delancy Avenue and that we'd like someone from the INS present at the interrogations so there's no perceived conflict of interest."

"Where?"

Boldt repeated the location and said, "This isn't an invitation."

"Coughlie?" LaMoia asked.

"You can't fish without bait," Boldt said. "You don't expect Talmadge to come downtown this time of night, do you?"

"You never know," LaMoia said.

"And if Coughlie shows up, stay glued to him, John."

As he drove the Chevy toward Delancy Avenue, Boldt remained in radio contact with detectives Heiman and Brown. Sometime in his years of service he had come to visualize the radio traffic—he actually saw the operation in his mind's eye as officers spoke back and forth.

Heiman was watching the construction site crane. Brown was a loose tail on one of the three suspect vehicles. When Brown reported his mark had just executed a U-turn, Boldt understood intuitively that these guys had been tipped to the live news report. With his car five blocks and closing to Delancy Avenue, Boldt issued the order to arrest while driving at breakneck speeds to join them as backup. The two guys who had hot-wired the crane topped his list of desirable arrests and he made this clear to Heiman. These two had trespassed and compromised machinery. A laundry list of possible criminal charges filled Boldt's head with delight. Cop work: There was nothing quite like it.

He wanted those two in an interrogation room. Despite the fact that Asian gang members were notorious for refusing to talk, if they were faced with the threat of multiple murder charges that carried the death penalty, Boldt believed tongues might wag.

The radio traffic won back Boldt's attention. As Brown's mark sped back toward Delancy Avenue, Heiman reported the two crane operators abandoning the machinery and heading for the fence. At the same time, a radio car recruited as further backup reported itself engaged in a high-speed chase and in need of assistance. The gang members had been smart enough to disperse in different directions, weakening the police. A block from Delancy Avenue Wharf, as Boldt rounded the last corner, a dark figure blurred through his headlights, and he reacted instinctively by slamming on the brakes and yanking the key from the ignition. Out of the corner of his eye he saw Heiman on foot heading the opposite direction. He heard the slowing siren of the remaining patrol car, and the distinctive pop of gunfire. He hated that sound.

Boldt jumped out of the Chevy and took off after that blur. The kid ran fast, turning down an alley into which Boldt followed. Behind him, a patrol car had pinned one of the vehicles, its officers engaged in a firefight. The adrenaline rush warped his sense of time. His gun was out, carried in his right hand. That blur up ahead, just rounding another corner, was all that mattered. Sirens wailed in the distance as additional backup made its way into the area. Boldt didn't have legs, or lungs, only adrenaline-induced purpose. He shouted a warning. It echoed off the brick and asphalt.

The kid rounded another corner. Boldt heard his own shoes slap the wet asphalt. More claps of gunfire from far behind him. He rounded that same corner and came to an immediate stop. A dead end. Brick on both sides. Concrete wall of a building at the far end. A Dumpster and some junked furniture to his left. A pile of black trash bags and debris to his right. The alley was perhaps twenty yards long. The wrought iron fire escape was empty. Sirens still approaching.

Boldt understood he was going to have to do this alone. He thought of Miles and Sarah and how much time he owed them, how many years they all had yet to go. He thought of how much he and Liz had been through together, how far they'd come. He moved quickly to his left until his shoulder brushed the cool brick wall, his right hand ready with his weapon. He smelled urine and stale beer and garbage and oil. He heard the firefight in the distance like a neighbor's TV through the wall.

"Police!" he announced sharply, very much aware that calling out made him a target, standing at the open end of the alley as he was.

The air was suddenly incredibly still. The distant sirens formed an uneasy curtain behind him. All else was silence and the beating of his own heart. Sweat prickled his scalp; his mouth was dry. He'd spent his life in this city; he had no intention of dying here. He saw the open graves at Hilltop. They seemed to call to him. All the petty politics suddenly seemed just that. This was the real police work. This was The Moment, and nothing else, the steady ticking off of seconds, each worth a lifetime. It was raw, visceral terror.

"We've got two options," Boldt announced, not wanting anything to do with a firefight. "One is you stand up with your arms high and walk out of here. The other is you come out feet first in a body bag. There's nothing in between. You hear those sirens? You think a couple hotheaded young uniforms just dying to try out their weapons are going to improve your situation any? Listen to me! I'm the best chance you'll ever have of walking out of here alive."

Silence. Had it been a few grunts, a few complaints, there would have been a dialogue started.

He took a series of deep breaths. He was guessing behind the Dumpster or hidden in the pile of bags and debris to his right.

He crept forward, eyes shifting: Dumpster, debris, Dumpster, debris. Every darkened shadow filled with an imaginary shape. He wanted none of this. He wanted to turn and walk away. The kid could be anywhere, most likely in the one place Boldt had not yet considered. He wanted to talk the kid out. He feared it wasn't going to happen.

His hand sweated against the gun's knurled stock. The sound of blood pumping clouded his ears. It was too damn dark in this alley.

He reached the Dumpster and wedged himself into the corner against the wall. He was in a full sweat. He hadn't heard the kid jump into the Dumpster but couldn't discount the possibility.

He glanced toward the mouth of the alley, ten yards behind him— thirty feet, most of it unprotected.

"Do you have any brothers?" he called out. "Sisters? A mother? Anyone who matters to you?"

That same sickening silence.

"You don't show yourself, make yourself known to me, I'm likely to shoot you. You understand that? I don't want to do that, but I will. You're not coming out of there. You're not getting past me."

"Bullshit."

Fast footsteps. A dark blur from the pile of trash bags. He ran low and incredibly fast.

Boldt had only one chance to intercept that blur. He lowered his shoulder, judged the distance and charged behind a loud scream meant to distract the kid. They made contact on the far side of the alley, Boldt just getting a small piece of the kid. They both spun like pinwheels and crashed down several feet apart. The kid came to his knees. Boldt lunged toward him and swatted. The kid went down a second time. Boldt scrambled forward, catching a gray glint of a metal blade. He fired a warning shot as he rolled out of the way and the blade came down where his chest had been. Boldt kicked out. The kid fell back. The slash of a flashlight beam painted the opposite brick wall. Backup was close.

The kid stood quickly and cocked his arm back, intending to throw the knife. Boldt fired once and missed. Fired again. Missed. That blade tumbled through the air end-over-end and clattered into the brick somewhere in the narrow space between Boldt's shoulder and head. The kid ran five paces, saw those flashlight beams paint him with their light and threw himself prostrate into the alley's urine-soaked litter, hands and legs outstretched.

"You're under arrest," Boldt called out, making himself known to his own people.

"I not do nothing," the kid called out.

Boldt checked his right ear to make sure it was still attached to his head as he reached for the handcuffs. This collar was his, no one else's.

CHAPTER 68

Whoever had designed the ventilation system for the interrogation rooms had either flunked engineering or had it in for detectives and suspects. The Box, as the largest of the rooms was referred to, smelled vaguely of tobacco smoke and strongly of the acrid, bitter body odor that accompanied panic and a person's last vestiges of freedom. The room was small nonetheless, impressively bland, and home to a cigarette-scarred table bolted to the floor and, on that night, three black formed-fiberglass chairs, one occupied by the shackled suspect, the other two by Daphne Matthews and Boldt.

Boldt understood the time pressures. With police closing in, with the SS *Hana* in custody of the Coast Guard and under investigation by the INS, with gang members in lockup, the sweatshop would be shut down as soon as physically possible. Boldt had a call into Mama Lu; LaMoia had detectives attempting to make contact with the Asian food distribution warehouse owned by one of the Great Lady's companies. But ultimately it came down to a bird in the hand: His best chance to locate the sweatshop remained with this one interrogation.

LaMoia had contacted Talmadge at home as ordered by Boldt. To everyone's surprise and disappointment, it was Talmadge himself, not Coughlie, who had come down to Public Safety to view the interrogation. Talmadge looked pale and visibly shaken, though he said nothing to explain his condition. LaMoia stood with the man on the other side of the one-way glass watching Boldt and Matthews work their magic. But LaMoia wasn't watching the interrogation; his eyes were on the shaky Adam Talmadge.

For Boldt and Matthews, teaming up on a suspect was like two singers joining in on a duet. They had done this enough times to communicate with only body language and voice inflection. As a psychologist, Matthews tended to humanize the event while Boldt used the existence of physical evidence to maintain pressure.

"You're in some kind of trouble," Boldt said to the kid.

He was a Chinese youth in his late teens, early twenties, with a neck like a water buffalo and pinprick eyes. His teeth were bad and he'd been in too many fights: Angry scars beaded from the edge of his lips, the turn of his nose and the slant of his eyes. He attempted a game face but the shine on his upper lip and the tinge of scarlet below his ears gave away his anxiety.

Daphne said, "You're alone in this room, and you'll be alone in a jail cell, but we know you're not alone in this."

"I no do nothing, bitch."

Boldt shifted in his chair as if to smack the guy, a fine performance. Daphne reached out and blocked him. Good cop, bad cop— "sweet and sour," as they called it. Boldt ran off a list of offenses including assault and attempted murder of a police officer, the last of which set the suspect to a vigorous blinking, a kind of tic that continued to manifest itself well into the interrogation.

Boldt said, "Your priors occupy two and a half pages. Your name appears on a roster compiled by our Gang Squad. You are in violation of your parole. Any judge gets one look at these charges and you're gone for good."

"So let's just see about that," the kid said. "You got the sheet, Butch," he said to Boldt. "How much hard time I done?" He grinned, "Butch and Bitch. What a pair you are!"

"You think you can duck this? You think anyone gives a rat's ass about stepping in and standing up for you?" Boldt said.

The kid smirked.

Boldt dropped the bomb early so that Daphne could get to work on him. "We're turning you over to the feds, my friend: transportation of illegals, three counts of murder—depraved indifference to life; two counts of rape; numerous RICO racketeering charges. This isn't staying in state courts."

The kid's face gave away his surprise. Perhaps Coughlie, or someone like him, had shielded the gang from prosecution in the past. With some money spread around to big-name attorneys or even under the table to the local judges, they ducked the heavy sentences and the hard time. That wasn't going to happen this time; Boldt had taken great pains to ensure SPD kept this one for themselves.

"After the federal trial, after you've been sentenced to who knows how many consecutive life terms," Boldt continued, "then you'll be remanded to state custody and tried well away from King County on the assault and attempted murder of a police officer."

Daphne cut in like a limber dancer tapping Boldt on the shoulder. "The latter of which carries the death penalty."

"Lethal injection," Boldt said, "although there's a lot of talk about bringing back hanging."

The kid's shiny black eyes tracked between them like a spectator at a tennis match. "No way you do this."

"Yes, way," Boldt replied. "You see that mirror? There's a federal agent on the other side of it. Federal prosecutors are on their way over. This is political, you see? Nothing worse to get screwed up in than a political case. I'm telling you—nothing worse. Everybody's got to look good, and the only way that happens is if someone pays the big price, and right now that someone is you, Mr. Tan."

"What we're offering," Daphne interrupted, "is to work with you on this. You didn't attack the lieutenant in that alley, you ran. That's in your favor here."

"I ran!" the kid pointed out to Boldt, who remained impassive.

Daphne said, "You did produce a knife and you did throw that knife, but maybe you were off balance to begin with, maybe that knife just kind of fell out of your hand on the way down. You see where I'm going?"

He didn't see much. While Mr. Tan listened to Daphne he concentrated on Boldt, well aware of where the trouble was coming from. "I dropped the knife," he spurted out, a well-trained mynah bird. "Off balance."

She said, "Which may indeed explain a lot and, it's conceivable, might help you present a defense, but it won't touch the federal charges, and that's really where your problems lie. You and Mr. Wong are our only two suspects at the moment. One of you was the leader, one the follower. Once we determine where that responsibility lies, then the breaking-and-entering, the trespassing charges will be filed along with the rest, all of which unfortunately suggest you intended to smuggle illegals into this country."

"We just playing around with a crane, man!" he pleaded to Boldt.

Boldt manipulated the truth, as was permitted him by the courts. Police had this one shot at a suspect who waived his right to an attorney—the interrogation. After that it was lawyers, courts and plea bargains. Both Tan and Wong had seen the court-appointed attorney side of the justice system enough times to believe they stood a better chance controlling their own destiny with the cops. Boldt advised him, "We seized the ship out in the bay. The captain gave up the Delancy Avenue marina. That's a gun aimed at your head, pal. You or Mr. Wong. We're not sure who."

"It's him, man. It's him!"

"What's him?" Daphne said.

Those untrusting eyes tried again, searching the two for whom to try. "The container," he said. "I'm the crane operator, but that's all! I'm telling you, I don't know shit about what's inside."

Boldt felt a wave of relief at the man's mention of the container. It connected a purpose to the operation of the crane. He needed the sweatshop's location; he needed Coughlie's involvement, but just the mention of that word opened doors previously shut.

"What we need is cooperation," Daphne said. "We need the particulars, Mr. Tan. If you're just the crane operator, if you're just a hired hand, then it's Mr. Wong we need to talk to. Unfortunately, if you can't help us out, you won't be buying yourself much of a break. Does that make sense to you?"

"No, it don't!"

"The way it works, the one with the most information for us gets the most breaks."

Boldt said, "We need to know where that container was headed once it landed."

"And we need to know who's been protecting you," she said. Answering his expression she continued, "Oh, yes, we know all about it."

"We have someone here with us tonight who is very interested in that—a federal agent."

"Well, bring him on," the suspect said. "Let's talk turkey." He leaned back and kicked his feet up onto the table in a bold and arrogant gesture. Boldt was about to reprimand him for the act when he noticed the bottom of the man's boots.

Clinging to the rubber between heel and worn-down sole was a small but unmistakable clot of fish scales.

CHAPTER 69

S tevie McNeal's final chance to find Melissa literally spilled out of her purse as she wrestled for her cellphone in the helicopter's tight confines and a city bus map fell out onto the clear plastic floor beneath her feet.

"Wait a minute!" she'd instructed the pilot, retrieving the map. "Can you fly this route for me?"

"We're low on fuel."

"As much as we have time for then," she said. "This area in particular." She pointed out the area where Coughlie had climbed aboard, distracting her. "We're looking for old canneries along here."

"Salmon Bay? Once upon a time. Mostly restaurants and boat-houses now."

"Let's take a look."

The helicopter veered north.

Turning to the technician, Stevie asked, "These binoculars? They can see heat?"

"You bet."

"Body heat?"

"That's the idea," he answered.

"Through a wall?"

"No way."

"A window?"

"A warm room would mean warm glass, which would produce some degree of green instead of black—so, sure. But it depends."

"But people crowded into a room," she suggested, "big machinery, people sweating."

The kid answered, "We'd get some kind of read on that I suppose.

Listen, I'd rather have that camera that Seven has, but we may have toasted that thing. All we can do is try."

At the edge of Lake Union they slowed, passing Fremont Bridge and moving west along the ship canal and into Salmon Bay. Hundreds, if not thousands, of boats of every kind crowded marinas along this stretch. Some of the boats glowed faintly green through the binoculars, holding out hope for Stevie. She trained the lenses onto the roofs and darkened windows of the buildings that lined the south shore of the waterway. The technician used another set of binoculars to view the north shore.

As they passed over a cluster of brick buildings in bad shape, Stevie asked the pilot to make a loop. She was studying those buildings as the kid said from the back, "Here's something interesting, but it isn't a warehouse." He directed her, "Up about a quarter mile. Your side. Check out the water next to that ship!"

Dozens of dark shapes. Perhaps forty or fifty boats all tied together haphazardly, side-to-side, bow to stern, unlike any of the marinas they had flown over. She spotted it then—clear out in the group—a glow of electronic green in the water, the binoculars picking up warmth.

The helicopter hovered.

"That's a lot of heat from below deck," the kid said.

"Where are we? What *is* that?" Stevie asked, pointing out the enormous cluster of shops and boats all tied together.

The pilot informed her, "They're the ones confiscated in drug busts and shit like that. The feds auction them off a couple times a year. A lot of 'em never sell. They end up rusting out there. Half of 'em are sinking."

"Confiscated?" Stevie asked, her skin tingling. "As in the feds? INS?"

The pilot said, "DEA, INS, FBI. Those boats are never going anywhere. They call it the graveyard."

Stevie shouted so loudly that both men grabbed for their headphones. "Get me down! Get me back to the station right now!"

CHAPTER 70

"I gotta tell ya," LaMoia said to Boldt as both men hurried down the fire stairs at Public Safety two at a time, "I'm a little pissed at Lofgrin for taking so long with that chain. Seems to me he coulda had something for us this afternoon."

"The chain takes a backseat to these fish scales," a winded Boldt said, carrying the evidence bag containing the gang kid's shoe in his left hand, while guiding himself with the banister in his right. LaMoia was suddenly leaping three stairs at a time. Youth! "Bernie's a perfectionist. He isn't going to speculate. It's not in his nature. If he's taking more time with the chain, then maybe that's in our favor. Maybe he's got something."

"Wouldn't count on it."

In a perfect choreography, LaMoia beat Boldt to the landing and held the door open. Boldt ran through without missing a step.

"Gentlemen!" Bernie Lofgrin said, looking up from the middle of his two-million-dollar playground. Two assistants worked at a bench nearby. Lofgrin's thick glasses leant him the nickname Magoo. He looked extraterrestrial with those eyes and the white lab jacket.

Boldt passed him the evidence bag. "Need to know if we're talking the same fish scales, Bernie. We've got a live one up in the Box."

"A match," LaMoia advised, "would put him with Jill and Jane Doe."

"I get the idea, Sergeant," Lofgrin replied. Detectives tried to influence the lab's findings by guiding and indicating where they wanted the evidence to lead. Lofgrin rarely played that game, though detectives never stopped trying.

They gave him the room to work and they kept their mouths shut, with Boldt twice reaching out to stop LaMoia from making any comment. Lofgrin always took his sweet time about it. To rush him was to get him talking; to get him talking was to suffer exasperatingly long explanations on a variety of subjects.

He prepared two fish scales onto a glass slide—one from the earlier evidence, and one from the shoe just delivered. He began speaking before the slide was fully inserted into the microscope. "Was just about to return your call, Sergeant," he said to LaMoia, though his attention remained on his equipment. "The reason we took so long on that chain that Dixie sent over was that we lifted a substance from a full third of the links. Ran a gas chromatograph on it—petroleum base—but couldn't establish a product identification for you. Knew you'd want it."

"Oil?" LaMoia asked.

"It has the viscosity of old oil, to be sure. Nothing automotive. The graph was a mess of chemicals. Couldn't get a clean enough sample for a good read. Because of its age maybe. We must have tried a dozen times or more, which accounted for the extra man-hours." He leaned his head into the microscope and made adjustments on the focus. "Bingo!" he said, stepping aside. "Have a look."

LaMoia moved to the microscope. He worked the focus. Nobody's eyes focused the same as Lofgrin's. "That's a match!" he said excitedly. The fish scales tied their suspect to the Hilltop homicides.

"I concur," Lofgrin said.

"The oil," Boldt encouraged. He knew the man well enough to know the importance of this evidence—Bernie Lofgrin always dragged out the really good stuff.

Lofgrin smiled at his old friend, letting Boldt know he was on the right track. "Grease, actually. Extremely heavy grease, used in winches, lifts. The substance that threw us off was nothing more than sea salt. Contaminated the hell out of our graphs."

"Sea salt," Boldt repeated. "Grease . . ." he mumbled. "And the only place we can confirm the use of those chains was in the sweat-shop."

"Ergo," Lofgrin said in his usual contemptuous tone, "that sweat-shop isn't in any cannery. It's on some ship."

"A trawler!" Boldt exclaimed.

"An old trawler," Lofgrin added. "If we're going to explain these fish scales, it had to be in operation over twenty-five years ago."

Boldt turned quickly on his heels and faced LaMoia. "Call in for backup. Two cars. Four uniforms. Have 'em waiting for us in the garage."

"Where we going?" LaMoia asked, the two men already on their way out of the lab.

"You're welcome!" shouted an annoyed Lofgrin. He lived for com-pliments.

Out in the hallway, at a full run, Boldt informed his sergeant, "We're going to do the one thing we should have done a long time ago: We're going to bluff."

CHAPTER 71

As Stevie agonized in bumper-to-bumper traffic caused by a series of weather-related accidents she left a long voice mail for Boldt, having no idea if he would ever get it. "I think I've found the 'graveyard' Melissa mentioned on the videos. It's complicated. We need to talk. Leave a way on my voice mail for me to reach you. If I don't hear from you, you'll hear from me. I'm going to get you the evidence you need." She hung up.

Back at the KSTV studios, she collected a camcorder—lightweight and easy to use. She was on her way back down the hall when the night watchman caught her with a shout.

"Ms. McNeal!"

She stopped and turned, impatient to her core.

"Damn glad to see you! Security people be looking everywhere for you! Police and feds been calling every fifteen minutes! They lost track of you. You had better stay put 'til I can hook you up with them again. They're all pissed off."

"Sure thing," Stevie said. "You make the call."

The man waved and turned into an office.

Stevie took off at a run.

With absolute certainty that she had found the sweatshop, it all began to add up for her: the darkness of Melissa's video, that echoing, reverberating sound. A ship!

The drive to Salmon Bay took less than ten minutes but occupied a lifetime. She accepted the danger she knew she faced as penance for involving Melissa in the first place. It seemed only right that she

341

should have to relive Melissa's hell in order to get Boldt the evidence he needed. No flashes of her life passing by, no nostalgia. She had a job to do. She was in her element.

She parked in the back lot of a marine supply store a hundred yards east of the impound area and went off on foot, staying away from the water's edge and electing to thread her way through two rows of boat storage that housed skiffs and rowboats and sailboats stacked five high on steel shelving and covered by a tin roof. The property included two warehouses—one for dry storage, the other a repair workshop, its northern boundary fenced off from the government impound by a rusted ten-foot chain-link fence that bore ancient NO TRESPASSING signs. Stevie moved carefully, shadow to shadow, alert for night watchmen or sentries, alert for any sign of activity that might confirm the existence of the sweatshop. At last she came to the end of the storage and tucked herself beneath the hull of a ski boat from where she had a view of the impound facility: dozens of rusting boats and ships, all tied one to the other in an unplanned confusion. Algae-green lines drooped and sagged toward the water like awkward smiles. A graveyard indeed. The ships were old ruins of rust and corrosion—fishing trawlers, small freighters, power cruisers, sailboats, tugs—all put into illegal service at some point: drug running, guns, human beings—a harsh and mechanical landscape overcome by decay and neglect.

She saw no hint of life, no evidence of the sweatshop to film. A wooden gangway lay on the asphalt next to a barge, the only indication of a way up to the flotilla, but it would require at least a couple men to move it into place. The assortment of boats and ships was secured to pylons where seagulls slept with their heads tucked into their wings. *See no evil* . . . she thought. Past these, any semblance of order was lost, the boats tied together at random one to the other in a patchwork of fiberglass and metal and inflatable bumpers, most crippled and listing.

However improbable, however unlikely, there was a sweatshop hiding among the carnage. Brian Coughlie had chosen well—the last place on earth one would expect the sweatshop, and a place under his professional control. The sweatshop. Melissa!

Reenvisioning what she had seen from the helicopter, she tried to locate the vessel rimmed in the electronic lime green of the binoculars. Somewhere in the middle of the pack she decided, resigned to getting out there. But in fact the aerial view did not translate well to a five-foot-seven-inch woman standing thirty yards away from the flotilla's perimeter, the first obstacle to which was a chain-link fence. In junior high maybe, when gymnastics had been a regular part of each afternoon, but suddenly the ten-foot-high rusted wire fence looked insurmountable.

Crouched beneath that ski boat, she heard a steady electrical hum. This hum meant electricity—electricity, power lines. The story slowly pieced together, her eyes found and followed a thick black cable that ran down a power pole at the farthest corner of the compound. The cable had been stuffed into the overgrowth to hide it, but it finally broke out of the bushes where it was tied to one of the massive rope lines that held the ships to the pilings, wrapped around the line like a fat snake. Stevie was no stranger to power cables, but as thick as her wrist, this one was clearly no simple ship-to-shore extension cord. This was some kind of major power supply—thousands of volts, like the one that fed KSTV's control room.

Big enough for a sweatshop, she thought. Big enough to follow.

The camcorder strapped to her, she considered her choices: The barge was the lowest of all the waterfront boats, clearly the more easily scaled, but it also offered the most exposure. The tanker to the left, on the other hand, although harder to scale, offered good cover, and the loading net that hung from its side appeared scalable, if not precarious.

She ran to the chain-link fence, exposed and vulnerable, the camcorder hanging at her back. Crossing that fence offered a finality for her. Once on the other side she was fully committed. But there was no moment of pause. Her fingers webbed tightly through the rusting wire and she pulled herself up, higher with each grasp. The fence wobbled and threatened to throw her off. She reached the top edge, a row of twisted wire spikes. Twice she tried to throw her right leg up and over. On her second attempt, the cellphone spilled from her coat pocket and clapped loudly down onto the asphalt. Mistaking it for a gunshot, she vaulted the fence effortlessly, clawing her way down the other side and jumping the final four feet. The camera slapped her back as she landed. She froze, her knees throbbing, ears ringing. Her cellphone lay broken in pieces on the other side. So much for the cavalry. But there was no turning back.

She hurried across the open wharf and into shadows thrown by the docked ships. Lightheaded, almost giddy, she felt like a teenager sneaking out of the house.

A wharf rat the size of a house cat skittered along the very edge where she stood, heading directly for her. She didn't scream, but her body locked, seized by fright, and she couldn't so much as take a step. The rodent saw Stevie and slithered out of sight, but the experience stung her. Su-Su would have said the rat was good luck, guiding her. That the rat had come to her as a teacher, not a threat. It was this flicker of remembrance of her former governess that supported Stevie's decision to do this, reminded her of her father's efforts to smuggle Melissa out of China alive. And it was there, standing on that deserted wharf, that for the first time Stevie confronted the small glances and occasional touches exchanged between Su-Su and her father. There, as an adult, she suddenly reinterpreted those glimpses of intimate contact. Realization charged through her: Father had been in China nearly a year before summoning Stevie from the school in Switzerland. The dread of truth crept into her. Those looks between Su-Su and her father. The occasional tears. The reality of the nickname Su-Su had given Mi Chow, the risks Father had taken to get Mi Chow to America. The legal adoption. Melissa was no political prisoner born to parents killed during the Cultural Revolution: all fiction for a necessary illusion. Melissa was, in fact, just as Su-Su called her from the very beginning: Little Sister.

True or not, at that moment Stevie accepted it, embraced it, the depth of her feelings for the girl making so much more sense. No matter what, she believed—a necessity perhaps born of the moment. No matter. Suddenly, there was no courage, no fear, no question about any of it. She felt bulletproof. Righteous.

The power cable climbed up the line toward the ship's bow. She climbed the net on the tanker's side, pulling herself higher and higher above the wharf, finally reaching the upper deck and the lip of slimy steel. She peered over this edge thinking there was no landscape as eerie as something man-made left abandoned. The lines creaked and sighed. Water slapped lazily all around her. The electric hum grew perceptibly louder.

She pulled herself under the rail and down onto the cold damp deck, and crawled into the shadow. She crouched and hurried toward the bow past ladders and winches, railing and line, the air thick with rust and algae. She reached the power cable and followed it to starboard, to where it spilled over the side and down to an abandoned river ferry listing badly to port, its stern also low in the water. The ferry's deck was a good fifteen to twenty feet below her, the heavy cable passing across it and on to the next ship. Elevated on the tanker, she took a moment to look around at the graveyard. Deck, rail, stacks and bridges.

Gray decaying steel. Rust the color of dried blood. To her right she saw a steady path of gangways, ladders and planks leading one deck to the next out to the center of the graveyard and a large fishing trawler where it stopped.

Below and to her left the black cable ran straight for that trawler, looking like a piece of thread dropped from the sky.

She could see Melissa here—could recall the videos. Excitement stole through her. Little Sister!

In the distance she heard the air brakes of a bus or truck. There was no mistaking that sound.

She crossed back around to the other side of the tanker in time to see a figure scramble down a steep path through the vegetation to the only gate in the chain-link fence. A big man. A man wearing a sweatshirt and a hood. Stevie ducked out of sight.

CHAPTER 72

Mama Lu looked like a prizefighter, dressed as she was in a pow-der blue silk robe embroidered in yellow and orange with scenes of peasants tilling the rice paddies. Her rich black hair was hoisted into a bun and secured with what looked to Boldt like an orphaned enameled chopstick, and her false teeth shined with the brilliance of having been recently dipped and cleaned. There were acres of cloth in that robe and years of wisdom in those agate eyes, and she could tell both from Boldt's solemn expression and his timing that they had problems.

"Come sit down. My legs tired."

The apartment above the small grocery was three or four times the size that Boldt had originally believed. The first room where she chose to receive guests and take her meals was simple and spare for the benefit of appearances; but as she led Boldt into the inner sanctum of room after room of stunning Asian antiques and artwork, of jade and scrolls and intricately carved ivory, he grabbed a glimpse of the real woman with whom he came to cut a deal.

"You are bothered, Mr. Both," she observed. "Please to sit."

He took a velvet-padded captain's chair with mahogany arms of lion's paws. She seemed to occupy the entire love seat where she sat. It fit her like a throne. "You like tea, don't you?" She rang a small glass bell summoning a young woman of twenty dressed in a simple black silk dress and rubber slaps. "Tea," she instructed. "He takes half-and-half and sugar in his," she said, surprising him.

"Is there anything you don't know?" he asked.

"We shall see," she said, allowing a smile.

He nodded. She had such an uncanny way of coming directly to the point without ever seeming direct at all.

"I know about the helicopter," she informed him. "And yes, even the arrests on Delancy Avenue. I know that you do not visit an old woman late at night looking the way you do without much on your mind. So what is it, Mr. Both?"

"It's bad," he said.

She bowed her formidable head slightly. "Whatever is, is," she said unexpectedly. "It is neither bad nor good. It exists for the reasons it exists. To qualify it is to contain it, to limit its undermining potential. Let us not judge too quickly, Mr. Both."

Boldt bit back his temptation to speak too quickly.

She sighed. "Are you here to arrest me?"

"I hope not," he conceded.

"The patrol cars," she said, explaining how she guessed this. "The press?"

"On its way."

"Most impolite."

The tea was delivered silently and artfully, a graceful dance of arms and hands and gold-rimmed cups of bone china. The young woman was beautiful and smelled of lilac. When she left the room her dress whispered them quiet again. Boldt sipped softly and drank a tea as rich as any he had tasted, hoping she might say something. He finally said, "I can connect your import company to the polarfleece recovered in that first container. If I have to, I'll use it."

"A Customs violation. A federal charge. This is not your business, Mr. Both."

He said nothing.

"What do you need?" She added, "What do you come for?"

"The grocery deliveries."

"I am not only person with groceries, Mr. Both."

"I know what I know, Great Lady, but I'm powerless to do much of anything with it. Our system is weak. It's flawed. It's corrupt. But it's all I have. It's my only tool." He added, "It's a ship." She twitched. "We *know* this. *You* know this. I need the location—now, tonight. Right now! I'll arrest you, embarrass you, if I'm forced to. I'm out of bullets."

She smiled, shocking him. "My problem is your problem," she said. "If I am the source of this information, if that should ever come out, I will make an early grave. That does not interest me."

"I can get Coughlie," he said, "but it has to be tonight. It has to be now before he can move his operations."

"You know much," she said.

"And if you don't tell me?" he asked, feeling her resistance to actually speak the information he needed. "If I figure it out myself?"

"Self-knowledge only true knowledge." She smiled again. Those teeth were perfect.

"A ship," he said. "A trawler. An old trawler."

"What does police do with cars belonging drug runners?"

"Forfeited assets," Boldt said, trying to follow. "We impound them. The court collects any property . . ." He caught himself.

Her eyes sparkled.

"Forfeited assets are auctioned off," he said.

"Not if no one wants to buy," she corrected.

"My God!" he gasped.

Another wide grin.

Boldt was dialing dispatch before he even reached the stairs.

CHAPTER 73

R odriguez waited on the wharf while Stevie watched through the camcorder's telephoto lens as two men hurried along the improvised path of ladders and wooden ramps connecting the various boats. Finally reaching the barge, these two secured a gangway for Rodriguez to use, and the three of them then hurried toward the trawler, their urgency and tension evident from the shouting. They were too far away and it was too dark for her to record their faces or anything they said, but she recorded them anyway.

Their route was unexpectedly long and involved, the path between the ships anything but a straight line. One finger on the camera's trigger, another pressed tightly to block the red light that showed while recording, she followed the three to the trawler where they disappeared around its far side.

She zipped the camera away in its case and worked herself down an accommodation ladder that led off the tanker's starboard side to the heavily listing ferry below. Reaching the deck, she faced a gap of six to eight feet to the next boat. With the stern submerged, she saw no other way off.

This next boat carried one of the planks, a stepping-stone in the improvised path forged between the shore and the trawler. That next deck would put her on the route to the sweatshop. She saw no choice but to jump.

A few feet into flight, a fraction of a second into the air, she knew she wasn't going to make it. She slammed into the adjacent hull, reached out and grabbed hold of a stanchion. Her face took the brunt of the miss, her left eye banged up and swelling. The black water below invited her to fall. She managed to pull her other arm up, swung herself like a pendulum, and hooked her heel on the edge of the deck. She pulled herself aboard, the camera following. Splayed out on the deck, struggling to find her breath, she took a moment to recover, testing the tender flesh around her eye.

She hurried to the stern and onto the man-made path. Three vessels later she descended a ladder to an old rusted cabin cruiser. She stopped. She wasn't alone.

She smelled the cigarette smoke too late, realizing all of a sudden that this funky old cabin cruiser was being used as a gatehouse along the route.

"Yo!" a man's voice called out.

She had literally rocked the boat when stepping down onto it, and the sentry called out accordingly. In a catlike motion, she leapt from the deck up over the wheelhouse as the sentry made a lazy effort to identify his visitor. She backed up, facing the stern but completely exposed, as first the sentry's head and then his incredibly wide shoulders appeared in the cabin hatch not five feet away from her. To move—even to breathe—would give her away. She stood absolutely still, her lungs filled to capacity, her breath held and burning in her chest. The black-haired head pivoted left to right and left again. Another inch or two and he'd pick her up in his peripheral vision.

"Yo?" he called out a second time, though more softly. "Kai? Timmy?" No answer.

She prepared to kick him in the face if he glanced back, cocking her right leg back in preparation. He'd never know what hit him.

Again, he looked to his left. Then he climbed back down the steep stairs and into the cabin.

She listened intently, not daring to move. A minute passed. Two. She felt the boat move and feared his coming topside again. But instead she heard him urinating. She crept slowly and quietly to the steep ladder leading off the boat's far side and climbed, her skin prickling. She moved much more slowly, boat to boat, carefully assessing her situation. Planks and gangways, ladders and crudely fashioned steps. The shore grew increasingly distant. She encountered a set of six garden hoses taped together, water gurgling inside. That mechanical hum grew ever louder. A snoring beast. She marveled at Melissa's resourcefulness. The woman had the footage to prove she had made it inside. No small feat.

The scavenged trawler loomed in front of her now, huge by comparison with the other boats around it, rising up out of the wreckage of ship decks, cabins and stacks—a rusting mass of iron and steel out of proportion with its neighbors, its joints frozen with rust and corrosion, consumed by decades of salt and storm, sun and wind. A skeleton of its former self. Huge sections missing, scavenged for resale or sold off as scrap, its profile a twisted torment of bent metal and ragged cuts.

She crossed the decks of the remaining two ships, staying low and in shadow, her full attention on that towering trawler. The hum developed different tones, no longer so indistinguishable, but split into a high whine, a tremendous metallic clatter and a low guttural growl. She thought her heart might explode in her chest.

Melissa had been caught. This fact remained foremost in her mind. The big man's arrival spoke volumes to Stevie. With all that had happened, would they move to close down shop? She resolved to get some footage, drive to Public Safety and make her case, providing Boldt the necessary probable cause to involve the FBI. Behind her, on shore, an eighteen-wheel truck arrived. A figure climbed out. She crouched and ran toward the trawler. She would have to hurry. The driver had left the truck running.

CHAPTER 74

"What the hell does that mean?" Boldt thundered, unable to believe what he was hearing.

"It's a federal impound. Federal property. It is beyond our jurisdiction." Lacey Delgato, the deputy prosecuting attorney with whom LaMoia had met, had a voice that could scratch glass. She was plump and wore her clothes too tight. She talked behind an ironic grin that leant her an imperial arrogance. "It's an INS impound, Lieutenant. If anyone's going to bust in there, it's them."

"But that's just the point. Right? That's exactly why we want in there ourselves." He had checked his voice mail only moments before. Suddenly McNeal's oblique message made more sense: She realized the graveyard was under Coughlie's jurisdictional control.

"I understand that, but it isn't going to happen. You crash those gates and you lose anything and everything you discover."

"So I have to go back to Talmadge."

"Right."

"And if he's in on it?"

She shrugged. "Chalk one up for the bad guys."

"Unacceptable."

"Suggestions?"

"Other fed agencies? Do they have access?"

Delgato pursed her lips and gave her next words considerable thought. "U.S. Attorney would have to be brought in. If you gave him enough evidence, enough probable cause, he might work the Bureau for the raid." She added, "The Bureau could invite you along for the ride. Nothing preventing that. Yeah. It could work, I suppose."

"Put it in motion," he said. "I'm going to get a surveillance team in place."

"Tomorrow, I'm talking about," Delgato complained. "No way this is going down tonight."

"Make the calls," Boldt ordered.

"It's late."

"Now."

"I'll wake him up."

"You want a hundred lives on your hands? You want this whole thing to come down to your refusal to make a call, to wake someone up? Fine," he said. "I'll make a note of it."

"You had better be right about this," she threatened.

"Amen," Boldt said.

CHAPTER 75

The constant coming and going had worn a trail through the rust and corrosion on the trawler's deck, beating a path around to the far side where any opening of a hatch or door was fully blocked from view of land. Even from across Salmon Bay, because of the trawler's angle in the graveyard, there was no chance of anyone being seen using this entrance. Coughlie had found himself the perfect hideaway.

The ship's deck vibrated underfoot like a kitchen appliance. She left the worn route and found her way along the determined shadow on the port side, moving incredibly slowly, every pore in her body alert, every hair at attention. She passed one door after another, having no idea where she was or which to use, and it was only her reporter's eye that finally spotted the fresh litter of cigarette butts accumulated around one particular door at her feet, causing her to stop and press her ear to this door.

A confusing rumble filled her head, the clatter louder but distant. She looked up to see the tractor trailer truck backing down between two rows in the boatyard. The trailer stopped just on the other side of the chain-link gate and the air brakes hissed.

She eased down on the levered handle and it moved, and she pulled the door open no more than it took to aim her eye inside.

The pitch-black foreground was accompanied by a warm yellow light to her left. She gathered her courage and slipped quickly inside, pressing her back to the cold metal and holding her breath for the benefit of her hearing. Blood pulsed so loudly in her ears that she heard nothing else. She stayed flat against the wall while her eyes adjusted to the limited light and her ears to the distant sounds. Although at first she thought she was in a room, she was in fact in some kind of hallway; the yellow light came from yet another passageway at the end. She gathered her courage and slowly walked toward that light, each footfall feeling like a lifetime, her mind cluttered with memory and thought to the point of confusion. She fought to clear her head but won little ground, conscious thought subverted by whatever process demands reflection at such moments. She saw her father, Melissa, Su-Su. She saw the studio set.

At the end of the long passageway she came across a narrow stairway leading down into the guts of the ship. An aluminum work light hung from an orange extension cord strung through the overhead metal beam at the bottom of the stairs. Stevie stood there, reluctant to descend, to risk putting herself into that light. But at last there seemed no choice in the matter.

She knew enough about ships to know that they were comprised of companionways, passageways, cabins, staterooms, holds, heads and galleys. But to her the trawler was a labyrinth of poorly lit gray steel corridors and steep ladder stairways, one leading to the other, leading to the next, lined with pipes and filled with the occasionally deafening groan of industry. The way they all connected seemed somebody's joke. For the most part, she followed the string of lights—crudely fashioned extension cords and bare bulbs strung at random, stretching shadows along the walls and turning a simple hallway into something at once both terrifying and mysterious. The farther she ventured, the less likely it seemed to her she would ever find her way out. And if those lights were to fail. . .

When there's nowhere else to go, try moving forward, Su-Su had once advised. She trusted that.

Stevie placed her foot onto the step, like a swimmer testing the water. Then the next step. The third. Down she went, into that light, a shadow stretching behind her. She assumed they would kill her if they caught her, or maybe not because of her celebrity—she wasn't sure. On reflection, Brian Coughlie had had ample opportunity to kill her, to make her disappear. So why not? Because he had missed on his first try? The hard metal walls amplified both her breathing and the grind of machinery, and thankfully covered her footfalls. She reached the bottom where the passageway turned sharply back on itself and she crept along, one hand touching the wall to give her reassurance. The smells were more caustic here: the salty tang of human toil and sea, urine and sweat, and a bitter taste like plastic in her mouth. The air grew hazy, and that haze grew thicker to her right where another passageway fed off this one. This new hallway was darker, and it led to a partially open door that was clearly the source of that sound. She felt drawn to it, unable to stop herself from entering the darker passageway and approaching that cacophony. Step by precious step she continued, checking both behind her and in front of her, expecting someone to jump out and grab her at any second. Beyond that partially open door was more darkness, but the locker-room smell of women grew more intense, and that sound—how could she describe that sound?—ever louder. Without being fully aware of her actions, her hands sought out the zipper on the camera case and blindly ran it down and around the corners to where the lid lifted open and the camera itself found its way into her hands. The lens cap came off. The switch went on. Stevie stepped up to the metal hatch and peered through. She jumped at the sound of her own gasp. She'd never seen anything like it.

This hatch led to a catwalk landing that hung like an observation balcony out over the enormous hold and in turn accessed a steel grate stairway that turned back and forth on itself descending through yet another landing before reaching the floor. She stood looking out over the forward hold of the ship, once intended to store tens of tons of fish, forty feet deep, forty wide, and perhaps sixty feet long, its floor converted to an industrial plant where dozens of women—a hundred or more—with their heads shaved bare, bowed over poorly lit sewing machines that echoed off the steel walls into a deafening noise. The machinery was crowded tightly in rows, the scraps of discarded fabric like a patchwork-quilt carpet on the floor, the lone Asian guard patrolling the aisles with what appeared to be a stun stick in his hand. The size of the operation overwhelmed her, as did the dusty air and the putrid stink. She raised the camera to her eye and began to shoot, mesmerized by it all, determined to capture it, painfully aware that as her eye took to the camera she lost all peripheral sense of her sur- roundings. She moved behind that steel hatch door, using it as a shield so she couldn't be seen from the hallway. It required both hands and a heavy pull to open it slightly farther in order to screen her from the stairway as well. She pushed herself more tightly into the far corner of the tiny landing, comfortable with her hiding spot and able to see and film the activities below.

This location gave her a momentary sense of protection, despite the fact that the catwalk balcony on which she stood allowed her to be seen from most anywhere on the floor. She reminded herself that she appeared as small to them as they appeared to her; and that if she remained perfectly still, it would take a good deal of concentration to pick her out up there. The recorder counted off its footage in time: thirty seconds . . . forty . . . fifty . . . She didn't need much. She could make her case by simply matching the images that Melissa had shot, for hers would look nearly identical, and the realization that she was standing in the exact spot where her little sister had stood before dis- appearing gave her a shudder of fear.

The camera's LOW LIGHT warning troubled her. Sometimes a cam- corder did fine in such light, despite the warning, but sometimes it recorded nothing but black. She could stop the recording, rewind and review her footage to make sure she had captured her proof. She was just about to do so when a bell rang out and all motion in the giant room stopped on cue.

Directly below her by some forty feet a man entered the room and spoke sharply in fluent Mandarin. "Stop your work! Line up!"

The women obeyed like terrified soldiers, hurrying to form two long lines in a scuffling of bare feet and bowed heads. They stood at attention as the room's lone guard moved from station to station, free- ing the few women chained to their machines. What footage! Stevie's eye remained glued to the camera. She panned from face to face hop- ing to see Melissa, excitement and anticipation pounding sharply in her chest. She wanted so desperately to confirm her among them.

"We are leaving ship at once," the man announced. "Groups of six. No more. No less. You will go orderly and quietly or you will get the stick," he said, hoisting the cattle prod.

The women mumbled amongst themselves.

"Silence!" this man roared. "Groups of six! Begin!"

The first six shuffled out of the hold in fast little steps, as if practiced in boot camp.

We are leaving ship at once . . .

Did they know someone had sneaked aboard? Had the sentry in the cabin cruiser raised the alarm? Or was this simply the plan, the reason for the semi truck?

Stevie heard the clap of quickened footsteps approaching from down the hallway behind her. Rodriguez's thickly Hispanic voice, not twenty feet away and closing, spoke with a chilling authority. "Three of them charges go forward, two in the back . . . We flood both them holds. Set the trip on the starboard door. You got that? *Only* the starboard door. That's important."

He stepped out onto the balcony not three feet away from her—so close she could have reached out and touched him—a huge man with wide shoulders and a sour smell. She cowered on the far side of the steel hatch as he leaned over the rail to watch the work progressing below. She knew that smell: It was the same man who had invaded her apartment. The temperature in the hold was in the low nineties. Stevie McNeal shuddered.

He said, "Only the starboard door. Make sure them others are sealed tight as a ten-year-old." As he spoke, great gushes of water began to pour into the hold from all four corners. The cold seawater rushed toward the feet of the women who stood at attention without saying a word. That power cord she had followed was strung along the floor like a snake. Its electricity wouldn't mix well with water.

Rodriguez said, "With them holds flooded she'll go down fast. Our guy'll be the first aboard when they get here—he'll make certain it trips. Get 'em in that truck. Fast. Hurry!"

"The machines," a guttural Asian voice objected. "What about the machines?" Hidden by the door, this man went unseen by her.

"He said lose 'em," Rodriguez replied. "It don't look right other-wise. With the mud down there it'll be a mess. We buy ourselves a day at least, maybe a week or more. That's all that matters. He thunk it through, I'm telling ya. It's sweet."

"Expensive."

"Not your worry. Not mine. His decision. He'll live with it."

"Maybe not," that Oriental voice replied.

Rodriguez coughed out an uptight laugh. "You got that right."

He turned and ducked through the hatch. She heard their foot-steps fade down the hallway. She exhaled and grabbed for air, soaked in sweat.

Huge conveyors hung suspended overhead and attached to the wall, apparently to lift the dead fish to the processing area where they would have been cleaned before being frozen while still out at sea. A metal wall ladder ran up to them. An enormous hatch half the size of a tennis court occupied the center of the ceiling—the deck hatch through which the catch was initially deposited. A catwalk ran along-side this hatch as well, maintenance access perhaps. She could make out only two other doors to the giant hold—steel hatches—both di-rectly below her: one on the ground level through which the women now passed in groups of six, and another that suddenly swung open at the middle landing. Seawater continued to flood the chamber. With the hatches left open, the entire ship would flood.

She heard a sound below and looked down to see Rodriguez step out onto the middle balcony directly below her, again leaning his head over to inspect the progress. He was a man charged with a particular task, and she could feel his impatience to see it through. Standing alongside him was an Asian with hands the size of oven mitts.

The plan was a simple one, she thought: evacuate the illegals—protect the investment—and then later let Coughlie raid the ship him-self, acting as an INS agent. If she had it right, Coughlie intended to scuttle the ship while he was aboard—another ploy intended to buy him both support and sympathy and to mislead any subsequent inves-tigations.

She looked down at her right hand: All this time the camcorder had been recording. She hadn't realized it, too caught up in Rodriguez's proximity, but his voice had been recorded on tape as he issued his instructions. This camcorder had the man dead to rights.

But it was all worthless if she didn't get to Boldt immediately. She had to move fast.

She stepped toward the hatch door, but in the process the strap to the camera case snagged behind her on a metal spur and tilted the case over, dumping its contents. Before she could react, a power cable, a blank tape and a spare battery spilled out noisily onto the steel landing, sounding like a drawer of kitchen utensils hitting the floor.

Stevie, who reached to catch the contents of the case a moment too late, found herself looking straight down through the slats under her feet and into the eyes of Rodriguez, directly below.

As the contents banged off the lower landing and rained down to the floor of the hold, every eye lifted up to look at her.

For a moment Stevie's heart simply seemed to stop. She was the center of attention—the very place she had made the focus of her professional life—and she suddenly wanted anonymity. Everything, everyone, stood still. She couldn't breathe; the pain was so great in her chest. Rodriguez, too, seemed frozen by the discovery of her. But then he moved to climb the stairs, taking them two at a time, and Stevie understood she was a dead woman.

The one thought that flashed before her was that Rodriguez controlled these women with fear. He and his men were grossly outnumbered. To disrupt that control—regardless of what happened to her and her tape—was all she had left. Rodriguez could offer them only fear; she had a far stronger weapon.

He had twenty or more feet to climb as Stevie stepped up to the rail and shouted in her best Mandarin. "Little Sisters! I am with the American press! The police are on their way! You are free!"

For a thousandth of a second there was absolute silence. Rodriguez stopped his climb and looked down below. But then their cheer arose—a unified cry of salvation—so loud as to be deafening, so exuberant as to bring tears to Stevie's eyes. The women broke ranks and charged the one guard. There was a great male scream from within them and the distinctive sound of bones breaking, like tree limbs in a storm.

As a group they made for the one door, but as the crowd bunched, others jumped onto the same metal stairs that ended at Stevie's landing, and they climbed as quickly as spreading fire. Rodriguez turned the corner to her, now only a few short stairsteps below.

Stevie rounded the hatch, jumped through into the hallway and pulled with all her strength, the camcorder dangling from the strap around her right forearm. The damn door was far heavier than she had expected. She knew that to seal that door was to seal Rodriguez's fate at the hands of his captives. She pulled and pulled, one eye cast through the slowly shrinking crack as the huge man grew ever larger with his approach. He bounded the final steps.

The screams of the excited women filled the ship now, shrill and electric. They came from every corner. Their feet shook the steel with a growing rumble. She heard two claps of gunfire, but then no more— that guard overwhelmed as well. Rodriguez had let loose the water, but Stevie had let loose the tide.

Her final tug pulled the door to closing, but it bumped and wouldn't catch, and it wasn't until she looked down that she saw the four stubby fingers—all broken and at odd angles, caught in the steel jamb—that she understood the impediment. Those fingers clenched and pulled despite their pain, and then four more appeared in the crack along with a pair of thumbs, and he overpowered her with his strength and slowly increased the gap, forcing the door back open.

Stevie held on tight and then let go the door all at once. Rodriguez, unprepared for this, flew back off balance and Stevie stepped forward and kicked him in the face, feeling the bone and gristle of his nose give way. Blood poured out. Rodriguez skidded face down along the metal stairs, his head rising and falling with each step.

He was caught there by his own captives. Three stepped over him and rushed for the hatch. But the next several stopped and took out their anger on him. A woman lifted herself up by the rail and came down fully on his head, then used his back as a trampoline. The others joined in. The fallen man glanced up the stairs at Stevie and they met eyes as the blows continued, as the blood flowed, as the defeat registered.

"Don't kill him!" Stevie shouted desperately in Mandarin. She looked down into those yellowed eyes. "Where is she?" she hollered—screamed. "Where?"

But the tide was not to be turned back. Blood was in the air. Three of the women continued to kick. His jaw hung off his face like a broken lampshade. He crawled blindly, his eyes bloodied and swollen. Crawled too close to the edge. One of the women shoved, then another. They launched him over the side to the steel floor below, where he landed with the final authority of death's brutal calling.

CHAPTER 76

Boldt's initial surveillance team arrived as illegals scattered from the trawler, some diving into the water, some jumping ship to ship, a carnival of terror as only those incarcerated against their will can impart, for their reckless run to freedom, and their mass hysteria, overcomes any and all reason, thought or plan. The moment those women left the graveyard, they also left federal property, meaning that Detectives Heiman and Ringwold possessed the necessary authority to detain these women for questioning; but it wasn't until Heiman thought to discharge his weapon—firing into the air over the water—that they gained any semblance of control, and by that time, as a few dozen of the women lay down flat on the wharf in response to the gunfire, far too many had escaped, leaving SPD, the Coast Guard and the INS coordinating their teams in the largest manhunt in city history. The public relations nightmare that arose over the course of the next few hours would eventually bring every member of the brass down to Public Safety for emergency meetings.

For his part, Boldt entered the "graveyard" as a guest of an Agent Prins, a U.S. Customs officer put onto the case by the U.S. Attorney. At the time of his arrival, Prins was in possession of a federal warrant entitling him to search and seizure for improperly imported goods, the product of quick thinking by the U.S. Attorney, whose reasoning was that a sweatshop required sewing machines and fabric, one or both of which had probably entered the country illegally. Furthermore, Customs had its own highly trained, heavily armed strike force—to conduct raids at warehouses, airports and aboard ships. Prins and his team, including a canine unit, followed in behind the chaos of the mass exodus of illegals in a militarylike operation that left two Chinese

363

gang members under arrest and two others wounded by gunfire. The dogs uncovered explosives in the hull of the ship based on information provided by McNeal. An FBI bomb squad was dispatched to assist.

Ambulances, fire trucks and every news team and crime reporter the city had to offer descended on the area, requiring overtime radio units for crowd control. When the third news helicopter appeared overhead and images began broadcasting live over CNN, a Coast Guard chopper was dispatched to disburse them and then to light the ship and the surrounding waters from where illegals were still being rescued. People living along Salmon Bay and the shore of the canal turned out onto their front porches in their pajamas to watch the spectacle despite the early hour. In an act of entrepreneurial ingenuity an ice cream truck showed up and toured the streets of Ballard, selling peach sticks and ice cream sandwiches at one o'clock in the morning. In police vernacular, the raid on the graveyard turned into a zoo scene.

By the time Coughlie and his INS Rapid Response Team arrived, a thorough search of the trawler was already under way, making for a heated argument between Prins and Coughlie. When Boldt walked into the captain's cabin, where this discussion was taking place, Coughlie stopped talking midsentence.

"You?" Coughlie said.

"Me," Boldt answered.

"This doesn't have to do with Customs."

"Sure it does."

"It's a sham."

"It's a crime scene. Prins offered for me to tag along."

"And I'm supposed to buy that?"

"I'm not selling," Boldt advised him. "Shots were fired. Federal property or not, it's within the county. It's ours."

"That may be; but the detention of the illegals, their captors and the ship itself are mine."

Sensing a knock-down-drag-out and briefed in advance by Boldt on what to do when Coughlie's team arrived, Prins excused himself from the room, pulling the door shut.

"Why the end run, Lieutenant?" Coughlie asked.

"What end run?"

"Why the end run?" Coughlie returned. Neither man would play according to the other's agenda. He held up one finger at a time. "Illegals? A sweatshop? A federal impound? If you had a lead, you should have called our house, not Customs, not FiBIes."

"I'm telling you—I'm here at the invitation of Customs."

"You're here because they had access to federal property and you didn't. They're here because you wanted them to be, no matter how you two act it out. But I'm here now, and that's all that matters. It's *our* scene. Thank you very much for all you've contributed."

"That's not my call to make," Boldt said. "Sorry. SPD is here to investigate shots fired. We have two deaths and several wounded."

"My team will do the search."

"It's not my call. You'll have to take that up with Prins. He showed me a warrant—"

"What the hell is going on, Lieutenant?"

"Just doing my job, Agent Coughlie."

"McNeal? Did I hear she was involved?"

"We haven't interviewed her yet. Haven't interviewed anyone."

"It smells," Coughlie said.

"It stinks," Boldt replied. On this, they struck their first moment of agreement.

There was a knock on the metal door followed by Prins. He was an athletic man in his mid-thirties. A sharp nose, vivid blue eyes. "Lookie what the boys found," he said, holding up a callused hand.

He held a small tape in his hand—a tape from a digital video camera. "Thing was sewed into the collar of one of the polarfleece vests. You believe that shit? We might have *never* found it!"

Coughlie coughed, his first uncontrolled, unchecked moment.

Boldt accepted the object from Prins and spun it around in the bad light. "It's a digital tape." He held it up for both to see and said, "This could make our entire case."

Prins said with astonishment, "We could have looked for this thing for weeks and never found it. Think of that!"

Coughlie held out his hand. "I'll take it, thank you."

Tension hung in the air as Boldt retained the tape.

Coughlie's hand remained outstretched. "Lieutenant," he said.

Boldt asked Prins about the chain of custody and the Customs man confirmed that since his boys had found it, it would have to go through their system.

"Ridiculous!" Coughlie hollered, stepping forward. Addressing Prins he said, "The lieutenant and I have just established between us that this is in fact an INS operation. Any evidence—all evidence—will go in under our umbrella."

Boldt corrected him. "We established that it was for you and Agent Prins and the U.S. Attorney's office to work out. SPD's only concern is the shootings and the homicides."

"Then shut up!" Coughlie said inappropriately, "and let me work this out with Agent Prins." He tried to forge a smile onto his face, but it wouldn't take, resulting instead in a snarl.

"The person who deserves this," Boldt told Prins, "is McNeal. She's been after this tape for two weeks. And in all honesty, the way it worked out for us in terms of the courts was that although the camera was ours, the intellectual property—the images—belong to the station. The sooner we get this to McNeal, the sooner we all find out what's on there."

"So I sign it off to McNeal to make a copy for us," Prins said. "Anybody have any problem with that?" he directed to Coughlie, who held his tongue. "We schedule a meeting for tomorrow morning when we'll all view it together—all of us in one room at the same time. That way nobody gets bent out of shape. Right? Okay with everyone?"

Coughlie's brow knitted angrily. His face looked the color of ash. He couldn't argue this.

Boldt said, "Fine. Makes sense to me."

"It's INS evidence," Coughlie objected one more time. "Anything and everything in this ship—"

"You want to do the dance, we'll do the dance," Prins said. "But tonight, right now, this is mine. I'm with Boldt. I say it goes to McNeal so at least we get a copy that we can view on a VCR. You want to battle me on this, you want to freeze this thing in some property room until the courts sort it out, you can do so in the morning. But tonight it's mine, and that's how it's playing out."

"We'll see about that," Coughlie challenged.

"The search warrant has my signature on it, Agent Coughlie. This tape was found inside a ship that is listed on the warrant as a target of that search. All of this went through the U.S. Attorney's office, which is—I might remind you—is the same office to which you will make your appeal. We're on the same side! We both want the bad guys! Don't fight me on this!"

Coughlie's paste complexion went scarlet. "We'll see." He stormed out past Boldt, his frustration following behind him like a vapor trail.

CHAPTER 77

Stevie McNeal stared at the image on the video monitor in KSTV's control room. Through the soundproofed glass she looked out on the news set where she had spent the last few years of her life. It was relatively dark out there on the set, a few overhead room lights throwing out just enough light to keep one from tripping on cords and wires. It looked foreign to her, this place. She wasn't sure she would ever sit in that chair again.

On the monitor was an image of the equally dark sweatshop—"the Sweatship," as the local news radio station had immediately dubbed it, a name that seemed likely to stick. Darkness pervaded her consciousness as well. She felt heavy with grief and burdened with guilt, and thought that the station was a lonely, even somewhat frightening place at three in the morning. A night watchman patrolled the building, checking up on Stevie about every half hour, but it did little to assuage her fears. She wouldn't have done any better at the hotel; not knowing what she and Boldt had worked out. Sleep wasn't an option.

Melissa was still missing. She had not been found among the recaptured population.

When the clock read exactly 3:00 A.M., she reluctantly placed the call to Coughlie's pager and dialed in the control room's direct line. When the phone rang a few minutes later its ringing jarred her, and she actually lifted out of her chair, despite the fact she was expecting the return call.

"McNeal," she answered.

"I've been calling your cellphone for the last two hours," Brian Coughlie said.

"It's broken."

"You're at the station. I tried the main line. A machine picks up."

"We need to talk, Brian." Despite her efforts, her voice sounded filled with defeat and sadness.

Steady breathing on the other end of the line. Coughlie said nothing.

She said, "We need to talk about this. Tonight. Before tomorrow morning. Before the meeting."

"I agree," he said.

"West side of the building. There are fire doors that lead into the studio. Knock, but not too loudly. There's a night watchman on duty. If you use the main entrance, your visit will be logged into the computer. I think we'd both rather avoid that. Am I right?"

"West side. Fire doors," he said.

"The guard makes his rounds every half hour. If you get here at thirty-five after, we've got twenty minutes or so in the clear. Can you make it?"

"Twenty-five of," he said. "I'll be there."

The twenty-some minutes passed interminably. She was not only emotionally drained but physically exhausted. She checked all the equipment for the third or fourth time—she'd lost count. Every monitor in the studio carried the freeze-frame image of the sweatshop floor with the sixty or seventy bareheaded women leaned over their sewing machines—overhead monitors, the huge SONY on the wall, the countertop monitors used by the anchors. The effect was overwhelming, magnifying the power of that image manyfold.

The guard passed through right on time, offered her a little wave, walked the studio and left by the door through which he had come. Her head ached, dull and heavy, a result of fatigue and her battered eye, but her heart beat quickly with a combination of anticipation and adrenaline. Everything she had worked for since Melissa's disappearance came down to these next ten or twenty minutes, and it was this compression of time that rattled her. That and the fact that every time she thought it was almost over, it came to life again, like something beaten but not killed. She found it difficult to concentrate, to hold a single thought in her head.

||||||||

When the knock came, it split her head open like an axe. She hurried out of the control room, down the three steps to the studio floor level and across to the fire doors. He knocked again, though she didn't immediately open the doors, for it took her longer than she thought to find her composure and collect herself. She exhaled slowly and pushed the door's panic bar. Aptly named, she thought privately.

Brian Coughlie stepped inside. Even given the dim light, she saw that his eyes were bloodshot and frantic. As he caught sight of the overhead monitors and the image of the sweatshop, he fell into a kind of trance.

"I have to hear your side of this," she whispered.

He snapped his attention away from the monitors to look at her, though it drew him back as she reached to pull the fire doors closed. She walked past him and toward the control room, saying nothing, knowing he would follow, relieved just the same when she heard his footsteps. A moment later he closed the control room door and took a seat in one of the producer's chairs. He gripped the arms of the chair like a person expecting an earthquake. "My *side*?" he inquired.

"I'm willing to believe there's an explanation." She wouldn't look at him, her attention riveted to the monitor and the image there, she wouldn't allow him to work on her with his controlled expressions.

"Explanation?"

"I could tell you what we're going to see on these videos tomorrow morning, or you could tell me why we're going to see it. And you can bullshit me or not—that's your decision. But it's late, and I'm exhausted, Brian." She carried that swollen eye like a badge of honor. "So maybe you just cut the shit and tell me what's going on here."

"I'm on the video?" he guessed.

His lip and forehead shined with perspiration. Stevie wore a cardigan, as the control room was kept in the middle to low sixties.

"Do I accept these images or not?" she asked.

"Maybe we had better watch and see," he suggested.

"No, no, no! That's just the point. I can't afford that. I can't have you adjusting your version of the truth to what you see on the tape."

"It's not a matter of me adjusting anything. Until tonight it was a matter of Need to Know. Not even Adam Talmadge knew about the operation. I couldn't tell anyone." He glanced to ensure the control room door was tightly shut. "I accepted my first bribe a year and a half ago. I laundered their cash and mine through the car wash. I documented every meeting, every bribe. The idea was for me to remain undercover until I had hard evidence against the people actually running things, not just the street-level thugs. It went much longer than I expected. Adam would have never approved it. I *still* don't have enough to convict. It blew up on me tonight. That happens. But the way it'll look now . . . the way it'll look if people see me on that video without knowing what was really going on . . . You see? If this tape gets out, then it's a year and a half of my life down the drain. My career."

"Melissa?"

"The count was off. I had a tough choice to make. I could blow the whole operation and save your friend, or I could stay in character and see her as a threat. You may not understand this right now, but I didn't have any choice. I had to weigh the benefits of one against the good of many."

"You killed her?"

"Listen to me. The system *does not work*. You can color it; you can spin it; I don't care. It's busted, and it's never going to be fixed. Not ever. It's corrupt. It's rigged. It's supply and demand, that's all. These people will do anything, risk everything, to live here. That's the demand. It's endless. It goes on at every border, every crossing, every port, every airport twenty-four hours a day, seven days a week. They want in, and they'll do anything to get it. If we catch them again, we slap their hands and send them home within the week. They try again. New contacts. More money. Another go. And if we catch them, we slap their hands and send them back." He checked the door again. "The point is, we had to chase this thing higher up the ladder. I took that upon myself. I've risked everything here."

She said softly, "You let those women die in that container."

"Not true," he objected. "I didn't run this thing, I protected it. Or I pretended to. They paid me to." He kept eyeing the equipment, trying to figure out what device drove the freeze-frame image of the darkened sweatshop.

"The captain of the *Visage*?" she asked.

He glanced around the small room nervously, as if he expected someone else. The sweat had returned to his forehead. He whispered to her hoarsely, "If I didn't pass information along, then they'd have found me out."

"You told them the police were going to question the captain."

"You know what it's like undercover for that long? You know what happens to you?"

"What happened to Melissa?"

"I changed the whole operation," he told her, avoiding an answer. "When I came in there was no way out for these women! No one ever intended to give them their freedom. They paid for a new freedom; what they got was slavery. It was me who got Klein involved, me who pointed out there was just as much profit in selling them a driver's license as there was reselling them into prostitution!" He was red in the face and practically coming out of his chair.

"Pointed out to whom?" she asked angrily. "I thought you hadn't made the connection to the higher-ups?"

Coughlie cocked his head at her like a puzzled dog.

"You know what I think, Brian? I think you've made it all up. I don't know if you fooled yourself at first into thinking you were running an undercover operation, but I doubt it. I think that was your fallback plan all along—to come up with some cockamamie story about a one-man sting. I think you slipped. You saw an agency swallowed by bureaucracy and a tide of humanity that was never going to be checked. You saw all that money, and all that opportunity—all the corruption around you—and you—"

"I've documented everything," he protested. "Every cent."

"And it doesn't mean a thing if it wasn't okayed by Talmadge."

"And if Talmadge is on the take? How could I risk that?"

"You've got it all figured, don't you? Getting people killed, accepting bribes. You can justify it all." She added, "Am I supposed to erase the video for you? Erase it and forget all about Melissa?"

"She infiltrated the operation. I didn't even know about it until you confirmed it."

"You're going to blame me? You . . . *bastard!*" She dove at him. The chair went over and she clawed his face, drawing blood. Coughlie dumped her and smacked her across the jaw and jumped to his feet. He grabbed hold of the cable running into the TV monitor and followed it to the console and began tearing equipment off the shelves, frantically ejecting cassettes and tearing the tape from them. "Where is it?" he roared.

"It doesn't exist!" she hollered back him, freezing him.

He turned, wild-eyed.

"There is no tape!" she said.

He drew his weapon. "I want it now."

Holding her hands out in front of her to ward him off, she sat up slowly and reached for the console. Her palm held down a square button. "Okay," she said, her voice echoing through overhead loudspeakers. She pointed into the studio, a dazed Brian Coughlie still holding his weapon on her.

An exhausted Lou Boldt stood on the other side of that glass. First one, then a second uniformed officer stepped out from behind the huge black curtains that surrounded the studio's walls. All held handguns trained on Coughlie.

She said, "The tape you saw on the ship? A blank. Boldt arranged to have it delivered. It was the psychologist's idea—Matthews. She said your ego would allow you to believe you could convince me to destroy it."

"I was undercover!" he shouted through the glass. "I can prove it!"

"Where's Melissa? What have you done with her?"

"Drop your weapon!" Boldt's muted voice shouted back.

Stevie tripped another button on the console. "I taped your visit, Brian. The whole confession. How's that for irony? I'll probably win that Emmy Melissa promised after all." She stepped up to him. "Where the hell is she?"

CHAPTER 78

"I n brothel by airport," the woman's deep voice said on the other end of Boldt's receiver. He knew that woman's voice, but he didn't bother to identify it by name. She gave him the address and said, "She in room on second floor. She not in good shape, but she alive. Best I could do. So sorry."

Boldt took McNeal with him and a radio car as backup. The drive to the airport was typically about twenty minutes. They made it in twelve.

"She just calls up and tells you this?" Stevie said.

"That's it." Boldt caught himself grinding his teeth and let his jaw hang slack to try to relax.

"No explanation?"

"She pressured them into keeping her alive. It's the only thing that makes sense."

"She has that kind of control?"

"And then some," he answered.

"And waits until Coughlie is indicted to tell us?"

"If he hadn't been indicted, we'd have never gotten the call. She's not an angel. She's a politician. She's buying herself a future break . . . and she'll get it."

"But Coughlie could have used Melissa to plea bargain. How stupid can you get?"

Boldt said, "Depends on what's left of her. How much Coughlie knows. A jury might not be too sympathetic."

"Torture?"

"They wanted that tape badly. I imagine that's what kept her alive until our friend stepped in."

"These people are not human beings."

"That's the way *they* think. That's where it all starts."

She nodded. "She's alive," she gasped.

They drove past neighborhoods where the houses all looked the same and the cars were the same. Big groups of sameness. He felt bothered and anxious.

"Another example of the wonderful cooperation between media and law enforcement."

She laughed out loud. "You win!"

"No one wins," he said. "Not ever." He pulled the car to a stop, a patrol vehicle parking alongside of him. The sign said NUDE GIRLS. The two-story building was painted Cape Cod gray and had enough parking for a convention center. "Are you prepared for this—for what we might find?"

"No," she admitted. "Are you?"

"Gloves?" Boldt said, handing her a pair.

"I'm not wearing gloves," Stevie replied, handing them back, hurrying from the car. "Come on!"

Boldt produced the warrant, but the uniforms led the way inside. It smelled foul, a combination of air freshener and human hell.

"She had a shaved head when she came in," Boldt told the obese manager, a sweaty man who couldn't, or wouldn't, get up out of the worn red couch. He was drinking a dark cocktail on the rocks. He smoked a thin foul cigar with a white plastic tip.

McNeal took off up the stairs. Boldt indicated for a uniform to follow her. He turned and climbed the stairs himself, leaving another uniform by the door. "No one goes anywhere," he told the kid. He remembered being that young—remembered the feel of the gun on his belt and the smell of the leather. He climbed the stairs heavily.

Stevie opened one door after another—bare buttocks, sweating flesh. A salesman's suit carefully arranged on a chair. The smell of pot and booze and familiarity. The uniform lingered a little too long at each door. Stevie moved faster and faster. Nine doors. No Melissa.

Her movements became frantic. She felt tears in her eyes and tension in every limb. An ache so deep inside her—an ache only a woman understood. Another flight of stairs. She ran now, out of breath, nearly out of life. The uniform lumbered up behind her, but she turned to see it was Boldt.

"Easy," he said. "We don't want to scare her."

"Scare her?" she barked back at him, incredulous.

"Just go easy," he repeated. He fired down to the uniform, "Where the hell are the EMTs? Get on the horn!"

"EMTs?" Stevie whined, now slowing as she reached the third floor.

Boldt handed her the gloves again, his arm outstretched. "Be smart," he said.

She accepted them limply. "Oh, God . . ."

They both paused by the only door that was locked.

Boldt whispered, "She mustn't see anything but joy in your face. You understand how important that is?"

Tears spilled down from her swollen eye.

"Freedom is a fragile thing," he said.

She nodded faintly.

"Are you ready?" he said, his shoulder against the door.

She struggled with the gloves, sniffled and drew in a deep breath. But the tears would not abate. Her shoulders shook. Her throat tightened. She nodded. "I'm ready," she said.

Boldt broke open the door.

"Thank God!" Stevie McNeal whimpered, running inside and falling to her knees.

CHAPTER 79

The late October sun played low and soft on the horizon, reminding Stevie McNeal of the yellow headlights on cars in Paris. She had thought about traveling, but it wasn't right yet for either of them. "You see the sailboat?"

Melissa didn't answer. She didn't rock the rocker. She just sat there staring out blankly.

Corwin had been good enough to loan them the cabin indefinitely. Marsh grass fluttered in the strong breeze that accompanied every sunset. A sturdy stand of cedar stood at water's edge like a wall.

She gave Melissa a bath every evening before bed, like a mother with her child. She soaped the skin where they'd used cigarettes to burn her, she cleaned the loins they had soiled with their filth. But she couldn't reach the woman's thoughts, couldn't clean there. They were trying a combination of massage, acupuncture and therapy. A woman psychiatrist recommended by Matthews made the ferry ride to the island twice a week. She said she was encouraged, but Stevie wasn't buying it. For all she could tell there had been no change whatsoever.

Melissa ate, though precious little. Stevie supplemented her diet with one of those chocolate drinks intended for the elderly. They slept together in the same bed because the nightmares and sweats could be horrible, and Stevie wanted to be right there when she was needed. The night before Melissa had crept across the bed in her sleep and had snuggled up to Stevie and had cried for the better part of an hour, though Stevie didn't think she'd ever been awake. Maybe it was an improvement; she intended to tell the shrink about it. The word was that she would come back slowly. Maybe the crying was a step forward, maybe a step back. Stevie wasn't leaving anytime soon.

She brought her a cardigan sweater and helped it around her bone-thin shoulders and stroked her cheek with the back of her hand and said, "I love you, Little Sister," as she did so many times each day. Love was what would heal. Stevie knew this. She trusted it. "You're safe here," she said, a knot in her throat.

Melissa reached up, took her hand and pulled it into her lap. Stevie dropped to her knees, tears coming now, for this was the first time anything like this had happened. It wasn't much, granted; but to Stevie it meant the world. She whispered to the woman in the rocker, "Every journey begins with but a single step." No reaction. Nothing.

Stevie started the rocker gently rocking. She thought Melissa liked that. She wasn't sure. She kneeled uncomfortably, but kept her hand there in her sister's lap, the grip weak but intentional. She wasn't going to move. She could barely breathe.

The sun became a yellow eye and then winked them into dusk. Stevie's legs went numb with the kneeling, and her arm fell asleep to where it was a bundle of needles. But she didn't move, didn't speak. The darkness played out on the western sky and the first stars appeared.

"The first stars are the strongest," Stevie said.

Nothing. No reaction whatsoever.

"As long as it takes," she whispered.

Still nothing.

The moon rose behind them and threw shadows into the trees. A satellite crossed the sky. Stevie watched as Melissa's dark eyes followed it higher. And then she noticed the rocker was still moving and realized that she was not the one driving it.

"I'll get dinner going," she said, reluctantly pulling her hand free. There would be other chances to hold hands; she would make sure of that. She stood, her tingling legs barely able to support her. The rocker continued to move. She backed up slowly across the porch, supporting herself against the shingled wall, unable to take her eyes off that slowly moving chair. A month earlier a rocking chair moving like that wouldn't have meant anything to her.

She was learning.

CHAPTER 80

B oldt slipped into bed, believing her asleep. He felt absolutely exhausted, and yet his mind was spinning. He wasn't sure he'd find sleep himself.

She said, "There's nothing there."

"Where?" he asked, his eyes still not accustomed to the dark.

"The tests. They came back negative."

Boldt switched on the bedside light. Both he and Liz squinted. He switched it back off. "You took the tests?"

"We can exist in separate beliefs," she said. "There's nothing wrong with that."

"A leap of faith," he whispered, remembering what Daphne had said.

She rolled away from him, but backed up to where her skin met his and together they made warmth. He slipped his arm over her and held her close.

She fell asleep first, her breathing stretching out, her ribs rising and falling against his arm. Her body twitched several times and then she was still again, her steady breathing the only sound.

Boldt dozed off after a while. Pulled down by a weighty fatigue, the darkness claimed him and he found a few hours' peace.